Deemed 'the father of the scien
Austin Freeman had a long and
a writer of detective fiction. He wa
tailor who went on to train as a pharmacist. After graduating as a surgeon at the Middlesex Hospital Medical College, Freeman taught for a while and joined the colonial service, offering his skills as an assistant surgeon along the Gold Coast of Africa. He became embroiled in a diplomatic mission when a British expeditionary party was sent to investigate the activities of the French. Through his tact and formidable intelligence, a massacre was narrowly avoided. His future was assured in the colonial service. However, after becoming ill with blackwater fever, Freeman was sent back to England to recover and finding his finances precarious, embarked on a career as acting physician in Holloway Prison. In desperation, he turned to writing and went on to dominate the world of British detective fiction, taking pride in testing different criminal techniques. So keen were his powers as a writer that part of one of his best novels was written in a bomb shelter.

BY THE SAME AUTHOR
ALL PUBLISHED BY HOUSE OF STRATUS

The D'Arblay Mystery
Dr Thorndyke Intervenes
Dr Thorndyke's Casebook
The Eye of Osiris
Felo De Se
Flighty Phyllis
The Golden Pool: A Story of a Forgotten Mine
The Great Portrait Mystery
Helen Vardon's Confession
John Thorndyke's Cases
Mr Polton Explains
Mr Pottermack's Oversight
The Mystery of 31 New Inn
The Mystery of Angelina Frood
The Penrose Mystery
The Puzzle Lock
The Red Thumb Mark
The Shadow of the Wolf
A Silent Witness
The Singing Bone
When Rogues Fall Out

A Certain Dr Thorndyke

R Austin Freeman

This edition published in 2001 by House of Stratus, an imprint of Stratus Holdings plc, 24c Old Burlington Street, London, W1X 1RL, UK. Also at: Suite 210, 1270 Avenue of the Americas, New York, NY 10020, USA.

www.houseofstratus.com

Typeset, printed and bound by House of Stratus.

A catalogue record for this book is available from the British Library and the Library of Congress.

ISBN 0-7551-0349-1

Contents

Book One: The Ishmaelite

Book Two: The Investigator

Book One

The Ishmaelite

Chapter One

The Fugitive

The tropic moon shone brightly on the village of Adaffia in the Bight of Benin as a fishing-canoe steered warily through the relatively quiet surf of the dry season towards the steep beach. Out in the roadstead an anchored barque stood up sharply against the moonlit sky, the yellow spark of her riding light glimmering warmly, and a white shape dimly discernible in the approaching canoe hinted of a visitor from the sea. Soon the little craft, hidden for a while in the white smother of a breaking wave, emerged triumphant and pushed her pointed nose up the beach; the occupants leaped out and, seizing her by her inturned gunwales, hauled her forthwith out of reach of the following wave.

"You know where to go?" the Englishman demanded, turning a grim, hatchet face towards the "headman." "Don't take me to the wrong house."

The headman grinned. "Only one white man live for Adaffia. Me sabby him proper." He twisted a rag of cotton cloth into a kind of turban, clapped it on his woolly pate and, poising on top a battered cabin-trunk, strode off easily across the waste of blown sand that separated the beach from a forest of coconut palms that hid the village. The Englishman followed less easily, his shod feet sinking into the loose sand; and as he went, he peered with a stranger's curiosity along the deserted beach and into the solemn gloom beneath the palms, whence came the rhythmical clamour of drums and the sound of many voices joining in a strange, monotonous chant.

Through the ghostly colonnade of palm trunks, out into the narrow, tortuous alleys that served for streets, between rows of mud-built hovels roofed with unkempt grass thatch, where all was inky blackness in the shadow and silvery grey in the light, the stranger followed his guide; and ever the noise of the drums and the melancholy chant drew nearer. Suddenly the two men emerged from an alley into a large open space and in an instant passed from the stillness of the empty streets into a scene of the strangest bustle and uproar. In the middle of the space was a group of men, seated on low stools, who held between their knees drums of various sizes, which they were beating noisily, though by no means unskilfully, some with crooked sticks, others with the flat of the hand. Around the musicians a circle of dancers moved in an endless procession, the men and the women forming separate groups; and while the former danced furiously, writhing with starting muscles and streaming skins, in gestures grotesque and obscene, the latter undulated languorously with half-closed eyes and rhythmically moving arms.

The Englishman had halted in the black shadow to look on at this singular scene and to listen to the strange chant that rang out at intervals from dancers and spectators alike, when his guide touched him on the arm and pointed.

"Look, Mastah!" said he; "dem white man live. You look um?"

The stranger looked over the heads of the dancers, and, sure enough, in the very midst of the revellers, he espied a fellow-countryman seated on a green-painted gin-case, the sides of which he was pounding with his fists in unsuccessful emulation of the drummers. He was not a spectacle to engender undue pride of race. To begin with, he was obviously drunk, and as he drummed on the case and bellowed discordantly at intervals, he was not dignified. Perhaps it is not easy to be drunk and dignified at one and the same time, and assuredly the task is made no easier by a costume consisting of a suit of ragged pyjamas, the legs tucked into scarlet socks, gaudy carpet slippers, and a skull-cap of plaited grass. But such was the garb of this representative of the superior race, and the final touch was given to a raffish *ensemble* by an unlit cigar that waggled from the corner of his mouth.

The stranger stood for a minute or more watching, in silence and with grim disapproval, this unedifying spectacle, when a sudden interruption occurred. One of the dancers, a big, powerful ruffian, in giving an extra flourish to his performance, struck his foot against the gin-case and staggered on to the seated white man, who, with a loud, foolish laugh, caught him playfully by the ankle. As a result, the big negro toppled over and fell sprawling amongst the drummers. In an instant all was confusion and uproar. The drummers pummelled the fallen man, the women howled, the men shouted, and the drunken white man yelled with idiotic laughter. Then the big negro leaped to his feet with a roar of fury, and rushing at the white man, closed with him. The gin-case turned turtle at the first onset, the two combatants flew off gyrating amongst the legs of the crowd, mowing down a little lane as they went; and for some moments nothing could be distinguished save a miscellaneous heap of black bodies and limbs with a pair of carpet slippers kicking wildly in the air. But the white man, if lacking in dignity and discretion, was not deficient in valour. He was soon on his feet and hitting out right and left with uncommon liveliness and spirit. This, however, could not, and did not, last long; a simultaneous rush of angry negros soon bore him once more to the ground and there seemed every prospect of his being very severely mauled.

It was at this moment that the stranger abandoned his rôle of a neutral spectator. Taking off his helmet and depositing it carefully in the angle of a mud wall, he lowered his head, thrust forward his shoulder, and charged heavily into the midst of the shouting mob. Now, the Slave Coast native is a sturdy, courageous fellow and truculent withal; but he does not play the Rugby game and he is a stranger alike to the subtler aspects of pugilism and the gentle art of ju-jitsu. Consequently the tactics of the new assailant created quite a sensation among the Adaffia men. Their heels flew up unaccountably, their heads banged together from unknown causes, mysterious thumps, proceeding from nowhere in particular with the weight of a pile-monkey, stretched them gasping on the earth; and when they would have replied in kind, behold! the enemy was not there! They rushed at him with outstretched hands and straightway fell upon their stomachs; they grabbed at his head and caught nothing but a pain in the shoulder or a tap under the chin; and the sledge-hammer blow that was to have annihilated him either spent itself on empty air or, impinging upon the countenance of an ally, led to misunderstanding and confusion. Hampered by their own numbers and baffled by the incredible quickness of their elusive adversary, they began to view his strange manoeuvres as feats of magic. The fire of battle died down, giving place to doubt, bewilderment, and superstitious fear. The space widened round the white, silent, swiftly-moving figure; the more faint-hearted made off with their hands clapped to their mouths, screeching forth the hideous Efé alarm cry; the panic spread, and the remainder first backed away and then fairly broke into a run. A minute later the place was deserted save for the two Europeans and the headman.

The stranger had pursued the retreating mob for some distance, tripping up the stragglers or accelerating their movements by vigorous hammerings from behind, and he now returned, straightening out his drill jacket and dusting the grimy sand from his pipe-clayed shoes with a silk handkerchief. The other white man had by this time returned to the gin-case, on which he was once more enthroned with one of the abandoned drums between his knees, and, as his compatriot approached, he executed a martial roll and would have burst into song but that the cigar, which had been driven into his mouth during the conflict, now dropped into his throat and reduced him temporarily to the verge of suffocation.

"Many thanks, dear chappie," said he, when he had removed the obstruction; "moral s'pport most valuable; uphold dignity of white man; congratulate you on your style; do credit to Richardsons.

Excuse my not rising; reasons excellent; will appear when I do." In fact his clothing had suffered severely in the combat.

The stranger looked down on the seated figure silently and with tolerant contempt. A stern-faced, grim-looking man was this new-comer, heavy-browed, square-jawed, and hatchet-faced, and his high-shouldered, powerful figure set itself in a characteristic pose, with the feet wide apart and the hands clasped behind the back as he stood looking down on his new acquaintance.

"I suppose," he said, at length, "you realize that you're as drunk as an owl?"

"I s'spected it," returned the other gravely. "Not's an owl, though, owls very temp'rate in these parts."

At this moment the headman rose from the cabin-trunk, on which he had seated himself to view the conflict, and, picking up the stranger's helmet, brought it to him.

"Mastah," said he, earnestly, "you go for house one time. Dis place no good. Dem people be angry too much; he go fetch gun."

"You hear that?" said the stranger. "You'd better clear off home."

"Ver' well, dear boy," replied the other, suavely. "Call hansom; we'll both go."

"Whereabouts do you live?" demanded the stranger.

The other man looked up with a bland smile. "Grosvenor Square, ol' fellow, A1; brass knocker 'stinguishers on doorstep. Tell cabby knock three times and ring bottom bell." He picked up the cigar and began carefully to wipe the sand from it.

"Do you know where he lives?" asked the stranger, turning to the headman.

"Yass; me sabby. He live for factory. You make him come one time, Mastah. You hear dat?"

The sound of the strange and dismal Efé alarm cry (produced by shouting or screaming continuously and patting the mouth quickly with the back of the hand) was borne down from the farther end of the village. The headman caught up the trunk and started off up the street, while the stranger, having hoisted the seated man off the gin-case with such energy that he staggered round in a half-circle, grasped him from behind by both arms and urged him forward at a brisk trot.

"Here, I say!" protested the latter, "nosso fast – d'ye hear? I've dropped my slipper. Lemme pick up my slipper."

To these protests the stranger paid no attention, but continued to hustle his captive forward with undiminished energy.

"Lemme go, confound you! You're shaking me all to bits!" exclaimed the captive; and, as the other continued to shove silently, he continued: "Now I un'stand why you boosted those niggers so neatly. You're a bobby, that's what you are. I know the professional touch. A blooming escaped bobby. Well, I'm jiggered!" He lapsed, after this, into gloomy silence, and a few minutes' more rapid travelling brought the party to a high palm-leaf fence. A primitive gate was unfastened, by the simple process of withdrawing a skewer from a loop of cord, and they entered a compound in the middle of which stood a long, low house. The latter was mud-built and thatched with grass like the houses in the village, from which, indeed, it differed only in that its mud walls were whitewashed and pierced for several windows.

"Lemme welcome you to my humble cot," said the proprietor, following the headman, who had unceremoniously walked into the house and dumped down the cabin-trunk. The stranger entered a small, untidy room lighted by a hurricane-lamp, and, having dismissed the headman with a substantial "dash," or present, turned to face his host.

"Siddown," said the latter, dropping into a dilapidated Madeira chair and waving his hand towards another. "Less have a talk. Don't know your name, but you seem to be a decent feller – for a bobby. My name's Larkom, John Larkom, agent for Foster Brothers. This is Fosters' factory."

The stranger looked curiously round the room – so little suggestive of a factory in the European sense – and then, as he seated himself, said: "You probably know me by name: I am John Walker, of whom you have – "

He was interrupted by a screech of laughter from Larkom, who flung himself back in his chair with such violence as to bring that piece of furniture to the verge of dissolution.

"Johnny Walker!" he howled. "My immortal scissors! Sh'ld think I do know you; more senses than one. I've got a letter about you – I'll show it to you. Where is that blamed letter?" He dragged out a table-drawer and rooted among a litter of papers, from which he at length extracted a crumpled sheet of paper. "Here we are. Letter from Hepburn. You 'member Hepburn? He and I at Oxford together. Merton, y'know. Less see what he says. Ah! Here you are; I'll read it: 'And now I want you to do me a little favour. You will receive a visit from a pal of mine who, in consequence of certain little indiscretions, is for the moment under a cloud, and I want you, if you can, to put him up and keep him out of sight. His name I am not permitted to disclose, since being, as I have said, *sub nube*, just at present, and consequently not in search of fame or notoriety, he elects to travel under the modest and appropriate name of Walker.' " At this point Larkom once more burst into a screech of laughter. "Funny devil, Hepburn! Awful rum devil," he mumbled, leering idiotically at the letter that shook in his hand; then, wiping his eyes on the gaudy "trade" tablecloth, he resumed his reading. " 'He need not cause you any inconvenience, and you won't mind his company as he is quite a decent fellow – he entered at Merton just after you went down – and he won't be any expense to you; in fact, with judicious management, he may be made to yield a profit, since he will have some money with him and is, between ourselves, somewhat of a mug.' Rum devil, awful rum devil," sniggered Larkom. "Doncher think so?" he added, grinning foolishly in the other man's face.

"Very," replied the stranger, stolidly. But he did not look particularly amused.

" 'I think that is all I have to tell you,' " Larkom continued, reading from the letter. " 'I hope you will be able to put the poor devil up, and, by the way, you need not let on that I have told you about his little misfortunes.' " Larkom looked up with a ridiculous air of vexation. "There now," he exclaimed, "I've given old Hepburn away like a silly fool. But no, it was he that was a silly fool. He shouldn't have told me."

"No, he should not," agreed Walker.

" 'Course not," said Larkom with drunken gravity. "Breach o' confidence. However, 's all right. 'Pend on me. Close as a lock-jawed oyster. What'll you drink?"

He waved his hand towards the table, on which a plate of limes, a stone gin jar, a bottle of bitters with a quill stuck through the cork, and a swizzle-stick, stained purple by long service, invited to conviviality.

"Have a cocktail," said Larkom. "Wine of the country. Good old swizzle-stick. I'll mix it. Or p'rhaps," he sniggered, slyly, "p'raps you'd rather have a drop of Johnny Walker – ha! ha! Hallo! Here they are. D'ye hear 'em?" A confused noise of angry voices was audible outside the compound and isolated shouts separated themselves now and again from the general hubbub.

"They're callin' us names," chuckled Larkom. "Good thing you don't un'stand the language. The nigger *can* be rude. Personal abuse as a fine art. Have a cocktail."

"Hadn't I better go out and send them about their business?" asked Walker.

"Lor' bless you, they haven't got any business," was the reply. "No, siddown. Lerrum alone and they'll go home. Have a cocktail." He compounded one for himself, swizzling up the pink mixture with deliberate care and pouring it down his throat with the skill of a juggler; and when Walker had declined the refreshment and lit his pipe, the pair sat and listened to the threats and challenges from the outer darkness. The attitude of masterly inactivity was justified by its results, for the noise subsided by degrees, and presently the rumble of drums and the sound of chanting voices told them that the interrupted revels had been resumed.

After the third application to the stone bottle Larkom began to grow sleepy and subsided into silence, broken at intervals by an abortive snore. Walker meanwhile smoked his pipe and regarded his host with an air of gloomy meditation. At length, as the latter became more and more somnolent, he ventured to rouse him up.

"You haven't said what you are going to do, Larkom," said he. "Are you going to put me up for a time?"

Larkom sat up in the squeaking chair and stared at him owlishly. "Put you up, ol' f'ler?" said he. "Lor bless you, yes. Wodjer think? Bed been ready for you for mor'n a week. Come'n look at it. Gettin' dam late. Less turn in." He took up the lamp and walked with unsteady steps through a doorway into a small, bare room, the whitewashed walls of which were tastefully decorated with the mud-built nests of solitary wasps. It contained two bedsteads, each fitted with a mosquito net and furnished with a mattress, composed of bundles of rushes lashed together, and covered with a grass mat.

"Thash your doss, ol' f'ler," said Larkom, placing the lamp on the packing-case that served for a table; "this is mine. Goo' night!" He lifted the mosquito-curtain, crept inside, tucked the curtain under the mattress, and forthwith began to snore softly.

Walker fetched in his trunk from the outer room, and, as he exchanged his drill clothes (which he folded carefully as he removed them) for a suit of pyjamas, he looked curiously round the room. A huge, hairy spider was spread out on the wall as if displayed in a collector's cabinet, and above him a brown cockroach of colossal proportions twirled his long antennae thoughtfully. The low, bumpy ceiling formed a promenade for two pallid, goggle-eyed lizards, who strolled about, defiant of the laws of gravity, picking up an occasional moth or soft-shelled beetle as they went. When he was half undressed an enormous fruit-bat, with a head like that of a fox-terrier, blundered in through the open window and flopped about the room in noisy panic for several minutes before it could find its way out again.

At length he put out the lamp, and creeping inside his curtain, tucked it in securely; and soon, despite the hollow boom of the surf, the whistle of multitudinous bats, the piping of the mosquitoes, and the sounds of revelry from the village, he fell asleep and slept until the sun streamed in on to the whitewashed wall.

Chapter Two

The Legatee

Larkom appeared to have that tolerance of alcohol that is often to be observed in the confirmed soaker. As he sat with his guest in the living-room, taking his early tea, although he looked frail and broken in health, there was nothing in his appearance to suggest that he had quite recently been very drunk. Nor, on the other hand, was his manner very different from that of the previous night, save that his articulation and his wits were both clearer.

"What made you pick out this particular health-resort for your little holiday?" he asked. "It isn't what you would call a fashionable watering-place."

"No," replied Walker. "That was the attraction. I heard about you from Hepburn – he is my brother-in-law, you know – and as it seemed, from what he said, that your abode was on the very outside edge of the world, I marked it down as a good place to disappear in."

Larkom grinned. "You are not a bad judge, old chappie. Disappearing is our speciality. We are famous for it. Always have been. How does the old mariners' ditty run? You remember it?

'Oh, the Bight of Benin, the Bight of Benin,
One comes out where three go in.'

But perhaps that wasn't exactly what was in your mind?"

"It wasn't. I could have managed that sort of disappearance without coming so far. But look here, Larkom, let us have a clear understanding. I came here on spec, not having much time to make arrangements, on the chance that you may be willing to put me up and give me a job. But I haven't come to fasten on to you. If my presence here will be in any way a hindrance to you, you've only got to say so and I will move on. And I shan't take it as unfriendly. I quite understand that you have your principles to consider."

"Principles be blowed!" said Larkom. "They don't come into it; and as to me, I can assure you, J W, that this is the first stroke of luck I've had for years. After vegetating in this God-forgotten hole with nobody but buck-niggers to speak to, you can imagine what it is to me to have a pukka white man – and a gentleman at that – under my roof. I feel like chanting 'Domine, non sum dignus'; but if you can put up with me, stay as long as you care to, and understand that you are doing me a favour by staying."

"It is very handsome of you, Larkom, to put it that way," said Walker, a little huskily. "Of course, I understand the position and I accept your offer gratefully. But we must put the arrangement on a business footing. I'm not going to sponge on you. I must pay my share of the expenses, and if I can give you any help in working the factory – "

"Don't you be afraid, old chappie," interrupted Larkom. "I'll keep your nose on the grindstone; and as to sharing up, we can see to that later when we cast up the accounts. As soon as we have lapped up our tea, we will go out to the store and I will show you the ropes. They aren't very complicated, though they are in a bit of a tangle just now. But that is where you will come in, dear boy."

Larkom's statement as to the "tangle" was certainly no exaggeration. The spectacle of muddle and disorder that the store presented filled Walker at once with joy and exasperation. After a brief tour of the premises, during which he listened in grim silence to Larkom's explanations, he deliberately peeled off his jacket –

which he folded up neatly and put in a place of safety – and fell to work on the shelves and lockers with a concentrated energy that reduced the native helper to gibbering astonishment and Larkom to indulgent sniggers.

"Don't overdo it, old chap," the latter admonished. "Remember the climate. And there's no hurry. Plenty of spare time in these parts. Leave yourself a bit for tomorrow." To all of which advice Walker paid no attention whatever, but slogged away at the confused raffle of stock-in-trade without a pause until close upon noon, when the cook came out to announce that "chop live for table." And even this was but a temporary pause; for soon after breakfast – or tiffin, as the Anglo-Indian calls it – when Larkom showed a tendency to doze in his chair with a tumbler of gin toddy, he stole away to renew his onslaught while the native assistant attended to the "trade."

During the next few days he was kept pretty fully occupied. Not that there was much business doing at the factory, but Larkom's hand having become of late so tremulous that writing was impossible, the posting of books and answering of letters had automatically ceased.

"You're a perfect godsend to me, old chappie," said Larkom, when, by dint of two days' continuous labour, the books had been brought up to date, and Walker attacked the arrears of correspondence. "The firm wouldn't have stood it much longer. They've complained of my handwriting already. If you hadn't come I should have got the order of the boot to a certainty. Now they'll think I've got a native clerk from somewhere at my own expense."

"How about the signature?" Walker asked. "Can you manage that?"

"That's all right, dear boy," said Larkom cheerfully. "You sign slowly while I kick the table. They'll never twig the difference."

By means of this novel aid to calligraphy the letter was completed and duly dispatched by a messenger to catch the land post at Quittah. Then Walker had leisure to look about him and study the methods of West Coast trade and the manners and customs of his host. Larkom sober was not very different from Larkom drunk – amiable, easy-going, irresponsible, and only a little less cheerful. Perhaps he was better drunk. At any rate, that was his own opinion, and he acted up to it consistently. What would have happened if there had been any appreciable trade at Adaffia it is impossible to guess. As it was, the traffic was never beyond the capacity of Larkom even at his drunkest. Once or twice during the day a party of bush natives would stroll into the compound with a demijohn of palm oil or a calabash full of kernels, or a man from a neighbouring village would bring in a bushel or so of copra, and then the premises would hum with business. The demijohn would be emptied into a puncheon or the kernels stowed in bags ready for shipment, and the vendors would receive their little dole of threepenny pieces – the ordinary currency of the coast. Then the vendors would change into purchasers. A length of baft or calico, a long, flint-lock gun with red-painted stock, a keg of powder, or a case of gin would replace the produce they had brought; the threepenny pieces would drift back into the chest whence they had come, and the deal would be completed.

At these functions Walker, owing to his ignorance of the language, appeared chiefly in the rôle of onlooker, though he took a hand at the scales, when he was about, and helped to fill the canvas bags with kernels. But he found plenty of time to wander about the village and acknowledge the appreciative grins of the men whom he had hammered on the night of his arrival or the courteous salutations of the women. Frequently in the afternoons he would stroll out to sit on the dry sand at high-water mark and, as the feathery leaves of the sea-washed palms pattered above him in the breeze, would gaze wistfully across the blue and empty ocean. One day a homeward-bound steamer came into the bay to anchor in Quittah roads; and then his gaze grew more wistful and the stern face softened into sadness. Presently Larkom hove in sight under the palms, carolling huskily and filling a gaudy trade pipe. He came and sat down by Walker, and having struck some two dozen Swedish matches without producing a single spark, gazed solemnly at the steamer.

"Yellow funnel boat," he observed; "that'll be the *Niger*, old Rattray's boat. She's going home, dear boy, home to England, where hansom cabs and green peas and fair ladies and lamb chops – "

"Oh, shut up, Larkom!" exclaimed the other, gruffly.

"Right, dear boy. Mum's the word," was the bland reply, as Larkom resumed his fruitless attack on the matches. "But there's one thing I've been going to say to you," he continued after a pause, "and it's this – confound these damstinkers; I've used up a whole box for nothing – I was going to say that you'd better not show yourself out on the beach unnecessarily. I don't know what your little affair amounts to, but I should say that, if it was worth your while to cut away from home, it's worth your while to stop away."

"What do you mean?"

"I mean that you are still within the jurisdiction of the English Courts; and if you should have been traced to the ship and you let yourself be seen, say, by any of the Germans who pass up and down from Quittah to Lomé or Bagidá, why, some fine day you may see an officer of the Gold Coast Constabulary bearing down on you with a file of Hausas, and then it would be ho! for England, home, and beauty. You sabby?"

"I must take that risk," growled Walker. "I can't stay skulking in the house, and I'm not going to."

"As you please, dear boy," said Larkom. "I only mentioned the matter. *Verbum sap*. No offence, I hope."

"Of course not," replied Walker.

"I don't think you are in any immediate danger," pursued Larkom. "Old chief Akolatchi looked in on me just now and he tells me that there are no white officers at Quittah. The doctor died of blackwater fever two days ago, and the commissioner is sick and is off to Madeira by this steamer. Still, you had better keep your weather eyelid lifting."

"I mean to," said Walker; and knocking out his pipe on the heel of his shoe, he rose and shook the sand from his clothes.

"If you'll excuse my harping on a disagreeable topic, old chappie," said Larkom, as they strolled homewards along the beach, "I think you would be wise to take some elementary precautions."

"What sort?" asked Walker.

"Well, supposing you were traced to that barque, the *Sappho*, it would be easy to communicate with her skipper when she comes to her station at Half-Jack. Then they might ascertain that a gent named Johnny Walker with a golden beard and a Wellington nose had been put ashore at Adaffia. You're a fairly easy chappie to describe, with that Romanesque boko, and fairly easy to recognize from a description."

"But, damn it, Larkom! You're not suggesting that I should cut off my nose, are you?"

"God forbid, dear boy! But you might cut off your beard and drop Johnny Walker. A clean shave and a new name would make the world of difference. No native would recognize you without your beard."

"Perhaps not. But a white police officer would spot me all right. A clean shave and a different name would not deceive him."

"Not if he really meant business. But the local officials here will be pretty willing to turn a blind eye. They are not keen on arresting a white man with a parcel of niggers looking on. Lowers the prestige of the race. If a constabulary officer came down here to arrest a bearded man named Walker and found only a clean-shaved covey of the name of Cook, he'd probably say that there was no one here answering the description and go back perfectly satisfied with his tongue in his cheek."

"Do you really think he would?"

"I do. At any rate, you may as well give the authorities a chance; meet 'em half-way. Don't you think so?"

"I suppose it is the reasonable thing to do. Very well, Larkom, I will take your advice and turn myself into a bald-faced stag – I noticed that you have some razors in the store. And as to the name, well, I will adopt your suggestion in that, too. 'Cook' will do as well as any other."

"Better, old chap. Distinguished name. Great man, James Cook. Circumnavigator; all round my hat."

"All the same," said Walker, *alias* Cook, "I fancy you are a trifle over-optimistic. If an officer were sent down here with a warrant, I think he would have to execute it if he could. He would be running a biggish risk if he let himself be bamboozled."

"Well, dear boy," replied Larkom, "you do the transformation trick and trust in Providence. It's quite likely that the local authorities will make no move; and if a GCC officer should turn up and insist on mistaking James Cook for Johnny Walker, I daresay we could find some way of dealing with him."

The other man smiled grimly. "Yes," he agreed. "I don't think he'd mistake James Cook for Mary's little lamb."

As they entered the compound a quarter of an hour later, a native rose from the kernel bag on which he had been seated, and disengaging from the folds of his cloth a soiled and crumpled letter, held it out to Larkom. The latter opened it with tremulous haste and, having glanced through it quickly, emitted a long, low whistle.

"Sacked, by jiggers!" he exclaimed, and handed the letter to his guest. It was a brief document and came to the point without circumlocution. The Adaffia factory was a financial failure, "whatever it might have been under other management," and the firm hereby dispensed with Mr Larkom's services. "But," the letter concluded, "as we are unwilling to leave a white man stranded on the Coast, we hereby make over to you, in lieu of notice, the factory and such stock as remains in it, the same to be your own property; and we hope that you will be able to carry on the trade to more advantage for yourself than you have for us."

"Devilish liberal of them," groaned Larkom, "for I've been a rotten bad servant to the firm. But I shall never make anything of it. I'm a regular waster, old chappie, and the sooner the land-crabs have me, the better it will be for everyone." He lifted the lid of a gin-case and dejectedly hoisted out a high-shouldered, square-faced Dutch bottle.

"Stop this boozing, Larkom," said Cook, late Walker. "Pull yourself together, man, and let us see if we can't make a do of it." He spoke gently enough, with his hand on the other man's shoulder, for the thought of his own wrecked life had helped him understand. It was not the mere loss of employment that had hit Larkom so hard. It was the realization, sudden and complete, of his utter futility; of his final irrevocable failure in the battle of life.

"It's awfully good of you, old chap," he said dismally; "but I tell you, I'm beyond redemption." He paused irresolutely and then added: "However, we'll stow the lush for the present and talk things over"; and he let the bottle slip back into its compartment and shut down the lid.

But he was in no mood for talking things over, at present. The sense of utter failure appeared to have overwhelmed him completely, and, though he made no further attempt upon the gin-case that evening, his spirits seemed to sink lower and lower until, about ten o'clock, he rose from his chair and silently tottered off to bed, looking pitiably frail and broken.

It was about two o'clock in the morning when Cook awoke to the consciousness of a very singular noise. He sat up in bed to listen. A strange, quick rattle, like the chatter of a jigsaw, came from the rickety bed on which Larkom slept, and with it was mingled a confused puffing that came and went in quick gusts.

"Anything the matter, Larkom?" he asked anxiously; and then, as a broken mumble and a loud chattering of teeth came in reply, he sprang from the bed and struck a match. A single glance made everything clear. The huddled body, shaking from head to foot, the white, pinched face, the bloodless hands with blue finger-nails, clutching the scanty bed-coverings to the trembling chin, presented a picture of African fever that even a newcomer could recognize. Hastily he lit a candle, and, gathering up every rag that he could lay hands on, from his own travelling-rug to the sitting-room table-cloth, piled them on to his shivering comrade until the sick man looked like a gigantic caddis-worm.

After an hour or so the violence of the shivering fit abated; gradually the colour returned to the white face until its late pallor gave place to a deep flush. The heaped coverings were thrown to the floor, the sufferer fidgeted restlessly about the bed, his breathing became hurried, and presently he began to babble at intervals. This state of affairs lasted for upwards of an hour. Then a few beads of perspiration appeared on the sick man's forehead; the chatterings and mumblings and broken snatches of song died away, and, as the parched skin broke out into dewy moisture, a look of intelligence came back to the vacant face.

"Cover me up, old chappie," said Larkom, turning over with a deep sigh. "Air strikes chilly. Thanks, old fellow; let's have the table-cloth, too. That's ripping. Now you turn in and get a bit of sleep. Sorry to have routed you up like this." He closed his eyes and at once began to doze, and Cook, creeping back to bed, lay and watched him by the light of the flickering candle. Then he, too, fell asleep.

When he awoke it was broad daylight, and through the open door he could see Larkom standing by the table in the sitting-room, wrapped in the rug. The Fanti cook was seated at the table and the solitary Kroo boy, who formed the staff of the factory, stood by his supplementary chair, his eyes a-goggle with curiosity.

"Now, Kwaku," Larkom was saying, "you see that pencil mark. Well, you take this pen and make a mark on top of it – so." He handed the pen to the cook, who evidently followed the instructions, for his tongue protruded several inches, and he presently rose, wiping his brow. The Kroo boy took his place and the ceremony was repeated, after which the two natives retired grinning with pride.

"Gad, Larkom," exclaimed Cook, when he came out and joined his host; "that dose of fever has taken the starch out of you. You oughtn't to be up, surely?" He looked earnestly at his comrade, shocked at the aspect of the pitiful wreck before him and a little alarmed at the strange, greenish-yellow tint that showed through the waxen pallor of the face.

"Shan't be up long, dear boy," Larkom said. "Just setting things straight before I turn in for good. Now, just cast your eye over this document – devil of a scrawl, but I expect you can make it out." He took up a sheet of paper and handed it to Cook. The writing was so tremulous as to be almost illegible, but with difficulty Cook deciphered it; and its purpose filled him with astonishment. It read thus:

> "This is the last will and testament of me John Larkom of Adaffia in the Gold Coast Colony, West Africa. I give and devise all my estate and effects, real and personal, which I may die possessed of or be entitled to, unto James Cook absolutely, and I appoint him the executor of this my will.
>
> "Dated this thirteenth day of November one thousand eight hundred and ninety-seven.
>
> "Signed by the testator in the presence of us, who thereupon made our marks in his and each other's presence.
>
> JOHN LARKOM
>
> Kwaku Mensah of Cape Coast.
> His + mark
>
> Pea Soup of Half-Jack.
> His + mark

"I've given you your new name, you see," Larkom explained. "Take charge of this precious document and keep that letter from the firm. Burn all other papers."

"But," exclaimed Cook, "why are you talking as if you expected to snuff out? You've had fever before, I suppose?"

"Rather," said Larkom. "But you're a newcomer; you don't sabby. I'm an old coaster, and I sabby proper. Look at that, dear boy. Do you know what that means?" He held out a shaking, lemon-coloured hand, and as his companion regarded it silently, he continued: "That means blackwater fever; and when a Johnny like me goes in for that luxury, it's a job for the gardener. And talking of that, you'd better plant me in the corner of the compound where the empty casks are kept, by the prickly-pear hedge; I shall be out of the way of traffic there, though graves are a damned nuisance in business premises, anyhow."

"Oh, dry up, Larkom, and get to bed," growled Cook; "and, I say, aren't there any doctors in this accursed place?"

Larkom grinned. "In the fossil state, dear boy, they are quite numerous. Otherwise scarce. The medico up at Quittah died three days ago, as I told you, and there are no others on tap just now. No good to me if they were. Remember what I've told you. Burn all papers and, when you've planted me, take over the factory and make things hum. There's a living to be made here and you'll make it. Leave the swizzle-stick alone, old chappie, and if ever you should chance to meet Hepburn again, give him my love and kick him – kick him hard. Now I'm going to turn in."

Larkom's forecast of the possible course of his illness bid fair to turn out correct. In the intervals of business – which, perversely enough, was unusually brisk on this day – Cook looked in on the invalid and at each visit found him visibly changed for the worse. The pale-lemon tint of his skin gave place to a horrible dusky yellow; his voice grew weaker and his mind more clouded, until at last he sank into a partial stupor from which it was almost impossible to rouse him. He wanted nothing, save an occasional sip of water, and nothing could be done to stay the march of the fell disease.

So the day passed on, a day of miserable suspense for Cook; the little caravans filed into the compound, the kernels and copra and knobs of rubber rolled out of the calabashes on to the ground, the oil gurgled softly into the puncheon, the bush people chattered vivaciously in the store and presently departed gleefully with their purchases; and still Larkom lay silent and pathetic and ever drawing nearer to the frontier between the known and the unknown. The evening fell, the store was locked up, the compound gate was shut, and Cook betook himself with a shaded lamp to sit by the sick man's bed.

But presently the sight of that yellow face, grown suddenly so strangely small and pinched, the sharpened nose, and the sunken eyes with the yellow gleam of the half-seen eyeballs between the lids, was more than he could bear, and he stole softly through to the sitting-room, there to continue his vigil. So hour after weary hour passed. The village sank to rest (for it was a moonless night) and the sounds that came in through the open window were those of beast and bird and insect. Bats whistled out in the darkness, cicadas and crickets chirred and chirruped, the bark of the genet and the snuffling mutter of prowling civets came from without the compound, while far away the long-drawn, melancholy cry of a hyaena could be heard in the intervals of the booming surf.

And all the while the sick man slowly drew nearer to the dread frontier.

It wanted but an hour to dawn when a change came. The feeble babblings and mumblings, the little snatches of forgotten songs chanted in a weak, quavering treble, had ceased for some time, and now through the open door came a new sound – the sound of slow breathing mingled with a soft, moist rattling. The watcher rose from his chair and once again crept, lamp in hand, into the dimly-lighted room, there to stand looking down gloomily at the one friend Fate had left him. Larkom was now unconscious and lay quite still, save for the heaving chest and the rise and fall of the chin at each breath.

Cook put down the lamp, and, sitting down, gently took the damp and chilly hand in his, while he listened, in agony at his own helplessness, to the monotonous, rattling murmur that went on and on, to and fro, like the escapement of some horrible clock.

By and by it stopped, and Cook fumbled at the tepid wrist; then, after a pause, it began again with an altered rhythm and presently paused again, and again went on; and so the weary, harrowing minutes passed, the pauses growing ever longer and the rattling murmur hoarser and more shallow. At last there came a pause so long that Cook leaned over the bed to listen. A little whispering sigh was borne to his ear, then all was still; and when, after waiting yet several minutes more, he had reverently drawn the gaudy table-cloth over the silent figure, he went back to his chair in the sitting-room, there to wait, with grim face and lonely heart, for the coming of the day.

The late afternoon sun was slanting eagerly over the palm-tops as he took his way to the far corner of the compound that faced towards the western beach. The empty barrels had been rolled away and, in the clear space, close to the low prickly-pear hedge, a smooth mound of yellow sand and a rough wooden cross marked the spot where Larkom, stitched up in sacking in lieu of a coffin, had been laid to rest. The cross had occupied most of Cook's scanty leisure since the hurried burial in the morning (for trade was still perversely brisk, despite the ragged house-flag half-mast on the little flag-pole), and he was now going to put the finishing touches to it.

It was a rude enough memorial, the upright fashioned from a board from one of the long gun-crates, and the cross-piece formed by a new barrel stave cut to the requisite length; and the lack of paint left it naked and staring.

Cook laid down on the sand a box containing his materials – a set of zinc stencil plates, used for marking barrels and cases, a stencil brush, and a pot of thin black paint – and sketched out lightly in pencil the words of the inscription:

JOHN LARKOM 14th November 1897

Then he picked out a J from the set of stencil plates, dipped the brush in the pot, and made the first letter, following it in order with O, H, and N. Something in the look of the familiar name – his own name as well as Larkom's – made him pause and gaze at it thoughtfully, and his air was still meditative and abstracted as he stooped and picked up the L to commence the following word. Rising with the fresh plate in his hand, he happened to glance over the low hedge along the stretch of beach that meandered away to a distant, palm-clad headland; and then he noticed for the first time a little group of figures that stood out sharply against the yellow background. They were about half a mile distant and were evidently coming towards the village; and there was something in their appearance that caused him to examine them narrowly. Four of the figures walked together and carried some large object that he guessed to be a travelling hammock; four others straggled some little distance behind; and yet three more, who walked ahead of the hammock, seemed to carry guns or rifles on their shoulders.

Still holding the plate and brush, Cook stood motionless, watching with grim attention the approach of the little procession. On it came, at a rapid pace, each step bringing it more clearly into view. The hammock was now quite distinct and the passenger could be seen lying in the sagging cloth; eight of the figures were evidently ordinary natives while the other three were plainly black men dressed in a blue uniform, wearing red caps and carrying rifles and bayonets.

Cook stooped and dropped the plate back into the box, picking out, in place of it, a plate pierced with the letter O. Dipping his brush into the paint, he laid the plate over the pencilled L on the cross and brushed in the letter. Quietly and without hurry, he followed the O with an S, M, O, N, and D; and he had just finished the last letter when an English voice hailed him from over the hedge.

He turned and saw, a little distance away, a fresh-faced Englishman in a quiet undress uniform and a cheese-cutter cap, peering at him curiously from the top of a sand-hill, at the base of which stood the group of hammockmen and the three Hausas.

"There's a gate farther down," said Cook; and, as the officer turned away, he dropped the plate that he was holding back into the box, laid down the brush, and took up a camel's-hair pencil. Dipping this into the paint-pot, he proceeded deliberately and with no little skill to write the date in small letters under the name. Presently the sound of footsteps was audible from behind. Cook continued his writing with deliberate care and the footsteps drew nearer, slowing down as they approached. Close behind him they halted, and a cheery voice exclaimed:

"Good Lord! What a let-off!" and then added, "Poor beggar! When did he die?"

"This morning, just before dawn," replied Cook.

"Phew!" whistled the officer. "He wasn't long getting his ticket. But, I say, how did you know his name? I thought he called himself Walker."

"So he did. But he wished his name to be put on his grave."

"Naturally," said the officer. "It's no use giving an *alias* at the last muster. Well, poor devil! He's had rough luck, but perhaps it's best, after all. It's certainly best for me."

"Why for you?" asked Cook.

"Because I've got a warrant in my pocket to arrest him for some trouble at home – signed the wrong cheque or something of that kind – and I wasn't very sweet on the job, as you may guess. Blood's thicker than water, you know, and the poor chap was an English gentleman after all. However, those black devils of mine don't know what I have come for, so now nothing need be said."

"No." He looked round into the bluff, rosy face and clear blue eyes of the officer and asked: "How did you manage to run him to earth?"

"He was traced to Bristol and to the barque *Sappho* after she had sailed. Then the *Sappho* was seen from Quittah to bring up here, right off her station – she trades to Half-Jack – and, as we were on the look-out, we made inquiries and found that a white man had come ashore here. Good thing we didn't find out sooner. Well, I'll be getting back to Quittah. I've just come down with a new doctor to take over there. My name's Cockeram, assistant inspector GCC. You're Mr Larkom, I suppose?"

"Won't you stop and have a cocktail?" asked Cook, ignoring the question.

"No, thanks. Don't take 'em. H_2O is the drink for this country."

He touched his cap and sauntered to the gate, and Cook saw him walk slowly up and down behind the hedge, apparently gathering something. Presently he sauntered back into the compound looking a little sheepish, and, as he came, twisting some blossoming twigs of wild cotton into a kind of grommet and shelling the little "prayer-beads" out of some Jequirity pods that he had gathered. He walked up to the sandy mound and, sprinkling the scarlet seeds in the form of a cross, laid the loop of cotton-blossoms above it.

"It's a scurvy wreath," he said, gruffly, without looking at Cook, "but it's a scurvy country. So long." He walked briskly out of the compound and, flinging himself into the hammock, gave the word to march.

The other looked after him with an unwonted softening of the grim face – yet grimmer and more lean now that the beard was gone – only resuming his writing when the little procession was growing small in the distance. The date was completed now, but, dipping his brush afresh, he wrote below in still smaller letters: "Now shall I sleep in the dust; and thou shalt seek me in the morning, but I shall not be."

Then he picked up the box and went back into the house.

Chapter Three

The Mutiny on the "Speedwell"

For a man in search of quiet and retirement, the village of Adaffia would seem to be an ideally eligible spot; especially if the man in question should happen to be under a rather heavy cloud. Situated in a little-frequented part of the Slave Coast, many miles distant from any town or settlement where white men had their abodes, it offered a haven of security to the Ishmaelite if it offered little else.

Thus reflected John Osmond, late John Walker, and now "Mr James Cook," if the need for a surname should arise. But hitherto it had not arisen; for, to the natives, he was simply "the white man" or "mastah," and no other European had passed along the coast since the day on which he had buried Larkom – and his own identity – and entered into his inheritance.

He reviewed the short interval with its tale of eventless and monotonous days as he sat smoking a thoughtful pipe in the shady coconut grove that encompassed the hamlet, letting his thoughts travel back anon to a more distant and eventful past, and all the while keeping an attentive eye on a shabby-looking brigantine that was creeping up from the south. It was not, perhaps, a very thrilling spectacle, but yet Osmond watched the approaching vessel with lively interest. For though, on that deserted coast, ships may be seen to pass up and down on the rim of the horizon, two or three, perhaps, in a month, this was the first vessel that had headed for the land since the day on which he had become the owner of the factory and the sole representative of European civilization in Adaffia. It was natural, then, that he should watch her with interest and curiosity, not only as a visitor from the world which he had left, but as one with which he was personally concerned; for if her people had business ashore, that business was pretty certainly with him.

At a distance of about a mile and a half from the shore the brigantine luffed up, fired a gun, hoisted a dirty red ensign, let go her anchor, scandalized her mainsail, lowered her head-sails, and roughly clewed up the square-sails. A fishing canoe, which had paddled out to meet her, ran alongside and presently returned shoreward with a couple of white men on board. And still Osmond made no move. Business considerations should have led him to go down to the beach and meet the white men, since they were almost certainly bound for his factory; but other considerations restrained him. The fewer white men that he met, the safer he would be; for, to the Ishmaelite, every stranger is a possible enemy, or, worse still, a possible acquaintance. And then, although he felt no distaste for the ordinary trade with the natives, he did not much fancy himself standing behind a counter selling gin and tobacco to a party of British shell-backs. So he loitered under the coconuts and determined to leave the business transactions to his native assistant, Kwaku Mensah.

The canoe landed safely through the surf; the two white men stepped ashore and disappeared towards the village. Osmond refilled his pipe and walked a little farther away. Presently a file of natives appeared moving towards the shore, each carrying on his head a green-painted gin-case. Osmond counted them – there were six in all – and watched them stow the cases in the canoe. Then, suddenly, the two white men appeared, running furiously. They made straight for the canoe and jumped in; the canoe men pushed off and the little craft began to wriggle its way cautiously through the surf. And at this moment another figure made its appearance on the beach and began to make unmistakable demonstrations of hostility to the receding canoe.

Now, a man who wears a scarlet flannelette coat, green cotton trousers, yellow carpet slippers, and a gold-laced smoking-cap is not difficult to identify even at some little distance. Osmond instantly recognized his assistant and strode away to make inquiries.

There was no need to ask what was the matter. As Osmond crossed the stretch of blown sand that lay between the palm-grove and the beach, his retainer came running towards him, flourishing his arms wildly and fairly gibbering with excitement.

"Dem sailor man, sah!" he gasped, when he had come within earshot, "he dam tief, sah! He tief six case gin!"

"Do you mean that those fellows didn't pay for that gin?" Osmond demanded.

"No, sah. No pay nutting. Dey send de case down for beach and dey tell me find some country cloth. I go into store to look dem cloth, den dey run away for deir canoe. Dey no pay nutting."

"Very well, Mensah. We'll go on board and collect the money or bring back the gin. Can you get a canoe?"

"All canoe go out fishing excepting dat one," said Mensah.

"Then we must wait for that one to come back," was the reply; and Osmond seated himself on the edge of dry sand that overhung the beach and fixed a steady gaze on the dwindling canoe. Mensah sat down likewise and glanced dubiously at his grim-faced employer; but whatever doubts he had as to the wisdom of the proposed expedition, he kept them to himself. For John Osmond – like Father O'Flynn – had a "wonderful way with him"; a way that induced unruly intruders to leave the compound hurriedly and rub themselves a good deal when they got outside. So Mensah kept his own counsel.

The canoe ran alongside the brigantine, and, having discharged its passengers and freight, put off for its return shorewards. Then a new phase in the proceedings began. The brigantine's head-sails, which lay loose on the jib-boom, began to slide up the stays; the untidy bunches of canvas aloft began to flatten out to the pull of the sheets. The brigantine, in fact, was preparing to get under way. But it was all done in a very leisurely fashion; so deliberately that the last of the square-sails was barely sheeted home when the canoe grounded on the beach.

Osmond wasted no time. While Mensah was giving the necessary explanations, he set his shoulder to the peak of the canoe and shoved her round head to sea, regardless of the cloud of spray that burst over him. The canoe-men were nothing loath, for the African is keenly appreciative of a humorous situation. Moreover, they had some experience of the white man's peculiar methods of persuasion and felt a natural desire to see them exercised on persons of his own colour – especially as those persons had been none too civil. Accordingly they pushed off gleefully and plunged once more into the breakers, digging their massive, trident-shaped paddles into the water to the accompaniment of those uncanny hisses, groans, and snatches of song with which the African canoe-man sweetens his labour.

Meanwhile their passenger sat in the bow of the canoe, wiping the sea water from his face and fixing a baleful glance on the brigantine, as she wallowed drunkenly on the heavy swell. Slowly the tack of the mainsail descended, and then, to a series of squeaks from the halyard-blocks, the peak of the sail rose by slow jerks. The canoe bounded forward over the great rollers, the hull of the vessel rose and began to loom large above the waters, and Osmond had just read the name "*Speedwell*, Bristol" on her broad counter, when his ear caught a new sound – the "clink, clink" of the windlass-pawl. The anchor was being hove up.

But the canoe-men had heard the sound, too, and, with a loud groan, dug their paddles into the water with furious energy. The canoe shot forward under the swaying counter and swept alongside, the brigantine rolled over as if she would annihilate the little craft, and Osmond, grasping a chain-plate, swung himself up into the channel, whence he climbed to the bulwark rail and dropped down on the deck.

The windlass was manned by six of the crew, who bobbed up and down slowly at the ends of the long levers; a seventh man was seated on the deck, with one of the gin-cases open before him, in the act of uncorking a bottle. The other five cases were ranged along by the bulwark.

"Good afternoon," said Osmond, whose arrival had been unnoticed by the preoccupied crew; "you forgot to pay for that gin."

The seated man looked up with a start, first at Osmond and then at Mensah, who now sat astride the rail in a strategic position that admitted of advance or retreat as circumstances might suggest. The clink of the windlass ceased, and the six men came sauntering aft with expectant grins.

"What are you doin' aboard this ship?" demanded the first man.

"I've come to collect my dues," replied Osmond.

"Have yer?" said the sailor. "You'll be the factory bug, I reckon?"

"I'm the owner of that gin."

"Now that's where you make a mistake, young feller. I'm the owner of this here gin."

"Then you've got to pay me one pound four."

The sailor set the bottle down on the deck and rose to his feet.

"Look here, young feller," said he, "I'm goin' to give you a valuable tip – gratis. You git overboard. Sharp. D'ye hear?"

"I want one pound four," said Osmond, in a misleadingly quiet tone.

"Pitch 'im overboard, Dhoody," one of the other sailors counselled. "Send 'im for a swim, mate."

"I'm a-goin' to," said Dhoody, "if he don't clear out"; and he began to advance, crabwise, across the deck in the manner of a wrestler attacking.

Osmond stood motionless in a characteristic attitude, with his long legs wide apart, his hands clasped behind him, his gaunt shoulders hunched up, and his chin thrust forward, swaying regularly to the heave of the deck, and with his grim, hatchet face turned impassively towards his adversary, presented a decidedly uninviting aspect. Perhaps Dhoody appreciated this fact; at any rate, he advanced with an ostentatious show of strategy and much intimidating air-clawing. But he made a bad choice of the moment for the actual attack, for he elected to rush in just as the farther side of the deck was rising. In an instant Osmond's statuesque immobility changed to bewilderingly rapid movement. There was a resounding "Smack, smack"; Dhoody flew backwards, capsizing two men behind him, staggered down the sloping deck, closely followed by Osmond (executing a continuous series of "postman's knocks" on the Dhoodian countenance), and finally fell sprawling in the scuppers, with his head jammed against a stanchion. The two capsized men scrambled to their feet, and, with their four comrades, closed in on Osmond with evidently hostile intentions. But the latter did not wait to be attacked. Acting on the advice of the Duke of Wellington – who, by the way, he somewhat resembled in appearance – to "hit first and keep on hitting," he charged the group of seamen like an extremely self-possessed bull, hammering right and left, regardless of the unskilful thumps that he got in return, and gradually drove them, bewildered by his extraordinary quickness and the weight of his well-directed blows, through the space between the foremast and the bulwark. Slowly they backed away before his continuous battering, hitting out at him ineffectively, hampered by their numbers and the confined space, until one man, who had had the bad luck to catch two upper cuts in succession, uttered a howl of rage and whipped out his sheath-knife. Osmond's quick eye caught the dull glint of the steel just as he was passing the fife-rail. Instantly he whisked out an unoccupied iron belaying-pin, whirled it over and brought it down on the man's head. The fellow dropped like a pole-axed ox, and as the belaying-pin rose aloft once more, the other five men sprang back out of range.

How the combat might have ended under other circumstances it is impossible to say. Dhoody had disappeared – with a bloody scalp and an obliterated eye; the man with the knife lay unconscious on the deck with a little red pool collecting by his head; the other five men had scattered and were hastily searching for weapons and missiles, so far as was possible with this bloodthirsty Bedlamite of a "factory bug" flying up and down the deck with a belaying-pin. Their principal occupation, in fact, was keeping out of reach; and they did not always succeed.

Suddenly a shot rang out. A little cloud of splinters flew from the side of the mainmast, and the five seamen ducked simultaneously. Glancing quickly forward, Osmond beheld his late antagonist, Dhoody, emerging from the forecastle hatch and taking aim at him with a still smoking revolver. Now, the "factory bug" was a pugnacious man and perhaps over-confident, too. But he had some idea of his limitations. You can't walk up twenty yards of deck to punch the head of a man who is covering you with a revolver. At the moment, Osmond was abreast of the uncovered main hatch. A passing glance had shown him a tier of kernel bags covering the floor of the hold. Without a moment's hesitation he stooped with his hands on the coaming, and, vaulting over, dropped plum on the bags, and then, picking himself up, scrambled forward under the shelter of the deck.

The hold of the *Speedwell*, like that of most vessels of her class, was a simple cavity, extending from the forecastle bulkhead to that of the after-cabin. Of this the forward part still contained a portion of the outward cargo, while the homeward lading was stowed abaft the main hatch. But the hold was two-thirds empty and afforded plenty of room to move about.

Osmond took up a position behind some bales of Manchester goods and waited for the next move on the part of the enemy. He had not long to wait. Voices from above told him that the crew had gathered round the hatch; indeed, from his retreat, he could see some of them craning over the coamings, peering into the dark recesses of the hold.

"What are yer goin' to do, Dhoody?" one of the men asked.

"I'm goin' below to finish the beggar off," was the reply in a tone of savage determination.

The place of a ladder was supplied by wooden footholds nailed to the massive stanchion that supported the deck and rested on the kelson. Osmond kept a sharp eye on the top foothold, clambering quickly on the closely-packed bales to get within reach; and as a booted foot appeared below the beam and settled on the projection, he brought down his belaying-pin on the toe with a rap that elicited a yell of agony and caused the hasty withdrawal of the foot. For a minute or more the air was thick with execrations, and, as Osmond crept back into shelter, an irregular stamping on the deck above suggested some person hopping actively on one leg.

But the retreat was not premature. Hardly had Osmond squeezed himself behind the stack of bales when a succession of shots rang out from above, and bullet after bullet embedded itself in the rolls of cotton cloth. Osmond counted five shots and when there came an interval – presumably to reload – he ventured to peer between the bales, and was able to see Dhoody frantically emptying the discharged chambers of the revolver and ramming in fresh cartridges, while the five sailors stared curiously into the hold.

"Now then," said Dhoody, when he had re-loaded, "you just nip down, Sam Winter, and see if I've hit him, and I'll stand by here to shoot if he goes for yer."

"Not me," replied Sam. "You 'and me the gun and just pop down yerself. I'll see as he don't hurt yer."

"How can I?" roared Dhoody, "with me fut hammered into a jelly?"

"Well," retorted Sam, "what about my feet? D'ye think I can fly?"

"Oh," said Dhoody contemptuously, "if you funk the job, I won't press yer. Bob Simmons ain't afraid, I know. He'll go."

"Will he?" said Simmons. "I'm jiggered if he will. That bloke's too handy with that pin for my taste. But I'll hold the gun while you go, Dhoody."

Dhoody cursed the whole ship's company collectively and individually for a pack of chicken-livered curs. But not one of them would budge. Each was quite willing, and even eager, to do the shooting from above; but no one was disposed to go below and "draw the badger." The proceedings seemed to have come to a deadlock when one of the sailors was inspired with a new idea.

"Look 'ere, mates," he said, oracularly; " 'Tis like this 'ere: 'ere's this 'ere bloomin' ship with a nomicidal maniac in 'er 'old. Now, none of us ain't a-goin' down there for to fetch 'im out. We don't want our 'eds broke same as what 'e's broke Jim Darker's 'ed. Contrarywise, so long as 'e's loose on this ship, no man's life ain't worth a brass farden. Wherefore I says, bottle 'im up, I says; clap on the hatch-covers and batten down. Then we've got 'im, and then we can sleep in our bunks in peace."

"That's right enough, Bill," another voice broke in, "but you're forgettin' that we've got a little job to do down below there."

"Not yet, we ain't," the other rejoined; "not afore we gets down Ambriz way, and he'll be quiet enough by then."

This seemed to satisfy all parties, including even the ferocious Dhoody, and a general movement warned Osmond that his incarceration was imminent. For one moment he was disposed to make a last, desperate sortie, but the certainty that he would be a dead man before he reached the deck decided him to lie low. Many things might happen before the brigantine reached Ambriz.

As the hatch-covers grated over the coaming and dropped into their beds, the prisoner took a rapid survey of his surroundings before the last glimmer of daylight should be shut out. But he had scarcely time to memorize the geographical features of the hold before the last of the hatch-covers was dropped into place. Then he heard the tarpaulin drag over the hatch, shutting out the last gleams of light that had filtered through the joints of the covers; the battens were dropped into their catches, the wedges driven home, and he sat, in a darkness like that of the tomb.

The hold was intolerably hot and close. The roasting deck above was like the roof of an oven. A greasy reek arose from the bags of kernels, a strange, mixed effluvium from the bales of cotton cloth. And the place was full of strange noises. At every roll of the ship, as the strain of the rigging changed sides, a universal groan arose; bulkheads squeaked, timbers grated, the masts creaked noisily in their housings, and unctuous gurgles issued from the tier of oil puncheons.

It was clear to Osmond that this was no place for a prolonged residence. The sweat that already trickled down his face meant thirst in the near future, and death if he failed to discover the tank or water-casks. A diet of palm kernels did not commend itself; and, now that the hatch was covered, the water in the bilge made its peculiar properties manifest. The obvious necessity was to get out; but the method of escape was not obvious at all.

From his own position Osmond's thoughts turned to the state of the vessel. From the first, it had been evident to him that there was something very abnormal about this ship. Apart from the lawless behaviour of the crew, there was the fact that since he had come on board he had seen no vestige of an officer. Dhoody had seemed to have some sort of authority, but the manner in which the men addressed him showed that he had no superior status. Then, where was the "afterguard"? They had not gone ashore. And there had been enough uproar to bring them on deck if they had been on board. There was only one reasonable conclusion from these facts, and it was confirmed by Dhoody's proprietary air and by a certain brown stain that Osmond had noticed on the deck. There had been a mutiny on the *Speedwell.*

The inveterate smoker invokes the aid of tobacco in all cases where concentrated thought is required. Osmond made shift to fill his pipe in the dark, and, noticing that his tobacco was low, struck a match. The flame lighted up the corner into which he had crept and rendered visible some objects that he had not noticed before; and, at the first glance, any lingering uncertainty as to the state of affairs on the *Speedwell* vanished in an instant. For the objects that he had seen comprised a shipwright's auger, a caulking mallet, and a dozen or more large pegs cut to a taper at one end.

The purpose of these appliances was unmistakable, and very clearly explained the nature of the "little job" that the sailors had to do down below. Those rascals intended to scuttle the ship. Holes were to be bored in the bottom with the auger and the plugs driven into them. Then, when the mutineers were ready to leave, the plugs would be pulled out, and the ship abandoned with the water pouring into her hold. It was a pretty scheme, if not a novel one, and it again suggested the question: Where were the officers?

Turning over this question, Osmond remembered that Dhoody had gone to the forecastle to fetch his revolver. Then the crew would appear to be still occupying their own quarters; whence it followed that, if the officers were on board, they were probably secured in their berths aft.

This consideration suggested a new idea. Osmond lit another match and explored the immediate neighbourhood in the hope of finding more tools; but there were only the auger and the mallet, the pegs having probably been tapered with a sheath-knife. As the match went out, Osmond quenched the glowing tip, and, picking up the auger and mallet, though for the latter he had no present use, began to grope his way aft. The part of the hold abaft the main hatch had a ground tier of oil-puncheons, above which was stowed a quantity of produce, principally copra and kernels in bags. Climbing on top of this, Osmond crawled aft until he brought up against the bulkhead that separated the cabin from the hold. Here he commenced operations without delay. Rapping with his knuckles to make sure of the absence of obstructing stanchions, he set the point of the auger against the bulkhead, and, grasping the cross lever, fell to work vigorously. It was a big tool, boring an inch and a half hole, and correspondingly heavy to turn; but Osmond drove it with a will, and was soon rewarded by feeling it give with a jerk, and when he withdrew it, there was a circular hole through which streamed the welcome daylight.

He applied his eye to the hole (which, in spite of the thickness of the planking, afforded a fairly wide view) and looked into what was evidently the cuddy or cabin. He could see a small, nearly triangular table fitted with "fiddles," or safety rims, between which a big water-bottle slid backwards and forwards as the ship rolled, pursued by a dozen or more green limes and an empty tumbler – a sight which made his mouth water. Opposite was the companion-ladder and at each side of it a door – probably those of the captain's and mate's cabins. Above the table would be the skylight, though he could not see it; but he could make out some pieces of broken glass on the floor and one or two on the table; and he now recalled that he had noticed, when on deck, that the skylight glass was smashed.

Having made this survey, he returned to his task. Above the hole that he had bored, he proceeded to bore another, slightly intersecting it, and above this another, and so on; tracing a continuous curved row of holes, each hole encroaching a little on the next, and the entire series looking, from the dark hold, like a luminous silhouette of a string of beads. It was arduous work, and monotonous, but Osmond kept at it with only an occasional pause to wipe his streaming face and steal a wistful look at the water-bottle on the cabin table. No sign did he perceive there of either officers or crew; indeed the latter were busy on deck, for he had heard the clink of the windlass, and when that had ceased, the rattle of running gear as the sails were trimmed. And meanwhile the curved line of holes extended along the bulkhead and began to define an ellipse some eighteen inches by twelve.

By the time he had made the twenty-fourth hole, a sudden weakening of the light that came through informed him that the sun was setting. He took a last peep into the cabin before the brief tropic twilight should have faded, and was surprised to note that the tumbler seemed to have vanished and that there appeared to be less water in the bottle. Speculating vaguely on the possible explanation of this, he fell to work again, adding hole after hole to the series, guiding himself by the sense of touch when the light failed completely.

The thirty-eighth hole nearly completed the ellipse, and was within an inch of the first one bored. Standing back from the bulkhead, Osmond gave a vigorous kick on the space enclosed by the last line of holes, and sent the oval piece of planking flying through into the cabin. Passing his head through the opening, he listened awhile. Sounds of revelry from the deck, now plainly audible, told him that the gin was doing its work and that the crew were fully occupied. He slipped easily through the opening, and, groping his way to the table, found the water-bottle and refreshed himself with a long and delicious draught. Then, feeling his way to the companion-ladder, he knocked with his knuckles on the door at its port side.

No one answered; and yet he had a feeling of some soft and stealthy movement within. Accordingly he knocked again, a little more sharply, and as there was still no answer, he turned the handle and pushed gently at the door, which was, however, bolted or locked. But the effort was not in vain, for as he gave a second, harder push, a woman's voice – which sounded quite near, as if the speaker were close to the door – demanded "Who is there?"

Considerably taken aback by the discovery of this unexpected denizen of the mutiny-ridden ship, Osmond was for a few moments at a loss for a reply. At length, putting his mouth near to the keyhole (for the skylight was open and the steersman, at least, not far away), he answered softly: "A friend."

The reply did not appear to have the desired effect, for the woman – also speaking into the keyhole – demanded sharply: "But who are you? And what do you want?"

These were difficult questions. Addressing himself to the first, and boggling awkwardly at the unaccustomed lie, Osmond stammered:

"My name is – er – is Cook, but you don't know me. I am not one of the crew. If you wouldn't mind opening the door, I could explain matters."

"I shall do nothing of the kind," was the reply.

"There's really no occasion for you to be afraid," Osmond urged.

"Isn't there?" she retorted. "And who said I was afraid? Let me tell you that I've got a pistol, and I shall shoot if I have any of your nonsense. So you'd better be off."

Osmond grinned appreciatively but decided to abandon the parley.

"Is there anyone aft here besides you?" he asked.

"Never you mind," was the tart reply. "You had better go back where you came from."

Osmond rose with a grim smile and began cautiously to feel his way towards the companion-steps and past them to the other door that he had seen. Having found it and located the handle, he rapped sharply but not too loudly.

"Well?" demanded a gruff voice from within.

Osmond turned the handle, and, as a stream of light issued from the opening door, he entered hastily and closed it behind him. He found himself in a small cabin lighted by a candle-lamp that swung in gimballs from the bulkhead. One side was occupied by a bunk in which reclined a small, elderly man, who appeared to have been reading, for he held an open volume, which Osmond observed with some surprise to be Applin's Commentary on the Book of Job. His head was roughly bandaged and he wore his left arm in a primitive sling.

"Well," he repeated, taking off his spectacles to look at Osmond.

"You are the captain, I presume," said Osmond.

"Yes. Name of Hartup. Who are you?"

Osmond briefly explained the circumstances of his arrival on board.

"Ah!" said the captain. "I wondered who was boring those holes when I went into the cabin just now. Well, you've put your head into a hornet's nest, young man."

"Yes," said Osmond, "and I'm going to keep it there until I'm paid to take it out."

The captain smiled sourly. "You are like my mate, Will Redford; very like him you are to look at, and the same quarrelsome disposition, apparently."

"Where is the mate now?"

"Overboard," replied the captain. "He got flourishing a revolver and the second mate stabbed him."

"Is the second mate's name Dhoody?"

"Yes. But he's only a substitute. The proper second mate died up at Sherbro, so I promoted Dhoody from before the mast."

"I take it that your crew have mutinied?"

"Yes," said the captain, placidly. "There is over a ton of ivory on board and two hundred ounces of gold dust in that chest that you are sitting on. It was a great temptation. Dhoody began it and Redford made it worse by bullying."

"Dhoody seems to be a tough customer."

"Very," said the captain. "A violent man. A man of wrath. I am surprised that he didn't make an end of you."

"So is he, I expect," Osmond replied with a grin; "and I hope to give him one or two more surprises before we part. What are you going to do?"

The captain sighed. "We are in the hands of Providence," said he.

"You'll be in the hands of Davy Jones if you don't look out," said Osmond. "They are going to scuttle the ship when they get to Ambriz. Can I get anything to eat?"

"There is corned pork and biscuit in that locker," said the captain, "and water and limes on the cabin table. No intoxicants. This is a temperance ship."

Osmond smiled grimly as a wild chorus from above burst out as if in commentary on the captain's statement. But he made no remark. Corned pork was better than discussion just now.

"You seem to have been in the wars," he remarked, glancing at the skipper's bandaged head and arm.

"Yes. Fell down the companion; at least, Dhoody shoved me down. I'll get you to fix a new dressing on my arm when you've finished eating. You'll find some lint and rubber plaster in the medicine-chest there."

"By the way," said Osmond, as he cracked a biscuit on his knee, "there's a woman in the next berth. Sounded like quite a ladylike person, too. Who is she?"

The captain shook his head. "Yes," he groaned, "there's another complication. She is a Miss Burleigh; daughter of Sir Hector Burleigh, the Administrator or Acting Governor, or something of the sort, of the Gold Coast."

"But what the deuce is she doing on an old rattletrap of a windjammer like this?"

The captain sat up with a jerk. "I'll trouble you, young man," he said, severely, "to express yourself with more decorum. I am the owner of this vessel, and if she is good enough for me she will have to be good enough for you. Nobody asked you to come aboard, you know."

"I beg your pardon," said Osmond. "Didn't mean to give offence. But you'll admit that she isn't cut out for the high-class passenger trade."

"She is not," Captain Hartup agreed, "and that is what I pointed out to the young woman when she asked for a passage from Axim to Accra. I told her we had no accommodation for females, but she just giggled and said that didn't matter. She is a very self-willed young woman."

"But why didn't she take a passage on a steamer?"

"There was no steamer due for the Leeward Coast. Her father, Sir Hector, tried to put her off; but she would have her own way. Said it would be a bit of an adventure, travelling on a sailing ship."

"Gad! She was right there," remarked Osmond.

"She was, indeed. Well, she came aboard and Redford gave her his berth, he moving into the second mate's berth, as Dhoody remained in the forecastle. And there she is; and I wish she was at Jericho."

"I expect she does, too. What happened to her when the mutiny broke out?"

"I told her to go to her berth and lock herself in. But no one attempted to molest her."

"I am glad to hear that," said Osmond, and as he broke another biscuit, he asked: "Did you secure the companion hatch?"

"Miss Burleigh did. She fixed the bar across the inside of the doors. But it wasn't necessary, for they had barricaded the doors outside. They didn't want to come down to us; they only wanted to prevent us from going up on deck."

"She was wise to bolt the doors, all the same," said Osmond; and for a time there was silence in the cabin, broken only by the vigorous mastication of stony biscuit.

Chapter Four

The Phantom Mate

When he had finished his rough and hasty meal, Osmond attended to his host's injuries, securing a pad of lint on the lacerated arm with strips cut from a broad roll of the sticky rubber plaster. Then he went out into the cabin to reconnoitre and take a drink of water, closing the door of the captain's berth so that the light should not be seen from above.

The hubbub on deck had now subsided into occasional snatches of indistinct melody. The men had had a pretty long bout and were – to judge by the tone of the songs – getting drowsy. Osmond climbed on to the table and began carefully to pick the remainder of the glass out of the skylight frame. The skylight had a fixed top – there being a separate ventilator for the cabin – and, instead of the usual guard-bars, had loose wooden shutters for use in bad weather. Hence the present catastrophe; and hence, when Osmond had picked away the remains of the glass, there was a clear opening through which he could, by hoisting himself up, thrust out his head and shoulders. To avoid this fatiguing position, however, he descended and placed on the table a case that he had noticed by daylight on a side-locker; then, mounting, he was able, by standing on this, to look out at his ease, and yet pop down out of sight if necessary.

When he cautiously thrust out his head to look up and down the deck, he was able at first to see very little, though there was now a moderate starlight. Forward, whence drowsy mumblings mingled with snores came from the neighbourhood of the caboose, he could see only a projected pair of feet; and aft, where a single voice carolled huskily at intervals, his view was cut off by the boat – which lay at the side of the deck – and by the hood of the companion-hatch. He craned out farther; and now he could catch a glimpse of the man at the wheel. The fellow was not taking his duties very seriously, for he was seated on the grating unhandily filling his pipe and letting the ship steer herself; which she did well enough, if direction was of no consequence, the light breeze being a couple of points free and the main-sheet well slacked out. Osmond watched the man light his pipe, recognizing that the flat, shaven face – which he had punched earlier in the day – and as he watched he rapidly reviewed the strategic position and considered its possibilities. The flat, shaven face, with its wide mouth, offered a vague suggestion. He considered; looked out again; listened awhile; and then descended with a distinctly purposeful air. First he crept silently up the steps of the companion and softly removed the bar from the inside of the doors. Then he made his way to the skipper's cabin.

As he entered, the "old man" looked up from his book inquiringly.

"I've come down for a bit of rubber plaster," said Osmond.

The skipper nodded towards the medicine-chest and resumed his studies, while Osmond cut off a strip of plaster some seven inches by four.

"You haven't got any thin rope or small-stuff in here, I suppose?" said Osmond.

"There's a coil of rope-yarn on the peg under those oilskins – those smart yellow ones; those were poor Redford's. He was too much of a dandy to wear common black oilies like the rest of us. What do you want the stuff for?"

"I want to try a little experiment," replied Osmond. "But I'll tell you about it afterwards"; and he took down the oilskins and the coil of line, the latter of which he carried away with him to the main cabin together with the roll of plaster and the scissors. Here, by the faint starlight that now mitigated the darkness, he cut off a couple of lengths of the line and, having pocketed one and made a bowline-knot or fixed loop in the end of the other, ascended the table and once more looked out on deck. Save for some resonant snoring from forward, all was quiet and the ship seemed to have settled down for the night. The helmsman, however, was still awake, for Osmond heard him yawn wearily; but he had left the wheel with a rope hitched round one of the spokes, and was now leaning over the quarter-rail, apparently contemplating the passing water.

It was an ideal opportunity. Grasping the frame of the skylight, Osmond gave a light spring and came through the opening like a very stealthy harlequin. Then, creeping along the deck in the shelter of the boat and that of the companion-hood, he rose and stole noiselessly on the toes of his rubber-soled shoes towards the preoccupied seaman. Nearer and nearer he crept, grasping an end of the line between the fingers of either hand, and holding the strip of plaster spread out on the palm of the left, until he stood close behind his quarry. Then, as the sailor removed his pipe to emit another enormous yawn, he slipped his left hand round, clapped the plaster over the open mouth, and instantly pinioned the man's arms by clasping him tightly round the chest. The fellow struggled furiously and would have shouted, but was only able to utter muffled grunts and snorts through his nose. His arms were gripped to his sides as if in a vice and his efforts to kick were all foreseen and adroitly frustrated. He had been taken by surprise by a man who was his superior in mere strength and who was an expert wrestler into the bargain; and he was further handicapped by superstitious terror and lack of breath.

The struggle went on with surprisingly little noise – since the sailor could not cry out – and meanwhile Osmond contrived to pass the end of the line through the loop of the bowline and draw it inch by inch until it was ready for the final pull. Then, with a skilful throw, he let the man down softly, face downwards, on the deck; jerked the line tight and sat on his prisoner's legs. He was now master of the situation. Taking another turn with the line round the man's body, he secured it with a knot in the middle of the back, and with the other length of line, which he had in his pocket, he lashed his captive's ankles together.

The almost noiseless struggle had passed unnoticed by the sleepers forward. No watch or look-out had been set and it had apparently been left to the helmsman to rouse up his relief when he guessed his "trick" at the wheel to have expired. Osmond listened for a few moments, and then, removing the batten with which the doors of the companion had been secured on the outside, opened the hatch, slid his helpless prisoner down the ladder; closed the doors again, replaced the batten, and, creeping through the opening of the skylight, let himself down into the cabin. Here he seized his writhing captive, and, dragging him across the cabin, thrust him head-first through the hole in the bulkhead and followed him into the hold, where he finally deposited him as comfortably as possible on the kernel bags under the main hatch.

"Now, listen," he said sternly. "I'm going to take that plaster off your mouth; but if you utter a sound, I shall stick it on again and fix it with a lashing." He peeled the plaster off, and, as the man drew a long breath, he demanded: "Do you hear what I say?"

"Yes," was the reply; "I hear. You've got me, governor, fair on the hop, you have. You won't hear no more of me. And if you can cop that there Dhoody the same way, there won't be no more trouble on this ship."

"I'll see what can be done," said Osmond; and with this he returned to the cabin, and, cutting off two fresh lengths of rope-yarn and another piece of plaster, prepared for a fresh capture.

But, at present, there was no one to capture. The wheel jerked to and fro in its lashing, the brigantine walloped along quietly before the soft breeze, the crew slumbered peacefully forward, and Osmond looked out of the skylight on an empty deck, listening impatiently to the chorus of snores and wondering if he would get another chance.

It is impossible to say how long this state of affairs would have lasted if nothing had happened to disturb it. As it was, a sudden accident dispelled the universal repose. The unsteered vessel, yawing from side to side, lifted her stern to a following sea and yawed so far that her mainsail got by the lee. The long boom swung inboard and the big sail jibed over with a slam that shook the entire fabric. The vessel immediately broached to with all her square-sails aback, and heeled over until the water bubbled up through her scupper-holes.

The noise and the jar roused some of the sleepers forward and a hoarse voice bawled out angrily: "Now you, Sam! What the devil are you up to? You'll have the masts overboard if you don't look out."

Immediately after, Dhoody came staggering aft along the sloping deck, followed by one or two bewildered sailors. The group stood gazing in muddled surprise at the unattended wheel, and Dhoody exclaimed:

"Where's the beggar gone to? Here, you Sam! Where are you?"

"P'raps he's gone down to the cabin," one of the men suggested.

"No, he ain't," said Dhoody. "The companion's fastened up."

"So it is, mate," agreed the other with a glance at the battened doors; and the party rambled slowly round the poop, peering out into the darkness astern and speculating vaguely on the strange disappearance.

"He's gone overboard," said Dhoody; "that's what he's done. So you'd better take the wheel now, Bob Simmons; and you just mind yer helm, or you'll be goin' overboard, too, with all that lush in yer 'ed."

Accordingly Simmons, protesting sleepily that it "wasn't his trick yet," took his place at the wheel. The vessel was put once more on her course, and the men, with the exception of Dhoody, crawled forward to the shelter of the caboose. The second mate remained awhile, yawning drearily and impressing on the somnolent Simmons the responsibilities of his position. Then, at last, he too went forward, and the ship settled down to its former quiet.

Osmond waited for some time in case Dhoody should return to see that the new helmsman was attending to his instructions; but as he made no reappearance and was now probably asleep, it seemed safe to resume operations. Osmond thrust his head and shoulders out through the opening, but, though he could see that the wheel was already deserted, the unfaithful Simmons was invisible. Presently, however, a soft snore from somewhere close by invited him to further investigation, and as he crept out on deck, the enormity of Simmons' conduct was revealed. He had not sunk overpowered at his post, but had deliberately seated himself against the doors of the companion, where he now reclined at his ease, wrapped in alcoholic slumber. If only Dhoody would keep out of the way, the capture was as good as made.

Osmond stole up to the sleeping seaman and softly encircled his arms with the noose, leaving it slack with the end handy for the final pull. Then he put the man's feet together, and passing the lashing round the ankles, secured it firmly. This aroused the sleeper, who began to mumble protests. Instantly, Osmond slapped the plaster on his mouth, jerked the arm-lashing tight and secured it with a knot; unbattened the doors, and, opening them, slid the wriggling captive down the ladder on to the cabin floor. Then he came up, closed and rebattened the doors, slipped down through the skylight, and, dragging his prisoner to the bulkhead, bundled him neck and crop through the opening and finally deposited him on the kernel-bags beside the other man, who was now slumbering peacefully. Having removed the plaster, he remained awhile, for Simmons was in no condition to give promises of good behaviour; but in a few minutes he gave what was more reassuring, a good healthy snore; on which Osmond departed, leaving him to sleep the sleep of the drunk.

The capture had been made none too soon. As Osmond came through into the cabin, he was aware of voices on deck and, climbing on to the table, put his head up to listen, but keeping carefully out of sight.

"It's a dam rum go," a hoarse voice exclaimed. "Seems as if there was somethink queer about this bloomin' ship. First of all this factory devil comes aboard like a roarin' lion seekin' who he can bash on the 'ed; then Sam goes overboard; then Bob Simmons goes overboard. 'Tain't nateral, I tell yer. There's somethink queer, and it's my belief as it's all along o' this mutiny."

"Oh, shut up, Bill," growled Dhoody.

"Bill's right, though," said another voice. "We ain't 'ad no luck since we broke out. I'm for chuckin' this Ambriz job and lettin' the old man out."

"And what about Redford?" demanded Dhoody.

"Redford ain't no affair of mine," was the sulky reply; to which Dhoody rejoined in terms that cannot, in the interests of public morality, be literally recorded; concluding with the remark that "if he'd got to swing, it wouldn't be for Redford only."

"Then," said the first speaker, "you'd better take the wheel yerself. I ain't goin' to."

"More ain't I," said another. "I don't want to go overboard."

A prolonged wrangle ensued, the upshot of which was that the men drifted away forward, leaving Dhoody to steer the ship.

Osmond quietly renewed his preparations, though he realized that a considerably tougher encounter loomed ahead. Dhoody was not only less drunk than the others; he was a good deal more alert and intelligent and he probably had a revolver in his pocket. And the other men would now be more easily roused after this second catastrophe. He peeped out from time to time, always finding Dhoody wide awake at his post, and sensible of drowsy conversation from the sailors forward.

It was fully an hour before a chance seemed to present itself; and Osmond was too wary to attack blindly without a chance. By that time the mumblings from forward had subsided into snores and the ship was once more wrapped in repose. Looking out at that moment, he saw Dhoody staring critically aloft, as if dissatisfied with the trim of the sails. Presently the second mate stepped away from the wheel, and, casting off one of the lee braces, took a long pull at the rope. Now was the time for action. Slipping out through the skylight, Osmond stole quickly along in the shelter of the boat, and, emerging behind Dhoody, stood up just as the latter stooped to belay the rope. He waited until his quarry had set a half-hitch on the last turn and rose to go back to the wheel; then he sprang at him, clapped the plaster on his mouth, and encircled him with his arms.

But Dhoody was a tough adversary. He was stronger, more sober, and less nervous than the others. And he had a moustache, which interfered with the set of the plaster, so that his breathing was less hampered. In fact, Osmond had to clamp his hand on it to prevent the man from calling out; and thus it was that the catastrophe befell. For as Osmond relaxed his bear-hug with one arm, Dhoody wriggled himself partly free. In a moment his hand flew to his pocket, and Osmond grabbed his wrist only just in time to prevent him from pointing the revolver. Then followed a struggle at the utmost tension of two strong men; a struggle, on Osmond's side, at least, for dear life. Gripping the other man's wrists, he watched the revolver, all his strength concentrated on the effort to prevent its muzzle from being turned on him. And so the two men stood for a space, nearly motionless, quite silent, trembling with the intensity of muscular strain.

Suddenly Dhoody took a quick step backwards. A fatal step; for the manoeuvre failed, and Osmond followed him up, pressing him farther backward. The bulwark on the poop was comparatively low. As Dhoody staggered against it with accumulated momentum, his body swung outboard and his feet rose from the deck. It was impossible to save him without releasing the pistol hand. He remained poised for an instant on the rail and then toppled over; and as he slithered down the side and his wrist slipped from Osmond's grasp, the revolver discharged, blowing a ragged hole in the bulwark and waking the echoes in the sails with the din of the explosion.

Osmond sprang back to the companion hatch and crouched behind the hood. There was no time for him to get back to the skylight; indeed he hardly had time to unfasten the doors and drop on to the ladder before the men came shambling aft, muttering and rubbing their eyes. Quietly closing the doors, he descended to the cabin and took up his old post of observation on the table.

"He's gone, right enough," said an awe-stricken voice, "and I reckon it'll be our turn next. This is a bad look-out, mates."

There was a brief and dismal silence; then a distant report was heard, followed quickly by two more.

"That's Dhoody," exclaimed another voice. "He's a-swimmin' and makin' signals. What's to be done? We can't let 'im drownd without doin' nothin'."

"No," agreed the first man, "we must have a try at pickin' 'im up. You and me, Tom, will put off in the dinghy, while Joe keeps the ship hove-to."

"What!" protested Joe. "Am I to be left alone on the ship with no one but Jim Darker, and him below in his bunk?"

"Well, yer can't let a shipmate drownd, can yer?" demanded the other. "And look here, Joe Bradley, as soon as you've got the ship hove-to, you just fetch up the fo'c'sle lamp and show us a glim, or we shall be goners, too. Now hard down with the helm, mate!"

Very soon the loud flapping of canvas announced that the ship had come up into the wind, and immediately after the squeal of tackle-blocks was heard. The *Speedwell* carried a dinghy, slung from davits at the taffrail, in addition to the larger boat on deck, and it was in this that the two men were putting out on their rather hopeless quest.

Osmond rapidly reviewed the situation. Of the original seven men one was overboard, two were in the hold, one was below in his bunk, and two were away in the boat. There remained only Joe Bradley. It would be pretty easy to overpower him and stow him in the hold; but a yet easier plan suggested itself. Joe was evidently in a state of extreme superstitious funk and the other two were in little better case. He recalled the captain's remark as to his resemblance to the dead mate and also the fact that Redford's oilskins were different from any others on board. These circumstances seemed to group themselves naturally and indicate a course of action.

He made his way to the captain's berth and, knocking softly and receiving no answer, entered. The skipper had fallen asleep over his book and lay in his bunk, a living commentary on the Book of Job. Osmond took the oilskins from the peg, and, stealing back silently to the cabin, invested himself in the borrowed raiment. Presently a passing gleam of light from above told him that Joe was carrying the forecastle lamp aft to "show a glim" from the taffrail. Remembering that he had left the companion hatch unfastened, he ascended the ladder, and, softly opening one door, looked out. At the moment, Joe was engaged in hanging the lamp from a fair-lead over the stern, and, as his back was towards the deck, Osmond stepped out of the hatch and silently approached him.

Having secured the lamp, Joe took a long look over the dark sea and then turned towards the deck; and as his eyes fell on the tall, oilskinned figure, obscurely visible in the gloom – for the lamp was below the bulwark – he uttered a gasp of horror and began rapidly to shuffle away backwards. Osmond stood motionless, watching him from under the deep shade of his sou'wester, as he continued to edge backwards. Suddenly his heel caught on a ring-bolt and he staggered and fell on the deck with a howl of terror; but in another instant he had scrambled to his feet and raced away forward, whence the slam of the forecastle scuttle announced his retirement to the sanctuary of his berth.

More than a quarter of an hour elapsed before a hoarse hail from the sea heralded the return of the boat.

"Joe ahoy! It's no go, mate. He's gone."

There was a pause. Then came the splash of oars, a bump under the counter, the sound of the hooking-on of tackles, and another hail.

"Joe ahoy! Is all well aboard?"

Osmond stepped away into the shadow of the mainsail, whence he watched the taffrail. Soon the two men came swarming actively up the tackle-ropes, their heads appeared above the rail, and they swung themselves on board simultaneously.

"Joe ahoy!" one of them sang out huskily, as he looked blankly round the deck. "Where are yer, Joe?" There was a brief silence; then, in an awe-stricken voice, he exclaimed: "Gawd-amighty, Tom! If he ain't gone overboard, too!"

At this moment the other man caught sight of Osmond, and, silently touching his companion on the shoulder, pointed to the motionless figure. Osmond moved a little out of the shadow and began to pace aft, treading without a sound. For one instant the two men watched as if petrified; then, with one accord, they stampeded forward, and once more the forecastle scuttle slammed. Osmond followed, and quietly thrusting a belaying-pin through the staple of the scuttle, secured them in their retreat.

Chapter Five

The New Afterguard

When Captain Hartup, brusquely aroused from his slumbers, opened his eyes and beheld a tall, yellow-oilskinned figure in his berth, the Book of Job faded instantly from his memory and he scrambled from his bunk with a yell of terror. Then, when Osmond took off his sou'wester, he recognized his visitor and became distinctly uncivil.

"What the devil do you mean by masquerading in this idiotic fashion?" he demanded angrily. "I don't want any of your silly schoolboy jokes on this ship, so you please understand that."

"I came down," said Osmond, smothering a grin and ignoring the reproaches, "to report progress. I have hove the ship to, but there is no one at the wheel and no look-out."

The skipper stared at him in bewilderment as he crawled back into his bunk. "What do you mean?" he asked. "*You've* hove the ship to? Isn't there anybody on deck?"

"No. The ship is taking care of herself at the moment."

"Queer," said the skipper. "I wonder what Dhoody's up to."

"Dhoody is overboard," said Osmond.

"Overboard!" exclaimed the skipper, staring harder than ever at Osmond. Then, after an interval of silent astonishment, he said severely:

"You are talking in riddles, young man. Just try to explain yourself a little more clearly. Do I understand that you have hove my second mate overboard?"

"No," replied Osmond. "He went overboard by accident. But it was all for the best"; and hereupon he proceeded to give the skipper a somewhat sketchy account of the stirring events of the last few hours, to which the latter listened with sour disapproval.

"I don't hold with deeds of violence," he said when the story was finished, "but what you have done is on your own head. Where do you say the crew are?"

"Two are in the hold and the other four are in the fo'c'sle, bolted in. They are all pretty drunk, but you'll find them as quiet as lambs when they've slept off their tipple. But the question is, what is to be done now. The men won't be any good for an hour or two, but there ought to be someone at the wheel and some sort of watch on deck. And I can't take it on until I have had a sleep. I've been hard at it ever since I came on board yesterday."

"Yes," Captain Hartup agreed, sarcastically, "I daresay you found it fatiguing, chucking your fellow-creatures overboard and breaking their heads. Well, you had better take the second mate's berth – the one Redford had – and I will go on deck and keep a look-out. But I can't do much with my arm in a sling."

"What about the lady?" asked Osmond. "Couldn't she hold on to the wheel if you stood by and told her what to do?"

"Ha!" exclaimed the skipper, "I had forgotten her. Yes, she knows how to steer – in a fashion. She used to wheedle Redford into letting her take a trick in his watch while he stood by and instructed her; a parcel of silly philandering, really, but it wasn't any affair of mine. I'd better go and rouse her up."

"Wait till I've turned in," said Osmond. "I am not fit to meet a lady until I have had a sleep and a wash. If you will show me my berth, I will go and cast the lashings off those two beggars in the hold and then turn in for an hour or two."

The captain smiled sardonically but made no comment; and when Osmond, furnished with a lantern, had visited the hold and removed the lashings from the still slumbering seamen, he entered the tiny berth that the skipper pointed out to him, closed the door, and, having taken off his jacket and folded it carefully, and wound his watch, blew out the candle in the lantern, stretched himself in the bunk and instantly fell asleep.

When he awoke, the gleam from the deck-light over his head – the berth had no port-hole – informed him that it was day. Reference to his watch showed the hour to be about half-past eight; and the clink of crockery and a murmur of voices – one very distinctly feminine – suggested that breakfast was in progress. Which, again, suggested that the conditions of life on board had returned to the, more or less, normal.

Osmond sprang out of the bunk, and, impelled by hunger and curiosity, made a lightning toilet with the aid of Redford's razor, sponge, and brushes. There was, of course, no bath; but a "dry" rub-down in the oven-like cabin was a fair substitute. In a surprisingly short time, with the imperfect means at hand, he had made himself almost incredibly presentable, and after a final "look over" in Redford's minute shaving-glass, he opened the door and entered the cuddy.

The little table, roughly laid for breakfast, was occupied by Captain Hartup and a lady, and a flat-faced seaman with a black eye officiated as cabin steward. They all looked up as Osmond emerged from his door and the sailor grinned a little sheepishly.

"Had a short night, haven't you?" said the captain. "Didn't expect you to turn out yet. Let me present you to our passenger. Miss Burleigh, this is Mr – Mr – "

"Cook," said Osmond, ready for the question this time.

"Mr Cook, the young man I was telling you about."

Miss Burleigh acknowledged Osmond's bow, gazing at him with devouring curiosity and marvelling at his cool, trim, well-groomed appearance.

"I think," she said, "we had a brief interview last night, if you can call it an interview when there was a locked door between us.

I am afraid I wasn't very civil. But you must try to forgive me. I've been sorry since."

"There is no need to be," replied Osmond. "It was perfectly natural."

"Oh, but it isn't mere remorse. I am so mad with myself for having missed all the excitements. If I had only known! But, you see, I had happened to look out of my door in the evening, hearing a peculiar sort of noise, and then I saw somebody boring holes in the partition, and of course I thought it was those wretches trying to get into the cabin. Then, when I heard your voice, I made sure it was Dhoody or one of those other ruffians, trying to entice me out. And so I missed all the fun."

Just as well that you did," said the captain. "Females are out of place in scenes of violence and disorder. What are you going to have, Mr Cook? There's corned pork and biscuit and I think there's some lobscouse or sea-pie in the galley, if the men haven't eaten it all."

Osmond turned suddenly to the sailor, who instantly came to "attention."

"You're Sam Winter, aren't you?"

"Aye, sir," the man replied, considerably taken aback by the "factory bug's" uncanny omniscience. "Sam Winter it is, sir."

"How is Jim Darker?"

"He's a-doin' nicely, sir," replied Sam, regarding Osmond with secret awe. "Eat a rare breakfast of lobscouse, he did."

"Is there any left?"

"I think there is, sir."

"Then I'll have some"; and, as the man saluted and bustled away up the companion-steps, he seated himself on the fixed bench by the table.

Captain Hartup smiled sourly, while Miss Burleigh regarded Osmond with delighted amusement.

"Seem quite intimate with 'em all," the former remarked. "Regular friend of the family. I suppose it was you who gave Winter that black eye?"

"I expect so," replied Osmond. "He probably caught it in the scrum when I first came on board. Did you have any trouble in getting the men to go back to duty?"

"The men in the fo'c'sle wouldn't come out till daylight, and the two men in the hold took a lot of rousing from their drunken sleep. Of course, I couldn't get through that hole with my arm in this sling, so I had to prod them with a boat-hook. It's a pity you made that hole. Lets the smell of the cargo and the bilge through into the cabin."

He looked distastefully at the dark aperture in the bulkhead and sniffed – quite unnecessarily, for the air of the cuddy was charged with the mingled aroma of bilge and kernels.

"Well, it had to be," said Osmond; "and it will be easy to cover up. After all, a smell in the cuddy is better than sea-water."

Here Sam Winter was seen unsteadily descending the companion-steps with a large enamelled-iron plate in his hands; which plate, being deferentially placed on the table before Osmond, was seen to be loaded with a repulsive-looking mixture of "salt horse," shreds of fat pork and soaked biscuit floating in a greasy brown liquid.

"That's all there was left, sir," said he, transferring a small surplus from his hands to the dorsal aspect of his trousers.

Osmond made no comment on this statement but fell-to on the unsavoury mess with wolfish voracity, while the captain filled a mug with alleged coffee and passed it to him.

"Who is at the wheel, Winter?" the captain asked.

"Simmons, sir," was the reply. "I woke him up again as I come aft."

"Well, you'd better go up and take it from him. Carry on till I come up."

As Winter disappeared up the companion-way Miss Burleigh uttered a little gurgle of enjoyment. "Aren't they funny?" she exclaimed. "Fancy waking up the man at the wheel! It's like a comic opera."

The captain looked at her sourly as he tapped the table with a piece of biscuit for the purpose of evicting a couple of fat weevils; but he made no comment, and for a time the meal proceeded in silence. The skipper was fully occupied in cutting up his corned pork with one hand and in breaking the hard biscuit and knocking out the weevils, while Osmond doggedly worked his way through the lobscouse with the silent concentration of a famished man, all unconscious of the interest and curiosity with which he was being observed by the girl opposite.

However, the lobscouse came to an end – all too soon – and as he reached out to the bread-barge for a handful of biscuit he met her eyes; and fine, clear, bright blue eyes they were, sparkling with vivacity and humour. She greeted his glance with an affable smile and hoped that he was feeling revived.

"That looked rather awful stuff," she added.

"It was all right," said he, "only there wasn't enough of it. But I hope you had something more suitable."

"She has had what the ship's stores provide, like the rest of us," snapped the captain. "This is not a floating hotel."

"No, it isn't," Osmond agreed, "and that's a fact. But it is something that she still floats; and it would be just as well to keep her floating."

"What do you mean?" demanded the skipper.

Osmond thoughtfully extracted a weevil with the prong of his fork as he replied: "You've got a crew of six, three to a watch, and one of them has got to do the cooking. But you have got no officers."

"Well, I know that," said the captain. "What about it?"

"You can't carry on without officers."

"I can and I shall. I shall appoint one of the men to be mate and take the other watch myself."

"That won't answer," said Osmond. "There isn't a man among them who could be trusted or who is up to the job; and you are not in a fit state to stand regular watches."

Captain Hartup snorted. "Don't you lay down the law to me, young man. I am the master of this ship." And then he added, a little inconsistently: "Perhaps you can tell me how I am to get a couple of officers."

"I can," replied Osmond. "There will have to be a responsible person on deck with each watch."

"Well?"

"Well, there are two responsible persons sitting at this table with you."

For a few moments the captain stared at Osmond in speechless astonishment (while Miss Burleigh murmured "Hear, hear!" and rapped the table with the handle of her knife). At length he burst out:

"What! Do I understand you to suggest that I should navigate this vessel with a landsman and a female as my mates?"

"I am not exactly a landsman," Osmond replied. "I am an experienced yachtsman and I have made a voyage in a sailing ship."

"Pah!" exclaimed the skipper. "Fresh-water sailor and a passenger! Don't talk nonsense. And a female, too!"

"What I am suggesting," Osmond persisted, calmly, "is that you should be about as much as possible in your condition and that Miss Burleigh and I should keep an eye on the men when you are below. I could take all the night watches and Miss Burleigh could be on deck during the day."

"That's just rank foolishness," said the skipper. "Talk of a comic opera! Why, you are wanting to turn the ship into a Punch and Judy show! I've no patience to listen to you," and the captain rose in dudgeon and crawled – not without difficulty – up the companion-steps. Miss Burleigh watched him with a mischievous smile, and as his stumbling feet disappeared she turned to Osmond.

"What a lark it would be!" she exclaimed, gleefully. "Do you think you will be able to persuade him? He is rather an obstinate little man."

"The best way with obstinate people," replied Osmond, "is to assume that they have agreed, and carry on. Can you steer – not that you need, being an officer. But you ought to know how to."

"I can steer by the compass. But I don't know much about the sails excepting that you have to keep the wind on the right side of them."

"Yes, that is important with a square-rigged vessel. But you will soon learn the essentials – enough to enable you to keep the crew out of mischief. We will go on deck presently and then I will show you the ropes and explain how the gear works."

"That will be jolly," said she. "But there's another thing that I want you to explain: about this mutiny, you know. Captain Hartup was awfully muddled about it. I want to know all that happened while I was locked in my berth."

"I expect you know all about it now," Osmond replied evasively. "There was a bit of a rumpus, of course, but as soon as Dhoody was overboard it was all plain sailing."

"Now, you are not going to put me off like that," she said, in a resolute tone. "I want the whole story in detail, if you please, sir. Does a second mate say 'sir' when he, or she, addresses the first mate?"

"Not as a rule," Osmond replied, with a grin.

"Then I won't. But I want the story. Now."

Osmond looked uneasily into the delicately fair, slightly freckled face and thought it, with its crown of red-gold hair, the prettiest face that he had ever seen. But it was an uncommonly determined little face, all the same.

"There really isn't any story," he began. But she interrupted sharply:

"Now listen to me. Yesterday there were seven ferocious men going about this ship like roaring and swearing lions. Today there are six meek and rather sleepy lambs – I saw them just before breakfast. It is you who have produced this miraculous change, and I want to know how you did it. No sketchy evasions, you know. I want a clear, intelligible narrative."

"It isn't a very suitable occasion for a long yarn," he objected. "Don't you think we ought to go on deck and keep an eye on the old man?"

"Perhaps we ought," she agreed. "But I'm not going to let you off the story, you know. That is understood, isn't it?"

He gave a reluctant assent, and when she had fetched her pith helmet from her cabin and he had borrowed a Panama hat of Redford's, they ascended together to the deck.

The scene was reminiscent of "The Ancient Mariner." The blazing sun shone down on a sea that seemed to be composed of oil, so smooth and unruffled was its surface. The air was absolutely still, and the old brigantine wallowed foolishly as the great, glassy rollers swept under her, her sails alternately filling and backing with loud, explosive flaps as the masts swung from side to side, and her long main-boom banging across with a heavy jar at each roll. Sam Winter stood at the wheel in a posture of easy negligence (but he straightened up with a jerk as Osmond's head rose out of the companion-hood); the rest of the crew, excepting Jim Darker, lounged about drowsily forward; and the skipper appeared to be doing sentry-go before a row of gin-cases that were ranged along the side of the caboose. He looked round as the newcomers arrived on deck, and pointing to the cases, addressed Osmond.

"These boxes of poison belong to you, I understand. I can't have them lying about here."

"Better stow them in the lazarette when I've checked the contents," replied Osmond.

"I can't have intoxicating liquors in my lazarette. This is a temperance ship. I've a good mind to chuck 'em overboard."

"All right," said Osmond. "You pay me one pound four, and then you can do what you like with them."

"Pay!" shrieked the captain. "I pay for this devil's elixir! I traffic in strong drink that steals away men's reason and turns them into fiends! Never! Not a farthing!"

"Very well," said Osmond, "then they had better go below. Here, you, Simmons and Bradley, bear a hand with these cases. Will you see them stowed away in the lazarette, Miss Burleigh?"

"Aye, aye, sir," the latter replied, touching her helmet smartly; whereupon the two men, with delighted grins, pounced upon two of the cases, while Miss Burleigh edged up close to Osmond.

"What on earth is the lazarette?" she whispered, "and where shall I find it?"

"Under the cuddy floor," he whispered in reply. "The trap is under the table."

As the two seamen picked up their respective loads and went off beaming, followed by Miss Burleigh, the captain stood gazing open-mouthed.

"Well, I'm – I'm – sure!" he exclaimed, at length. "What do you mean by giving orders to my crew? And I said I wouldn't have that gin in my lazarette."

"Can't leave it about for the men to pinch. You'll have them all drunk again. And what about the watches? We can't have the regular port and starboard watches until you are fit again. Better do as I suggested. Let me keep on deck during the night, and you take charge during the day. Miss Burleigh can relieve you if you want to go below."

"I'll have no women playing the fool on my ship," snapped the skipper; "but as to you, I don't mind you staying on deck at night if you undertake to call me up when you get into a mess – as you certainly will."

"Very well," said Osmond, "we'll leave it at that. And now you'd better come below and let me attend to your bandages. There's nothing to do on deck while this calm lasts."

The skipper complied, not unwillingly; and when Osmond had very gently and skilfully renewed the dressings and rebandaged the injured arm and head – the captain reclining in his bunk for the purpose – he retired, leaving his patient to rest awhile with the aid of the Commentary on the Book of Job.

As soon as he arrived on deck, he proceeded definitely to take charge. The stowage of the gin was now completed and the crew were once more collected forward, gossiping idly but evidently watchful and expectant of further developments from the "afterguard." Osmond hailed them in a masterful tone.

"Here, you men, get a pull on the main-sheet and stop the boom from slamming. Haul her in as taut as she'll go."

The men came aft with ready cheerfulness, and as Osmond cast off the fall of the rope and gave them a lead, they tailed on and hauled with a will until the sheet-blocks were as close as they could be brought. Then, when the rope had been belayed, Osmond turned to the crew and briefly explained the arrangements for working the ship in her present, short-handed state.

"So you understand," he concluded, "I am the mate for the time being, and Miss Burleigh is taking the duties of the second mate. Is that clear?"

"Aye, aye, sir," was the reply, accompanied by the broadest of grins, "we understands, sir."

"Who is the cook?" inquired Osmond.

"Bill Foat 'as been a-doin' the cookin', sir," Simmons explained.

"Then he'd better get on with it. Whose watch on deck is it?"

"Starboard watch, sir," replied Simmons; "that's me and Winter and Darker."

"I must have a look at Darker," said Osmond. "Meanwhile you take the wheel, and you, Winter, keep a look-out forward. I haven't heard the ship's bell sounded this morning."

"No, sir," Winter explained. "The clock in the companion has stopped and none of us haven't got the time."

"Very well," said Osmond. "I'll wind it up and start it when I make eight bells."

The routine of the duties being thus set going, Osmond went forward and paid a visit to the invalid in the forecastle, with the result that Jim Darker presently appeared on deck with a clean bandage and a somewhat sheepish grin. Then the chief officer turned his attention to the education of his subordinate, observed intently by six pairs of inquisitive eyes.

"I think, Miss Burleigh," he said, "you had better begin by learning how to take an observation. Then you will be able to do something that the men can't, as an officer should. Do you know anything about mathematics?"

"As much as is necessary, I expect. I took second-class honours in maths. Will that do?"

"Of course it will. By the way, where did you take your degree?"

"Oxford – Somerville, you know?"

"Oh," said Osmond, rather taken aback. "When were you up at Oxford?"

She regarded him with a mischievous smile as she replied: "After your time, I should say. I only came down a year ago."

It was, of course, but a chance shot. Nevertheless, Osmond hastily reverted to the subject of observations. "It is quite a simple matter to take the altitude of the sun, and you work out your results almost entirely from tables. You will do it easily the first time. I'll go and get Redford's sextant, or better still, we might go below and I can show you how to use a sextant and how to work out your latitude."

"Yes," she agreed, eagerly, "I would sooner have my first lesson below. Our friends here are so very interested in us."

She bustled away down to the cabin, and Osmond, following, went into his berth, whence he presently emerged with two mahogany cases and a portly volume, inscribed *Norie's Navigation*.

"I've found the second mate's sextant as well as Redford's, so we can have one each," he said, laying them on the table with the volume. "And now let us get to work. We mustn't stay here too long or we shall miss the transit."

The two mates seated themselves side by side at the table, and Osmond, taking one of the sextants out of its case, explained its construction and demonstrated its use. Then the volume was opened, the tables explained, the mysteries of "dip" refraction and "parallax" expounded, and finally an imaginary observation was worked out on the back of an envelope.

"I had no idea," said Miss Burleigh, as she triumphantly finished the calculation, "that the science of navigation was so simple."

"It isn't," replied Osmond. "Latitude by the meridian altitude of the sun is the ABC of navigation. Some of it, such as longitude by lunar distance, is fairly tough. But it is time we got on deck. It is past eleven by my watch and the Lord knows what the time actually is. The chronometer has stopped. The skipper bumped against it when he staggered into his berth on the day when the mutiny broke out."

"Then how shall we get the longitude?" Miss Burleigh asked.

"We shan't. But it doesn't matter much. We must keep on a westerly course. There is nothing, in that direction, between us and America."

The appearance on deck of the two officers, each armed with a sextant, created a profound impression. It is true that, so far as the "second mate" was concerned, the attitude of the crew was mere;y that of respectful amusement. But the effect, in the case of Osmond, was very different. The evidence that he was able to "shoot the sun" established him in their eyes as a pukka navigator, and added to the awe with which they regarded this uncannily capable "factory bug." And there was plenty of time for the impression to soak in; for the first glance through the sextant showed that the sun was still rising fairly fast; that there was yet some considerable time to run before noon. In fact, more than half an hour passed before the retardation of the sun's motion heralded the critical phase. And at this moment the skipper's head rose slowly above the hood of the companion-hatch.

At first his back was towards the observers, but when he emerged and, turning forward, became aware of them, he stopped short as if petrified. The men ceased their gossip to watch him with ecstatic grins, and Sam Winter edged stealthily towards the ship's bell.

"What is the meaning of this play-acting and tomfoolery?" the skipper demanded, sourly. "Women and landsmen monkeying about with nautical instruments."

Osmond held up an admonitory hand, keeping his eye glued to the eyepiece of the sextant.

"I'm asking you a question," the captain persisted.

There was another brief silence. Then, suddenly, Osmond sang out "Eight bells!" and looked at his watch. Winter, seizing the lanyard that hung from the clapper of the bell, struck the eight strokes, and the second mate – prompted in a hoarse whisper – called out:

"Port watch, there! Bradley will take the first trick at the wheel."

"Aye, aye, sir – Miss, I means," responded Bradley, and proceeded, purple-faced and chuckling aloud, to relieve the gratified Simmons.

At these proceedings the captain looked on in helpless bewilderment. He watched Osmond wind and set the clock in the companion and saw him disappear below, followed by his accomplice, to work out the reckoning, and shook his head with mute disapproval. But yet to him, as to the rest of the ship's company, there came a certain sense of relief. Osmond's brisk, confident voice, the cheerful sound of the ship's bell, and the orderly setting of the watch, seemed definitely to mark the end of the mutiny and the return to a reign of law and order.

Chapter Six

Betty Makes a Discovery

For reasons best known to herself, Miss Burleigh made no further attempt that day to satisfy her curiosity as to the quelling of the mutiny. There was, in fact, little opportunity. For shortly after the midday meal – sea-pie and corned pork with biscuit – Osmond turned in regardless of the heat, to get a few hours' sleep before beginning his long night vigil. But on the following day the captain was so far recovered as to be able to take the alternate watches – relieved to some extent in the daytime by the second mate – and this left ample time for Osmond to continue the education of his junior, which now extended from theoretical navigation to practical seamanship.

In was during the afternoon watch, when the two mates were seated on a couple of spare cases in the shadow of the main-sail, practising the working of splices on some oddments of rope, that the "examination-in-chief" began; and Osmond, recognizing the hopelessness of further evasion, was fain to tell the story of his adventure, dryly enough, indeed, but in fairly satisfying detail. And, as he narrated, in jerky, colourless sentences, with his eyes riveted on the splice that he was working, his spellbound listener let her rope's-end and marlinspike lie idle on her lap while she watched his impassive face with something more than mere attention.

"I wonder," she said when the tale was told, "whether the men realize who the spectre mate really was."

"I don't think they can quite make out what happened. But I fancy they look upon me as something rather uncanny; which is all for the best, seeing how short-handed we are and what a helpless worm the skipper is."

"Yes, they certainly have a holy fear of you," she agreed, smiling at the grim, preoccupied face. She reflected awhile and then continued: "But I don't quite understand what brought you on board. You say that Dhoody had stolen those cases of gin. But what business was that of yours?"

"It was my gin."

"Your gin! But you don't drink gin."

"No, I sell it. I am a trader. I run a store, or factory, as they call it out here."

As Osmond made this statement, her look of undisguised admiration changed to one of amazement. She smothered an exclamation and managed to convert it at short notice into an unconcerned "I see"; but her astonishment extinguished her powers of conversation for the time being. She could only gaze at him and marvel at the incongruity of his personality with his vocation. She had encountered a good many traders, and though she had realized that the "palm-oil ruffian" was largely the invention of the missionary and the official snob and that West African traders are a singularly heterogeneous body, still that body did not ordinarily include men of Osmond's class. And her sly suggestion of his connection with Oxford had been something more than a mere random shot. There are certain little tricks of speech and manner by which members of the ancient universities can usually be recognized, especially by their contemporaries; and though Osmond was entirely free from the deliberate affectations of a certain type of "varsity" man, her quick ear had detected one or two turns of phrase that seemed familiar. And he had not repudiated the suggestion.

"I wonder," she said, after an interval of somewhat uncomfortable silence, "what made you take to trading. The *métier* doesn't seem to fit you very well."

"No," he admitted with a grim smile; "I am a bit of a mug at a business deal."

"I didn't mean that," she rejoined hastily. "But there are such a lot of things that would suit you better. It is a sin for a man of your class and attainments to be keeping a shop – for that is what it amounts to."

"That is what it actually is," said he.

"Yes. But why on earth do you do it?"

"Must do something, you know," he replied, lamely.

"Of course you must, but it should be something suitable, and selling gin is not a suitable occupation for a gentleman. And it isn't as if you were a 'lost dog.' You are really extremely capable."

"Yes," he admitted with a grin, "I'm pretty handy in a scrum."

"Don't be silly," she admonished, severely. "I don't undervalue your courage and strength – I shouldn't be a natural woman if I did – but I am thinking of your resourcefulness and ingenuity. It wasn't by mere thumping that you got your ascendancy over the men. You beat them by sheer brains."

"Jim Darker thinks it was an iron belaying-pin."

"Now don't quibble and prevaricate. You know as well as I do that, if it had been a matter of mere strength and courage, you would never have got out of the hold, and we should have been at the bottom of the sea by now. It was your mental alertness that saved us all."

"I'm glad to hear it," said Osmond. "But you aren't getting on very fast with that splice. Have you been watching me?"

"Oh! Bother the splice!" she exclaimed, impatiently. "I want you to tell me why you are throwing yourself away on this ridiculous factory."

"It isn't a bad sort of life," he protested. "I don't think I mind it."

"Then you ought to," she retorted. "You ought to have some ambition. Think of all the things that you might have done – that you still might do with your abilities and initiative."

She looked at him earnestly as she spoke; and something that she saw in his face as she uttered those last words gave her pause. Suddenly it was borne in on her that she had met other men who seemed to be out of their element; men who, report whispered, had been driven by social misadventure – by debt, entanglements, or drink – to seek sanctuary on the remote West Coast. Was it possible that he might be one of these refugees? He was obviously not a drinker and he did not look like a wastrel of any kind. Still, there might be a skeleton in his cupboard. At any rate, he was extraordinarily reticent about himself.

She changed the subject rather abruptly.

"Is your factory in the British Protectorate?"

"Yes. At Adaffia, a little out-of-the-way place about a dozen miles east of Quittah."

"I know it – at least I have heard of it. Isn't it the place where that poor fellow Osmond died?"

"Yes," he replied, a little startled by the question.

"What was he like? I suppose you saw him?"

"Yes. A biggish man. Short moustache and Vandyke beard."

"Quite a gentlemanly man, wasn't he?"

"He seemed to be. But he didn't have a great deal to say to anybody."

"It was rather pathetic, his dying that way, like a hunted fox that has run into a trap."

"Well," said Osmond, "there wasn't much to choose. If the climate hadn't had him, the police would."

"I am not so sure," she replied. "We all hoped he would get away, especially the officer who was detailed to arrest him. I think he meant to make a fussy search of all the wrong houses in the village by way of giving notice that he was there and scaring the fugitive away. Still, I think he was rather relieved when he found that trader man – what was his name? – Larkin or Larkom? – painting the poor fellow's name on the cross above his grave. You heard about that, I suppose?"

"Yes. Queer coincidence, wasn't it?"

"Don't be so callous. I think it was a most pathetic incident."

"I suppose it was," Osmond agreed. "And now, don't you think you had better have another try at that splice?"

With a little grimace she took up the piece of rope and began obediently to unlay its ends and the interrupted course of practical seamanship was resumed, with intervals of desultory conversation, until eight bells, when the teapot was brought forth from the galley and conveyed below to the cabin. After tea, through what was left of the first dog-watch, there was another spell of knots and splices; and then, when the sun set and darkness fell on the sea, more desultory talk, in which Osmond mostly played the rôle of listener, which – with an interval for dinner – lasted until it was time for the second mate to turn in.

So life went on aboard the *Speedwell* day after day. The calm persisted, as calms are apt to do in the Doldrums, with nothing to suggest any promise of a change. Now and again, at long intervals, the oily surface of the sea would be dimmed by a little draught of air – just enough to "put the sails asleep" and give momentary life to the steering-wheel. But in a few minutes it would die away, leaving the sails to back and fill as the vessel rolled inertly on the glassy swell. The first observation had shown the ship's position to be about four degrees north of the equator, with the coast of the Bight of Benin some eighty miles away to the north; and subsequent observations revealed a slow southerly drift. It was pretty certain that she had a more rapid easterly drift on the Guinea current, but as the chronometer was out of action, there was no means of ascertaining this or of determining her longitude. Sooner or later, if the calm continued, she would drift into the Bight of Biafra, where she might pick up the land and sea breezes or find an anchorage where she could bring up and get the chronometer rated.

To a seaman there is nothing more exasperating than a prolonged calm. The crew of the *Speedwell* were not sailors of a strenuous type, but the inaction and monotony that prevailed on the idly-rolling ship bored them – if not to tears, as least to bad language and chronic grumbling. They lounged about with sulky looks and yawned over the odd jobs that Osmond found for them, whistling vainly for a breeze and crawling up the rigging from time to time to see if anything – land or another ship – was in sight. As to the captain, he grew daily more sour and taciturn as he saw his stores of provisions dwindling with nothing to show for the expenditure.

But by two of the ship's company the calm was accepted with something more than resignation. The two mates had no complaint whatever to make. They were, indeed, cut off from all the world; marooned on a stationary ship in an unfrequented sea. But they had one another and asked for nothing better; and the longer the calm lasted the more secure they were of the continuance of this happy condition. For the inevitable thing had happened. They had fallen in love.

It was very natural. Both were more than commonly attractive, and circumstances had thrown them together in the closest and most intimate companionship through every hour of the long days. They had worked together, though the work was more than half play; they had a common interest which kept them apart from the others. Together they had sat, talking endlessly, in little patches of shadow when the sun was high in the heavens, or leaned upon the bulwark rail and watched the porpoises playing round the idle ship or the Portuguese men-of-war gliding imperceptibly past on their rainbow-tinted floats. They had paced the heaving deck together when the daylight was gone and earnestly studied the constellations "that blazed in the velvet blue," or peered down into the dark water alongside where the Noctilucae shone like submarine stars and shoals of fish darted away before the pursuing dolphin with lurid flashes of phosphorescent light. No more perfect setting for a romance could be imagined.

And then the personality of each was such as to make a special appeal to the other. In the eyes of the girl, Osmond was a hero, a paladin. His commanding stature, his strength, his mastery of other men, and above all his indomitable courage, had captured her imagination from the first. And in his rugged way he was a handsome man; and if he could be a little brutal on occasion, he had always been, to her, the soul of courtesy and chivalry. As to the "past" of which she had a strong suspicion, that was no concern of hers; perhaps it even invested him with an added interest.

As to Osmond, he had been captivated at once, and, to do him justice, he had instantly perceived the danger that loomed ahead. But he could do nothing to avoid it. Flight was impossible from this little self-contained world, so pleasantly cut off from the unfriendly world without; nor could he, even if he had tried, help being thrown constantly into the society of this fascinating little lady. And if, during the long, solitary night-watches, or in his stifling berth, he gnashed his teeth over the perverseness of Fate and thought bitterly of what might have been, that did not prevent him from succumbing during the day to the charm of her frank, unconcealed friendliness.

It was in the forenoon of the eighth day of the calm that the two cronies were leaning on the rail, each holding a stout line. The previous day Osmond had discovered a quantity of fishing tackle among Redford's effects, and a trial cast had provided, not only excellent sport, but a very welcome addition to the ship's meagre diet. Thereupon an epidemic of sea-angling had broken out on board, and Bill Foat, the cook, had been kept busy with the preparation of snappers, horse-mackerel, and other deep-sea fish.

"I wonder," the girl mused, as she peered over the side, "how much longer this calm is going to last."

"It may last for weeks," Osmond replied. "I hope it won't for your sake. You must be getting frightfully bored."

"Indeed, I'm not," she rejoined. "It is the jolliest holiday I have ever had. The only fly in the ointment is the fear that my father may be a little anxious about me. But I don't suppose he is really worrying. He is like me – not much given to fussing; and he knows that I am fairly well able to take care of myself, though he doesn't know that I have got a Captain James Cook to stand by me. But I expect you are getting pretty sick of this monotonous life, aren't you, Captain J.?"

Osmond shook his head. "Not a bit," he replied. "It has been a delightful interlude for me. I should be perfectly satisfied for it to go on for the rest of my life."

She looked at him thoughtfully, speculating on the inward meaning of this statement and noting a certain grave wistfulness that softened the grim face.

"That sounds rather as if Adaffia were not a perfect Paradise, for it has been a dull life for you since the mutiny collapsed and the calm set in, with no one to talk to but me."

"Adaffia would be all right under the same conditions," said he.

"What do you mean by the same conditions?" she asked, flushing slightly; and as he did not immediately answer, she continued: "Do you mean that life would be more pleasant there if you had your second mate to gossip with?"

"Yes," he answered, reluctantly, almost gruffly. "Of course that is what I mean."

"It is very nice of you, Jim, to say that, but you needn't have spoiled it by speaking in that crabby tone. It is nothing to be ashamed of. I don't mind admitting that I shall miss you most awfully if we have to separate when this voyage is over. You have been the best of chums to me."

She flushed again as she said this and then looked at him a little shyly. For nearly a minute he made no response, but continued to gaze intently and rather gloomily at the water below. At length he said, gravely, still looking steadily at the water:

"There is something, Miss Burleigh, that I feel I ought to tell you; something that I wouldn't tell anyone else in the world."

"Thank you, Jim," she said. "But please don't call me Miss Burleigh. It is so ridiculously stiff between old chums like us. And, Jim, you are not to tell me anything that it might be better for you that I should not know. I am not in the least inquisitive about your affairs."

"I know that," he replied. "But this is a thing that I feel you ought to know. It has been on my mind to tell you for some days past." He paused for a few seconds and then continued: "You remember, Betty, that man Osmond that you spoke about?"

"Yes; but don't call him 'that man Osmond.' Poor fellow! I don't suppose he had done anything very dreadful, and at any rate we can afford to speak kindly of him now that he is dead."

"Yes, but that is just the point. He isn't dead."

"Isn't dead?" she repeated. "But Captain Cockeram saw that other man, Larkom, painting the name on his grave. Was it a dummy grave?"

"No. But it was Larkom who died. The man Cockeram saw was Osmond."

"Are you sure? But of course you would be. Oh, Jim! You won't tell anybody else, will you?"

"I am not very likely to," he replied with a grim smile, "as I happen to be the said John Osmond."

"Jim!" she gasped, gazing at him with wide eyes and parted lips. "I am astounded! I can't believe it."

"I expect it has been a bit of a shock," he said bitterly, "to find that you have been associating for more than a week with a man who is wanted by the police."

"I didn't mean that," she exclaimed, turning scarlet. "You know I didn't. But it is so astonishing. I can't understand how it happened. It seems so extraordinary, and so – so opportune."

Osmond chuckled grimly. "It does," he agreed. "Remarkably opportune. Almost as if I had polished Larkom off *ad hoc*. Well, I didn't."

"Of course you didn't. Who supposed for a moment that you did? But do tell me exactly how it happened."

"Well, it was quite simple. Poor old Larkom died of blackwater fever. He was a good fellow. One of the very best, and the only friend I had. He knew all about me – or nearly all – and he did everything he could to help me. It was an awful blow to me when he died. But he never had a chance when once the fever took hold of him. He was an absolute wreck and he went out like the snuff of a candle, though he managed to make a will before he died, leaving the factory and all his effects to his friend James Cook. It was he who invented that name for me.

"Well, of course, when he was dead, I had to bury him and stick up a cross over his grave. And – then I just painted the wrong name on it. That's all."

She nodded without looking at him and a shadow seemed to fall on her face. "I see," she said, a little coldly. "It was a tempting opportunity; and events have justified you in taking it."

Something in her tone arrested his attention. He looked at her sharply and with a somewhat puzzled expression. Suddenly he burst out:

"Good Lord, Betty! You don't think I did this thing in cold blood, do you?"

"Didn't you?" she asked. "Then how did you come to do it?"

"I'll tell you. Poor old Larkom's name was John, like mine. I had painted in the 'John' and was just going to begin the 'Larkom' when I happened to look along the beach. And there I saw Cockeram with his armed party bearing down on Adaffia. Of course, I guessed instantly what his business was, and I saw that there was only one thing to be done. There was the blank space on the cross. I had only to fill it in with my own name and the situation would be saved. So I did."

Her face cleared at this explanation. "I am glad," she said, "that it was only done on the spur of the moment. It did seem a little callous."

"I should think so," he agreed, "if you thought of me sitting by the poor old fellow's bedside and calmly planning to use his corpse to cover my retreat. As it was, I hated doing it; but necessity knows no law. I have thought more than once of making a dummy grave for myself and shifting the cross to it and of setting up a proper memorial to Larkom. And I will do it when I get back."

She made no comment on this; and as, at the moment, her line tightened, she hauled it in, and impassively detaching a big red snapper from the hook, rebaited and cast the line overboard with a curiously detached, preoccupied air. Apparently, she was reflecting profoundly on what she had just learned, and Osmond, glancing at her furtively from time to time, abstained from interrupting her meditations. After a considerable interval she turned towards him and said in a low, earnest tone:

"There is one thing that I want to ask you. Just now you said that you felt you ought to tell me this; that I ought to know. I don't quite see why."

"There was a very good reason," he replied, "and I may as well make a clean breast of it. To put it bluntly, I fell in love with you almost as soon as I saw you, and naturally, I have grown to love you more with each day that has passed."

She flushed deeply, and glancing at him for an instant, turned her eyes once more on her line.

"Still," she said in a low voice, "I don't see why you thought I ought to know."

"Don't you?" he rejoined. "But surely it is obvious. You accepted me as your chum and you seemed to like me well enough. But you had no inkling as to who or what I was. It was my clear duty to tell you."

"You mean that there was the possibility that I might come to care for you and that you felt it your duty to warn me off?"

"Yes. It wasn't very likely that there would be anything more than friendship on your side; but still it was not impossible. Women fall in love with the most unlikely men."

At this she smiled and looked him squarely in the face. "I thought you meant that," she said, softly, "and, of course, you were quite right. But if your intention was to put me on my guard and prevent me from caring for you, your warning has come too late. You would have had to tell me before I had seen you – and I don't believe it would have made a scrap of difference even then. At any rate, I don't care a fig what you have done – I know it was nothing mean. But all the same, I am glad you told me. I should have hated to find it out afterwards by myself."

He gazed at her in dismay. "But, Betty," he protested, "you don't seem to grasp the position. There is a warrant out for my arrest."

"Who cares?" she responded. "Besides, there isn't. John Osmond is dead and there is no warrant out for Captain James Cook. It is you who don't grasp the position."

"But," he expostulated, "don't you realize that I can never go home? That I can't even show my face in Europe?"

"Very well," said she. "So much the worse for Europe. But there are plenty of other places; and what is good enough for you is good enough for me. Now, Jim dear," she added, coaxingly, "don't create difficulties. You have said that you love me – I think I knew it before you told me – and that is all that matters to me. Everything else is trivial. You are the man to whom I have given my heart, and I am not going to have you crying off."

"Good God, Betty," he groaned, "don't talk about 'crying off.' If you only know what it means to me to look into Paradise and be forced to turn away! But, my dearest love, it has to be. I would give my life for you gladly, joyfully. I am giving more than my life in refusing the sacrifice that you, in the nobleness of your heart, are willing to make. But I could never accept it. I could never stoop to the mean selfishness of spoiling the life of the woman who is more to me than all the world."

"I am offering no sacrifice," she said. "I am only asking to share the life of the man I love. What more does a woman want?"

"Not to share such a life as mine," he replied, bitterly. "Think of it, Betty, darling! For the rest of my days I must sneak about the world under a false name, hiding in obscure places, scanning the face of every stranger with fear and suspicion lest he should discover my secret and drag me from my sham grave. I am an outcast, an Ishmaelite. Every man's hand is against me. Could I allow a woman – a beautiful girl, a lady of position – to share such a sordid existence as mine? I should be a poor lover if I could think of such contemptible selfishness."

"It isn't so bad as that, Jim, dear," she pleaded. "We could go abroad – to America – and make a fresh start. You would be sure to do well there with your abilities, and we could just shake off the old world and forget it."

He shook his head, sadly. "It is no use, darling, to delude ourselves. We must face realities. Mine is a wrecked life. It would be a crime, even if it were possible, for me to take you from the surroundings of an English lady and involve you in the wreckage. It was a misfortune, at least for you, that we ever met, and there is only one remedy. When we separate, we must try to forget one another."

"We shan't, Jim," she exclaimed, passionately. "You know we shan't. We aren't, either of us, of the kind that forgets. And we could be so happy together! Don't let us lose everything for a mere scruple."

At this moment all on deck were startled by a loud hail from aloft. One of the men had climbed up into the swaying foretop and stood there holding on to the topmast shrouds and with his free hand pointing to the north. Osmond stepped forward and hailed him.

"Foretop there! What is it?"

"A steamer, sir. Seems to be headin' straight on to us."

Osmond ran below, and having fetched Redford's binocular from the berth, climbed the main rigging to just below the cross-tree. There, securing himself with one arm passed round a shroud, he scanned the northern horizon intently for a minute or two and then descended slowly with a grave, set face. From his loftier station he had been able to make out the vessel's hull; and the character of the approaching ship had left him in little doubt as to her mission. His comrade met him with an anxious, inquiring face as he jumped down from the rail.

"Small man-o'-war," he reported in response to the unspoken question; "barquentine-rigged, buff funnel, white hull. Looks like a gun-boat."

"Ha!" she exclaimed. "That will be the *Widgeon*. She was lying off Accra."

The two looked at one another in silence for a while as they look who have heard bad tidings. At length Osmond said, grimly:

"Well, this is the end of it, Betty. She has been sent out to search for you. It will be 'goodbye' in less than an hour."

"Not 'goodbye,' Jim," she urged. "You will come too, won't you?"

"No," he replied; "I can't leave the old man in this muddle."

"But you'll have to leave him sooner or later."

"Yes; but I must give him a chance to get another mate, or at least to ship one or two native hands."

"Oh, let him muddle on as he did before. My father will be wild to see you when he hears of all that has happened. Don't forget, Jim, that you saved my life."

"I saved my own," said he, "and you chanced to benefit. But I couldn't come with you in any case, Betty. You are forgetting that I have to keep out of sight. There may be men up at headquarters who know me. There may be even on this gun-boat."

She gazed at him despairingly and her eyes filled. "Oh, Jim," she moaned, "how dreadful it is. Of course I must go. But I feel that we shall never see one another again."

"It will be better if we don't," said he.

"Oh, don't say that!" she pleaded. "Think of what we have been to one another and what we could still be for ever and ever if only you could forget what is past and done with. Think of what perfect chums we have been and how fond we are of one another. For we are, Jim. I love you with my whole heart and I know that you are just as devoted to me. It is a tragedy that we should have to part."

"It is," he agreed, gloomily, "and the tragedy is of my making."

"It isn't," she dissented, indignantly; and then, softly and coaxingly, she continued: "But we won't lose sight of each other altogether, Jim, will we? You will write to me as soon as you get ashore. Promise me that you will."

"Much better not," he replied; but with so little decision that she persisted until, in the end, and much against his judgement, he yielded and gave the required promise.

"That makes it a little easier," she said, with a sigh. "It leaves me something to look forward to."

She took the glasses from him and searched the rim of the horizon, over which the masts of the approaching ship had begun to appear.

"I suppose I ought to report to the old man," said Osmond, and he was just turning towards the companion when Captain Hartup's head emerged slowly and was in due course followed by the remainder of his person. His left arm was now emancipated from the sling and in his right hand he carried a sextant.

"Gun-boat in sight, sir," said Osmond. "Seems to be coming our way."

The captain nodded, and stepping to the taffrail, applied his eye to the eyepiece of the sextant.

"It has gone seven bells," said he. "Isn't it about time you got ready to take the latitude – you and the other officer?" he added, with a sour grin.

In the agitating circumstances, Osmond had nearly forgotten the daily ceremony – a source of perennial joy to the crew. He now ran below and presently returned with the two sextants, one of which he handed to "the other officer."

"For the last time, little comrade," he whispered. "And we'll work the reckoning together. *Norie's Navigation* will be a sacred book to me after this."

She took the instrument from him and advanced with him to the bulwark. But if the truth must be told, her observation was a mere matter of form, and twice before the skipper called "eight bells" she had furtively to wipe a tear from the eyepiece. But she went below to the cuddy and resolutely worked out the latitude (from the reading on Osmond's sextant), and when the brief calculation was finished, she silently picked up the scrap of paper on which Osmond had worked out the reckoning and laid hers in its place. He took it up without a word and slipped it in his pocket.

"They are queer keepsakes," she said in a half-whisper as the door of the captain's cabin opened, "but they will tell us exactly when and where we parted. Who knows when and where we shall meet again – if we ever do?"

"If we ever do," he repeated in the same tone; and then, as the captain came out and looked at them inquiringly, he reported the latitude that they had found, and followed him up the companion-steps.

When they arrived on deck they found the crew ranged along the bulwark watching the gun-boat, which was now fully in view, end-on to the brigantine, and approaching rapidly, her bare masts swinging like pendulums as she rolled along over the big swell.

"I suppose we shall make our number, sir," said Osmond; and as the skipper vouchsafed no reply beyond an unintelligible grunt, he added: "The flag locker is in your cabin, isn't it?"

"Never you mind about the flag locker," was the sour reply. "Our name is painted legibly on the bows and the counter, and I suppose they've got glasses if they want to know who we are." He took the binocular from Osmond, and after a leisurely inspection of the gun-boat, continued: "Looks like the *Widgeon*. Coming to pick up a passenger, I reckon. About time, too. I suppose you are both going – if they'll take you?"

"I am not," said Osmond. "I am going to stay and see you into port."

The skipper nodded and emitted an ambiguous grunt, which he amplified with the addition: "Well, you can please yourself," and resumed his inspection of the approaching stranger.

His forecast turned out to be correct, for the gun-boat made no signal, but, sweeping past the *Speedwell*'s stern at a distance of less than a quarter of a mile, slowed down and brought-to on the port side, when she proceeded to lower a boat; whereupon Captain Hartup ordered a rope ladder to be dropped over the port quarter. These preparations Miss Burleigh watched anxiously and with an assumption of cheerful interest, and when the boat ran alongside, she joined the skipper at the head of the ladder, while Osmond, lurking discreetly in the background, kept a watchful eye on the officer who sat in the stern-sheets until the lessening distance rendered him distinguishable as an undoubted stranger, when he also joined the skipper.

As the newcomer – a pleasant-faced, clean-shaved man in a lieutenant's uniform – reached the top of the ladder, he exchanged salutes with the skipper and the lady, who advanced and held out her hand.

"Well, Miss Burleigh," said the lieutenant as he shook her hand, heartily, "this is a relief to find you safe and sound and looking in the very pink of health. But you have given us all a rare fright. We were afraid the ship had been lost."

"So she was," replied Betty. "Lost and found. I think I have earned a fatted calf, don't you, Captain Darley?"

"I don't know," rejoined the lieutenant (the honorary rank was in acknowledgement of his position as commander of the gunboat); "we must leave that to His Excellency. But it doesn't sound very complimentary to your shipmates or to your recent diet. I needn't ask if you are coming back with us. My cabin has been made ready for you."

"But how kind of you, Captain Darley. Yes, I suppose I must come with you, though I have been having quite a good time here; mutinies, fishing, and all sorts of entertainments."

"Mutinies, hey!" exclaimed Darley, with a quick glance at the captain. "Well, I am sorry to tear you away from these entertainments, but orders are orders. Perhaps you will get your traps packed up while I have a few words with the captain. I shall have to make a report of what has happened."

On this there was a general move towards the companion. Betty retired – somewhat precipitately – to her berth and the lieutenant followed Captain Hartup to his cabin.

Both parties were absent for some time. The first to reappear was Betty, slightly red about the eyes and carrying a small handbag. Having dispatched Sam Winter below to fetch up her portmanteau, she drew Osmond away to the starboard side.

"Jack," she said, in a low, earnest tone – "I may call you by your own name just for once, mayn't I? – you have made me a promise. You won't go back on it, will you, Jack?"

"Of course I shan't, Betty," he replied.

"I want you to have my cabin when I've gone," she continued. "It is a better one than yours and it has a tiny port-hole. And if you open the locker, you will find a little note for you. That is all. Here they come. Goodbye, Jack, darling!"

She turned away abruptly as he murmured a husky farewell, and having shaken hands with Captain Hartup and thanked him for his hospitality, was stepping on to the ladder when she paused suddenly and turned back.

"I had nearly forgotten," said she. "I haven't paid my passage."

"There is no passage-money to pay," the skipper said, gruffly. "My contract was to deliver you at Accra, and I haven't done it. Besides," he added, with a sour grin, "you've worked your passage."

"Worked her passage!" exclaimed the lieutenant. "What do you mean?"

"She has been taking the second mate's duties," the skipper explained.

Darley stared open-mouthed from the skipper to the lady. Then, with a fine, hearty British guffaw, he assisted the latter down to the boat.

Chapter Seven

The Mate Takes His Discharge

As an instance of the malicious perversity which the forces of nature often appear to display, the calm which had for so many days cut off Miss Betty from any communication with the world at large seemed unable to survive her departure. Before the gun-boat was fairly hull down on the horizon, a dark line on the glassy sea announced the approach of a breeze, and a few minutes later the brigantine's sails filled, her wallowings subsided, and a visible wake began to stream out astern.

The change in the vessel's motion brought the captain promptly on deck, and Osmond listened somewhat anxiously for the orders as to the course which was to be set. But he knew his commander too well to make any suggestions.

"Breeze seems to be about sou'-sou'-west," the skipper remarked with one eye on the compass-dial and the other on the upper sails. "Looks as if it was going to hold, too. Put her head west-nor'-west."

"Did the lieutenant give you our position?" Osmond inquired.

"No, he didn't," the skipper snapped. "He wasn't asked. I don't want any of your brass-bound dandies teaching me my business. The continent of Africa is big enough for me to find without their help."

Osmond smothered a grin as he thought of the chronometer, restarted and ticking away aimlessly in the captain's cabin, its error and rate alike unknown. But again he made no comment, and presently the skipper resumed:

"I suppose you will be wanting to get back to Adaffia?"

"I'm not going to leave you in the lurch."

"Well, you can't stay with me for good excepting as a seaman, as you haven't got a ticket – at least, I suppose you haven't."

"No. I hold a master's certificate entitling me to navigate my own yacht, but, of course, that is no use on a merchant vessel, excepting in an emergency. But I don't quite see what you are going to do."

"It is a bit of a problem," the skipper admitted. "I shall take on one or two native hands to help while we are on the Coast, and appoint Winter and Simmons to act as mates. Then perhaps I shall be able to pick up an officer from one of the steamers for the homeward trip."

"I will stay with you until you are fixed up, if you like," said Osmond; but the captain shook his head.

"No," he replied. "I shall put you ashore at Adaffia. I can manage all right on the Coast, and I must have a regular mate for the homeward voyage."

Thus the programme was settled, and, on the whole, satisfactorily to Osmond. It is true that, if there had been no such person as Elizabeth Burleigh, he would have held on to his position, even with the rating of ordinary seaman, for the homeward voyage, on the chance of transferring later to some ship bound for South America or the Pacific Islands. But although he had renounced all claim to her and all hope of any future connected with her, he still clung to the ill-omened land that was made glorious to him by her beloved presence.

The captain's forecast was justified by the event. The breeze held steadily and seemed inclined to freshen rather than to fail. The old brigantine heeled over gently and forged ahead with a pleasant murmur in her sails and quite a fine wake trailing astern. It was a great relief to everybody after the long calm, with its monotony and inaction and the incessant rolling of the ship and flapping of the sails. The captain was almost pleasant and the crew were cheerful and contented, though they had little to do, for when once the course was set there was no need to touch sheet or brace, and the trick at the wheel was the only active duty apart from the cook's activities.

To Osmond alone the change brought no obvious satisfaction. All that had recently happened had been, as he could not but recognize, for the best. The parting had to come, and every day that it was delayed forged his fetters only the more firmly. But this reflection offered little consolation. He loved this sweet, frank, open-hearted girl with an intensity possible only to a man of his strength of will and constancy of purpose. And now she was gone; gone out of his life for ever. It was a final parting. There was no future to look forward to; not even the most distant and shadowy. The vision of a great happiness had floated before him and had passed, leaving him to take up again the burden of his joyless life, haunted for ever by the ghost of the might-have-been.

Nevertheless, he went about his duties briskly enough, finding jobs for the men and for himself, overhauling the cordage, doing small repairs on the rigging, and even, with his own hands, putting a patch on a weak spot on the bottom of the long-boat and lining it inside and out with scraps of sheet copper. And if he was a little grimmer and more silent than before, the men understood and in their rough way sympathized, merely remarking that "Pore old Cook do seem cut up along o' losin' his Judy."

At dawn on the third day the land was in sight; that is to say to the north there was an appearance as if a number of small entomological pins had been stuck into the sea-horizon in irregular groups. Viewed from the fore-top, however, through Redford's glasses, this phenomenon resolved itself into a narrow band of low-lying shore, dotted with coconut palms, the characteristic aspect of the Bight of Benin.

As the day wore on, the brigantine gradually closed in with the land. Before noon, the captain was able, through his telescope, to identify a group of white buildings as the German factories at the village of Bagidá. Then the neighbouring village of Lomé came in sight and slowly crept past; and as the *Speedwell* drew yet nearer to the land, Osmond was able to recognize, among a large grove of coconuts, the white-washed bungalow at Denu, and, a few miles ahead, the dark mass of palms that he knew to be Adaffia.

"Well, Mr Cook," said the captain, "you'll soon be back by your own fireside. If the breeze holds, we ought to be in Adaffia roads by four at the latest. I suppose you have got all your portmanteaux packed?"

"I'm all ready to go ashore, if you are still of the same mind."

"I never change my mind," replied the skipper; and Osmond believed him.

"Are you making any stay at Adaffia?" he asked.

"I am going to put you ashore," the captain answered. "What I shall do after that is my business."

"I asked," said Osmond, "because I thought I might be able to get you one or two native hands. However, you can let me know about that later. Now, as it is your watch on deck, I will go below and take a bit of a rest."

He went down to the berth, into which he had moved when Betty departed, and, shutting the door, looked thoughtfully round the little apartment. Nothing had been altered since she left. All the little feminine tidinesses had been piously preserved. It was still, to the eye, a woman's cabin, and everything in its aspect spoke to him of the late tenant. Presently he lay down on the bunk – the bunk in which she had slept – and for the hundredth time drew from his pocket the letter which she had left in the locker. It was quite short – just a little note hastily written at the last moment when the boat was waiting. But to him it was inexhaustible; and though by now he knew it by heart, he read it again as eagerly as when he had first opened it.

"MY DEAREST JIM," it ran. "I am writing to you a few words of farewell (since we must say 'goodbye' in public) to tell you that when you read them I shall be thinking of you.

I shall think of you, best and dearest comrade, every day of my life, and I shall go on hoping that somehow we shall meet again and be as we have been on this dear old ship. And Jim, dearest, I want you to understand that I am always yours. Whenever you want me – no, I don't mean that; I know you want me now – but whenever you can cast away things that ought to be forgotten, remember that I am waiting for you. Try, dear, to forget everything but your love and mine.

"Au revoir!

"Your faithful and loving

"BETTY."

It was a sweet letter, written in all sincerity; and even though Osmond never wavered in the renunciation that honour demanded, still it told him in convincing terms that the door was not shut. The gate of Paradise was still ajar. If he could forget all justice and generosity; if he, who had nothing to give, could bring himself to accept the gift so generously held out to him, he still had the option to enter. He realized that – and never, for an instant, entertained the thought. Perhaps there were other ways out. But if there were, he dismissed them, too. Like Captain Hartup, he was not given to altering his mind. Free as he was from the captain's petty obstinacy, he was a man of inflexible purpose, even though the purpose might have been ill-considered.

His long reverie was at length interrupted by a voice which came in through the little port-hole.

"No soundings!"

He glanced up at the tell-tale compass which formed a rather unusual fitting to the mate's bunk and noted that the ship's course had been altered three points to the north. She was now heading almost directly for the land and was presumably nearly opposite Adaffia. He refolded the letter and put it away, but his thoughts went back to its message and the beloved writer. Presently the voice of the man in the channel who was heaving the lead was heard again; and this time it told of a nearer approach to that dreary shore.

"By the deep, eighteen!"

He noted the depth with faint interest and began to think of the immediate future. As soon as he got ashore he must write to her. It was quite wrong, but he had promised and he could not but be glad that she had exacted the promise. It would be a joy to write to her, and yet he could feel that he was doing it under compulsion. But it must be a careful letter. There must be in it no sign of weakening or wavering that might mislead her. She must be free and she must fully realize it; must realize that he belonged to her past and had no part in her future. It would be a difficult letter to write; and here he set himself to consider what he should say. And meanwhile the leadsman's voice came in from time to time, recording the gradual approach to the land.

"By the deep, ele-vern!" "By the mark, ten!" "By the deep, eight!"

At this point he was aware of sounds in the cuddy as if some heavy objects were being moved, and he surmised that the gin-cases were being disinterred from the lazarette. Then he heard the trap fall and heavy footsteps stumbled up the companion-stairs. A moment later the leadsman sang out: "By the mark, se-vern!" and as Osmond rose from the bunk there came a thumping at his door and a voice sang out:

"The captain wants you on deck, sir, and there's a canoe a-comin' alongside."

Osmond cast a farewell glance round the little cabin and followed the man up on deck, where he found the captain waiting on the poop, standing guard, apparently, over two leathern bags and one of canvas. Looking forward, he saw the crew gathered at the open gangway, regarding with sheepish grins four unopened gin-cases, while a canoe, bearing a scarlet-coated grandee, was just running alongside. As he stepped out of the companion, the captain picked up the three bags, and walking with him slowly towards the gangway, addressed him in a gruff tone and a somewhat aggressive manner.

"According to law," said he, "I believe you are entitled to a third of the ship's value for salvage services. There are nearly two hundred ounces of gold-dust in these two leather bags – that is, roughly, eight hundred pounds – and there is forty-eight pounds ten in sovereigns and half-sovereigns, in the canvas bag. Will that satisfy you?"

"Rubbish," said Osmond. "I want eight shillings for two cases of gin broached by your men."

"You won't get it from me," snapped the skipper. "I'll have nothing to do with intoxicating liquor."

"If you don't pay, I'll sue you," said Osmond.

"I haven't had the gin," retorted the skipper. "It was brought on board without my authority. You must recover from the men who had it. But what do you say about the question of salvage?"

"Hang the salvage!" replied Osmond. "I want to be paid for my gin."

"You won't get a ha-penny from me for your confounded poison," exclaimed the skipper, hotly. "I hold very strict views on the liquor traffic. There are the men who drank the stuff. Make them pay. It's no concern of mine. But about this salvage question: are you satisfied with what I offer?"

Osmond glanced through the gangway. The gin-cases were all stowed in the canoe; Mensah was beaming up at him with an expectant grin and the canoe-men grasped their paddles. He felt in his pocket, and then, taking the canvas bag from the skipper, thrust his hand in and brought out a handful of coins. From these he selected a half-sovereign, and returning the others, dropped in a couple of shillings from his pocket.

"Two shillings change," he remarked. He threw the bag down on the deck, and pocketing the half-sovereign, dropped down into the canoe. But he had hardly taken his seat on the tie-tie thwart when two heavy thumps on the floor of the canoe, followed by a jingling impact, announced the arrival of the two bags of gold-dust and the bag of specie.

Osmond stood up in the dancing canoe with a leather bag in each hand.

"Now, Mensah," he sang out, "tell the boys to get away one time."

The paddles dug into the blue water; the canoe bounded forward. Aiming skilfully at the open gangway, Osmond sent the heavy leathern bags, one after the other, skimming along the deck, and the little bag of specie after them. The skipper grabbed them up and rushed to the gangway. But he was too late. The canoe was twenty yards away and leaping forward to the thud of the paddles. Looking back at the brigantine with a satisfied smile, Osmond saw a row of six grinning faces at the rail, and at the gangway a small figure that shook its fist at the receding canoe with valedictory fury.

His homecoming was the occasion of a pleasant surprise. At intervals during his absence he had given a passing thought to his factory and the little solitary house by the beach and had wondered how they would fare while their master was away. Now he found that in Kwaku Mensah he had a really faithful steward, and not only faithful but strangely competent in his simple way. The house was in apple-pie order and the store was neatly kept and evidently a going concern, for when he arrived, Mensah's pretty Fanti wife was behind the counter, chaffering persuasively with a party of "bush" people from Agotimé, and a glance into the compound showed a good pile of produce, awaiting removal to the produce store. Accounts, of course, there were none, since Mensah "no sabby book," but nevertheless that artless merchantman had kept an exact record of all the transactions with that uncanny precision of memory that one often observes in the intelligent illiterate.

So Osmond settled down at once, with a satisfaction that rather surprised him, into the old surroundings; and as he sat that evening at the table, consuming with uncommon relish a dinner of okro soup, "chickum cotrecks,"and "banana fritters," the product of Mrs Mensah's skill (her name was Ekua Bochwi, from which one learned that she had been born on Wednesday and was the eighth child of her parents), he was inclined to congratulate himself on Captain Hartup's refusal to retain him as the provisional mate of the *Speedwell.*

But in spite of the triumphant way in which he had outmanoeuvred the skipper, Osmond had a suspicion that he had not seen the last of his late commander. For the brigantine, which he had left hove-to and apparently ready to proceed on her voyage, had presently let go her anchor and stowed her sails as if the captain contemplated a stay at Adaffia. And the event justified his suspicions. On the following morning, while he was seated at the breakfast table, with a fair copy of his letter to Betty before him, he became aware of shod feet on the gravelled compound, and a few moments later the doorway framed the figure of Captain Hartup, while in the background lurked Sam Winter, grinning joyfully and carrying two leathern bags.

The captain entered, and regarding his quondam mate with an expression that almost approached geniality, wished him "good morning" and even held out his hand. Osmond grasped it cordially, and drawing up a second chair, pressed his visitor to join him.

"A little fresh food," he remarked, untactfully, with his eye on the leathern bags, "and a cup of real coffee will do you good."

"I don't know what you mean by that," snorted the skipper. "I'm not starving, and neither are you. The ship's grub hasn't killed you. Still," he added, "as I see you are breakfasting like a Christian and not in the beastly Coast fashion, I don't mind if I do try a bit of shore tack with you. And you needn't look at those bags like that. I am not going to force anything on you. I am not an obstinate man" (which was a most outrageous untruth).

"What have you brought them here for?" Osmond demanded stolidly.

"I'll tell you presently," replied the skipper. "Bring 'em in, Winter, and dump 'em on that sideboard."

Winter deposited the two bags on the stack of empty cases thus politely designated and then backed to the doorway, where he was encountered by Kwaku, who was directed to take him to the store and feed him.

"I've come ashore," the captain explained, when they were alone, "to see if I can make one or two little arrangements with you."

Osmond nodded as he helped his guest to stuffed okros and fried eggs (eggs are usually served, on the Coast, fried or poached or in some other overt form, as a precaution against embryological surprises).

"To begin with," continued the skipper, "I want about half a dozen niggers – a cook, a cabin-boy, and a few hands to do the rough work. Do you think you can manage that for me?"

"I've no doubt I can," was the reply.

"Good. Well, then, there is this gold-dust. If you care to change your mind, say so, and the stuff is yours."

Osmond shook his head. "I came on board for my own purposes," said he, "and I am not going to take any payment for looking after my own business."

"Very well," the skipper rejoined: "then if you won't have it, I may as well keep it; and I shan't if it remains on board. It was that gold-dust that tempted Dhoody and the others. Now I understood from you that you have got a safe. Is it a pretty strong one?"

"It's strong enough. There are no skilled burglars out here."

"Then I'm going to ask you to take charge of this stuff for me. You see that both bags are sealed up, and there is a paper inside each giving particulars of the contents and full directions as to how they are to be disposed of if anything should happen to me. Will you do this for me – as a matter of business, of course?"

"Not as a matter of business," replied Osmond. "That would make me responsible for the safe custody of the bags, which I can't be, as I may have to be absent from Adaffia and leave my man,

Mensah, in charge of the factory. I will put the stuff in my safe with pleasure, and I think it will be perfectly secure there; but I won't take any payment or accept any responsibility beyond exercising reasonable care. Will that do?"

"Yes," replied the captain, "that will do. What is good enough for your own property is good enough for mine. So I will ask you to lock the stuff up for me and keep it till I ask for it; but if you should hear that anything has happened to me – that I am dead, in fact – then you will open the bags and read the papers inside and dispose of the property according to the directions written in those papers. Will you do that? It will be a weight off my mind if you will."

"Certainly I will," said Osmond. "But have you any reason to expect that anything will happen to you?"

"Nothing immediate," the captain replied. "But, you see, I am not as young as I was, and I am not what you would call a very sound man. I am subject to occasional attacks of giddiness and faintness. I don't know how much they mean, but my doctor at Bristol warned me not to treat them too lightly. He gave me a supply of medicine, which I keep in the chest, and when I feel an attack coming on, I turn in and take some. But still, 'in the midst of life we are in death,' you know; and I'm ready to answer to my name when the call comes."

"Well," said Osmond, "let us hope it won't come until you have got your goods safely home to Bristol. But in any case, you can depend on me to carry out your instructions."

"Thank you, Mr Cook," said the captain. "I am glad to get that little matter settled. The only anxiety that is left now is the ivory. I had thought of asking you to take charge of that, too, but it would be awkward for you to store. And, after all, it's fairly safe in the hold. A man can't nip off with a dozen eighty-pound tusks in his pocket. So I think we will leave that where it is, ready stowed for the homeward voyage. By the way, have you got any produce that you want to dispose of?"

"Yes, I have a ton or two of copra and a couple of puncheons of oil; and I can let you have some kernels and rubber. Perhaps you would like to take some of the produce in exchange for trade goods."

The arrangement suited Captain Hartup exactly, and accordingly, when they had finished breakfast and stowed the gold-dust in the safe, they adjourned to the produce store to settle the details of the exchange. Then half a dozen canoes were chartered, the new hands mustered by Kwaku, and for the rest of the day the little factory compound and the usually quiet beach were scenes of unwonted bustle and activity. Sam Winter (secretly fortified with a substantial "tot" of gin) was sent on board to superintend the stowage and breaking-out of cargo, while the skipper remained ashore to check off the goods landed and embarked.

The sun was getting low when the two white men set forth to follow the last consignment down to the beach. When they had seen it loaded into the canoes and watched its passage through the surf, Captain Hartup turned to Osmond, and having shaken his hand with almost unnatural cordiality, said, gruffly but not without emotion:

"Well, goodbye, Mr Cook. I've a good deal to thank you for, and I don't forget it. Providence brought us together when I badly needed a friend, and He will bring us together again, no doubt, in His own good time. But how or when, no one can foresee."

He shook Osmond's hand again and, stepping into the waiting canoe, took his seat on a parcel of rubber. The incoming breaker surged up and spent its last energy in a burst of spray on the canoe's beak. The little craft lifted and, impelled by a hearty shove from the canoe-men, slid down the beach on the backwash and charged into the surf. For a few minutes Osmond stood at the brink of the sea watching the canoe as it hovered amidst clouds of spray, dodging the great combers and waiting for its chance to slip through the "shouting seas" to the quiet rollers outside. At length the periodical "lull" came; the paddles drummed furiously on the green-blue water; the canoe leaped at the following wave, disappeared in a burst of snowy foam, and reappeared prancing wildly but safely outside the line of surf. A little figure in the canoe turned and waved its hand; and Osmond, after a responsive flourish of his hat and a glance at the anchored brigantine, turned away from the beach with an odd feeling of regret and walked slowly back to the factory, pondering on the captain's curious and rather cryptic farewell.

Chapter Eight

The Last of the "Speedwell"

For a couple of months Osmond's life at Adaffia drifted on monotonously enough, yet not at all drearily to a man of his somewhat solitary habits and self-contained nature. The factory prospered in a modest way with very little attention on his part, causing him often to reflect regretfully on poor Larkom's melancholy and unnecessary failure. That kindly wastrel was now secured – for a time – from oblivion by a neatly-made wooden cross, painted white and inscribed with his name, a date, and a few appreciative words, which had been set above his grave when the other cross had been removed to grace an elongated heap of sand which represented the resting-place of the late John Osmond.

Moreover, there were breaks in the monotony which had not existed before the adventure of the *Speedwell*. His letter to Betty (in which, among other matters, he had related with naïve satisfaction the incident of the leathern bags and the defeat of Captain Hartup) had evoked a lengthy reply with a demand for a further letter; and so, much against his judgement, he had been drawn into a regular correspondence which was the occasion of alternate and conflicting emotions. Every letter that he wrote racked his conscience and filled him with self-contempt. But the arrival of the inevitable and always prompt reply was a delight which he accepted and enjoyed without a qualm. It was very inconsistent. To the half-naked native who acted as the semi-official postman, he would hand his letter shamefacedly, with a growl of disapproval, admonishing himself that "this sort of thing has got to stop." And then on the day when the reply was expected, he would take a telescope out on the sand-hills and remain for hours watching the beach for the appearance in the remote distance of that same native postman.

These letters, mostly written from headquarters, kept him informed respecting events of local interest, and, what was much more to the point, of Betty's own doings and movements. He learned, for instance, that there were rumours of a native rising in Anglóh (officially spelt Awuna), the region at the back of Adaffia; and that – regardless of this fact – Betty was trying to get her father's permission for a little journey of exploration into this very district.

This latter item of news set his emotional see-saw going at double speed. His judgement denounced the project violently. First, there was the danger – obvious, though not so very great; for the African is essentially a gentlemanly fighter, if rather heavy-handed, and would avoid injuring a white woman. But he is a shockingly bad marksman and uses slugs and gravel for ammunition, so that accidents are very likely to happen. But apart from the danger, this expedition was highly undesirable, for it would bring Betty into his neighbourhood, and of course they would meet – she would see to that. And that meeting ought not to take place. It would only prolong a state of affairs that was disturbing to him and ruinous to her future prospects. He felt this very sincerely, and was foolish enough to say so in his reply to her letter.

From time to time his thoughts wandered to Captain Hartup, and always with a tendency to speculate on the meaning – if there were any – of the note of foreboding which he thought he had detected in the captain's last words as they said "goodbye" on the beach. Those words – together with something final and testamentary in his manner when he had deposited the bags of gold-dust in the safe – seemed to hint at an uncertainty of life and distrust of the future on the captain's part, on which Osmond reflected uneasily. And at last, there came a day on which the skipper's meaning was made clear.

One morning, in the short interval between the night and the dawn, he awoke suddenly and became aware of a dusky figure between his bed and the window.

"Mastah!" the voice of Mensah exclaimed, excitedly, "dat ship, *Speedwell!*" I look um. He fit for come on de beach."

Osmond lifted the mosquito-curtain and, springing out of bed, dropped into his slippers, snatched up the telescope, and followed Mensah out to the end of the compound whence there was a clear view of the sea. And there she was looming up sharp and clear against the grey dawn; and the first glance of a nautical eye read tragedy and disaster in every detail of her aspect. No telescope was needed. She was close in shore, within a couple of cable-lengths of the surf, with her square-sails aback and head-sails shivering, drifting slowly but surely to the destruction that roared under her lee. Obviously, there was no one at the wheel, nor was there any sign of life on board. She was a perfect picture of a derelict.

For a few moments Osmond stared at her in horrified amazement. Then, with a sharp command to Mensah to "get canoe one time," he ran out of the compound and made his way to the beach.

But his order had been anticipated. As he and Mensah came out on the shore, they found a group of excited fishermen dragging a canoe down to the water's edge, while another party were already afloat and paddling out through the surf towards the derelict brigantine. Osmond and his henchman at once joined the fishermen, and though the latter looked askance at the white man – for the accommodation of the little craft was rather limited – they made no demur, experience having taught them that he would have his own way – and pay for it. Accordingly they hauled and shoved with a will, and in a very few moments got the canoe down to the water's edge. Osmond and Mensah stepped in and took their seats, the fishermen grasped the gunwales, and when a big wave swept in and lifted the canoe, they shoved off and went sliding down on the backwash and charged into the surf.

Meanwhile the brigantine continued to drift by the wind and current nearly parallel to the shore, but slowly approached the latter. At the moment she was turning sluggishly and beginning to "pay off" on the starboard tack. Her sails filled and she began to move ahead. If anyone had been on board she might even now have been saved, for there was still room for her to "claw off" the lee shore. Osmond gazed at her with his heart in his mouth and urged the canoe-men to greater efforts; though they wanted little urging, seeing that their friends in the other canoe were now quite near to the receding ship. Moment by moment his hopes rose as the brigantine gathered way, though she was now less easy to overtake. Breathlessly he watched the leading canoe approach her nearer and nearer until at last the fishermen were able to lay hold of the vacant tackles that hung down from the stern davits and swarm up them to the poop. And even as they disappeared over the taffrail, the flicker of life that the old brigantine had displayed faded out. Under the pressure of the mainsail she began slowly to turn to windward. The head-sails shivered, the square-sails blew back against the mast; she ceased to move ahead, and then began once more to drift stern-foremost towards the white line of surf.

As Osmond's canoe ran alongside, where the other canoe was now towing, the first arrivals came tumbling over the side in a state of wild excitement, jabbering as only an excited African can jabber. Mensah proceeded hastily to interpret.

"Dose fishermen say dis ship no good. Dead man live inside him."

Osmond acknowledged the information with an inarticulate growl, and grasping a chain-plate, hauled himself up into the channel, whence he climbed over the rail and dropped on deck.

His first act was to run to the wheel, jam it hard over to port and fix it with a lashing. Then he ran forward to look at the anchors; but both of them were stowed securely and – for the present purposes – useless. He looked up despairingly at the sails, and for a moment thought of trying to swing the yards; but a glance over the stern at the snowy line of surf showed him that the time for manoeuvring was past. For an instant he stood scanning the deck; noting the absence of both boats and the yawning main hatch. Then he ran aft and scrambled down the companion-steps.

The door of the captain's cabin was open – had been left open by the fishermen – and was swinging idly as the ship rolled. But though the whereabouts of the dead man was evident enough before he reached it, he entered without hesitation, intent only on learning exactly what had happened on that ill-omened ship.

The little cabin was just as he had last seen it – with certain differences. And in the bunk lay something that had once been Captain Hartup. It was a dreadful thing to look upon, for the Tropics deal not kindly with the unsepulchred dead. But as Osmond stood looking down on the bunk, mere physical repulsion was swallowed up in a profound feeling of pity for the poor, cross-grained, honest-hearted little shipmaster. There he lay – all that was left of him. There, in the bunk, still lightly held by the blackened, puffy hand, was the inexhaustible Commentary, and on the deck, by the bunk-side, an open box containing a tumbler and a large medicine-bottle the label of which bore written directions and a Bristol address.

Osmond picked up the bottle and read the minute directions with a sense of profound relief. Its presence suggested what his inspection of the dead man confirmed; that at least death had come to Captain Hartup peaceably and decently. The traces of a murderous attack which he had feared to find were not there. Everything tended to show that the captain had died, as he had seemed to expect, from the effects of some long-standing malady.

From the dead man Osmond turned a swift attention to the cabin. He had noticed, when he entered, that the chronometer was not in its place on the little chart-table. He now observed that other things had disappeared – the telescope, the marine glasses, the sextant, and the mathematical instrument case. In short, as he looked around, he perceived that the little cabin had been gutted. Every portable thing of value had been taken away.

His observations were interrupted by the voice of Mensah calling to him urgently to come away "one time," and at the same moment he felt the ship give a heavy lurch followed by a quick recovery. He backed out of the cabin and was about to run up the companion-steps when his glance fell on the door of the adjoining berth, which had been his own and Betty's, and he was moved irresistibly to take a last, farewell look at the little hutch which held so many and so dearly prized memories. He thrust the door open and looked in; and even as he looked, a flash of dazzling white came through the tiny porthole, and a moment later a thunderous crash resounded and the ship trembled as if struck by a thousand monstrous hammers.

He waited no more, but, springing up the steps, thrust his head cautiously out of the companion-hatch. Glancing seaward, he saw a great, sparkling green mass sweeping down on the ship. In another instant, its sharp, tremulous crest whitened; a hissing sound was borne to his ears and quickly rose to a hoarse roar which ended in a crash that nearly shook him off his feet. Then sea and sky, masts and deck, were swallowed up in a cloud of blinding white; there was another roar, and the snowy cataract descended, filling the deck with a seething torrent of foaming water.

Osmond sprang out of the hatch and took a quick glance round. The two canoes were hovering on the outside edge of the surf and obviously unable to approach the ship. Towards the land, the sea was an unbroken expanse of white, while to seaward the long ranks of sharp-crested waves were turning over and breaking as they approached. Warned by a hissing roar from the nearest wave, he stepped back into the shelter of the companion. Again the ship staggered to the crashing impact. Again the visible world was blotted out by the white cloud of spray and foam; and then, as the deluge fell, came a sickening jar with loud cracking noises as the ship struck heavily on the ground. Twice she lifted and struck again, but the third time, rending sounds from below told that her timbers had given way and she lifted no more. Then, under the hammering of the surf, which filled her lower sails with green water, she heeled over towards the shore until the deck was at an angle of nearly forty-five degrees.

Osmond looked out from his shelter and rapidly considered what he should do. There was not much time to consider, for the ship would soon begin to break up. He thought of dropping overboard on the land side and swimming ashore; but it was not a very safe plan, for at any moment the masts might go over the side, and it would not do for him to be underneath when they fell.

Still, he had to act quickly if he were to escape from the impending collapse of the whole fabric, and he looked about eagerly to find the least perilous method. Suddenly his glance fell upon a large cork fender which was washing about in the lee scuppers. The way in which it floated showed that it was dry and buoyant, and it appeared to him that with its aid he might venture into the surf beyond the shelter of the ship and wash safely ashore.

He watched for an opportunity to secure it. Waiting for the brief interval between the descent of the deluge and the bursting of the next wave, he slipped out, and grasping the end of the main sheet, which had washed partly loose from the cleat, ran down to the scupper, seized the fender, and hauling himself up again, crept into his shelter just in time to escape the next wave. When this had burst on the ship and the cataract had fallen, he kicked off his slippers, darted out, and clawing his way past the wheel, reached the taffrail. Holding on firmly to the fender with one hand, with the other he grasped the lee davit-tackle, and springing out, let the tackle slip through his hand.

Just as he reached the water, the next wave burst on the ship; and for the next few moments he was conscious of nothing but a roaring in his ears, a sudden plunge into darkness, and a sense of violent movement. But he still clung tenaciously to the fender, and presently his head rose above the seething water. He took a deep breath, shook the water from his eyes, and began to strike out with his feet, waiting anxiously for the next wave and wondering how much submersion he could stand without drowning. But when the next wave came, its behaviour rather surprised him. The advancing wall of hissing foam seemed simply to take hold of the fender and bear it swiftly shoreward, leaving him to hold on and follow with his head comfortably above the surface.

In this way, amidst a roar like that of steam from an engine's escape-valve, he was borne steadily and swiftly for about a quarter of a mile. Then the spent wave left him and he could see it travelling away towards the shore. But the following wave overtook him after a very short interval and carried him forward another stage. And so he was borne along with surprising ease and speed until he was at last flung roughly on the beach and forthwith smothered with foaming water. He clawed frantically at the wet sand and strove to rise. But the beach was steep and the undertow would have dragged him back but for the help of a couple of fishermen, who, holding on to a grass rope that was held by their companions, waded into the surf, and grabbing him by the arms, dragged him up on to the dry sand beyond the reach of the waves.

As he rose to his feet, he turned to look at the ship. But she was a ship no longer. The short time occupied by his passage ashore had turned her into a mere wreck. Her masts lay flat on the water and her deck had been burst through from below; and through the yawning spaces where the planks had been driven out, daylight could be seen in several places where her side was stove in. The two canoes had already come ashore, and their crews stood at the water's edge, watching the flotsam that was even now beginning to drift shoreward on the surf. Osmond, too, watched it with interest, for he now recalled that the instantaneous glance that he had cast through the open main hatch had shown an unexpectedly empty condition of the hold. And this impression was confirmed when Mensah joined him (apparently quite unmoved by the proceedings of his eccentric employer) and remarked:

"Dose fishermen say only small-small cargo live inside dat ship. Dey say de sailor-man tief de cargo and go away in de boats."

Osmond made no comment on this. Obviously the cargo could not have been taken away in two small boats. But equally obviously it was not there, nor were the boats. It was clear that the ship had been abandoned – probably after the skipper's death – and she had been abandoned at sea. The suggestion was that the crew had transhipped on to some passing vessel and that the cargo had been transferred with them. It might be a perfectly legitimate transaction. But the presence in the cabin of the unburied body of the captain, and the open main hatch, hinted at hurried proceedings of not very scrupulous agents. A responsible shipmaster would certainly have buried the dead captain. Altogether it was a mysterious affair, on which it was possible only to speculate.

The spot where the brigantine had come ashore was about halfway between Adaffia and the adjoining village of Denu. Osmond decided to walk the three or four miles into Adaffia, and when he had washed, dressed, and breakfasted, to return and examine the wreckage. Meanwhile, he left Mensah on guard to see that nothing was taken away – or at any rate, to keep account of anything that was removed by the natives, who were now beginning to flock in from the two villages. Accordingly, having borrowed from the fishermen a large, shallow calabash to put over his head – for the sun was now well up and making itself felt – he strode away westward along the beach, walking as far as was possible on the wet sand to avoid delivering his bare feet to the attacks of the chiggers – sand-fleas – which infested the "aeolian sands" above the tidemarks.

When he returned some three hours later all that remained of the *Speedwell* was a litter of wreckage and flotsam strewn along the margin of the sea or on the blown sand, to which some of the more valuable portions had been carried. The vessel's keel, with the stem and stern-posts and a few of the main timbers still attached, lay some distance out, but even this melancholy skeleton was gradually creeping shoreward under the incessant pounding of the surf. The masts, spars and sails were still in the water, but they, too, were slowly creeping up the beach as the spent waves struck them every few seconds. As to the rest, the ship seemed almost to have decomposed into her constituent planks and beams. There is no ship-breaker like an Atlantic surf.

Osmond cast a pensive glance over the disorderly raffle that had once been a stout little ship, and as Mensah observed him and approached, he asked:

"How much cargo has come ashore, Kwaku?"

Mensah flung out his hands and pointed to the litter on the shore. "Small, small cargo come," said he. "One, two puncheons of oil, two or tree dozen bags ob kernels, some bags copra, two, tree bales Manchester goods – finish."

"I don't see any Manchester goods," said Osmond.

"No, sah. Dem country people. Dey dam tief. Dey take eberyting. Dey no leave nutting"; and in confirmation he pointed to sundry little caravans of men, women and children, all heavily laden and all hurrying homeward, which were visible, mostly in the distance. Indeed, Osmond had met several of them on his way.

"You have not seen any ivory?"

"No sah. I look for um proper but I no see um."

"Nor any big crates or cases?"

"No, sah. Only de bales and crates of Manchester goods, and de country people break dem up."

"Has the captain – the dead man – come ashore?"

"Yas, sah. He live for dat place," and Mensah pointed to a spot at the eastern end of the beach where a clump of coconut palms grew almost at high-water mark. Thither Osmond proceeded with Mensah, and there, at the spot indicated, he found the uncomely corpse of the little skipper lying amidst a litter of loose planks and small flotsam, on the wet sand in the wash of the sea, and seeming to wince as the spent waves alternately pushed it forward and drew it back.

"Mensah," said Osmond, looking down gravely at the body, "this man my countryman, my friend. You sabby?"

"Yas, sah. I sabby he be your brudder."

"Well, I am going to bury him in the compound with Mr Larkom and Mr Osmond."

"Yas, sah," said Mensah, with a somewhat puzzled expression. That second grave was a mystery that had caused him much secret cogitation. But discretion had restrained him from asking questions.

"You think," pursued Osmond, "these people fit for bring the dead man to Adaffia?"

"Dey fit," replied Mensah, "s'pose you dash um plenty money."

"Very well," said Osmond, with characteristic incaution, "see that he is brought in and I will pay them what they ask."

"I go look dem people one time," said Mensah, who had instantly decided that, on these advantageous terms, he would undertake the contract himself.

Before starting to walk back, Osmond took another glance at the wreckage and at the crowd of natives who were, even now, carrying it away piecemeal. For a moment he had a thought of constituting himself Lloyd's agent and taking possession of what was left. But he had no authority, and as the mere wreckage was of no realizable value, and as the little cargo there had been was already carried away, he dismissed the idea and set out homeward, leaving the delighted natives in undisputed possession.

His first proceeding on arriving home was to unlock the safe and break open the leathern bags to see what directions Captain Hartup had given as to the disposal of his property. He was not entirely unprepared to find that the captain had formally transferred the gold-dust to him. But he was totally unprepared for the contents of the bulky paper which he drew out of the second bag, and as he opened and read it he could hardly believe the evidence of his eyesight. The paper was a regularly-drawn will, witnessed by Winter and Simmons, which made "my friend and temporary mate, Mr James Cook," sole executor and legatee.

It began with a preamble, setting forth that "I, Nicholas Hartup, being a widower without offspring, dependants, or near relations, give and bequeath my worldly possessions to the man who has dealt with me honestly, faithfully, and without thought of material profit or reward," and then went on to make the specific bequests, describing each of the items clearly and in detail. These included the gold-dust, giving the exact weight, a consignment of ivory, consisting of "thirty-nine large tusks in three large crates, at present in the hold of the brigantine *Speedwell*, and fifty-one scribellos in a large canvas bag, wired up and sealed, also in the hold"; also the vessel herself, and, most astonishing of all, "my freehold house in Bristol, known as number sixty-five Garlic Street," and a sum of about three thousand pounds, a part invested in certain named securities and the remainder lying on deposit at a specified bank in Bristol. It was an amazing document. As Osmond read and reread it he found himself wondering at the perverseness of the little shipmaster in hiding his kindly, appreciative feelings under so forbidding an exterior; but, to judge by the wording of the preamble, his experience of men would seem not to have been happy. Osmond, having put back the will in the bag, tied up that and the other and put them in the safe. As he locked the door and pocketed the key, he reflected on the irony of his present position. In all the years during which he had lived amidst his friends and relatives, no one had ever bequeathed to him a single penny. Yet in the course of a few months, in this unfrequented and forgotten corner of the world, he had twice been made the sole legatee of almost complete strangers. And now he had become a man of modest substance, an owner of landed property; and that in a country which prudence insisted that he must never revisit.

Chapter Nine

Arms and the Man

Speaking in general terms, Welshmen cannot be fairly described as excessively rare creatures; in fact, there are some parts of the world – Wales, for instance – in which they are quite common. But circumstances alter cases. When Jack Osmond, busily engaged in posting up his account-books, lifted his eyes and beheld a specimen of this well-known type of mammal, he was quite startled; not merely because he had never before heard anyone say "Good mor*ning*" with an accent on the "ning" – which the present example did, although it was actually three in the afternoon – but because no ship had called in the neighbourhood quite lately and he had not known of the presence of any European in the village.

The stranger introduced himself by the name of Jones, which being not entirely without precedent was accepted without difficulty. He had an additional name, but as Osmond failed to assimilate it, and it could be expressed in writing only by an extravagant expenditure of l's and double d's, it is omitted from this merely Saxon chronicle. He shook Osmond's hand exuberantly and smiled until his face – particularly the left side – was as full of lines as a ground-plan of Willesden Junction.

"I come to you, Mr Larkom," said the visitor, retaining Osmond's unwilling hand and apparently adopting the name that remained unaltered over the door of the factory, "as a fellow-countryman in distress, craving a charitable judgement and a helping hand."

He would have been well advised to leave it at that; for Osmond's natural generosity needed no spur, and the memory of his own misfortunes was enough to ensure his charity to others. But Mr Jones continued, smiling harder than ever:

"I come to you confidently for this help because of the many instances of your kindness and generosity and good-fellowship that I have heard – "

"From whom?" interrupted Osmond.

"From – er – from – well, I may say, from everyone on the Coast who knows you."

"Oh," said Osmond; and his face relaxed into a grim smile. Jones saw that he had made a mistake and wondered what the deuce it was.

"Come into my room," said Osmond, "and tell me what you want me to do. Have a cocktail?"

Mr Jones *would* have a cocktail, thank you; and while Osmond twirled the swizzle-stick and raised a pink froth in the tumbler, he cautiously opened his business.

"I am taking some risk in telling you of my little affair, but I am sure I can trust you not to give me away."

"Certainly you can," Osmond replied, incautiously.

"You promise on your honour as a gentleman not to give me away?"

"I have," said Osmond, handing him the cocktail.

Jones still hesitated somewhat, as if desirous of further formalities, but at length plunged into the matter in a persuasive whisper, with much gesticulation and a craftily watchful eye on Osmond's face.

It was not an encouraging face. A portrait of the "Iron Duke" at the age of thirty, executed in very hard wood by a heavy-handed artist with a large chisel and mallet, would give you the kind of face that Mr Jones looked upon; and as the "little affair" unfolded itself, that face grew more and more wooden. For Osmond's charity in respect of errors of conduct did not extend to those that were merely in contemplation.

It transpired gradually that Mr Jones' sufferings and distress were occasioned by a little cargo that he had been unable to land; which cargo happened to include – er – in fact, to be quite candid, consisted largely of Mauser rifles, together with some miscellaneous knick-knacks – such as Mauser cartridges, for instance – all of which were at present rolling in the hold of a privately-chartered vessel (name not mentioned). It also appeared that the Colonial Government had most unreasonably prohibited the importation of arms and ammunition on account of the silly little insurrection that had broken out inland; which very circumstance created an exceptional opportunity – don't you understand? – for disposing of munitions of war on profitable terms. It appeared, finally, that Mr Larkom's factory was an ideal place in which to conceal the goods and from which to distribute them among local sportsmen interested in target-practice or partridge-shooting.

"To put it in a nutshell," said Osmond, "you're doing a bit of gun-running and you want to use me as a cat's paw; and to put it in another nutshell, I'll see you damned first."

"But," protested Jones, "you sell arms yourself, don't you?"

"Not while this row is on. Besides, the niggers don't buy my gas-pipes for war-palaver. My customers are mostly hunters from the bush."

Mr Jones lingered a while to ply the arts of persuasion and consume two more cocktails; and when at last he departed, more in sorrow than in anger, he paused on the threshold to remark:

"You have promised, on your honour, not to give me away."

"I know I have, like a fool," replied Osmond. "Wish I hadn't. Know better next time. Good day." And he followed his departing guest to the compound gate and shut it after him.

From that moment Mr Jones seemed to vanish into thin air. He was seen no more in the village, and no whispers as to his movements came from outside. But a few nights later Osmond had a rather curious experience that somehow recalled his absent acquaintance. He had gone out, according to his common custom, to take a quiet stroll on the beach before turning in, and think of his future movements and of the everlasting might-have-been. Half a mile west of the village he came on a fishing canoe, drawn up above tide-marks, and as he had just filled his pipe, he crept under the lee of the canoe to light it – for one learns to husband one's matches in West Africa. Having lighted his pipe, he sat down to think over a trading expedition that he had projected, but, finding himself annoyed by the crabs, which at nightfall pour out of their burrows in myriads, he shifted to the interior of the canoe. Here he sat, looking over the spectral breakers out into the dark void which was the sea, and immersed in his thoughts until he was startled by the sudden appearance of a light. He watched it curiously and not without suspicion. It was not a ship's anchor-light, nor was it a flare-lamp in a fishing-canoe. By the constant variation in its brightness Osmond judged it to be a bull's-eye lantern which was being flashed to and fro along the coast from some vessel in the offing to signal someone ashore.

He looked up and down the dark beach for the answering signal, and presently caught a dull glimmer, as of a bull's-eye lantern seen from one side, proceeding from the beach a short distance farther west. Watching this spot, he soon made out a patch of deeper darkness which grew in extent, indicating that a crowd of natives had gathered at the water's edge; and, after a considerable interval a momentary flash of the lantern fell on a boat dashing towards the beach in a smother of spray.

Soon after this a number of dark shapes began to separate themselves from the mass and move in single file across the low sand-dunes, passing within a few dozen yards of the canoe. Osmond could see them distinctly, though himself unseen; a long procession of carriers, each bearing a load on his head; and whereas some of these loads were of an oblong shape, like small gun-crates – about the length of a Mauser rifle – the others were more nearly cubical and quite small, though obviously heavy. Osmond watched the file of carriers and counted upwards of forty loads. Perhaps it was none of his business. But as those parcels of death and destruction were borne silently away into the darkness to swell the tale of slaughter in the inland villages, he cursed Mr Jones and his own folly in giving that unconsidered promise.

The last of the carriers had vanished and he had just risen from the canoe to return up the now deserted beach when a new phenomenon presented itself. The clouds which had hidden the rising moon, thinned for a few moments, leaving a patch of coppery light in the eastern sky; and against this, sharp and distinct as if cut out of black paper, stood the shape of a schooner. But not an ordinary trading schooner. Brief as was the gleam that rendered her visible, her character was perfectly obvious to a yachtsman's eye. She was a large yacht of the type that was fashionable when the America Cup was new; when spoon-bows and bulb keels were things as yet undreamed of. Osmond stared at her in astonishment; and even as he looked, the clouds closed up, the sky drew dark, and she was lost in the blackness of the night.

He was up betimes on the following morning and out on the beach in the grey dawn to see if any confirmatory traces of these mysterious proceedings were visible. But his questioning eye ranged over the grey sea in vain. The schooner had vanished as if she had never been. There were, however, multitudinous tracks of bare feet leading up from the shore to the sand-hills, where they were lost; deep footprints such as would be made by heavily-laden men. And there was something else, even more significant. Just at high-water mark, hardly clear of the wash of the sea, was a ship's boat, badly battered, broken-backed, and with one bilge stove in. Some fool, who knew not the West Coast surf, had evidently landed a heavy lading in her with this inevitable result.

But it was not her condition alone that caused Osmond to stride so eagerly towards her. There was something in her size and build that he seemed to recognize. As he reached her, he walked round to examine her stern. There had, of course, been a name painted on her transom, but it had been scraped out and the stern repainted. Then Osmond stepped in and lifted one of the bottom-boards; and there, on the starboard side close to the keel, was a patch covered with sheet-copper, while inspection from without showed an external covering of copper. There was no mistaking that patch. It was his own handiwork. This poor battered wreck was the *Speedwell*'s long-boat; and as he realized this, he realized, too, what had become of the *Speedwell*'s cargo.

The discovery gave Osmond considerable food for thought for the remainder of the morning. But about midday an unlooked-for letter from Betty arrived and for the time being occupied his attention to the exclusion of all other matters. And not entirely without reason. For it conveyed tidings of a somewhat disturbing kind. The message was, indeed, smuggled in inconsequently, as important messages often are in ladies' letters, at the end. But there it was; and Osmond read it with deep disapproval and no small uneasiness.

"You will probably not hear from me again for a week or two as I am going for a little trip inland and may not have a chance to send a letter. I shall let you know directly I get back, and until you hear from me you had better not write – or, at least, you can write, and make it a nice long letter, but don't send it until you get mine."

That was the message. She did not give a hint as to the region into which the "little trip" would take her. But Osmond had a strong and uncomfortable suspicion that her route would take her into the country at the back of the great lagoon and would bring her finally to Adaffia.

He pondered the situation at length. As to the danger of such a journey, it was probably negligible – if the reports were correct. The disturbed area was far away to the north, on the borders of Krepi. The country at the back of the lagoon was believed to be quite peaceful and safe. But one never knew. These Efé peoples were naturally warlike and turbulent. At any moment they might break out in support of their inland relatives. Even now they might have provided themselves with some of Mr Jones' knick-knacks and be preparing for "war-palaver."

The result of his cogitations was somewhat curious and not very easy to understand. For some time past he had been turning over in his mind a project which had really been held up by the regular arrival of Betty's letters. That project was concerned with a trading expedition to the interior – to the country at the back of the lagoon. But that "little trip" would have taken him out of the region in which the receipt of letters was possible, and he had accordingly put it off to some more opportune time. Now that more opportune time seemed to have arrived. There would be no more letters for a week or two, so there was nothing to prevent him from starting. That was how he put it to himself. What was actually in his mind it is impossible to guess. Whether his purpose was to be absent from Adaffia when Betty should make her inevitable visit, to avoid the meeting for which he had yearned but which he felt to be so undesirable; or whether he had some vague hopes of a possible encounter on the road: who can say? Certainly not the present chronicler, and probably not Osmond himself. At any rate, the upshot of it was that he decided on the journey, and with characteristic promptitude set about his preparations forthwith; and as they were far from elaborate and had been well considered beforehand, a single day's work saw everything ready for the start.

On the following morning he set forth, leaving the faithful Mensah in charge of the factory. A dozen carriers bore the loads of goods for the trading venture, and his recently engaged servant, Koffi Kuma, carried his simple necessaries in a light box. In spite of his anxieties and haunting regrets, he was in high spirits at the promised change from the monotony of Adaffia, which, but for the infinitely precious letters, would have been intolerably wearisome. The universal sand, varied only by the black lagoon mud, the everlasting coconut palms chattering incessantly in the breeze, and the bald horizon of the unpeopled sea, had begotten in him an intense yearning for a change of scene; for the sight of veritable trees with leaves, growing in actual earth, and of living things other than the sea-birds and the amphibious denizens of the beach.

A couple of hours' steady marching carried him and his little party across the bare plain of dry mud that had once been part of the great lagoon and brought him to the mainland and the little nine-inch trail that did duty as a road. Gleefully he strode along in the rear of his little caravan, refreshing his eyes and ears with the novel sights and sounds. The tiresome boom of the surf had faded into a distant murmur that mingled with the stirring of leaves; strange birds, unseen in the bush, piped queer little Gregorian chants, while others, silent, but gorgeous of plumage – scarlet cardinals and rainbow-hued sun-birds – disported themselves visibly among the foliage. Little striped Barbary mice gambolled beside the track, and great, blue-bodied lizards with scarlet heads and tails perched on the tall ant-hills that rose on all sides like pink monuments, and nodded their heads defiantly at the passing strangers. It was a new world to Osmond. The bright pink soil, the crowded bush, the buttressed forest trees, the uncouth baobabs, with their colossal trunks and absurdly dwarfed branches – all were new and delightful after the monotony of the beach village, and so fully occupied his attention that when they entered a hamlet of pink-walled houses, he was content to leave the trading to Koffi, while he watched a troop of dog-faced monkeys who seemed to have established a sort of *modus vivendi* with the villagers.

Thus, with occasional halts for rest or barter, the caravan worked its way through the bush until about four o'clock in the afternoon; when Osmond, who had lagged behind to avoid the chatter of his carriers, rounded a sharp turn in the road and found himself entering the main street of a village. But he was not the only visitor. An instantaneous glance showed him a couple of stands of piled arms, by the side of which some half-dozen bare-footed native soldiers were seated on the ground eating from a large calabash; a fierce and sullen looking native, secured with manacles and a leading-rope and guarded by two more of the Hausa soldiers as he was fed by some of the villagers; and two white officers, seated under the village shade tree and engaged at the moment in conversation with Koffi, who seemed to have been captured by a Hausa sergeant.

As Osmond came in sight the two officers looked at one another and rose with a rather stiff salutation.

"You are Mr Cook of Adaffia, I understand?" one of them said.

"Yes," Osmond replied; and as the two officers again looked at one another with an air of some embarrassment, he continued, bluntly:

"I suppose you want to know if I have got any contraband of war?"

"Well, you know," was the half-apologetic reply, "someone has been selling rifles and ammunition to the natives, so we have to make inquiries."

"Of course you do," said Osmond; "and you'd better have a look at my goods. Koffi, tell the carriers to bring their loads here and open them."

A very perfunctory inspection was enough to satisfy the constabulary officers of the harmless character of the trade goods, and having made it, they introduced themselves by the respective names of Stockbridge and Westall and invited Osmond to join them in their interrupted tea under the shade tree.

"Troublesome affair this rising," said Westall, as he handed Osmond a mug of tea; "there'll be wigs on the green before it's over. Now that the beggars have got rifles, they are ready to stand up to the constabulary. Think they're as good as we are; and they're not so far wrong, either."

"Where are you bound for now?" Osmond asked.

"We are going back to Quittah with some prisoners from Agotimé." Westall nodded at the manacled native and added: "That's one of the ring-leaders – a rascal named Zippah; a devil of a fellow, vicious as a bush-cat and plucky, too. Stockbridge and I are keeping him with us, in case of a rescue, but there are over a dozen other prisoners with the main body of Hausas. They marched out of the village just before you turned up."

"And we'd better be marching out, too," said Stockbridge, "or we shan't catch them up. Will you have any more tea, Cook? If not, we'd better get on the road. There's only a native sergeant-major with those men ahead. Are you coming our way?"

"Yes," replied Osmond, "I'll come with you as far as Affieringba, and then work my way home along the north shore of the lagoon."

The three Englishmen rose, and, as Westall's servant repacked the tea apparatus, the little procession formed up. The six Hausas led with fixed bayonets; then came Westall followed by the prisoner, Zippah, and his guard; next came half a dozen carriers loaded with bundles of confiscated muskets and powder-kegs; then Osmond and Stockbridge; and the rear was brought up by Osmond's carriers and the three servants.

The road, or path, after leaving the village, passed through a number of yam and cassava plantations and then entered a forest of fan-palms; a dim and ghostly place now that the sun was getting low, pervaded by a universal rustling from the broad, ragged leaves above and a noisy crackling from the dry branches underfoot. For nearly an hour the party threaded its way through the gloomy aisles, then the palms gradually thinned out, giving place to ordinary forest trees and bush.

"Quite pleasant to get a look at the sky again," Osmond remarked as they came out into the thin forest.

"Yes," said Stockbridge; "but you won't see it for long. There's a bamboo thicket just ahead."

Even as he spoke there loomed up before them an immense, cloudy mass of soft, blue-green foliage; then appeared a triangular black hole like the entrance to a tunnel, into which the Hausas, the prisoners, and the carriers successively vanished. A moment later and Osmond himself had entered through that strange portal and was groping his way in almost total darkness through a narrow passage, enclosed and roofed in by solid masses of bamboo stalks. Ahead, he could dimly make out the shapes of the carriers, while all around the huge clusters of bamboo rose like enormous piers, widening out until they met overhead to form a kind of groined roof. It was an uncanny place; a place in which voices echoed weirdly, mingling with strange, unexplained noises and with the unceasing, distant murmur of the soft foliage far away overhead.

Osmond stumbled on over the crackling canes that formed the floor, gradually growing accustomed to the darkness until there appeared ahead a triangular spot of light that grew slowly larger, framing the figures of the Hausas and carriers; and then, quite suddenly, he emerged, blinking, into broad daylight in the margin of a smallish but deep and rapid river, which at this spot was spanned by a primitive bridge.

Now a native bridge is an excellent contrivance – for natives; for the booted European it is much less suitable. The present one was formed of the slender trunk of a young silk-cotton tree, barkless and polished by years of wear, and Osmond watched enviously as the Hausas strolled across, grasping the cylindrical surface handily with their bare feet, and wondered if he had not better take off his boots. However, Westall had no false pride. Recognizing the disabilities involved by boots, he stooped, and, getting astride the slender log, crossed the river with ease and safety, if without much dignity; and the other two white men were not too proud to follow his example.

Beyond the river the path, after crossing a narrow belt of forest, entered a valley bordered by hills covered with dense bush, which rose steeply on either side. Osmond looked at the little party ahead, straggling in single file along the bottom of the valley, and inwardly wondered where Westall had picked up his strategy.

"It's to be hoped, Stockbridge," he remarked, "that there are none of Mr Zippah's friends hanging about here. You couldn't want a prettier spot for an ambush."

He had hardly spoken when a tall man, wearing a hunter's lionskin cap and carrying a musket, stepped quietly out of the bush on to the track just in front of Westall. The prisoner, Zippah, uttered a yell of recognition and held up his manacled hands. The deep, cannon-like report of the musket rang out and the narrow gorge was filled with a dense cloud of smoke.

There was an instant's silence. Then a scattering volley was heard from the Hausas ahead, the panic-stricken carriers came flying back along the trail, shouting with terror, and the two white men plunged forward into the stinking smoke. Leaping over the prostrate Zippah, who was being held down by two Hausas, they came upon Westall, lying across the path, limp and motionless. A great ragged patch on his breast, all scorched and bloody, told the tale that his pinched, grey face and glazing eyes confirmed. Indeed, even as they stooped over him, heedless of the bellowing muskets and the slugs that shrieked past, he drew one shallow breath and was gone.

There was no time for sentiment. With set faces the two men turned from the dead officer and ran forward to where the shadowy forms of the Hausas appeared through the smoke, holding their ground doggedly and firing right and left into the bush. But a single glance showed the hopelessness of the position. Two of the Hausas were down, and of the remaining four, three, including the sergeant, were more or less wounded. Not a man of the enemy was to be seen, but from the wooded slope on either hand came jets of flame and smoke, accompanied by the thunderous reports of the muskets and the whistle of flying slugs, while a thick cloud of smoke rolled down the hillsides and filled the bottom of the valley as with a dense fog.

Osmond snatched up the rifle of one of the fallen Hausas and, clearing out the man's cartridge-pouch, began firing into likely spots in the bush when Stockbridge interposed.

"It's no go, Cook. We must fall back across the bridge. You clear out while you've got a whole skin. Hallo! Did you hear that? Those weren't trade guns."

As he spoke there were heard, mingling with the noisy explosions of the muskets, a succession of sharp, woody reports, each followed by the musical hum of a high-speed bullet.

"Back you go, Cook," he urged. "This is no place for – "

He stopped short, staggered back a few paces, and fell, cursing volubly, with a bloody hand clasped on his leg just below the knee.

Osmond stooped over him, and, finding that the bone was not broken, quickly tied his handkerchief over the wound to restrain the bleeding. "That will do for the present," said he. "Now you tell the men to fall back, and I'll bring the prisoner."

"Never mind the prisoner," said Stockbridge. "Get the wounded back and get back yourself."

"Not at all," said Osmond. "The prisoner is going to cover our retreat. Put your arm round the sergeant's neck and hop along on your sound leg."

In spite of the galling fire, the retreat was carried out quickly and in good order. Stockbridge was hustled away by the sergeant – who was only disabled in one arm – and the two helpless men and the dead officer were borne off by the three native servants. Meanwhile Osmond took possession of the prisoner – just as one of his guards was preparing to cut his throat with a large and very unofficial-looking knife – and, rapidly pinioning his arms with the leading-rope, held him up with his face towards the enemy; in which position he served as excellent cover, not only for Osmond but also for the two Hausas, who were able to keep up a brisk fire over his shoulders.

In this fashion Osmond and his two supporters slowly backed after the retreating party. The firing from the bush practically ceased, since the enemy had no mark to fire at but their own chief; and though they continued to follow up, as the moving bushes showed, their wholesome respect for the Snider rifle – with which the Hausas were armed – prevented them from coming out of cover or approaching dangerously near.

In less than a quarter of an hour the open space by the river was reached; and here Osmond's retreat was covered by the rest of the party, who had crossed the river and had taken up a safe position in the bamboo thicket, whence they could, without exposing themselves, command the approaches to the bridge. The two Hausas were turning to run across the log when Osmond noticed a large basket of produce – containing, among other things, a number of balls of shea butter – which one of his carriers had dropped in his retreat.

"Hi!" he sang out, "pick up that basket and take him across"; and then, as a new idea suggested itself: "Put those balls of shea tulu in my pocket."

The astonished Hausa hesitated, especially as a Mauser bullet had just hummed past his head, but when Osmond repeated the order impatiently he hurriedly grabbed up the unsavoury-looking balls of grease and crammed them into Osmond's pocket. Then he turned and ran across the bridge.

Osmond continued to back towards the river, still holding the struggling Zippah close before him as a shield. Arriving at the end of the bridge, he cautiously sat down and got astride the log, pulling his captive, with some difficulty, into the same position, and began to wriggle across. Once started, Zippah was docile enough, for, with his pinioned arms, he could not afford to fall into the swirling water. He even assisted his captor so far as he was able, being evidently anxious to get the perilous passage over as quickly as possible. When they had crept about a third of the way across, Osmond took one of the balls of shea butter from his pocket, and, reaching past his prisoner, smeared the greasy mass thickly on the smooth surface of the log; and this proceeding he repeated at intervals as he retired, leaving a thick trail of the solid grease behind him. Zippah was at first profoundly mystified by the white man's manoeuvres, which he probably regarded as some kind of fetish ceremonial or magic; but when its purpose suddenly dawned on him, his sullen face relaxed into a broad and appreciative grin, and as he was at length dragged backwards from the head of the bridge, through the opening into the dark bamboo thicket, he astonished the besieged party (and no doubt the besiegers also) by letting off a peal of honest African guffaws.

Chapter Ten

Betty's Appeal

As the prisoner was withdrawn by his guard into the dark opening of the thicket, Osmond halted for a moment to look back across the river. Not a sign of the enemy was to be seen excepting the pall of smoke that hung over the wooded shore. But the reports of unseen muskets and rifles and the hum of slugs and bullets warned him of the danger of exposing himself – though he, too, was probably hidden from the enemy by the dense smoke of the black powder. Accordingly he turned quickly and, plunging into the dark tunnel-like passage, groped his way forward, unable, at first, to distinguish anything in the all-pervading gloom. Presently he perceived a little distance ahead a cluster of the great bamboo stalks faintly lighted as if by a hidden fire or torch, and a moment later, a turn of the passage brought him in view of the light itself, which seemed to be a rough shea-butter candle or lamp, set on the ground and lighting up dimly the forlorn little band whose retreat he had covered.

This much he took in at the first glance. But suddenly he became aware of a new presence, at the sight of which he stopped short with a smothered exclamation. Stockbridge, sitting beside his dead comrade, had uncovered his wounded leg; and kneeling by him as she applied a dressing to the wound was a woman. He could not see her face, which was partly turned away from him and concealed by a wide pith helmet; but the figure was – to him –

unmistakable, as were the little, dainty, capable hands on which the flickering light shone. He approached slowly, and as Stockbridge greeted him with a wry grin, she turned her head quickly and looked up at him. "Good evening, Mr Cook," she said, quietly. "What a fortunate chance it is that you should be here."

"Yes, by Jove," agreed Stockbridge; "at least a fortunate chance for us. He is a born tactician."

Osmond briefly acknowledged the greeting, and in the ensuing silence, as Betty methodically applied the bandage, he looked about him and rapidly assessed the situation. Stockbridge looked weak and spent and was evidently in considerable pain, though he uttered no complaint; the wounded Hausas lay hard by, patiently awaiting their turn to have their injuries attended to, and the carriers crouched disconsolately in gloomy corners out of the way of chance missiles. A continuous firing was being kept up from the other side of the river, and slugs and Mauser bullets ploughed noisily through the bamboo, though none came near the fugitives. The position of the latter, indeed, was one of great natural strength, for the river made a horse-shoe bend at this spot and the little peninsula enclosed by it was entirely occupied by the bamboo. An attack was possible in only two directions; by the bridge, or by the path that entered the thicket at the other end.

"Well," said Osmond, as Betty, having finished the dressing, transferred her attention to one of the wounded Hausas, "here we are, safe for the moment. They can't get at us in here."

"No," agreed Stockbridge. "It's a strong position, if we could stay here, though they will probably try to rush the bridge when it's dark."

Osmond shook his head with a grim smile. "They won't do that," said he. "I've taken the precaution to grease the log; so they'll have to crawl across carefully, which they won't care to do with the Hausas potting at them from shelter. But we can't stay here. We'd better clear out as soon as it is dark; and the question is, which way?"

"We must follow the river, I suppose," said Stockbridge, in a faint voice. "But you'd better arrange with the sergeant. I'm no good now. Tell him he's to take your orders. Our carriers know the country."

The sergeant, who had witnessed Osmond's masterly retreat, accepted the new command without demur. A guard was posted to watch the bridge from safe cover, and the carriers were assembled to discuss the route.

"Now," said Osmond, "where is the next bridge?"

There was apparently no other bridge, but there was a ford some miles farther up, and a couple of miles below there was a village which possessed one or two of the large, punt-shaped canoes that were used for trading across the lagoon.

"S'pose dey no fit to pass de bridge," said the head carrier, "dey go and fetch canoe for carry um across de river."

"I see," said Osmond. "Then they'd attack us from the rear and we should be bottled up from both sides. That won't do. You must get ready to march out as soon as it is dark, sergeant. Your carriers can take Mr Westall's body and some of the wounded and the sound men must carry the rest. And send my carriers back the way they came. There are too many of us as it is."

"And dem muskets and powder, dat we bring in from the villages?" said the sergeant. "What we do wid dem?"

"We must leave them here or throw them in the river. Anyhow, you get off as quickly as you can."

The sergeant set about his preparations without delay and Osmond's carriers departed gleefully towards the safe part of the country. Meanwhile Osmond considered the situation. If the enemy obtained canoes from the lower river, they would probably ferry a party across and attack the bamboo fortress from front and rear simultaneously. Then they would find the nest empty, and naturally would start in pursuit; which would be unpleasant for the helpless fugitives, crawling painfully along the river bank. He turned the position over again and again with deep dissatisfaction, while Stockbridge watched him anxiously and Betty silently continued her operations on the wounded. If they were pursued, they were lost. In their helpless condition they could make no sort of stand against a large body attacking from the cover of the bush. And the pursuit would probably commence before they had travelled a couple of miles towards safety.

Suddenly his eye fell on the heap of captured muskets and powder-kegs that were to be left behind or destroyed. He looked at them meditatively, and, as he looked, there began to shape itself in his mind a plan by which the fugitives might at least increase their start by a mile or so. A fantastic scheme, perhaps, but yet, in the absence of any better, worth trying.

With characteristic energy, he set to work at once, while the carriers hastily fashioned rough litters of bamboo for the dead and wounded. Broaching one of the powder-kegs, he proceeded to load all but two of the muskets – of which there were twenty-three in all – cramming the barrels with powder and filling up each with a heavy charge of gravel. Six of the loaded and primed muskets he laid on the ground about fifty yards from the bridge end of the long passage, with their muzzles pointing towards the bridge; the remaining fifteen he laid in batches of five about the same distance from the opposite entrance, towards which their muzzles pointed. Then, taking a length of the plaited cord with which the muskets had been lashed into bundles, he tied one end to the stock of one of the unloaded guns and the other to the trigger of one of the wounded Hausas' rifles. Fixing the rifle upright against the bamboo with its muzzle stuck in the half-empty powder-keg, of which he broke out two or three staves, he carried the cord – well greased with shea butter – through a loop tied to one of the slanting bamboos. Then he propped the musket in a standing position on two bamboo sticks, to one of which he attached another length of cord. It was the mechanism of the common sieve bird-trap. When the cord was pulled, the stick would be dislodged, the musket would fall, and in falling jerk the other cord and fire the rifle.

Broaching another keg, he carried a large train of powder from the first keg to the row of loaded muskets, over the pans of which he poured a considerable heap. Leaving the tripping-cord loose, he next proceeded to the opposite end of the thicket and set up a similar trap near the landward entrance, connecting it by a large powder train with the three batches of loaded muskets.

"You seem to be deuced busy, Cook," Stockbridge remarked as Osmond passed the hammock in which he was now reclining.

"Yes," Osmond replied; "I am arranging a little entertainment to keep our friends amused while we are getting a start. Now, sergeant, if you are ready, you had better gag the prisoner and move outside the bamboos. It will be dark in a few minutes. And give me Mr Westall's revolver and pouch."

At this moment, Betty, having applied as much "first aid" as was possible to the wounded Hausas, came up to him and said in a low voice:

"Jim, dear, you will let me help you, if I can, won't you?"

"Certainly I will, dearest," he replied, "though I wish to God you weren't here."

"I don't," said she. "If it comes to the worst, we shall go out together. But it won't. I am not a bit frightened now you are with me."

"I see you have given Stockbridge your hammock," said he. "How far do you think you can walk?"

"Twenty miles, easily, or more at night. Now, Jim, don't worry about me. Just tell me what I am to do and forget me. You have plenty to think about."

"Well, then, I want you and Stockbridge to keep to the middle of the column. The carrier who knows the way will lead, and the sergeant and I will march at the rear to look out for the pursuers. And you must get along as fast as you can."

"Aye, aye, sir," she replied, smiling in his face and raising her hand smartly to the peak of her helmet; and without another word she turned away to take her place in the retiring column.

As the little procession moved towards the opening, Osmond ran back to the bridge end of the track to clear out the guard before he set his traps. A brisk fusillade was proceeding from the concealed enemy when he arrived, to which the guards were replying from their cover.

"I tink dey fit for come across de bridge," one of the Hausas remarked as Osmond gave them the orders to retire.

"Very well," he replied; "you be off one time. I stop to send them back."

The two Hausas accordingly retired, reluctant and protesting, and Osmond took their place behind the screen of bamboo, from which he looked out across the river. It was evident by the constant stirring of the bush and the occasional appearance of men in the openings that some sort of move was in progress, and in fact the footsteps of the two Hausas had hardly died away when it took definite shape. The attack opened with a thundering volley which sent the leaves and splinters of bamboo flying in all directions; then, out of the bush, a compact body of warriors each armed with a Mauser rifle, emerged in single file and advanced towards the bridge at a smart trot. Osmond watched them with a grim smile. Down the narrow track they came in perfect order and on to the foot of the bridge, stepping along the smooth log with perfect security – until they reached the greased portion. Then came the catastrophe. As the leading warrior stepped on the greasy surface, his feet flew from under him and down he slithered, grabbing frantically at the legs of the next man, who instantly clawed hold of his neighbour and thus passed on the disturbance. In a moment the whole file was capsized like a row of ninepins, and as each man's rifle exploded as he fell and the whole body broke out into simultaneous yells of rage and terror, the orderly dignity of the attack was destroyed utterly.

The cause of the disaster was not immediately perceived, and as soon as the struggling warriors had been rescued from the river or had drifted down stream, the attack was renewed, to end in another wholesale capsize. After the third attempt, however, it apparently began to dawn on the warriors that there was something unnatural about the bridge. A noisy consultation followed, and when Osmond opened a smart fire with his revolver, the entire body retreated hastily into the bush.

As it was pretty certain that there would be no further attempt to rush the bridge at present, and as the darkness was fast closing in, Osmond proceeded to finish his arrangements before evacuating the fortress. Having set the tripping-cord across the path about six inches from the ground, he loaded and cocked the rifle. The trap was now set. If the warriors should presently manage to crawl across the bridge and enter the thicket, the first comer would certainly strike the cord; and the musket volley and the flying gravel, though they would probably do little harm, would send the attacking party back to the cover of the bush.

Having set the trap, Osmond knocked in the heads of the remaining powder-kegs and spread the powder about among the dry dead bamboo stalks that covered the ground. Then he retired to the landward end of the thicket, and, having set the second trap, started in pursuit of his friends.

The fugitives had evidently travelled at a good pace despite their encumbrances, for he had walked nearly a mile along the riverside track before he overtook them. As he turned a sharp bend he came on them quite suddenly, crouching down in the undergrowth as if in hiding; and, as he appeared, the two Hausas who formed the rearguard motioned to him to crouch down too.

"What is it?" he whispered, kneeling beside the last Hausa.

"S't! Someone live for river. You no hear um, sah?"

Osmond listened attentively. From somewhere down the river came a sound of muffled voices and the rhythmical swish of something moving through water. He crept nearer to the brink and cautiously peered through the bushes across the dark river. The sounds drew nearer, and soon he could dimly make out the shapes of two long canoes poling up-stream in the shallows on the other side. Each canoe held only three or four men, just enough to drive it swiftly against the stream; but in spite of this, there could be little doubt as to the business on which these stealthily-moving craft were bent. As they faded into the darkness, Osmond touched the Hausa on the shoulder, and, whispering to him to follow, began softly to retrace his steps. His experience of the happy-go-lucky native had inspired him with a new hope.

Attended by the puzzled but obedient Hausa, he followed the sound of the retreating canoes until it suddenly ceased. Then he crept forward still more cautiously and presently caught sight of the two craft, brought up under the opposite bank and filling rapidly with men. He crouched down among the bushes and watched. Very soon the canoes, now crowded with men, put out, one after the other, and swiftly crossing the river, grounded on a small beach or hard under the high bank; when the men, each of whom, as Osmond could now see, carried a gun or rifle, landed and crept up a sloping path. The canoe immediately put off and returned to the other side, whence, having taken up a fresh batch of passengers they crossed to the hard. This manoeuvre was repeated six times, and, as each canoe carried over a dozen men, there were now assembled on the near bank about a hundred and fifty warriors, who remained in a mass, talking in hoarse undertones and waiting for the word to advance.

The last load apparently completed the contingent, for, this time, all the passengers landed and crept up the path, leaving the two canoes drawn up on the hard. This was what Osmond had hoped for and half expected. Feverishly he watched the mob of warriors form up and move off in orderly single file, each shouldering his musket or rifle and no one making a sound. As the silent procession vanished towards the lately evacuated fortress, he craned forward to see if any guards had been posted. But not a soul was in sight. Then he stole along the track until he was above the hard, when he turned to the Hausa.

"Wait," he whispered, "until I get the canoes. Then go back quickly and tell the sergeant I come."

He crept down the path to the hard, and, stepping into one of the canoes, walked to the stern, holding on to the second canoe.

As his weight depressed the stern, the bow lifted from the ground and he was able to push off, walking slowly forward as the craft went astern. Then, from the bow, he threw his weight on the stern of the second canoe, which lifted free of the ground in the same manner, and the two craft began silently to drift away down stream on the swift current.

Osmond waved his free hand to the Hausa, and, when he had seen the man steal away to carry the good tidings to the fugitives, he set himself to secure the two canoes together. Each had a primitive painter of grass rope rove through a hole in the bluff bow and a small thwart or cross-band of the same material close to the stern to strengthen the long sides. By making fast the painter of the second canoe to the stern thwart of the one he was in, he secured them together and left himself free to ply the pole; which he began to do as noiselessly as possible, when he had drifted down about a quarter of a mile from the hard, steering the canoes close along the side on which his friends would be waiting. Presently there came a soft hail from the bank; on which, checking their way with the pole, he brought the two canoes up on a spit of sandy mud close underneath.

As he stepped ashore, holding on to the painter of the leading canoe, a little, white-skirted figure came scrambling down the bank, and running to him, seized both his hands.

"Jim!" she whispered, "you are a wonder! You have saved us all! Of course you have! I knew you would!" She gave his hands a final squeeze and then abruptly returned to business. "I will see to the wounded if you tell me where they are to go."

Osmond indicated the larger of the two canoes, and she at once climbed up the bank to arrange the embarkation, while Osmond, having drawn both canoes up on the spit, called to two of the Hausas to take charge of the painters so that the craft should not get adrift while loading. Then he went up to superintend. The first problem, that of canoe-men, was easily solved, for the carriers, who were natives of the lagoon country, all had some skill in the use of the pole and cheerfully volunteered for duty.

But it was not without some difficulty that the three rough litters – one of them containing the body of poor Westall – were lowered down the steep bank and the wounded men helped down to the spit; but when once they were there, the roomy, punt-like canoes afforded ample and comfortable accommodation for the whole party. The sound men, with three canoe-men and the prisoner, were packed into the smaller canoe, leaving plenty of space in the other for the wounded to lie at their ease. Stockbridge's hammock was stowed in the bows, so that he should not be disturbed by the movements of the canoe-men, the body of Westall came next, decently covered with a country cloth, and then the rest of the wounded. When all was ready, Betty and Osmond stepped on board and took their places side by side in the stern.

As they pushed off into the river Stockbridge settled himself comfortably on his pillow with a sigh of relief at exchanging the jolting of the bush road for the easy motion of the canoe.

"By Jove, Cook!" he exclaimed, "it was a stroke of luck for us that you happened to overtake us. But for your wits they would have made a clean sweep of us. Hallo! What the deuce is that?"

From up the river came three thunderous volleys in quick succession, followed by a confused noise of shouting and the reports of muskets and rifles; then the sound of another volley, more shouts and rattling reports; and as they looked back, the sky was lighted for a few moments by a red glare. Osmond briefly explained the nature of his "little arrangements," while the alarmed carriers poled along the shallows for dear life.

"But," said Stockbridge, after listening awhile, "what are the beggars going on firing for? Just hark at them! They're blazing away like billy-oh!"

"I take it," replied Osmond, "that they have gorged the bait. Apparently, a party has managed to crawl across the bridge to attack the bamboo thicket from the front while the other force, which ferried across the river, attacked from the rear, and that each party is mistaking the other for us. The trifling error ought to keep them amused for quite a long time; in fact until we are beyond reach of pursuit."

Stockbridge chuckled softly. "You are an ingenious beggar, Cook," he declared with conviction; "and how you managed to keep your wits about you in that hurly-burly, I can't imagine. However, I think we are safe enough now." With this comfortable conclusion, he snuggled down into his hammock and settled himself for a night's rest.

"Oh, Jim dear," whispered Betty, "how like you! To think out your plans calmly with the bullets flying around and everybody else in a hopeless twitter. It reminds me of the 'phantom mate' on the dear old *Speedwell*. By the way, how *did* you happen to be there in that miraculously opportune fashion?"

Osmond chuckled. "Well," he exclaimed, "you are a pretty cool little fish, Betty. You drop down from the clouds and then inquire how I happened to be there. How did you happen to be there?"

"Oh, that is quite simple," she replied. "I got Daddy's permission to take a trip from Accra across the Akwapim Mountains to Akusé; and when I got there I thought I should like to have a look at the country where the bobbery was going on. So I crossed the river and was starting off gaily towards the Krepi border when an interfering though well-meaning old chief stopped me and said I mustn't go any farther because of war-palaver. I wanted to go on, but my carriers wouldn't budge; so back I came, taking the road for Quittah, and by good luck dropped into a little war-palaver after all."

"Why were you going to Quittah?"

"Now, Jim, don't ask silly questions. You know perfectly well. Of course I was going to run over to Adaffia to call on my friend Captain J.; and by the same token, I shouldn't have found him there. Now tell me how you came to be in the bush at this particular time."

Osmond stated baldly the ostensible purpose of his expedition, to which Betty listened without comment. She had her suspicions as to the ultimate motive, but she asked no questions. The less said on that subject, the better.

This was evidently Osmond's view, for he at once plunged into an account of the loss of the *Speedwell* and of Captain Hartup's testamentary arrangements. Betty was deeply affected, both by the loss of the ship and the death of the worthy but cross-grained little skipper.

"How awfully sad!" she exclaimed, almost in tears. "The dear old ship, where I spent the happiest days of my life! And poor Captain Hartup! I always liked him really. He was quite nice to me, in spite of his gruff manner. I used to feel that he was just a little human porcupine with india-rubber quills. And now I love him because, in his perverse little heart, he understood and appreciated my Captain Jim. May I come, one day, and put a wreath on his grave?"

"Yes, do, Betty," he replied. "I buried him next to Osmond's new grave, and I put up an oaken cross which I made out of some of the planking of the old *Speedwell*. He was very fond of his ship. And I have kept a couple of her beams – thought you might like to have something made out of one of them."

"How sweet of you, Jim, to think of it!" she exclaimed, nestling close to him and slipping her hand round his arm, "and to know exactly what I should like! But we do understand each other, don't we, Jim, dear?"

"I think we do, Betty, darling," he replied, pressing the little hand that had stolen into his own.

For a long time nothing more was said. After the turmoil and the alarms of the escape, it was very peaceful to sit in the gently-swaying canoe and listen to the voices of the night; the continuous "chirr" of countless cicadas, punctuated by the soft "swish" of the canoe-poles as they were drawn forward for another stroke; the deep-toned, hollow whistle of the great fox-bats, flapping slowly across the river; the long-drawn cry, or staccato titter, of far-away hyaenas, and now and again, the startling shriek of a potto in one of the lofty trees by the river bank. It was more soothing than absolute silence. The sounds seemed so remote and unreal, so eloquent of utter solitude; of a vast, unseen wilderness with its mysterious population of bird and beast, living on its strange, primeval life unchanged from the days when the world was young.

After a long interval, Betty spoke again. "It seems," she said, reflectively, "dreadfully callous to be so perfectly happy. I wonder if it is."

"Why should it be?" her companion asked.

"I mean," she explained, "with poor Mr Westall lying there dead, only a few feet away."

Osmond felt inwardly that Westall had not only thrown away his own life but jeopardized the lives of the others which were in his custody. But he forbore to express what he felt and answered, simply:

"I don't suppose the poor chap would grudge us our happiness. It won't last very long."

"Why shouldn't it, Jim?" she exclaimed. "Why should we part again and be miserable for the want of one another? Oh, Jim, darling, my own mate, won't you try to put away your scruples – your needless scruples, though I love and respect you for having them? But don't let them spoil our lives. Forget John Osmond. He is dead and buried. Let him rest. I am yours, Jim, and you know it; and you are mine, and I know it. Those are the realities, which we could never change if we should live for a century. Let us accept them and forget what is past and done with. Life is short enough, dear, and our youth is slipping away. If we make a false move, we shall never get another chance. Oh, say it, Jim. Say you will put away the little things that don't matter and hold fast to the reality of our great love and the happiness that is within our reach. Won't you, Jim?"

He was silent for a while. This was what he had dreaded. To have freely offered, yet again, the gift beside which all the treasures of the earth were to him as nothing; and, even worse, to be made to feel that he, himself, had something to give which he must yet withhold; it was an agony. The temptation to yield – to shut his eyes to the future and snatch at the golden present – was almost irresistible. He knew that Betty was absolutely sincere. He knew quite well that whatever might befall in the future, she would hold him blameless and accept all mischances as the consequences of her own considered choice. His confidence in her generosity was absolute, nor did he undervalue her judgement. He even admitted that she was probably right. John Osmond was dead. The pursuit was at an end and the danger of discovery negligible. In a new country and in a new character he was sure that he could make her life all that she hoped. Then why not forget the past and say "yes"?

It was a great temptation. One little word, and they would possess all that they wished for, all that mattered to either of them. And yet –

"Betty," he said at length, in a tone of the deepest gravity, "you have said that we understand one another. We do; perfectly; absolutely. There is no need for me to tell you that I love you, or that if there were any sacrifice that I could make for you, I would make it joyfully and think it an honour and a privilege. You know that as well as I do. But there is one thing that I cannot do. Whatever I may be or may have done, I cannot behave like a cad to the woman I love. And that is what I should do if I married you. I should accept your sterling gold and give you base metal in exchange. You would be the wife of an outlaw, you would live under the continual menace of scandal and disaster. Your children would be the children of a nameless man and would grow up to the inheritance of an ancestry that could not be spoken of.

"Those are the realities, Betty. I realize, and I reverence, your great and noble love for me, unworthy as I am. But I should be a selfish brute if I accepted what you offer to me with such incredible generosity. I can't do it, Betty. It was a disaster that you ever met me, but that we cannot help. We can only limit its effects."

She listened silently while he pronounced the doom of her newly-born hopes, holding his hand tightly grasped in hers and scarcely seeming to breathe. She did not reply immediately when he ceased speaking, but sat a while, her head resting against his shoulder and her hand still clasped in his. Once she smothered a little sob and furtively wiped her eyes. But she was very quiet, and, at length, in a composed, steady voice, though sadly enough, she rejoined:

"Very well, Jim, dear. It must be as you think best, and I won't tease you with any more appeals. At any rate, we can go on loving each other, and that will be something. The gift of real love doesn't come to everyone."

For a long time they sat without further speech, thinking each their own thoughts. To Betty the position was a little puzzling. She understood Osmond's point of view and respected it, for she knew that the sacrifice was as great to him as to her. And though, woman-like, she felt their mutual devotion to be a full answer to all his objections, yet – again, woman-like – she approved, though reluctantly, of his rigid adherence to a masculine standard of conduct.

But here came another puzzle. What was it that he had done? What could it possibly be that a man like this should have done? He had said plainly – and she knew that it was true – that there had been a warrant for his arrest. He had been, and in a sense still was, a fugitive from justice. Yet his standard of honour was of the most scrupulous delicacy. It had compelled him quite unnecessarily to disclose his identity. It compelled him now to put away what she knew was his dearest wish. Nothing could be more unlike a criminal; who, surely, is above all things self-indulgent. Yet he was an offender against the law. Now, what, in the name of Heaven, is the kind of offence against the law of which a man of this type could be guilty? He had never given a hint upon the subject, and of course she had never sought to find out. She was not in the least inquisitive now. But the incongruity, the discrepancy between his character and his circumstances, perplexed her profoundly.

Finally, she gave up the puzzle and began to talk to him about Captain Hartup and the pleasant old times on board the *Speedwell*.

He responded with evident relief at having passed the dreaded crisis; and so, by degrees, they got back to cheerful talk and frank enjoyment of one another's society, letting the past, the future, and the might-have-been sink into temporary oblivion.

Chapter Eleven

The Order of Release

It was a long journey down the winding river and across the great lagoon. How long Osmond never knew; for, as hour after hour passed and the canoe sped on noiselessly through the encompassing darkness, the fatigues of the day began to take effect, not only on him, but on his companion too. Gradually the conversation slackened, the intervals of silence grew longer and longer, merging into periods of restful unconsciousness and punctuated by little smothered yawns on the part of Betty; until, at length, silence fell upon the canoe, unbroken save by the sounds of sleeping men and the rhythmical "swish" of the poles.

At the sound of a distant bugle Osmond opened his eyes and became aware that the day was breaking and that the journey was nearly at an end. Also that his head was very comfortably pillowed on the shoulder of his companion, who now slumbered peacefully at his side. Very softly he raised himself and looked down at the sleeping girl, almost holding his breath lest he should disturb her. How dainty and frail she looked, this brave, hardy little maid! How delicate, almost childlike, she seemed as she lay, breathing softly, in the easy posture of graceful youth! And how lovely she was! He gazed adoringly at the sweet face, so charmingly wreathed with its golden aureole, at the peacefully-closed eyes with their fringes of long, dark lashes, and thought half-bitterly, half-proudly, that she was his own for the asking; and even as he looked, she opened her eyes and greeted him with a smile.

"What are you looking so solemn about, Jim?" she asked, as she sat up and reached for her helmet.

"Was I looking solemn? I expect it was only foolishness. Most fools are solemn animals."

"Don't be a guffin, Jim," she commanded, reprovingly.

"What is a guffin?" he asked.

"It is a thing with a big, Roman nose and a most abnormal amount of obstinacy, which makes disparaging comments on my Captain Jim."

"A horrid sort of beast it must be. Well, I won't, then. Is that Quittah, where all those canoes are?"

"I suppose it is, but I've never been there. Yes, it must be. I can see Fort Firminger – that thing like a Martello tower out in the lagoon opposite the landing-place. Mr Cockeram says it is an awfully strong fort. You couldn't knock it down with a croquet-mallet."

Osmond looked about him with the interest of a traveller arriving at a place which he has heard of but never seen. Behind and on both sides, the waste of water extended as far as the eye could see. Before them was a line of low land with occasional clumps of coconut palms that marked the position of beach villages. Ahead was a larger mass of palms, before which was a wide "hard" or landing-place, already thronged with market people, towards which numbers of trading canoes were converging from all parts of the lagoon.

As they drew nearer, an opening in the palms revealed a whitewashed fort above which a flag was just being hoisted; and now, over the sandy shore, the masts of two vessels came into view.

"There is the *Widgeon*," said Betty, pointing to the masts of the barquentine, "and there is another vessel, a schooner. I wonder who she is."

Osmond had observed and was also wondering who she was; for he had a suspicion that he had seen her before. Something in the appearance of the tall, slim masts seemed to recall the mysterious yacht-like craft that he had seen one night at Adaffia revealed for a moment in "the glimpses of the moon."

They were now rapidly approaching the landing-place. The other canoe had already arrived, and its disembarked crew could be seen on the hard surrounded by a crowd of natives.

"That looks like a naval officer waiting on the beach," said Osmond, looking at a white-clad figure which had separated itself from the crowd and appeared to be awaiting their arrival.

"It is," replied Betty. "I believe it is Captain Darley. And there is a constabulary officer coming down, too. I expect they have heard the news. You'll get a great reception when they hear Mr Stockbridge's story – and mine. But they will be awfully upset about poor Mr Westall. You are coming up to the fort with me, of course?"

Osmond had intended to go straight on to Adaffia, but he now saw that this would be impossible. Besides, there was the schooner.

"Yes," he replied, "I will see you to your destination."

"It isn't my destination," said she. "I shall rest here for a day – the German deaconesses will give me a bed, I expect – and then I am coming on with you to Adaffia to put a wreath on Captain Hartup's grave. You can put up either at the fort or with one of the German traders or missionaries. There are no English people here excepting the two officers at the fort."

Osmond made no comment on this, for they were now close inshore. The canoe slid into the shallows and in a few moments more was hauled up by a crowd of willing natives until her bows were high and dry on the hard.

The officer who had joined Darley turned out to be the doctor, under whose superintendence Stockbridge's hammock was carefully landed and the rest of the wounded brought ashore. Then the litter containing the body of the dead officer was lifted out and slowly borne away, while Darley and the native soldiers stood at the salute, and the doctor, having mustered the wounded, led the way towards the little hospital. As the melancholy procession moved off, Darley turned to greet Betty and Osmond, who had stepped ashore last.

"How do you do, Miss Burleigh? None the worse for your adventures, I hope. Been having rather a strenuous time, haven't you?"

"We have rather," she replied. "Isn't it a dreadful thing to have lost poor Mr Westall?"

"Yes," he replied, as they turned away from the lagoon and began to walk towards the fort. "Shocking affair. Still, fortune of war, you know. Can't make omelettes without breaking eggs. And here is Mr Cook, in the thick of the bobbery, as usual. What a fellow you are, Cook! Always in hot water."

As he shook Osmond's hand heartily, the latter replied:

"Well, the bobbery wasn't of my making, this time. I found it ready made and just bore a hand. By the way, what schooner is that out in the roads?"

"That," replied Darley, "is an ancient yacht named the *Primula* – a lovely old craft – sails like a witch. But she has come down in the world now. We met her coming up from the leeward coast and brought her in here."

"Brought her in? Is she in custody, then?"

"Well, we brought her in to overhaul her and make some inquiries. There is just a suspicion that she has been concerned in the gun-running that has been going on. But we haven't found anything up to the present. She seems to be full up with ordinary, legitimate cargo."

"Ha!" exclaimed Osmond.

"Why 'ha'?" demanded Darley with a quick look at Osmond. "Do you know anything about her?"

"Let us hear some more," said Osmond. "Is there a Welshman named Jones on board?"

"There is. He's the skipper, purser, and supercargo all combined."

"Have you looked through her manifest?"

"I have; and I've jotted down some notes of the items of her lading."

"Is there any ivory on board?"

"Yes," replied Darley, with growing excitement.

"Three large crates and a big canvas bag?"

"*Yes!*"

"Containing in all, thirty-nine large tusks and fifty-one scribellos?"

Darley dragged a pocket-book out of his pocket and feverishly turned over the leaves. "Yes, by Jove!" he fairly shouted. "The very numbers. Now, what have you got to tell us?"

"I think you can take it that the ivory and probably the rest of the lading, too, is stolen property."

"Why," exclaimed Betty, "that must be your ivory, Jim."

Darley flashed an astonished glance at her and then looked inquiringly at Osmond. "Is that so?" he asked.

"I have no doubt that it is," the latter replied. "But if it should happen that there is a man on board named Sam Winter – "

"There is," interrupted Darley.

"And another named Simmons, and others named Foat, Bradley, and Darker, I think, if you introduce me to them, that we shall get the whole story. And as to the gun-running, I can't make a voluntary statement, but if you were to put me in the witness-box, I should have to tell you all I know; and I may say that I know a good deal. Will that do, for the present?"

Darley smiled complacently. "It seems like a pretty straight tip," said he. "I will just skip on board, now, and take possession of the manifest; and if you will give me that list of names again, I will see if those men are on board, and bring them ashore, if they are. You will be staying at the fort, I suppose? There are only Cockeram and the doctor there."

"Yes," said Betty, "I shall ask Mr Cockeram to put him up, for tonight, at any rate."

"Very well," said Darley, "then I shall see you again later. And now I will be off and lay the train."

He touched his cap, and as they emerged into an open space before the gateway of the fort, he turned and walked away briskly down a long, shady avenue of wild fig-trees that led towards the shore.

Quittah fort was a shabby-looking, antique structure adapted to the conditions of primitive warfare. It was entered by an arched gateway graced by two ancient cannon set up as posts and guarded by a Hausa sentry in a blue serge uniform and a scarlet fez. Towards the gateway Osmond and Betty directed their steps, and as they approached, the sentry sprang smartly to attention and presented arms; whereupon Betty marched in with impressive dignity and two tiny fingers raised to the peak of her helmet.

"This seems to be the way up," she said, turning towards a mouldering wooden staircase, as a supercilious-looking pelican waddled towards them and a fish-eagle on a perch in a corner uttered a loud yell. "What a queer place it is! It looks like a menagerie. I wonder if there is anyone at home."

She tripped up the stairs, followed by Osmond and watched suspiciously by an assemblage of storks, coots, rails, and other birds which were strolling about at large in the quadrangle, and came out on an open space at the top of a corner bastion. Just as they reached this spot a man came hurrying out of a shabby building which occupied one side of the square; and at the first glance Osmond recognized him as the officer who had come to Adaffia to execute the warrant on the day when he had buried poor Larkom. The recognition was mutual, for as soon as he had saluted Betty, the officer turned to him and held out his hand.

"Larkom, by Jove!" said he.

"My name is Cook," Osmond corrected.

"Oh," said the other; "glad you set me right, because I have been going to send you a note. You remember me – Cockeram. I came down to Adaffia, you know, about that poor chap Osmond."

"I remember. You said you had been going to write to me."

"Yes. I was going to send you something that I thought would interest you. I may as well give it to you now." He began to rummage in his pockets and eventually brought forth a bulging letter-case, the very miscellaneous contents of which he proceeded to sort out. "It's about poor Osmond," he continued, disjointedly, and still turning over a litter of papers. "I felt that you would like to see it. Poor chap! It was such awfully rough luck."

"What was?" asked Osmond.

"Why, you remember," replied Cockeram, suspending his search to look up, "that I had a warrant to arrest him. It seemed that he was wanted for some sort of jewel robbery and there had been a regular hue-and-cry after him. Then he managed to slip away to sea and had just contrived to get into hiding at Adaffia when the fever got him. Frightful hard lines!"

"Why hard lines?" demanded Osmond.

"Why? Because he was innocent."

"Innocent!" exclaimed Osmond, staring at the officer in amazement.

"Yes, innocent. Had nothing whatever to do with the robbery. No one can make out why on earth he scooted."

As Cockeram made his astounding statement, Betty turned deathly pale.

"Is it quite certain that he was innocent?" she asked in a low, eager tone.

"Perfectly," he replied, turning an astonished blue eye on the white-faced girl and then hastily averting it. "Where is that confounded paper – newspaper cutting? I cut it out to send to Lark – Cook. There is no doubt whatever. It seems that they employed a criminal lawyer chap – a certain Dr Thorndyke – to work up the case against Osmond. So this lawyer fellow got to work. And the upshot of it was that he proved conclusively that Osmond couldn't possibly be the guilty party."

"How did he prove that?" Osmond demanded.

"In the simplest and most satisfactory way possible," replied Cockeram. "He followed up the tracks until he had spotted the actual robber and held all the clues in his hand. Then he gave the police the tip; and they swooped down on my nabs – caught him fairly on the hop with all the stolen property in his possession. There isn't the shadow of a doubt about it."

"What was the name of the man who stole the gems?" Osmond asked anxiously.

"I don't remember," Cockeram replied. "What interested me was the name of the man who didn't steal them."

Betty, still white-faced and trembling, stood gazing rather wildly at Osmond. For his face bore a very singular expression – an expression that made her feel sick at heart. He did not look relieved or joyful. Surprised he certainly was. But it was not joyous surprise. Rather was it suggestive of alarm and dismay. And meanwhile Cockeram continued to turn over the accumulations in his letter-case. Suddenly he drew forth a crumpled and much-worn envelope from which he triumphantly extracted a long newspaper cutting.

"Ah!" he exclaimed, as he handed it to Osmond, "here we are. You will find full particulars in this. You needn't send it back to me. I have done with it. And now I must hook off to the court-house. You will take possession of the mess-room, Miss Burleigh, won't you? And order whatever you want. Of course, Mr Cook is my guest." With a formal salute he turned, ran down the rickety stairs and out at the gate, pursued closely as far as the wicket by the pelican.

But Betty's whole attention was focussed on Osmond; and as he fastened hungrily on the newspaper cutting, she took his arm and drew him gently through a ramshackle lattice porch into the shabby little white-washed mess-room, where she stood watching with mingled hope and terror the strange, enigmatical expression on his face as he devoured the printed lines.

Suddenly – in the twinkling of an eye – that expression changed. Anxiety, even consternation, gave place to the wildest astonishment; his jaw fell, and the hand which held the newspaper cutting dropped to his side. And then he laughed aloud; a weird, sardonic laugh that made poor Betty's flesh creep.

"What is it, Jim, dear?" she asked nervously.

He looked in her face and laughed again.

"My name," said he, "is not Jim. It is John. John Osmond."

"Very well, John," she replied meekly. "But why did you laugh?"

He placed his hands on her shoulders and looked down at her with a smile.

"Betty, darling," said he, "do I understand that you are willing to marry me?"

"Willing indeed!" she exclaimed. "I am going to marry you."

"Then, my darling," said he, "you are going to marry a fool."

Book Two
The Investigator

Chapter Twelve

The Indictment

Mr Joseph Penfield sat behind his writing-table in a posture of calm attention, allowing his keen grey eyes to travel back and forth from the silver snuff-box which lay on the note-pad before him to the two visitors who confronted him from their respective chairs. One of these, an elderly, hard-faced man, square of jaw and truculent of eye, was delivering some sort of statement, while the other, a considerably younger man, listened critically, with his eyes cast down, but stealing, from time to time, a quick, furtive glance either at the speaker or at Mr Penfield. He was evidently following the statement closely; and to an observer there might have appeared in his concentrated attention something more than mere interest; something inscrutable, with, perhaps, the faintest suggestion of irony.

As the speaker came, somewhat abruptly, to an end, Mr Penfield opened his snuff-box and took a pinch delicately between finger and thumb.

"It is not quite clear to me, Mr Woodstock," said he, "why you are consulting me in this matter. You are an experienced practitioner, and the issue is a fairly simple one. What is there against your dealing with the case according to your own judgement?"

"A good deal," Mr Woodstock replied. "In the first place, I am one of the interested parties – the principal one, in fact. In the second, I practise in a country town, whereas you are here in the very heart of the legal world; and in the third, I have no experience whatever of criminal practice; I am a conveyancer pure and simple."

"But," objected Mr Penfield, "this is not a matter of criminal practice. It is just a question of your liability as a bailee."

"Yes, true. But that question is closely connected with the robbery. Since no charge was made for depositing this property in my strong-room, obviously, I am not liable unless it can be shown that the loss was due to negligence. But the question of negligence turns on the robbery."

"Which I understand was committed by one of your own staff?"

"Yes, the man Osmond, whom I mentioned; one of my confidential clerks – Hepburn, here, is the other – who had access to the strong-room and who absconded as soon as the robbery was discovered."

"When you say he had access," said Mr Penfield, "you mean – "

"That he had access to the key during office hours. As a matter of fact, it hangs on the wall beside my desk, and when I am there the strong-room is usually kept open – the door is in my private office and opposite to my desk. Of course, when I leave at the end of the day, I lock up the strong-room and take the key away with me."

"Yes. But in the interval – hm? It almost looks as if a claim might be – hm? But you have given me only an outline of the affair. Perhaps a more detailed account might enable us better to form an opinion on the position. Would it be troubling you too much?"

"Not at all," replied Mr Woodstock; "but it is rather a long story. However, I will cut it as short as I can. We will take the events in the order in which they occurred; and you must pull me up, Hepburn, if I overlook anything.

"The missing valuables are the property of a client of mine named Hollis; a retired soap manufacturer, as rich as Croesus, and like most of these over-rich men, having made a fortune was at his wit's end what to do with it. Eventually, he adopted the usual plan. He became a collector. And having decided to burden himself with a lot of things that he didn't want, he put the lid on it by specializing in goldsmith's work, jewellery and precious stones. Wanted a valuable collection, he said, that could be kept in an ordinary dwelling-house.

"Well, of course, the acquisitive mania, once started, grew by what it fed on. The desire to possess this stuff became an obsession. He was constantly planning expeditions in search of new rarities, scouring the Continent for fresh loot, flitting from town to town and from dealer to dealer like an idiotic bee. And whenever he went off on one of these expeditions he would bring the pick of his confounded collection to me to have it deposited in my strong-room. I urged him to take it to the bank; but he doesn't keep an account with any of the local branches and didn't want to take the stuff to London. Moreover, he had inspected my strong-room and was a good deal impressed by it."

"It is really strong, is it?" asked Mr Penfield.

"Very. Thick reinforced concrete lined with steel. Very large, too. Not that the strength is material as it was not broken into. Well, eventually I agreed to deposit the things in the strong-room – couldn't refuse an important client – but I resolutely declined to make any charge or accept any sort of consideration for the service. I wasn't going to make myself responsible for the safety of things of that value. And I explained my position to Hollis; but he said that a strong-room that was good enough for my valuable documents was good enough for his jewels. Which was talking like a fool. Burglars don't break into safes to steal leases.

"Well, this business began about six years ago, and – so far as I can tell – nothing amiss occurred until quite lately. I say so far as I can tell, for of course we can't date the robbery. We only know when it was discovered. But I assume that the theft was committed pretty recently or it would surely have been discovered sooner."

"And when was it first ascertained that a robbery had been committed?" asked Mr Penfield, dipping a quill into the ink.

"On the fourth of October," replied Mr Woodstock; and having paused while Mr Penfield noted the date, he continued: "On that day Hollis took a great ruby up to South Kensington, where it had been accepted for a loan exhibition. He delivered it himself to the keeper of the precious stones, and was a little taken aback when that gentleman, after a preliminary inspection, began to pore over it with a magnifying glass and then sent for one of his colleagues. The second expert raised his eyebrows when he had looked at the gem, and he, too, made a careful scrutiny with the lens. Finally, they sent for a third official; and the upshot of it was that the three experts agreed that the stone was not a ruby at all but only a first-class imitation.

"Of course Hollis didn't believe them, and said so. He had bought the stone for four thousand pounds from a well-known dealer and had shown it to a number of connoisseurs, who had all been enthusiastic about the colour and lustre of the gem. There had never been any question that it was not merely a genuine ruby, but a ruby of the highest class. However, when he had heard the verdict of the experts, he pocketed his treasure and went straight off to Cawley's in Piccadilly. But when Mr Cawley shook his head over the gem and pronounced it an unquestionable counterfeit, he became alarmed and danced off in a deuce of a twitter to the dealer from whom he had bought it.

"That interview settled the matter. The dealer remembered the transaction quite well and knew all about the stone, for he had full records of the circumstances under which he had acquired it. Moreover, he recognized the setting – a pendant with a surround of small diamonds – but he was quite clear that the stone in it was not the stone that he had sold to Hollis. In fact, it was not a stone at all; it was just a good-class paste ruby. The original had been picked out of the setting and the counterfeit put in its place; and the person who had done the job was apparently not a skilled jeweller, for there were traces on the setting of some rather amateurish work."

"There is no doubt, I suppose," said Mr Penfield, "of the *bona-fides* of the dealer?"

"Not the slightest," was the reply. "He is a man of the highest reputation; and as a matter of fact, no regular dealer would palm off a counterfeit. It wouldn't be business. But the question doesn't really arise, as you will see when I proceed with the story.

"As soon as Hollis was convinced that a substitution had been effected, he commissioned an independent expert to come down and make a critical survey of his collection; and it was then ascertained that practically every important gem in his cabinets was a counterfeit. And in every case in which the stone was a false one, the same traces of clumsy workmanship were discoverable by an expert eye.

"The conclusion was obvious. Since the original gems had come from all sorts of different sources, there could be no question of fraud on the part of the various vendors; to say nothing of the fact that Hollis – who has practically no knowledge of stones himself – always obtained an expert opinion before concluding a deal. It was obvious that a systematic robbery had been carried out, and the question that arose was, who could the robber be?

"But that question involved certain others; as, for instance, when had the robbery been committed? where were the jewels at that time? and who had access to the place in which they were?

"These were difficult questions. At first it seemed as if they were unanswerable, and perhaps some of them would have been if the robber had not lost his nerve. But I am anticipating. Let us take the questions in their order.

"First as to the date of the robbery. It happens that a little less than two years ago Professor Eccles came down by invitation and made a careful inspection of Hollis' collection with a view to a proposed bequest to the nation, and marked off what he considered to be the most valuable specimens. Now, I need not say that if Professor Eccles detected counterfeit stones, we may take it that no counterfeits were there. Consequently, the collection was then intact and the robbery must have been committed since that date. But it happens that that date coincides almost exactly with the arrival of Osmond at my office. Just two years ago Hepburn introduced him to me; and as he is Hepburn's brother-in-law, I accepted him with perfect confidence.

"The other questions seemed more difficult. As to Hollis' own premises, the jewel-room had a Chubb detector lock on its only door, the cabinets have similar locks, the windows are always kept securely fastened, and no attempt has ever been made to break into the place. Besides, burglars would simply have taken the jewels away. They would not have left substitutes. The personnel of his household – a lady secretary, a housekeeper and two maids – appear beyond suspicion. Moreover, they had all been with him many years before the robbery occurred. In short, I think we may consider Hollis' premises as outside the field of inquiry."

"Do you really?" said Mr Penfield, in a tone which clearly indicated that he did not.

"Certainly; and so will you when you hear the rest of the story. We now come to the various occasions on which the more valuable parts of this collection were deposited in my strong-room. Let me describe the procedure. In the first place, Hollis himself packed the jewels in a number of wooden boxes which he had had made specially for the purpose, each about fourteen inches by nine by about five inches deep. Every box had a good lock with a sunk disc on each side of the keyhole for the seals. When the boxes were packed they were locked and a strip of tape put across the keyhole and secured at each end with a seal. They were then wrapped in strong paper and sealed at all the joints with Hollis' seal – an antique Greek seal set in a ring which he always wears on his finger. On the outside of the cover was written a list of the contents in Hollis' own handwriting and signed by him, and each box bore in addition a number. The boxes were brought to my office by Hollis and by him delivered personally to me; and I gave him a receipt, roughly describing and enumerating the boxes, but, of course, not committing myself in respect of the contents. I then carried them myself into the strong-room and placed them on an upper shelf which I reserved for them; and there they remained until Hollis fetched them away, when he used to give me a receipt in the same terms as my own. That concluded the particular transaction.

"Now, it happened that at the time when the robbery was discovered, several of the boxes which Hollis had taken back from me about a month previously still remained packed and in their paper wrappings. And it further happened that one of these – there were eight in all – contained an emerald which Hollis had bought only a few days before he packed it. There was no question as to the genuineness of this stone; and when the box was opened, there was no question as to the fact that it had been replaced by a counterfeit. Even Hollis was able to spot the change. So that seemed to fix the date of the robbery to the period during which the box had been in my strong-room."

"Apparently," Mr Penfield agreed. But you speak of the box as being still in its paper wrapping. What of the seals?"

"Ah!" exclaimed Woodstock, "that is the most mysterious feature of this whole affair. The seals were unbroken and, so far as Hollis could see, the package was absolutely intact, just as it had been handed to me."

Mr Penfield pursed his lips and took snuff to the verge of intemperance.

"If the seals were unbroken," said he, "and the package was in all other respects intact, that would seem to be incontestable proof that it had never been opened since it was closed and sealed."

"That was what I pointed out," interposed Hepburn, "when Mr Woodstock talked the matter over with Osmond and me. The unbroken seals seemed a conclusive answer to any suggestion that the robbery took place in our office."

"So they did," Woodstock agreed, "and so they would still if Osmond had kept his head. But he didn't. He had evidently reckoned on the question of a robbery from our strong-room never being raised, and I imagine that it was that emerald that upset his nerve. At any rate, within a week of our discussion he bolted, and then, of course, the murder was out."

Mr Penfield nodded gravely and asked, after a short pause: "And how is Mr Hollis taking it? Is he putting any pressure on you?"

"Oh, not at all – up to the present. He has not suggested any claim against me; he merely wants to lay his hand on the robber and, if possible, get his jewels back. He entirely approves of what I have done."

"What have you done?" Mr Penfield asked.

"I have done the obvious thing," was the reply, delivered in a slightly truculent tone. "As soon as it was clear that Osmond had absconded, I communicated with the police. I laid an information and gave them the leading facts."

"And do they propose to take any action?"

"Most undoubtedly; in fact, I may say that they have been most commendably prompt. They have already traced Osmond to Bristol, and I have every hope that in due course they will run him to earth and arrest him."

"That is quite probable," said Mr Penfield. "And when they have arrested him – ?"

"He will be brought back and charged before a magistrate, when we may take it that he will be committed for trial."

"It is possible," Mr Penfield assented, doubtfully. "And then – "

"Then," replied Woodstock, reddening and raising his voice, "he will be put on his trial and, I make no doubt, sent to penal servitude."

Mr Penfield took snuff depracatingly and shook his head.

"I think not," said he; "but perhaps there is some item of evidence which you have omitted to mention?"

"Evidence!" Woodstock repeated impatiently. "What evidence do you want? The property has been stolen and the man who had an opportunity to steal it has absconded. What more do you want?"

Mr Penfield looked at his brother solicitor with mild surprise.

"The judge," he replied, "and I should think the magistrate, too, would want some positive evidence that the accused stole the jewels. There appears to be no such evidence. The unexplained disappearance of this man is a suspicious circumstance; but it is useless to take suspicions into court. You have got to make out a case, and at present you have no case. If the charge were not dismissed by the magistrate, the bill would certainly be thrown out by the Grand Jury."

Mr Woodstock glowered sullenly at the old lawyer, but he made no reply, while Hepburn sat with downcast eyes and the faintest trace of an ironical smile.

"Consider," Mr Penfield resumed, "what would be the inevitable answer of the defence. They would point out that there is not a particle of evidence that the robbery – if there has really been a robbery – occurred in your office at all, and that there are excellent reasons for believing that it did not."

"What reasons are there?"

"There are the unbroken seals. Until you can show how the jewels could have been abstracted without breaking the seals, you have not even a *prima-facie* case. Then there is the method of the alleged robbery. It would have required not merely access but undisturbed possession for a considerable time. It was not just a matter of picking out the stones. They were replaced by plausible counterfeits which had to be made or procured. Take the case of the ruby that you mentioned. It deceived Hollis completely. Then it must have been very like the original in size, form, and colour. It could not have been picked up casually at a theatrical property dealer's; it must have been made *ad hoc* by careful comparison with the original. But all this and the subsequent setting and finishing would take time. It would be quite possible while the jewels were lying quietly in Hollis' cabinets, but it would seem utterly impossible under the alleged circumstances. In short," Mr Penfield concluded, "I am astounded that you ever admitted the possibility of the robbery having occurred on your premises. What do you say, Mr Hepburn?"

"I agree with you entirely," the latter replied. "My position would have been that we had received certain sealed packages and that we had handed them back in the same condition as we received them. I should have left Hollis to prove the contrary."

"And I think he could have done it," said Woodstock doggedly. "You seem to be forgetting that emerald. But in any case I have accepted the suggestion and I am not going to draw back, especially as my confidential clerk has absconded and virtually admitted the theft. The question is, what is to be done? Hollis is mad to get hold of the robber and recover his gems, and he is prepared to stand the racket financially."

"In that case," said Mr Penfield, taking a final pinch and pocketing his snuff-box, "I will venture to make a suggestion. This case is out of your depth and out of mine. I suggest that you allow me to take counsel's opinion; and the counsel I should select would be Dr John Thorndyke."

"Thorndyke – hm!" grunted Woodstock. "Isn't he an irregular practitioner of some sort?"

"Not at all," Mr Penfield dissented warmly. "He is a scientific expert with an unrivalled knowledge and experience of criminal practice. If it is possible for anyone to unravel this tangle, I am confident that he is the man; and I know of no other."

"Then," exclaimed Woodstock, "for God's sake get hold of him, and let me know what he says, so that I can report to Hollis. And let him know that there will be no trouble about costs."

With this Mr Woodstock rose and, after an unemotional leave-taking, made his way out of the office, followed by Hepburn.

CHAPTER THIRTEEN

Thorndyke Takes Up the Inquiry

Mr Penfield's visit to Dr Thorndyke's chambers in King's Bench Walk, Inner Temple, was productive of some little surprise, as such visits were rather apt to be. For the old solicitor had definitely made up his mind that Woodstock's theory of the robbery was untenable and that the burden of proof ought to be cast on Hollis; and he was therefore not a little disconcerted to find Thorndyke tending to favour the view that the probabilities pointed to the strong-room as the scene of the robbery.

"After all," the latter said, "we must not ignore the obvious. It is undeniable that Osmond's disappearance – which has the strongest suggestion of flight – is a very suspicious circumstance. It occurred almost immediately after the discovery of the thefts and the suggestion that the gems had been stolen from the strong-room. Osmond had access to the strong-room – though I admit that a good many other persons had, too. Then there is the striking fact that the period of the robberies coincides exactly with the period of Osmond's presence at the office. During the four years which preceded his arrival no robbery appears to have occurred, although all the other conditions seem to have been the same. So far as we can see, the robberies must have commenced very shortly after his arrival. These are significant facts which, as I have said, we cannot ignore."

"I am entirely with you," Mr Penfield replied, "when you say that we must not ignore the obvious. But are you not doing so? These packages were most carefully and elaborately sealed; and it is admitted that they were returned to the owner with the seals unbroken. Now, it seems to me obvious that if the seals were unbroken, the packages could not have been opened. But apparently you think otherwise. Possibly you attach less importance to seals than I do?"

"Probably," Thorndyke admitted. "It is easy to exaggerate their significance. For what is a seal, when all is said? It is an artificial thing which some artist or workman has made and which another artist or workman could copy if necessary. There is no magic in seals."

"Dear, dear!" Mr Penfield exclaimed with a wry smile. "Another illusion shattered! But I think a Court of Law would share my erroneous view of the matter. However, we will let that pass. I understand that you look upon Osmond as the probable delinquent?"

"The balance of probabilities is in favour of that view. But I am keeping an open mind. There are other possibilities, and they will have to be explored. We must take nothing for granted."

Mr Penfield nodded approvingly. "And suppose," he asked, "the police should arrest Osmond?"

"Then," replied Thorndyke, "Mr Woodstock would be in difficulties, and so would the police – who have shown less than their usual discretion – unless the prisoner should get in a panic and plead 'guilty.' There is not even a *prima-facie* case. They can't call upon Osmond to prove that he did not steal the gems."

"Exactly," Mr Penfield agreed. "That is what I tried to impress on Woodstock – who is really a most extraordinarily unlegal lawyer. But have you any suggestion to offer?"

"I can only suggest that, as we are practically without data, we should endeavour to obtain some. The only fact that we have is that the stones have been removed from their settings and replaced by imitations. There seems to be no doubt about that. As to how they came to be removed, there are evidently four possibilities. First, they may have been taken from Hollis' cabinets by some person unknown. Second, the substitution may have been effected by Hollis himself, for reasons unknown to us and by no means easy to imagine. Third, they may have been stolen from the strong-room by some person other than Osmond. Fourth, they may have been stolen from the strong-room by Osmond. The last is, I think, the most probable. But all of the four hypotheses must be impartially considered. Do I understand that Hollis is prepared to offer facilities?"

"He agrees to give every assistance, financial or other."

"Then," said Thorndyke, "I suggest that we make a beginning by inspecting the boxes. I understand that there are still some unopened."

"Yes; six. Hollis reserved them to be opened in the presence of witnesses."

"Let Hollis bring those six boxes together with those that have been opened, with their packings and wrappings, if he has them. If we can fix a day, I will arrange for an expert to be present to witness the opening of the six boxes and give an opinion on the stones in them. If it appears that any robbery has been committed, I shall ask Hollis to leave the boxes and the counterfeit jewels that I may examine them at my leisure."

Mr Penfield chuckled softly and helped himself to a pinch of snuff.

"Your methods, Dr Thorndyke," said he, "are a perennial source of wonder to me. May I ask what kind of information you expect to extract from the empty boxes?"

"I have no specific expectations at all," was the reply; "but it will be strange indeed if we learn nothing from them. They will probably have little enough to tell us; but, seeing that we have, at present, hardly a single fact beyond that of the substitution – and that is not of our own observing – a very small addition to our knowledge would be all to the good."

"Very true, very true," agreed Mr Penfield. "A single definite fact might enable us to decide which of those four possibilities is to be adopted and pursued; though how you propose to extract such a fact from an empty box, or even a full one, I am unable to imagine. However, I leave that problem in your hands. As soon as you have secured your expert, perhaps you will kindly advise me and I will then make the necessary arrangements with Mr Hollis."

With this Mr Penfield rose and took his departure, leaving Thorndyke to read over and amplify the notes that he had taken during the consultation.

As matters turned out, he was able to advise Mr Penfield within twenty-four hours that he had secured the services of an expert who was probably the greatest living authority on gem stones; with the result that a telegram arrived from Mr Hollis accepting the appointment for the following day at eleven in the forenoon, that time having been mentioned by the expert as the most suitable on account of the light.

It wanted several minutes to the appointed hour when the first visitor arrived; for the Treasury clock had hardly struck the third quarter when, in response to a smart rat-tat on the little brass knocker, Thorndyke opened the door and admitted Professor Eccles.

"I am a little before my time," the latter remarked as he shook hands, "but I wanted to have a few words with you before Mr Hollis arrived. I understand that you want me to give an opinion on some doubtful stones of his. Are they new ones? Because I may say that I looked over his collection very carefully less than two years ago and I can state confidently that it contained no gems that were not unquestionably genuine. But I have heard some rumours of a robbery – unfounded, I hope, seeing that Hollis proposes to bequeath his treasures to the national collection."

"I am afraid," replied Thorndyke, "that the rumours are correct; but that is what you are going to help us to decide. It is not a case of simple robbery. The stolen stones seem to have been replaced by imitations; and as you examined the collection when it was undoubtedly intact, you will see at once if there has been any substitution."

He proceeded to give the professor a brief account of the case and the curious problem that it presented, and he had barely finished when a cab was heard to draw up below. A minute later, as the two men stood at the open door, the visitor made his appearance, followed by the cabman, each carrying a bulky but apparently light wooden case.

Mr Hollis was a typical business man – dry, brisk, and shrewd-looking. Having shaken hands with the professor and introduced himself to Thorndyke, he dismissed the cabman and came to the point without preamble.

"This case, marked A, contains the full boxes. The other, marked B, contains the empties. I will leave you to deal with that at your convenience. My concern and Professor Eccles' is with the other, which I will open at once and then we can get to work."

He thrust the despised case B into a corner, and hoisting the other on to the table, unbuckled the straps, unlocked it, threw open the lid, and took out six sealed packages, which he placed side by side on the table.

"Shall I open them?" he asked, producing a pocket-knife, "or will you?"

"Before we disturb them," said Thorndyke, "we had better examine the exteriors very carefully."

"I've done that," said Hollis. "I've been over each one most thoroughly and, so far as I can see, they are in exactly the same condition as they were when I handed them to Woodstock. The writing on them is certainly my writing and the seals are impressions of my seal, which, as you see, I carry on my finger in this ring."

"In that case," said Thorndyke, "we may as well open them forthwith. Perhaps I had better take off the wrappings, as I should like to preserve them and the seals intact."

He took up the first package and turned it over in his hands, examining each surface closely. And as he did so, his two visitors watched him – the professor with slightly amused curiosity, the other with a dry, rather impatient manner not without a trace of scepticism. The package was about fourteen inches in length by nine wide and five inches deep. It was very neatly covered with a strong, smooth white paper bearing a number – thirteen – and a written and signed list of the contents, and sealed at each end in the middle. The paper was further secured by a string, tied tightly and skilfully, of which the knot was embedded in a mass of wax on which was an excellent impression of the seal.

"You see," Hollis pointed out, "that the parcel has been made as secure as human care could make it. I should have said that it was perfectly impossible to open it without breaking the seals."

"But surely," exclaimed the professor, "it would be an absolute impossibility! Don't you agree, Dr Thorndyke?"

"We shall be better able to judge when we have seen the inside," the latter replied. With a small pair of scissors he cut the string, which he placed on one side, and then, with great care, cut round each of the seals, removing them with the portions of paper on which they were fixed and putting them aside with the string. The rest of the paper was now taken off, disclosing a plain, white-wood box, the keyhole of which was covered by a strip of tape secured at each end by a seal seated in a small circular pit. Thorndyke cut the tape and held the box towards Hollis, who already held the key in readiness. This having been inserted and turned, Thorndyke raised the lid and laid the box on the table.

"There, Professor," said he; "you can now answer your own question. The list of contents is on the cover. It is for you to say whether that list correctly describes the things which are inside."

Professor Eccles drew a chair up to the table, and lifting from the inside of the box a thick pad of tissue paper (which Thorndyke took from him and placed with the string and the seals), ran his eye quickly over the neatly-arranged assemblage of jewels that reposed on a second layer of tissue. Very soon a slight frown began to wrinkle his forehead. He bent more closely over the box, looked narrowly first at one gem, then at another, and at length he picked out a small, plain pendant set with a single oval green stone about half an inch in diameter.

"Leaf-green jargoon," said he, reading from the list as he produced a Coddington lens from his pocket; "that is the one, isn't it?"

Hollis grunted an assent as he watched the professor inspecting the gem through his lens.

"I remember the stone," said the professor. "It was one of the finest of the kind that I have ever seen. Well, this isn't it. This is not a jargoon at all. It is just a lump of green sass – flint glass, in fact. But it is quite well cut. The lapidary knew his job better than the jeweller. There has been some very rough work on the setting."

"How much was the stone worth?" Thorndyke asked.

"The original? Not more than thirty pounds, I should say. It was a beautiful and interesting stone, but rather a collector's specimen than a jeweller's piece. The public won't give big prices for out-of-the-way stones. They like diamonds, rubies, sapphires, and emeralds."

"Is this counterfeit a true facsimile of the original? I mean as to size and style of cutting?"

Professor Eccles took from his pocket a small leather case, from which he extracted a calliper gauge. Applying this delicately to the exposed edges of the "girdle" between the claws, he read the vernier and then reapplied it in the other diameter.

"Seven-twelfths by three-quarters of an inch, brilliant cut," he announced. "Do you happen to remember the dimensions, Mr Hollis? These can't be far out as the stone fits the setting."

"I've brought my catalogue," said Hollis, producing a small, fat volume from his pocket. "Thought we might want it. What's the number? Three-sixty-three. Here we are. 'Jargoon. Full leaf-green. Brilliant cut. Seven-twelfths by three-quarters.' "

"Then," said the professor, "this would seem to be a perfect replica. Queer, isn't it? I see your point, Doctor. This fellow has been to endless pains and some expense in lapidary's charges – unless he is a lapidary himself – to say nothing of the risk; and all to get possession of a stone worth only about thirty pounds, and not easily marketable at that."

"Some of the other stones are worth more, though," remarked Hollis.

"True, true," agreed the professor. "Let us look at some of the others. Ha! Here is one that looks a little suspicious, if my memory serves."

He picked out a gold ornament set with a large cat's-eye bordered with small diamonds and exhibited it to Hollis, who bent down to inspect it.

"Cat's-eye," he commented, after a long and anxious inspection. "Well, it looks all right to me. What's the matter with it?"

"Oh, it is a cat's-eye, sure enough, but not the right kind, I think. What does the catalogue say?"

Hollis turned over a page and read out: "Chrysoberyl. Cymophane or cat's-eye. Brown, oval, cut *en cabochon*. Five-eighths by half an inch. Bordered by twelve diamonds."

"I thought so," said the professor. "This is a cat's-eye, but not a chrysoberyl. It is a quartz cat's-eye. But I should hardly have thought it would have been worth the trouble and expense of making the exchange. You see," he added, taking the dimensions with his gauge, "this stone is apparently a facsimile of the missing one in size and shape and not a bad match in colour. The diamonds don't appear to have been tampered with."

"What about that emerald?" Hollis asked anxiously, indicating a massive ring set with a large, square stone bordered with diamonds. Professor Eccles picked up the ring, and at first glance he pursed up his lips, dubiously. But he examined it carefully through his lens, nevertheless.

"Well?" demanded Hollis.

The professor shook his head sadly. "Paste," he replied. "A good imitation as such things go, but unmistakable glass. Will you read out the description?"

Hollis did so and once again the correspondence in dimensions and cutting showed the forgery to be a carefully-executed facsimile.

"This fellow was a conscientious rascal," said the professor. "He did the thing thoroughly – excepting the settings."

"Yes, damn him!" Hollis agreed, savagely. "That ring cost me close on twelve hundred pounds. It came from Lord Pycroft's collection."

Professor Eccles was deeply concerned; naturally enough, for any robbery of precious things involves a wicked waste. And then there was the depressing fact that the valuable "Hollis bequest" was melting away before his eyes. Gloomily, he picked out one after another of the inmates of the box and regretfully added them to the growing heap of the rejected.

When the first box had been emptied, the second was attacked with similar procedure, and so on with the remainder, until the last box had been probed to the bottom, when the professor sat back in his chair and drew a deep breath.

"Well," he exclaimed, "it is a terrible disaster and profoundly mysterious. In effect, the collection has been skimmed of everything of real value. Even the moonstones have been exchanged for cheap specimens with the rough native cutting untouched. I have never heard of anything like it. But I don't understand why the fellow took all this trouble. He couldn't have supposed that the robbery would pass undetected."

"It might easily have remained undetected long enough to confuse the issues," said Thorndyke. "If the jewels had been returned to the cabinets and left there undisturbed for a few months, it would have been very difficult to determine exactly when, or where, or how the robbery had been carried out."

"Yes," growled Hollis. "The scoundrel must have known that I am no expert and reckoned on my not spotting the change. And I don't suppose I should, for that matter. However, the cat slipped out of the bag sooner than he expected and now the police are close on his heels. I'll have my pound of flesh out of him yet."

As he snapped out this expression of his benevolent intentions, Mr Hollis gathered up the remnant of unrifled jewels and was about to deposit them in one of the empty boxes when Thorndyke interposed.

"May I lend you a deed-box with some fresh packing? I think we agreed that the empty boxes and the packing should be left with me, that I might examine them thoroughly before returning them."

"Very well," said Hollis, "though it seems a pretty futile thing to do. But I suppose you know your own business. What about those sham stones?"

"I should like to examine them too, as they are facsimile imitations; and we may possibly learn something from the settings."

"What do you expect to learn?" Hollis inquired in a tone which pretty plainly conveyed *his* expectations.

"Very little," Thorndyke replied (on which Hollis nodded a somewhat emphatic agreement). "But," he continued, "this case will depend on circumstantial evidence – unless the robber confesses – and that evidence has yet to be discovered. We can do no more than use our eyes to the best advantage in the hope that we may light on some trace that may give us a lead."

Hollis nodded again. "Sounds pretty hopeless," said he. "However, Mr Penfield advised me to put the affair in your hands, so I have done so. If you should discover anything that will help us with the prosecution, I suppose you will let me know."

"I shall keep Mr Penfield informed as to what evidence, if any, is available, and he will, no doubt, communicate with you."

With this rather vague promise Mr Hollis appeared to be satisfied, for he pursued the subject no farther, but, having packed the poor remainder of his treasures in the deed-box, prepared to depart.

"Before you go," said Thorndyke, "I should like to take a trial impression of your seal, if you would allow me."

Hollis stared at him in amazement. "My seal!" he exclaimed. "Why, good God, sir, you have already got some seventy impressions – six from each of these boxes and all those from the empties!"

"The seals that I have," Thorndyke replied, "are the questioned seals. I should like to have what scientists call a 'control.' "

"I don't know what you mean by 'questioned seals,' " Hollis retorted. "I haven't questioned them. I have acknowledged them as my own seals."

"I think," Thorndyke rejoined with a faint smile, "that Mr Penfield would advise you to acknowledge nothing. But, furthermore, none of these seals is a really perfect impression such as one would require for purposes of comparison."

"Comparison!" exclaimed Hollis. "Comparison with what? But there," he concluded with a sour smile, "it's no use arguing. Have it your own way. I suppose you know what you are about."

With this, he drew off the ring, and, laying it on the table, bestowed a glance of defiance on Thorndyke. The latter had, apparently, made his preparations, for he promptly produced from a drawer a small box, the opening of which revealed a supply of sealing-wax, a spirit-lamp, a metal plate, a little crucible or melting-ladle with a wooden handle, a bottle of oil, a camel's-hair brush, and a number of small squares of white paper. While he was setting out his apparatus the professor examined the seal through his lens.

"A fine example," he pronounced. "Syracusan, I should say, fourth or fifth century BC. Not unlike the decadrachm of that period – the racing Quadriga with the winged Victory above and the panoply of armour below seem to recall that coin. The stone seems to be green chalcedony. It is a beautiful work. Seems almost a pity to employ it in common use."

He surrendered it regretfully to Thorndyke, who, having taken an infinitesimal drop of oil on the point of the brush and wiped it off on the palm of his hand, delicately brushed the surface off the seal. Then he laid a square of paper on the metal plate, broke of a piece from one of the sticks of sealing-wax and melted it in the crucible over the lamp. When it was completely liquefied, he poured it slowly on the centre of the square of paper, where it formed a circular, convex pool. Having given this a few seconds to cool, he took the ring and pressed it steadily on the soft wax. When he raised it – which he did with extreme care, steadying the paper with his fingers – the wax bore an exquisitely perfect impression of the seal.

Hollis was visibly impressed by the careful manipulation and the fine result; and when Thorndyke had repeated the procedure, he requested that a third impression might be made for his own use. This having been made and bestowed in the deed-box, he replaced the ring on his finger, bade the professor and Thorndyke a curt farewell, and made his way down to the waiting cab.

As the door closed behind him, the professor turned to Thorndyke with a somewhat odd expression on his face.

"This is a very mysterious affair, Doctor," said he.

The curiously significant tone caused Thorndyke to cast a quick, inquiring glance at the speaker. But he merely repeated the latter's remark.

"A very mysterious affair, indeed."

"As I understand it," the professor continued, "Hollis claims that these gems were stolen from the boxes while they were in the solicitor's strong-room; and that they were taken without breaking the seals. But that sounds like sheer nonsense. And yet the solicitor appears to accept the suggestion."

"Yes. Hollis claims that the gems that were put into the boxes were the real gems; and both he and the solicitor, Woodstock, base their beliefs on the fact that Woodstock's confidential clerk appears to have absconded immediately after the discovery of the robbery."

"H'm!" grunted the professor. "Is it quite clear that the clerk has really absconded?"

"He has disappeared for no known reason."

"H'm. Not quite the same thing, is it? But has it been established that the real stones were actually in the boxes when they were handed to the solicitor?"

"I wouldn't use the word 'established,' " Thorndyke admitted. "There is evidence that one stone, at least, was intact a day or two before the boxes were deposited; and that stone – a large emerald – was found to have been changed when the box was opened."

The professor grunted dubiously and reflected awhile. Then he looked hard at Thorndyke and appeared to be about to make some observation; and then he seemed to alter his mind, for he concluded with the somewhat colourless remark: "Well, I daresay you are quite alive to all the possibilities"; and with this he prepared to take his departure.

"Do you happen," asked Thorndyke, "to know the addresses of any lapidaries who specialize in imitation stones?"

Professor Eccles reflected. "Imitations are rather out of my province," he replied. "Of course any lapidary could cut a paste gem or make a doublet or triplet, and would if paid for the job. I will write down the addresses of one or two men who have worked for me and they will probably be able to give you any further information." He wrote down two or three addresses, and as he put away his pencil, he asked: "How is your colleague, Jervis? He is still with you, I suppose?"

"Jervis," was the reply, "is at present an independent practitioner. He accepted, on my advice, a whole-time appointment at the 'Griffin' Life Assurance Office. But he drops in from time to time to lend me a hand. I will tell him you asked after him. And let me tender you my very warmest thanks for your invaluable help today."

"Tut, tut," said the professor, "you need not thank me. I am an interested party. If Hollis doesn't recover his gems, the national collection is going to lose a valuable bequest. Bear that in mind as an additional spur to your endeavours. Goodbye, and good luck!"

With a hearty handshake and a valedictory smile, Professor Eccles let himself out and went his way, apparently in a deeply thoughtful frame of mind, as Thorndyke judged by observing his receding figure from the window.

Chapter Fourteen

Thorndyke Makes a Beginning

The profound cogitations of Professor Eccles set up in the mind of Thorndyke a sort of induced psychic current. As he turned from the window and began to occupy himself in sorting his material preparatory to examining it, his thoughts were busy with his late visitor. The professor had been about to say something and had suddenly thought better of it. Now, what could it have been that he was about to say? And why had he not said it? And what was the meaning of that strangely intent look he had bestowed on Thorndyke, and that rather odd expression that his face had borne? And, finally, what were those "possibilities" at which he had hinted?

These were the questions that Thorndyke asked himself as he carried out, quietly and methodically, the preliminaries to his later investigations; with the further questions: Did the professor know anything that bore on the mystery? and if so, what was it that he knew? He evidently had no knowledge either of Woodstock or of Osmond, but he was fairly well acquainted with Hollis. It was manifest that he rejected utterly the alleged robbery from the strong-room; which implied a conviction that the exchange of stones had been made either before the boxes were handed to Woodstock or after they had been received back from him.

It was a perfectly natural and reasonable belief. Mr Penfield had been of the same opinion. But Mr Penfield had no special knowledge of the matter. His opinion had been based exclusively on the integrity of the seals. Was this the professor's case, too? Or was he in possession of some significant facts which he had not disclosed? His manner rather suggested that he was. Perhaps it might be expedient, later, to sound him cautiously. But this would depend on the amount and kind of information that was yielded by other sources.

By the time he reached this conclusion the sorting process was completed. The six boxes with their contents replaced were set out in order, the empties put together as well as was possible, and the seals from the wrapping of each box put into a separate envelope on which the number and description was written. A supply of white paper was laid on the table together with a number of new paper bags, and a little simple microscope which consisted of a watchmaker's compound eye-glass mounted on a small wooden stand. Thorndyke ran his eye over the collection to see that everything was in order; then, dismissing the professor from his mind, he drew a chair up to the table and fell to work.

He began with the seals. Opening one of the envelopes, he took out the four seals – including that on the knot, which he had cut off – and laying them out on the table, examined them quickly, one after the other. Then he picked up one of them, laid it on a card and placed the card on the stage of the magnifier, through which he made a more prolonged examination, turning the card from time to time to alter the incidence of the light, and jotting down on a note-block a few brief memoranda. The same procedure was followed with the other three seals, and when they had all been examined they were returned to their envelope, the top sheet of the note-block was detached and put in with them, the envelope was put aside and a fresh one opened. Finally he came to the envelope that contained the two impressions that he had, himself, taken from Hollis' seal, but these were not subjected to the minute scrutiny that the others had received. They were merely laid on the card, slipped under the magnifier, and after a single, brief glance, returned to their envelope and put aside. Next, the seals in the recesses by the keyholes of the boxes were scrutinized, the eyeglass being swung clear of its stand for the purpose, and when this had been done, the fresh set of notes was detached and slipped into one of the envelopes.

But this did not conclude the examination. Apparently there was some further point to be elucidated. Rising from his chair, Thorndyke fetched from a cabinet a microscope of the kind used for examining documents – a heavy-based instrument with a long-pivoted arm and a bull's-eye condenser. With this he re-examined the seals in succession, beginning with the two impressions that he had, himself, taken; and it might have been noticed that this examination concerned itself exclusively with a particular spot on the seal – a portion of the background just in front of the chariot and above the back of the near horse.

He had just finished and was replacing the microscope in the cabinet when the door opened silently and a small, clerical-looking man entered the room and regarded him benevolently.

"I have laid a cold lunch, sir, in the small room upstairs," he announced, "and I have put everything ready in your laboratory. Can I help you to carry anything up?" As he spoke, he ran an obviously inquisitive eye over the row of boxes and the numbered envelopes.

"Thank you, Polton," Thorndyke replied. "I think we will take these things up out of harm's way and I will just look them over before lunch. But meanwhile there is a small job that you might get on with. I have here a collection of seals of which I want enlarged photographs made – four diameters magnification and each set on a separate negative and numbered similarly to the envelopes."

He exhibited the collection to his trusty coadjutor with a few words of explanation, when Polton tenderly gathered together the seven envelopes, and master and man betook themselves to the upper regions, each laden with a consignment of Mr Hollis' boxes, full and empty.

The laboratory of which Polton had spoken was a smallish room which Thorndyke reserved for his own use, and which was on the same floor as the large laboratory and the workshop over which Polton presided. Its principal features were a large work-bench, covered with polished linoleum and at present occupied by a microscope and a tray of slides, needles, forceps, and other accessories, a side-table, a cupboard, and several sets of shelves.

"Is there anything more, sir?" Polton asked when the boxes had been stacked on the side-table. He looked at them wistfully as he spoke, but accepted with resignation the polite negative and stole our, shutting the door silently behind him. As soon as he had gone, Thorndyke fell to work with a rapid but unhurried method suggestive of a fixed purpose and a considered plan. He began by putting on a pair of thin rubber gloves. Then, spreading on the bench a sheet of white demy paper such as chemists use for wrapping bottles, he took one of the boxes, detached its wrapping paper, opened the box, and taking out the jewels and the pads of tissue paper, deposited the former at one end of the table and the latter at the other, together with the empty box. First he dealt with the pads of tissue paper, one of which he placed on the sheet of white paper, and having opened it out and smoothed it with an ivory paper-knife, examined it closely on both sides with the aid of a reading-glass. Then he took from a drawer a large tuning-fork, and holding the packing paper vertically over the middle of the sheet on the bench, he struck the tuning-fork sharply, and while it was vibrating, lightly applied its tip to the centre of the suspended paper, causing it to hum like a gigantic bumble-bee and to vibrate visibly at its edges. Having repeated this proceeding two or three times, he laid the paper aside and with the reading-glass inspected the sheet of demy, on which a quite considerable number of minute specks of dust were now to be seen. This procedure he repeated with the other pads of tissue paper from the box, and as he worked, the sheet of white paper on the bench became more and more conspicuously sprinkled with particles of dust until, by the time all the pads had been treated, a quite appreciable quantity of dust had accumulated. Finally, Thorndyke took the box itself and, having opened it, placed it bottom upwards on the sheet of paper and with a small mallet tapped it lightly but sharply all over the bottom and sides. When he lifted it from the paper, the further contribution of dust could be plainly seen in a speckling of the surface corresponding to the shape of the box.

For some moments Thorndyke stood by the bench looking down on this powdering of grey that occupied the middle of the sheet of white paper. Some of the particles, such as vegetable fibres, were easily recognizable by the unaided eye; and there were two hairs, evidently moustache hairs, both quite short and of a tawny brown colour. But he made no detailed examination of the deposit. Taking from the cupboard a largish flat pill-box, he wrote on its lid the number of the box, and then, having lightly folded the sheet of paper, carefully assembled the dust into a tiny heap in the middle and transferred it to the pill-box, applying the tuning-fork to the sheet to propel the last few grains to their destination. Then, having put the box aside and deposited the sheets of tissue paper – neatly folded – in a numbered envelope, he spread a fresh sheet of demy on the bench, and taking up another box from the side-table, subjected it to similar treatment; and so, carefully and methodically, he dealt with the entire collection of boxes, never pausing for more than a rapid glance at the sprinkling of dust that each one yielded.

He was just shooting the "catch" from the last package into the pill-box when a quick step was audible on the stairs, and after a short interval Polton let himself in silently.

"Here's Dr Jervis, sir," said he, "and he says he hasn't had lunch yet. It is past three o'clock, sir."

"A very delicate hint, Polton," said Thorndyke. "I will join him immediately – but here he is, guided by instinct at the very psychological moment."

As he spoke, Dr Jervis entered the room and looked about him inquisitively. From the row of pill-boxes his glance travelled to the little heaps of jewellery, each on a numbered sheet of paper.

"This is a quaint collection, Thorndyke," said he, stooping to inspect the jewels. "What is the meaning of it? I trust that my learned senior has not, at last, succumbed to temptation; but it is a suspicious-looking lot."

"It does look a little like a fence's stock-in-trade or the product of a super-burglary," Thorndyke admitted. "However, I think Polton will be able to reassure you, when he has looked over the swag. But let us go and feed; and I will give you an outline sketch of the case in the intervals of mastication. It is quite a curious problem."

"And I take it," said Jervis, "that these pill-boxes contain the solution. There is a necromantic look about them that I seem to recognize. You must tell me about them when you have propounded the problem."

He followed Thorndyke into the little breakfast-room, and when they had taken their seats at the table and fairly embarked on their immediate business, the story of the gem robbery was allowed to transpire gradually. Jervis followed the narrative with close attention and an occasional chuckle of amusement.

"It is an odd problem," he commented when the whole story had been told. "There doesn't seem to be any doubt as to who committed the robbery; and yet if you were to put this man Osmond into the dock, although the jury would be convinced to a man of his guilt, they would have to acquit him. I wonder what the deuce made him bolt."

"Yes," said Thorndyke, "that is what I have been asking myself. He may be a nervous, panicky man, but that does not look like the explanation. The suggestion is rather that he knew of some highly incriminating fact which he expected to come to light, but which has not come to light. As it is, the only incriminating fact is his own disappearance; which is evidentially worthless by itself."

"Perfectly. And you are now searching for corroborative facts in the dust from those boxes. It doesn't look a very hopeful quest."

"It doesn't," Thorndyke agreed. "But still, circumstantial evidence gains weight very rapidly. A grain of positive evidence would give quite a new importance to the disappearance. For instance, no less than seven of those boxes have yielded moustache hairs, all apparently from the same person – a fair man with a rather closely cropped moustache of a tawny colour. Now, if it should turn out that Osmond has a moustache of that kind and that no other person connected with those boxes has a moustache of precisely that character, this would be a really important item of evidence, especially coupled with the disappearance."

"It would, indeed; and even the number might be illuminating. I mean that, although moustache hairs are shed pretty freely, one would not have expected to find so many. But if the man had the not uncommon habit of stroking or rubbing his moustache, that would account for the number that had got detached."

Thorndyke nodded approvingly. "Quite a good point, Jervis. I will make a note of it for verification. And now, as we seem to have finished, shall we take a look at one or two of the samples?"

"Exactly what I was going to propose," replied Jervis; and as they rose and repaired to the small laboratory, he added: "It's quite like old times to be pursuing a mysterious unknown quantity with you. I sometimes feel like chucking the insurance job and coming back."

"It is better to come back occasionally and keep the insurance job," Thorndyke rejoined as he placed two microscopes on the bench facing the window and drew up a couple of chairs. "You had better note the number of each box that you examine, though it is probably of no consequence."

He took up the collection of pill-boxes, and having placed them between the two microscopes, sat down, and the two friends then fell to work, each carefully tipping the contents of a box on to a large glass slip and laying the latter on the stage of the microscope.

For some time they worked on in silence, each jotting down on a note-block brief comments on the specimens examined. When about half of the boxes had been dealt with – and their contents very carefully returned to them – Jervis leaned back in his chair and looked thoughtfully at his colleague.

"This is very commonplace, uncharacteristic dust in most respects," said he, "but there is one queer feature in it that I don't quite make out. I have found in every specimen a number of irregularly oval bodies, some of them with pointed ends. They are about a hundredth of an inch long by a little more than a two hundredth wide; a dull pink in colour and apparently of a granular homogeneous substance. I took them at first for insect eggs, but they are evidently not, as they have no skin or shell. I don't remember having seen anything exactly like them before. Have you found any of them?"

"Yes. Like you, I have found some in every box."

"And what do you make of them? Do you recognize them?"

"Yes," replied Thorndyke. "They are the castings of a wood-boring beetle; particles of that fine dust that you see in the worm-holes of worm-eaten wood. Quite an interesting find."

"Quite; unless they come from the boxes that the jewels were packed in."

"I don't think they do. Those boxes are white wood, whereas these castings are from a red wood. But we may as well make sure."

He rose and took up the empty boxes one by one, turning each one over and examining it closely on all sides.

"You see, Jervis," he said as he laid down the last of them, "there is not a trace of a worm-hole in any of them. No, that worm-dust came from an outside source."

"But," exclaimed Jervis, "it is very extraordinary. Don't you think so? I mean," he continued in response to an inquiring glance from his colleague, "that the quantity is so astonishing. Just think of it. In every one of these boxes we have found an appreciable number of these castings – quite a large quantity in the aggregate. But the amount of dust that will fall from a piece of worm-eaten furniture must be infinitesimal."

"I would hardly agree to that, Jervis. A really badly wormed piece – say an old walnut chair or armoire – will, in the course of time, shed a surprisingly large amount of dust. But, nevertheless, my learned friend has, with his usual perspicacity, laid his finger on the point that is of real evidential importance – the remarkable quantity of this dust and its more or less even distribution among all these boxes. And now you realize the truth of what I was saying just now as to the cumulative quality of circumstantial evidence. Here we have a number of boxes which have undoubtedly been tampered with by some person. That person is believed to be the man Osmond on the ground that he has absconded. But his disappearance, by itself, furnishes no evidence of his guilt. It merely offers a suggestion. He may have gone away for some entirely different reason.

"Then we find in these boxes certain moustache hairs. If it should turn out that Osmond has a moustache composed of similar hairs, that fact alone would not implicate him, since there are thousands of other men with similar moustaches. But taken in conjunction with the disappearance, the similarity of the hairs would constitute an item of positive evidence.

"Then we find some dust derived from worm-eaten wood. Its presence in these boxes, its character, and its abundance offer certain suggestions as to the kind of wood, the nature of the wooden object, and the circumstances attending its deposition in the boxes. Now, if it should be possible to ascertain the existence of a wooden object of the kind suggested and associated with the suggested circumstances, and if that object were the property of, or definitely associated with, the man Osmond, that fact, together with the hairs and the disappearance, would form a really weighty mass of evidence against him."

"Yes, I see that," said Jervis; "but what I don't see is how you arrive at your inferences as to the object from which the dust was derived."

"It is a question of probabilities," replied Thorndyke. "First, as to the kind of wood. It is a red wood. It is pretty certainly not mahogany, as it is too light in colour and mahogany is very little liable to 'the worm.' But the abundance of dust suggests one of those woods which are specially liable to be worm-eaten. Of these the fruit woods – walnut, cherry, apple, and pear – are the most extreme cases, cherry being, perhaps, the worst of all and therefore usually avoided by the cabinet-maker. But this dust is obviously not walnut. It is the wrong colour. But it might be either cherry, apple, or pear, and the probabilities are rather in favour of cherry; though, of course, it might be some other relatively soft and sappy red wood."

"But how do you infer the nature of the object?"

"Again, by the presence of the dust in these boxes, by the properties of that dust and the large quantity of it. Consider the case of ordinary room dust. You find it on all sorts of surfaces, even high up on the walls or on the ceiling. There is no mystery as to how it gets there. It consists of minute particles, mostly of fibres from textiles, so small and light that they float freely in the air. But this wood-dust consists of relatively large and heavy bodies – over a hundredth of an inch long. From the worm-holes it will fall to the floor; and there it will remain even when the floor is being swept. It cannot rise in the air and become deposited like ordinary dust, and it must therefore have made its way into these boxes in some other manner."

"Yes, I realize that; but still I don't see how that fact throws any light on the nature of the wooden object."

"It is merely a suggestion," replied Thorndyke; "and the inference may be quite wrong. But it is a perfectly obvious one. Come now, Jervis, don't let your intellectual joints get stiff. Keep them lissom by exercise. Consider the problem of this dust. How did it get into these boxes and why is there so much of it? If you reason out the probabilities, you must inevitably reach a conclusion as to the nature of the wooden object. That conclusion may turn out to be wrong; but it will be logically justifiable."

"Well, that is all that matters," Jervis retorted with a sour smile, as he rose and glanced at his watch. "The mere fact of its being wrong we should ignore as an irrelevant triviality; just as the French surgeon, undisturbed by the death of the patient, proceeded with his operation and finally brought it to a brilliantly successful conclusion. I will practise your logical dumb-bell exercise, and if I reach no conclusion after all I shall still be comforted by the mental vision of my learned senior scouring the country in search of a hypothetical worm-eaten chest of drawers."

Thorndyke chuckled softly. "My learned friend is pleased to be ironical. But nevertheless his unerring judgement leads him to a perfect forecast of my proceedings. The next stage of the inquiry will consist in tracing this dust to its sources, and the goal of my endeavours will be the discovery and identification of this wooden object. If I succeed in that, there will be, I imagine, very little more left to discover."

"No," Jervis agreed, "especially if the owner of the antique should happen to be the elusive Mr Osmond. So I wish you success in your quest, and only hope it may not resemble too closely that of the legendary blind man, searching in a dark room for a black hat – that isn't there."

With this parting shot and a defiant grin, Jervis took his departure, leaving Thorndyke to complete the examination of the remaining material.

CHAPTER FIFTEEN

Mr Wampole is Highly Amused

On a certain Saturday afternoon at a few minutes to three the door of Mr Woodstock's office in High Street, Burchester, opened somewhat abruptly and disclosed the figures of the solicitor himself and his chief clerk.

"Confounded nuisance all this fuss and foolery," growled the former, pulling out his watch and casting an impatient glance up the street. "I hope he is not going to keep us waiting."

"He is not due till three," Hepburn remarked, soothingly; and then, stepping out and peering up the nearly empty street, he added: "Perhaps that may be he – that tall man with the little clerical-looking person."

"If it is, he seems to be bringing his luggage with him," said Mr Woodstock, regarding the pair, and especially the suitcases that they carried, with evident disfavour; "but you are right. They are coming here."

He put away his watch, and as the two men crossed the road, he assumed an expression of polite hostility.

"Dr Thorndyke?" he inquired as the newcomers halted opposite the doorway; and having received confirmation of his surmise, he continued: "I am Mr Woodstock, and this is my colleague, Mr Hepburn. May I take it that this gentleman is concerned in our present business?" As he spoke he fixed a truculent blue eye on Thorndyke's companion, who crinkled apologetically.

"This is Mr Polton, my laboratory assistant," Thorndyke explained, "who has come with me to give me any help that I may need."

"Indeed," said Woodstock, glaring inquisitively at the large suit-case which Mr Polton carried. "Help? I gathered from Mr Penfield's letter that you wished to inspect the office, and I must confess that I found myself utterly unable to imagine why. May I ask what you expect to learn from an inspection of the premises?"

"That," replied Thorndyke, "is a rather difficult question to answer. But as all my information as to what has occurred here is second- or third-hand, I thought it best to see the place myself and make a few inquiries on the spot. That is my routine practice."

"Ah, I see," said Woodstock. "Your visit is just a matter of form, a demonstration of activity. Well, I'm sorry I can't be present at the ceremony. My colleague and I have an engagement elsewhere; but my office-keeper, Mr Wampole, will be able to tell you anything that you may wish to know and show you all there is to see excepting the strong-room. If you want to see that, as I suppose you do, I had better show it to you now, as I must take the key away with me."

He led the way along the narrow hall, half-way down which he opened a door inscribed "Clerks' Office," and entered a large room, now unoccupied save by an elderly man who sat at a table with the parts of a dismembered electric bell spread out before him. Through this Mr Woodstock passed into a somewhat smaller room furnished with a large writing-table, one or two nests of deed-boxes, and a set of bookshelves. Nearly opposite the table was the massive door of the strong-room, standing wide open with the key in the lock.

"This is my private office," said Mr Woodstock, "and here is the strong-room. Perhaps you would like to step inside. I am rather proud of this room. You don't often see one of this size. And it is absolutely fire-proof; thick steel lining, concrete outside that, and then brick. It is practically indestructible. Those confounded boxes occupied that long upper shelf."

Thorndyke did not appear to be specially interested in the strong-room. He walked in, looked round at the steel walls with their ranks of steel shelves, loaded with bundles of documents, and then walked out.

"Yes," he said, "it is a fine room, as strong and secure as one could wish; though, of course, its security has no bearing on our case, since it must have been entered either with its own key or a duplicate. May I look at the key?"

Mr Woodstock withdrew it from the lock and handed it to him without comment, watching him with undisguised impatience as he turned it over and examined its blade.

"Not a difficult type of key to duplicate," he remarked as he handed it back, "though these wardless pin-keys are more subtle than they look."

"I suppose they are," Woodstock assented indifferently. "But really, these investigations appear to me rather pointless, seeing that the identity of the thief is known. And now I must be off; but first let me introduce you to my deputy, Mr Wampole."

He led the way back to the clerks' office, where his subordinate was busily engaged in assembling the parts of the bell.

"This is Dr Thorndyke, Wampole, who has come with his assistant, Mr – er – Bolton, to inspect the premises and make a few inquiries. You can show him anything that he wants to see and give him all the assistance that you can in the way of answering questions. And," concluded Mr Woodstock, shaking hands stiffly with Thorndyke, "I wish you a successful issue to your labours."

As Mr Woodstock and his colleague departed, closing the outer door after them, Mr Wampole laid down his screwdriver and looked at Thorndyke with a slightly puzzled expression.

"I don't quite understand, sir, what you want to do," said he, "or what sort of inspection you want to make; but I am entirely at your service, if you will kindly instruct me. What would you like me to show you first?"

"I don't think we need to interrupt your work just at present, Mr Wampole. The first thing to be done is to make a rough plan of the premises, and while my assistant is doing that, perhaps I might ask you a few questions if it will not distract you too much."

"It will not distract me at all," Mr Wampole replied, picking up his screwdriver. "I am accustomed to doing odd jobs about the office – I am the handy man of the establishment – and I am not easily put out of my stride."

Evidently he was not; for even as he was speaking his fingers were busy in a neat, purposive way that showed clearly that his attention was not wandering from his task. Thorndyke watched him curiously, not quite able to "place" him. His hands were the skilful, capable hands of a mechanic, and this agreed with Woodstock's description of him and his own. But his speech was that of a passably educated man and his manner was quite dignified and self-possessed.

"By the way," said Thorndyke, "Mr Woodstock referred to you as the office-keeper. Does that mean that you are the custodian of the premises?"

"Nominally," replied Wampole. "I am a law-writer by profession; but when I first came here, some twenty years ago, I came as a caretaker and used to live upstairs. But for many years past the upstairs rooms have been used for storage – obsolete books, documents, and all sorts of accumulations. Nobody lives in the house now. We lock the place up when we go away at night. As for me, I am, as I said, the handy man of the establishment. I do whatever comes along – copy letters, engross leases, keep an eye on the state of the premises, and so on."

"I see. Then you probably know as much of the affairs of this office as anybody."

"Probably, sir. I am the oldest member of the staff, and I am usually the first to arrive in the morning and the last to leave at night. I expect I can tell you anything that you want to know."

"Then I will ask you one or two questions, if I may. You probably know that my visit here is connected with the robbery of Mr Hollis' gems?"

"The alleged robbery," Mr Wampole corrected. "Yes, sir. Mr Woodstock told me that."

"You appear to be somewhat doubtful about the robbery."

"I am not doubtful at all," Wampole replied in a tone of great decision. "I am convinced that the whole thing is a mare's nest. The gems may have been stolen. I suppose they were as Mr Hollis says they were. But they weren't stolen from here."

"You put complete trust in the strong-room?"

"Oh no, I don't, sir. This is a solicitor's strong-room, not a banker's. It is secure against fire, not against robbery. It was designed for the custody of things such as documents, of great value to their owners but of no value to a thief. It was no proper receptacle for jewels. They should have gone to a bank."

"Do I understand, then, that unauthorized persons might have obtained access to the strong-room?"

"They might, during business hours. Mr Woodstock unlocks it when he arrives and it is usually open all day; or if it is shut, the key is left hanging on the wall. But it has never been taken seriously as a bank strong-room is. Mr Hepburn and Mr Osmond kept their cricket-bags and other things in it, and we have all been in the habit of putting things in there if we were leaving them here overnight."

"Then, really, any member of the staff had the opportunity to make away with Mr Hollis' property?"

"I wouldn't put it as strongly as that," replied Wampole, with somewhat belated caution. "Any of us could have gone into the strong-room; but not without being seen by some of the others. Still, one must admit that a robbery might have been possible; the point is that it didn't happen. I checked those boxes when I helped to put them in, and I checked them when we took them out. They were all in their original wrappings with Mr Hollis' handwriting on them and all the seals intact. It is nonsense to talk of a robbery in the face of those facts."

"And you attach no significance to Mr Osmond's disappearance?"

"No, sir. He was a bachelor and could go when and where he pleased. It was odd of him, I admit, but he sometimes did odd things; a hasty, impulsive gentleman, quick to jump at conclusions and make decisions and quick to act. Not a discreet gentleman at all; rather an unreasonable gentleman, perhaps, but I should say highly scrupulous. I can't imagine him committing a theft."

"Should you describe him as a nervous or timid man?"

Mr Wampole emitted a sound as if he had clockwork in his inside and was about to strike. "I never met a less nervous man," he replied with emphasis. "No, sir. Bold to rashness would be my description of Mr John Osmond. A buccaneering type of man. A yachtsman, a boxer, a wrestler, a footballer, and a cricketer. A regular hard nut, sir. He should never have been in an office. He ought to have been a sailor, an explorer, or a big-game hunter."

"What was he like to look at?"

"Just what you would expect – a big, lean, square-built man, hatchet-faced, Roman-nosed, with blue eyes, light-brown hair, and a close-cropped beard and moustache. Looked like a naval officer."

"Do you happen to know if his residence has been examined?"

"Mr Woodstock and the Chief Constable searched his rooms, but of course they didn't find anything. He had only two small rooms, as he took his meals and spent a good deal of his time with Mr Hepburn, his brother-in-law. He seemed very fond of his sister and her two little boys."

"Would it be possible for me to see those rooms?"

"I don't see why not, sir. They are locked up now, but the keys are here and the rooms are only a few doors down the street."

Here occurred a slight interruption, for Mr Wampole, having completed his operations on the bell, now connected it with the battery – which had also been under repair – when it emitted a loud and cheerful peal. At the same moment, as if summoned by the sound, Polton entered holding a small drawing-board on which was a neatly executed plan of the premises.

"Dear me, sir!" exclaimed Mr Wampole, casting an astonished glance at the plan. "You are very thorough in your methods. I see you have even put in the furniture."

"Yes," Thorndyke agreed, with a faint smile; "we must needs be thorough even if we reach no result."

Mr Wampole regarded him with a sly smile. "Very true, sir," he chuckled – "very true, indeed. A bill of costs needs something to explain the total. But, God bless us! what is this?"

"This" was, in effect, a diminutive vacuum cleaner, fitted with a little revolving brush and driven by means of a large dry battery, which Polton was at the moment disinterring from his suitcase. Thorndyke briefly explained the nature of the apparatus while Mr Wampole stared at it with an expression of stupefaction.

"But why have you brought it here, sir?" he exclaimed. "The premises would certainly be the better for a thorough cleaning, but surely – "

"Oh, we are not going to 'vacuum clean' you," Thorndyke reassured him. "We are just going to take samples of dust from different parts of the premises."

"Are you, indeed, sir? And, if I may take the liberty of asking, what do you propose to do with them?"

"I shall examine them carefully when I get home," Thorndyke replied, "and I may then possibly be able to judge whether the robbery took place here or elsewhere."

As Thorndyke furnished this explanation, Mr Wampole stood gazing at him as if petrified. Once he opened his mouth, but shut it again tightly as if not trusting himself to speak. At length he rejoined: "Wonderful! wonderful!" and then, after an interval, he continued meditatively: "I seem to have read somewhere of a wise woman of the East who was able, by merely examining a hair from the beard of a man who had fallen downstairs, to tell exactly how many stairs he had fallen down. But I never imagined that it was actually possible."

"It does sound incredible," Thorndyke admitted, gravely. "She must have had remarkable powers of deduction. And now, if Mr Polton is ready, we will begin our perambulation. Which was Mr Osmond's office?"

"I will show you," replied Mr Wampole, recovering from his trance of astonishment. He led the way out into the hall and thence into a smallish room in which were a writing-table and a large, old-fashioned, flap-top desk.

"This table," he explained, "is Mr Hepburn's. The desk was used by Mr Osmond and his belongings are still in it. That second door opens into Mr Woodstock's office."

"Is it usually kept open or closed?" Thorndyke asked.

"It is nearly always open; and as it is, as you see" – here he threw it open – "exactly opposite the door of the strong-room, no one could go in there unobserved unless Mr Woodstock, Mr Hepburn, and Mr Osmond had all been out at the same time."

Thorndyke made a note of this statement and then asked:

"Would it be permissible to look inside Mr Osmond's desk? Or is it locked?"

"I don't think it is locked. No, it is not," he added, demonstrating the fact by raising the lid; "and, as you see, there is nothing very secret inside."

The contents, in fact, consisted of a tobacco-tin, a couple of briar pipes, a ball of string, a pair of gloves, a clothes-brush, a pair of much-worn hair-brushes, and a number of loose letters and bills. These last Thorndyke gathered together and laid aside without examination, and then proceeded methodically to inspect each of the other objects in turn, while Mr Wampole watched him with the faintest shadow of a smile.

"He seems to have had a pretty good set of teeth and a fairly strong jaw," Thorndyke remarked, balancing a massive pipe in his fingers and glancing at the deep tooth-marks on the mouth-piece, "which supports your statement as to his physique."

He peered into the tobacco-tin, smelt the tobacco, inspected the gloves closely, especially at their palmar surfaces, and tried them on; examined the clothes-brush, first with the naked eye and then with the aid of his pocket-lens, and, holding it inside the desk, stroked its hair backwards and forwards, looking closely to see if any dust fell from it. Finally, he took up the hair-brushes one at a time and, having examined them in the same minute fashion, produced from his pocket a pair of fine forceps and a seed-envelope. With the forceps he daintily picked out from the brushes a number of hairs which he laid on a sheet of paper, eventually transferring the collection to the little envelope, on which he wrote: "Hairs from John Osmond's hair-brushes."

"You don't take anything for granted, sir," remarked Mr Wampole, who had been watching this proceeding with concentrated interest (perhaps he was again reminded of the wise woman of the East).

"No," Thorndyke agreed. "Your description was hearsay testimony, whereas these hairs could be produced in Court and sworn to by me."

"So they could, sir; though, as it is not disputed that Mr Osmond has been in this office, I don't quite see what they could prove."

"Neither do I," rejoined Thorndyke. "I was merely laying down the principle."

Meanwhile, Polton had been silently carrying out his part of the programme, not unobserved by Mr Wampole; and a pale patch about a foot square, between Mr Hepburn's chair and the front of the table, where the pattern of the grimy carpet had miraculously reappeared, marked the site of his operations. Tenderly removing the little silken bag, now bulging with its load of dust, he slipped it into a numbered envelope and wrote the number on the spot on the plan to which it corresponded.

Presently a similar patch appeared on the carpet in front of Osmond's desk, and when the sample had been disposed of and the spot on the plan marked, Polton cast a wistful glance at the open desk.

"Wouldn't it be as well, sir, to take a specimen from the inside?" he asked.

"Perhaps it would," Thorndyke replied. "It should give us what we may call a 'pure culture.' " He rapidly emptied the desk of its contents, when Polton introduced the nozzle of his apparatus and drew it slowly over every part of the interior. When this operation was completed, including the disposal of the specimen and the marking of the plan, the party moved into Mr Woodstock's office, and from thence back into the clerks' office.

"I find this investigation intensely interesting," said Mr Wampole, rubbing his hands gleefully. "It seems to combine the attractions of a religious ceremony and a parlour game. I am enjoying it exceedingly. You will like to have the names of the clerks who sit at those desks, I presume."

"If you please," replied Thorndyke.

"And, of course, you will wish to take samples from the insides of the desks. You certainly ought to. The informal lunches which the occupants consume during the forenoon will have left traces which should be most illuminating. And the desks are not locked, as there are no keys."

Mr Wampole's advice produced on Polton's countenance a smile of most extraordinary crinkliness, but Thorndyke accepted it with unmoved gravity and it was duly acted upon. Each of the desks was opened and emptied of its contents – instructive enough as to the character and personal habits of the tenant – and cleared of its accumulation of crumbs, tobacco-ash, and miscellaneous dirt, the "catch" forming a specimen supplementary to those obtained from the floor. At length, when they had made the round of the office, leaving in their wake a succession of clean squares on the matting which covered the floor, Mr Wampole halted before an old-fashioned high desk which stood in a corner in company with a high office-stool.

"This is my desk," said he. "I presume that you are going to take a little souvenir from it?"

"Well," replied Thorndyke, "we may as well complete the series. We operated on Mr Hollis' premises this morning."

"Did you indeed, sir! You went there first; and very proper too. I am sure Mr Hollis was very gratified."

"If he was," Thorndyke replied with a smile, "he didn't make it obtrusively apparent. May I compliment you on your desk? You keep it in apple-pie order."

"I try to show the juniors an example," replied Mr Wampole, throwing back the lid of the desk and looking complacently at the neatly stowed contents. "It is a miscellaneous collection," he added as he proceeded to transfer his treasures from the desk to a cleared space on the table.

It certainly was. There were a few tools – pliers, hacksaw, hammer, screwdriver, and a couple of gimlets – a loosely folded linen apron, one or two battery terminals and a coil of insulated wire, a stamp-album, a cardboard tray full of military buttons, cap-badges, and old civilian coat buttons, and a smaller tray containing one or two old copper and silver coins.

"I see you are a stamp collector," remarked Thorndyke, opening the album and casting a glance of lukewarm interest over its variegated pages.

"Yes," was the reply, "in a small way. It is a poor man's hobby, unless one seeks to acquire costly rarities, which I do not. As a matter of fact, I seldom buy specimens at all. This album has been filled principally from our foreign correspondence. And the same is true of the coins. I don't regularly collect them; I just keep any odd specimens that come my way."

"And the buttons? You have a better opportunity there, for you have practically no competitors. And yet it seems to me that they are of more interest than the things that conventional collectors seek so eagerly."

"I entirely agree with you, sir," Mr Wampole replied, warmly. "It is the common things that are best worth collecting – the things that are common now and will be rare in a few years' time. But the collector who has no imagination neglects things until they have become rare and precious. Then he buys at a high price what he could have got a few years previously for nothing. Look at these old gilt coat-buttons. I got them from an old-established tailor who was clearing out his obsolete stock. Unfortunately, he had thrown away most of them and nearly all the steel button-dies. I just managed to rescue these few and one or two dies, which I have at home. They are of no value now, but when the collectors discover the interest of old buttons, they will be worth their weight in gold. I am collecting all the buttons I can get hold of."

"I think you are wise, from a collector's point of view. By the way, did you ever meet with any of those leather-bound sample wallets that the old button-makers used to supply to tailors?"

"Never," replied Mr Wampole. "I have never even heard of them."

"I have seen one or two," said Thorndyke, "and each was a collection in itself, for it contained some two or three hundred buttons, fixed in sheets of millboard, forming a sort of album; and, of course, every button was different from every other."

Mr Wampole's eyes sparkled. "What an opportunity you had, sir!" he exclaimed. "But probably you are not a collector. It was a pity, though, for, as you say, one of those wallets was a museum in itself. If you should ever chance to meet with another, would it be too great a liberty for me to beg you to secure an option for me, at a price within my slender means?"

"It is no liberty at all," Thorndyke replied. "It is not likely that I should ever come across one again, but if I should, I will certainly secure it for you."

"That is most kind of you, sir," exclaimed Mr Wampole. "And now, as Mr Polton seems to have completed the cleansing of my desk – the first that it has had, I am afraid, for a year or two – we may continue our exploration. Did you wish to examine the waiting-room?"

"I think not. I have just looked into it, but its associations are too ambiguous for the dust to be of any interest. But I should like to glance at the rooms upstairs."

To the upstairs rooms they accordingly proceeded, but the inspection was little more than a formality. They walked slowly through each room, awakening the echoes as they trod the bare floors, and as they went, Thorndyke's eye travelled searchingly over the shelves and rough tables, stacked with documents and obsolete account-books, and the few rickety Windsor chairs. There was certainly an abundance of dust, as Mr Wampole pointed out, but it did not appear to be of the brand in which Thorndyke was interested.

"Well," said Mr Wampole, as they descended to the ground-floor, "you have now seen the whole of our premises. I think you said that you would like to inspect Mr Osmond's rooms. If you will wait a few moments, I will get the keys."

He disappeared into the principal's office, and meanwhile Polton rapidly packed his apparatus in the suitcase, so that by the time Mr Wampole reappeared, he was ready to start.

"Mr Osmond's rooms," said Mr Wampole, as they set forth, "are over a bookseller's shop. This is the place. If you will wait for a moment at the private door, I will notify the landlord of our visit."

He entered the shop and after a short interval emerged briskly and stepped round to the side-door, into which he inserted a latch-key. He led the way along the narrow hall, past a partially open door, in the opening of which a portion of a human face was visible, to the staircase, up which the little procession advanced until the second-floor landing was reached. Here Mr Wampole halted and, selecting a key from the small bunch, unlocked and opened a door, and preceded his visitors into the room.

"It is just as well that you came today," he remarked, "for I understand that Mrs Hepburn is going to take charge of these rooms. A day or two later and she would have been beforehand with you in the matter of dust. As it is, you ought to get quite a good haul."

"Quite," Thorndyke agreed. "There is plenty of dust; but in spite of that, the place has a very neat, orderly appearance. Do you happen to know whether the rooms have been tidied up since Mr Osmond left?"

"They are just as he left them," was the reply, "excepting that the Chief Constable and Mr Woodstock came and looked them over. But I don't think they disturbed them to any extent. There isn't much to disturb, as you see."

Mr Wampole was right. The furnishing of the room did not go beyond the barest necessities, and when Thorndyke opened the door of communication and looked into the bedroom, it was seen to be characterized by a like austere simplicity. Whatever might be the moral shortcomings of the vanished tenant, softness or effeminate luxuriousness did not appear to be among them.

As his assistant refixed the "extractor," Thorndyke stood thoughtfully surveying the room, trying to assess the personality of its late occupant by the light of his belongings. And those belongings and the room which held them were highly characteristic. The late tenant was clearly an active man, a man whose interests lay out-of-doors; an orderly man, too, with something of a sailor's tidiness. He had the sailor's knack of keeping the floor clear by slinging things aloft out of the way. Not only small articles such as rules, dividers, marlinspike, and sheath-knife, but a gun-case, fishing-rods, cricket-bats, and a bulky roll of charts were disposed of on the walls by means of picture-hooks and properly made slings – the height of which gave a clue as to the occupant's stature and length of arm. And the nautical flavour was accentuated by the contents of a set of rough shelves in a recess, which included a boat compass, a nautical almanack, a volume of sailing directions, and a manual of naval architecture. The only touch of ornament was given by a set of four photographs in silver frames, which occupied the mantelpiece in company with a pipe-rack, a tobacco-jar, an ash-bowl, and a box of matches.

Thorndyke stepped across to the fireplace to look at them more closely. They were portraits of five persons: a grave-looking, elderly clergyman; a woman of about the same age with a strong, alert, resolute face and markedly aquiline features; and a younger woman, recognizably like the clergyman; and two boys of about seven and eight, photographed together.

"Those," said Mr Wampole, indicating the older persons, "are Mr Osmond's parents, both, I regret to say, deceased. The younger lady is Mrs Hepburn, Mr Osmond's sister, and those little boys are her sons. Mr Osmond was very devoted to them, as I believe they were to him."

Thorndyke nodded. "They are fine little fellows," he remarked. "Indeed it is a good-looking family. I gather from your description that Mr Osmond must have taken rather strongly after his mother."

"You are quite right, sir," replied Mr Wampole. "From that portrait of his mother you would recognize Mr Osmond without the slightest difficulty. The likeness is quite remarkable."

Thorndyke nodded again as he considered long and earnestly the striking face that looked out of the frame so keenly under its bold, straight brows. Strength, courage, determination, were written in every line of it; and as he stood with his eyes bent upon those of the portrait and thought of this woman's son – of the mean, avaricious crime, so slyly and craftily carried out, of the hasty, pusillanimous flight, unjustified by any hint of danger – he was sensible of a discrepancy between personality and conduct to which his experience furnished no parallel. A vast amount of nonsense has been talked and believed on the subject of physiognomy; but within the body of error there lies a soul of truth. "Character reading" in the Lavater manner is largely pure quackery; but there is a certain general congruity between a man's essential character and his bodily "make-up," including his facial type. Here, however, was a profound incongruity. Thorndyke found it difficult to identify the sly, cowardly knave whom he was seeking with the actual man who appeared to be coming into view.

But his doubts did not affect his actions. He had come here to collect evidence; and that purpose he proceeded to execute with a perfectly open mind. He pointed out to Polton the most likely spots to work for characteristic dust; he examined minutely every piece of furniture and woodwork in both the rooms; he made careful notes of every fact observed by himself or communicated by Wampole that could throw any light on the habits or occupations of the absent man. Even the secretly-amused onlooker was impressed by the thoroughness of the investigation, for, as Polton finally packed his apparatus, he remarked:

"Well, sir, I have told you what I think – that you are following a will-o'-the-wisp. But if you fail to run him to earth, it certainly won't be for lack of painstaking effort. You deserve to succeed."

Thorndyke thanked him for the compliment and retired slowly down the stairs while the rooms were being locked up. They called in at the office to collect Thorndyke's green canvas-covered case and then made their adieux.

"I must thank you most warmly, Mr Wampole," said Thorndyke, "for the kind interest that you have taken in our investigations. You have given us every possible help."

Mr Wampole bowed. "It is very good of you to say so. But it has really been a great pleasure and a most novel and interesting experience." He held the door open for them to pass out, and as they were crossing the threshold he added: "You won't forget about that button-wallet, sir, if the opportunity should arrive."

"I certainly will not," was the reply. "I will secure an option – or better still, the wallet itself and send it to you. By the way, should it be sent here or to your private address?"

Mr Wampole reflected for a few moments. Then he drew from his pocket a much-worn letter-case from which he extracted a printed visiting-card.

"I think, sir, it would be best to send it to my private address. One doesn't want it opened by the wrong hands. This is my address; and let me thank you in advance, even if only for the kind intention. Good evening, sir. Good evening, Mr Polton. I trust that your little dusty souvenirs will prove highly illuminating."

He stood on the threshold and gravely watched his two visitors as they retired down the street. At length, when they turned a corner, he re-entered, shutting and locking the outer door. Then in an instant his gravity relaxed, and flinging himself into a chair, he roused the echoes with peal after peal of joyous laughter.

Chapter Sixteen

Which Treats of Law and Buttons

"This seems highly irregular," said Mr Penfield, settling himself comfortably in the easy-chair and smilingly regarding a small table on which were a decanter and glasses. "I don't treat my professional visitors in this hospitable fashion. And you don't even ask what has brought me here."

"No," replied Thorndyke, as he filled a couple of glasses; "I accept the gifts of fortune and ask no questions."

Mr Penfield bowed. "You were good enough to say that I might call out of business hours, which is a great convenience, so here I am, with a twofold purpose; first, to seek information from you; and second, to give you certain news of my own. Perhaps I may take them in that order and begin by asking one or two questions?"

"Do so, by all means," replied Thorndyke.

"I have heard," pursued Mr Penfield, "from our friends Hollis and Woodstock, and perhaps you will not be surprised to learn that you have made yourself somewhat unpopular with them. They have even applied disrespectful epithets to you."

"Such as mountebank, impostor, quack, and so forth," suggested Thorndyke.

Mr Penfield chuckled as he sipped his wine. "Your insight is remarkable," said he. "You have quoted the very words. They complain that, after making a serious appointment with them and occupying their time, you merely asked a number of foolish and irrelevant questions, and then proceeded to sweep the floor. Is that an exaggeration, or did you really sweep the floor?"

"I collected a few samples of dust from the floor and elsewhere."

Mr Penfield consumed a luxurious pinch of snuff and regarded Thorndyke with delightful amusement.

"Did you indeed? Well, I am not surprised at their attitude. But a year or so ago it would have been my own. It must have looked like sheer wizardry. But tell me, have your investigations and floor-sweepings yielded any tangible facts?"

"Yes," replied Thorndyke, "they have; and those facts I will lay before you on the strict understanding that you communicate them to nobody. As to certain further inferences of a more speculative character, I should prefer to make no statement at present. They may be entirely erroneous."

"Exactly, exactly. Let us keep scrupulously to definite facts which are susceptible of proof. Now, what have you discovered?"

"My positive results amount to this: in the first place I have ascertained beyond the possibility of any reasonable doubt that those boxes had been opened by some person other than Mr Hollis. In the second place it is virtually certain that the person who opened them was in some way connected with Mr Woodstock's office."

"Do you say that the boxes were actually opened in his office?"

"No. The evidence goes to prove that they were taken from the office and opened elsewhere."

"But surely they would have been missed from the strong-room?"

"That, I think was provided for. I infer that only one box was taken at a time and that its place was filled by a dummy."

"Astonishing!" exclaimed Mr Penfield. "It seems incredible that you should have been able to discover this – or, indeed, that it should be true. The seals seem to me to offer an insuperable difficulty."

"On the contrary," replied Thorndyke, "it was the seals that furnished the evidence. They were manifest forgeries."

"Were they really! The robber had actually had a counterfeit seal engraved?"

"No. The false seal was not engraved. It was an electrotype made from one of the wax impressions; a much simpler and easier proceeding, and one that the robber could carry out himself and so avoid the danger of employing a seal engraver."

"No doubt it would be the safer plan, and probably you are right in assuming that he adopted it; but – "

"I am not assuming," said Thorndyke. "There is direct evidence that the seal used to make the false impressions was an electrotype."

"Now, what would be the nature of that evidence – or is it, perhaps, too technical for an ignorant person like me to follow?"

"There is nothing very technical about it," replied Thorndyke. "You know how an electrotype is made? Well, to put it briefly, the process would be this: one of the wax impressions from a box would be carefully coated with black lead or some other conducting material and attached to one of the terminals of an electric battery; and to the other terminal a piece of copper would be attached. The black-leaded wax impression and the piece of copper would be suspended from the wires of the battery, close together but not touching, in a solution of sulphate of copper. Then, as the electric current passed, the copper would dissolve in the solution and a film of metallic copper would become deposited on the black-leaded wax and would gradually thicken until it became a solid shell of copper. When this shell was picked off the wax it would be, in effect, a copper seal which would give impressions on wax just like the original seal. Is that clear?"

"Perfectly. But what is the evidence that this was actually done?"

"It is really very simple," replied Thorndyke. "Let us consider what would happen in the two alternative cases. Take first that of the seal engraver. He has handed to him one or more of the wax impressions from the boxes and is asked to engrave a seal which shall be an exact copy of the seal which made the impressions. What does he do? If the wax impression were absolutely perfect, he would simply copy it in intaglio. But a seal impression never is perfect unless it is made with quite extraordinary care. But the wax impressions on the boxes were just ordinary impressions, hastily made with no attempt at precision, and almost certainly not a perfect one among them. The engraver, then, would not rigorously copy a particular impression, but, eliminating its individual and accidental imperfections, he would aim at producing a seal which should be a faithful copy of the original seal, without any imperfections at all.

"Now take the case of the electrotype. This is a mechanical reproduction of a particular impression. Whatever accidental marks or imperfections there may be in that impression will be faithfully reproduced. In short, an engraved seal would be a copy of the original seal; an electrotype would be a copy of a particular impression of that seal."

Mr Penfield nodded approvingly. "An excellent point and very clearly argued. But what is its bearing on the case?"

"It is this: since an electrotype seal is a mechanical copy of a particular wax impression, including any accidental marks or imperfections in it, it follows that every impression made on wax with such a seal will exhibit the accidental marks or imperfections of the original wax impression, in addition to any defects of its own. So that, if a series of such impressions were examined, although each would probably have its own distinctive peculiarities, yet all of them would be found to agree in displaying the accidental marks or imperfections of the original impression."

"Yes, I see that," said Mr Penfield with a slightly interrogative inflexion.

"Well, that is what I have found in the series of seal-impressions from Mr Hollis' boxes, They are of all degrees of badness, but in every one of the series two particular defects occur; which, as the series consists of over thirty impressions, is utterly outside the limits of probability."

"Might those imperfections not have been in Hollis' seal itself?"

"No. I took, with the most elaborate care, two impressions from the original seal, and those impressions are, I think, as perfect as is possible. At any rate, they are free from these, or any other visible defects. I will show them to you."

He took from a drawer a portfolio and an envelope. From the latter he produced one of the two impressions that he had made with Mr Hollis' seal and from the former a half-plate photograph.

"Here," he said, handing them to Mr Penfield, "is one of the seal impressions taken by me, and here is a magnified photograph of it. You can see that every part of the design is perfectly clear and distinct and the background quite free from indentations. Keep that photograph for comparison with these others, which show a series of thirty-two impressions from the boxes, magnified four diameters. In every one of them you will find two defects. First the projecting fore-legs of the left-hand horse are blurred and faint; second, there is, just in front of the chariot and above the back of the near horse, a minute pit in the background. It is hardly visible to the naked eye in the wax impressions, but the photographs show it plainly. It was probably produced by a tiny bubble of air between the seal and the wax.

"Now, neither of these defects is to be seen in Mr Hollis' seal. Either of them might have occurred accidentally in one or two impressions. But since they both occur in every case, whether the impressions are relatively good or bad, it is practically certain that they existed in the matrix or seal with which the impressions were made. And this conclusion is confirmed by the fact that, in some cases, the defect in the horse's fore-legs is inconsistent with other defects in the same impression."

"How inconsistent?" Mr Penfield demanded.

"I mean that the faint impression of the horse's legs is due to insufficient pressure of the left side of the seal; the seal has not been put down quite vertically. But here – in number 23, for instance –

the impression of the chariot and the driver on the right-hand side is quite faint and shallow. In that case, the left-hand side of the impression should have been deep and distinct. But both sides are faint, whereas the middle is deep."

"Might not the seal have been rocked from side to side?"

"No, that would not explain the appearances; for if the seal were rocked from side to side, both sides would be deep, though the middle might be shallow. It is impossible to imagine any kind of pressure which would give an impression shallow on both sides and deep in the middle. The only possible explanation is that the matrix, itself, was shallow on one side."

Mr Penfield reflected, helping his cogitations with a pinch of snuff.

"Yes," he agreed. "Incredible as the thing appears, I think you have made out your case. But doesn't it strike you as rather odd that this ingenious rascal should not have taken more care to secure a good impression from which to make his false seal?"

"I imagine that he had no choice," replied Thorndyke. "On each box were six seals; three on the paper wrapping, two in the recesses by the keyhole, and one on the knot of the string. Now, as the paper had to be preserved, the seals could not be torn or cut from that. It would be impossible to get them out of the recesses. There remained only the seals on the knots. These were, of course, much the least perfect, though the string was little more than thread and the knots quite small. But they were the only ones that it was possible to remove, and our friend was lucky to have got as good an impression as he did."

Mr Penfield nodded. "Yes," said he, "you have an answer to every objection. By the way, if the paper had to be preserved so carefully, how do you suppose he got the parcels open? He would have had to break the seals."

"I think not. I assume that he melted the seals by holding a hot iron close to them and then gently opened the packets while the wax was soft."

Mr Penfield chuckled. "Yes," he admitted, "it is all very complete and consistent. And now to go on to the next point. You say that there is evidence that these boxes were opened by some person other than Hollis himself; a person connected in some way with Woodstock's office. Further that they were opened, not in the office itself, but in some other place to which they had been taken. I should like to hear that evidence; especially if it should happen to be connected with those mysterious floor-sweepings."

"As a matter of fact, it is," Thorndyke replied, with a smile. "But the floor-sweeping was not the first stage. The investigation began with Mr Hollis' boxes, from which I extracted every particle of dust I could obtain; and this dust I examined minutely and exhaustively. The results were unexpectedly illuminating. For instance, from every one of the untouched boxes I obtained one or more moustache hairs."

"Really! But isn't that very remarkable?"

"Perhaps it is. But moustache hairs are shed very freely. If you look at the dust from a desk used by a man with a moustache, you will usually see in it quite a number of moustache hairs."

"I have not noticed that," said Mr Penfield, "having no moustache myself. And what else did you obtain by your curious researches?"

"The other result was really very remarkable indeed. From every one of the boxes I obtained particles – in some cases only one or two, in others quite a number – of the very characteristic dust which is shed by worm-eaten furniture."

"Dear me!" exclaimed Mr Penfield. "And you were actually able to identify it! Astonishing! Now, I suppose – you must excuse me," he interpolated with an apologetic smile, "but I am walking in an enchanted land and am ready to expect and believe in any marvels – I suppose you were not able to infer the character of the piece of furniture?"

"Not with anything approaching certainty," replied Thorndyke. "I formed certain opinions; but they are necessarily speculative, and we are dealing with evidence."

"Quite so, quite so," said Mr Penfield. "Let us avoid speculation. But I now begin to see the inwardness of the floor-sweeping. You were tracing this mysterious dust to its place of origin."

"Exactly. And, naturally, I began with Mr Hollis' premises – though the forgery of the seals seemed to put him outside the field of inquiry."

"Yes; he would hardly have needed to forge his own seal."

"No. But I examined his premises thoroughly, with an entirely negative result. There was no one on them with a moustache of any kind; the dust from the floors showed not a particle of the wood-dust, and I could find no piece of furniture in his house which could have yielded such dust.

"I then proceeded to Mr Woodstock's office, and there I obtained abundant samples both of hairs and wood-dust. I found Osmond's hair-brushes in his desk, and from them obtained a number of moustache hairs which, on careful comparison, appear to be identically similar to those found in the boxes."

"Ha!" exclaimed Mr Penfield in what sounded like a tone of disapproval. "And as to the wood-dust?"

"I obtained traces of it from every part of the floor. But it was very unequally distributed; so unequally as to associate it quite distinctly with a particular individual. I obtained abundant traces of it from the floor around that individual's desk, and even more from the inside of the desk; whereas, from the interiors of the other desks I recovered hardly a particle."

"You refer to a 'particular individual.' Do you mean John Osmond?"

"No," replied Thorndyke. "Osmond's desk contained no wood-dust."

"Ha!" exclaimed Mr Penfield in what sounded very like a tone of satisfaction.

"As to the individual referred to," said Thorndyke, "I think that, for the present, it might be better – "

"Certainly," Mr Penfield interrupted emphatically, "certainly. It will be much better to mention no names. After all, it is but a coincidence, though undoubtedly a striking one. But we must keep an open mind."

"That is what I feel," said Thorndyke. "It is an impressive fact, but there is the possibility of some fallacy. Nevertheless it is the most promising clue that offers, and I shall endeavour to follow it up."

"Undoubtedly," Mr Penfield agreed, warmly. "It indicates a new line of inquiry adapted to your peculiar gifts, though to me I must confess it only adds a new complication to this mystery. And I do really find this a most perplexing case. Perhaps you do not?"

"I do, indeed," replied Thorndyke. "It bristles with contradictions and inconsistencies. Take the case against Osmond. On the one hand it is in the highest degree convincing. The robberies coincide in time with his presence in the office. His disappearance coincides with the discovery of the robbery; and then in the rifled boxes we find a number of hairs from his moustache."

"Can you prove that they are actually his?" Mr Penfield asked.

"No," Thorndyke replied. "But I have not the slightest doubt that they are, and I think they would be accepted by a jury – in conjunction with the other circumstances – as good evidence. These facts seem to point quite clearly to his guilt. On the other hand, the wood-dust is not connected with him at all. None was found in his desk or near it; and when I examined his rooms – which by a fortunate chance I was able to do – I not only found no trace whatever of wood-dust, but from the appearance of the place I was convinced that the boxes had not been opened there. And furthermore, so far as I could ascertain, the man's personality was singularly out of character with a subtle, cunning, avaricious crime of this type; not that I would lay great stress on that point."

"No," agreed Mr Penfield; "the information is too scanty. But tell me: you inferred that the boxes were not opened in Woodstock's office, but were taken away and opened in some other place. How did you arrive at that?"

"By means of the wood-dust. The place in which those boxes were opened and refilled must have contained some worm-eaten wooden object which yielded that very distinctive dust, and yielded it in very large quantities. But there was no such object on Woodstock's premises. I searched the house from top to bottom and could not find a single piece of worm-eaten woodwork."

"And may I inquire – mind, I am not asking for details – but may I inquire whether you have any idea as to the whereabouts of that piece of furniture?"

"I have a suspicion," replied Thorndyke. "But there is my dilemma. I have a strong suspicion as to the place where it might be found; but, unfortunately, that place is not accessible for exploration. So, at present, I am unable either to confirm or disprove my theory."

"But supposing you were able to ascertain definitely that the piece of furniture is where you believe it to be? What then?"

"In that case," Thorndyke replied, "provided that this worm-eaten object turned out to be the kind of object that I believe it to be, I should be disposed to apply for a search-warrant."

"To search for what?" demanded Mr Penfield.

"The stolen property – and certain other things."

"But surely the stolen property has been disposed of long ago."

"I think," replied Thorndyke, "that there are reasons for believing that it has not. But I would rather not go into that question at present."

"No," said Mr Penfield. "We agreed to avoid speculative questions. And now, as I think I have exhausted your supply of information, it is my turn to contribute. I have a rather startling piece of news to communicate. John Osmond is dead."

Thorndyke regarded Mr Penfield with raised eyebrows. "Have you heard any particulars?" he asked.

"Woodstock sent me a copy of the police report, of which I will send you a duplicate if you would like one. Briefly, it amounts to this: Osmond was traced to Bristol, and it was suspected that he had embarked on a ship which traded from that port to the west coast of Africa. That ship was seen, some weeks later, at anchor off the African coast at a considerable distance from her usual trading-ground, and on her arrival at her station – a place called Half-Jack on the Grain Coast – was boarded by an inspector of constabulary who had been sent up from the Gold Coast to make inquiries. To him the captain admitted that he had landed a passenger from Bristol at a place called Adaffia in the Bight of Benin. The passenger was a man named Walker whose description agreed completely with that of Osmond. Thereupon, the inspector returned to Accra to report; and from thence was sent down to Adaffia with an armed party to find the man and arrest him.

"But he was too late. He arrived only in time to find a trader named Larkom setting up a wooden cross over the grave. Walker had died early that morning or the night before."

"Is it quite clear that this man was really John Osmond?"

"Quite," replied Mr Penfield. "Larkom had just painted the name John Osmond on the cross. It appeared that Osmond, when he realized that he was dying, had disclosed his real name and asked to have it written above his grave – naturally enough. One doesn't want to be buried under an assumed name."

"No," Thorndyke agreed. "The grave is a sufficiently secure sanctuary. Does the report say what was the cause of death?"

"Yes, though it doesn't seem very material. He is said to have died from blackwater fever – whatever that may be."

"It is a peculiarly malignant type of malaria," Thorndyke explained; and he added after a pause: "Well, 'the White Man's Grave' is a pestilential region, but poor Osmond certainly wasted no time in dying. How does his death affect our inquiry?"

Mr Penfield took snuff viciously. "Woodstock's view is – I can hardly speak of it with patience – that as the thief is dead, the inquiry comes automatically to an end."

"And Hollis, I take it, does not agree?"

"Indeed he does not. He wants his property traced and recovered."

"And do I understand that you instruct me to proceed with my investigations?"

"Most certainly; especially in view of what you have told me."

"I am glad of that," said Thorndyke. "I dislike exceedingly leaving an inquiry uncompleted. In fact, I should have completed the case for my own satisfaction and as a matter of public policy. For if Osmond stole these gems, the fact ought to be proved lest any other person should be suspected; and if he did not, his character ought to be cleared as a matter of common justice."

"That is exactly my own feeling," said Mr Penfield. "And then, of course, there is the property. That ought to be recovered if possible, especially if, as you seem to think, it is still intact. And now," he added, draining his glass and rising, "it is time for me to depart. I have to thank you for a most interesting and pleasant evening."

As Thorndyke stood on the landing looking down upon his retreating guest, he was dimly aware of a presence on the stair above; and when he turned to re-enter his chambers, the presence materialized into the form of Polton. With silent and stealthy tread the "familiar spirit" stole down the stairs and followed his principal into the room, where, having closed both doors with a secret and portentous air, he advanced to the table.

"What have you got under your arm, Polton?" Thorndyke asked.

By way of reply, Polton regarded his employer with a smile of the most extraordinary crinkliness and began very deliberately to untie the string of a small parcel. From the latter he at length disengaged a kind of leathern wallet marked in gold lettering with what appeared to be a tradesman's name and address. This he bore, slowly and ceremoniously, to the table, where with a sudden movement he unrolled it, displaying a glittering constellation of metal buttons.

"Well done, Polton!" Thorndyke exclaimed. "What a man you are! Now, where might you have unearthed this relic?"

"I discovered it, sir," replied Polton, blushing with pleasure like a dried apricot, "in a little, old-fashioned tailor's trimming-shop in one of the courts off Carnaby Street. It is quite a well preserved specimen, sir."

"Yes, it is in wonderful condition, considering its age. Mr Wampole will be delighted with it. He will be set up with buttons for life. I think, Polton, it would add to his pleasure if you were to run down and make the presentation in person. Don't you?"

Polton's features crinkled to the point of obliteration. "I do, indeed, sir," he replied. "At his private residence, I think, sir."

"Certainly; at his private residence. And we shall have to find out at what time he usually returns from the office."

"We shall, sir," Polton agreed; and thereupon proceeded to crinkle to a perfectly alarming extent.

CHAPTER SEVENTEEN

The Lapidary

In a small street hard by Clerkenwell Green is a small shop of antique and mouldy aspect, the modest window of which is so obscured by a coat of paint on the inside as to leave the unaided observer to speculate in vain as to the kind of wares concealed within. A clue to the mystery is, however, furnished by an inscription in faded gilt lettering on the fascia above, which sets forth that the tenant's name is Lambert and that his vocation is that of a lapidary and dealer in precious stones.

On a certain afternoon, a few days after his interview with Mr Penfield, Dr John Thorndyke might have been seen to turn into the small street with a brisk, decisive air suggestive of familiarity with the neighbourhood and a definite purpose; and the latter suggestion would have been confirmed when, having arrived at the shop, he pushed open the door and entered. A faded, elderly man confronted him across the counter and inquired what might be his pleasure.

"I have called," said Thorndyke, "to make some inquiries concerning artificial stones."

"Did you want them for theatrical purposes?"

"No. Those are usually cast or moulded, aren't they?"

"Sometimes. Not as a rule. Can't get much sparkle out of moulded glass, you know. But what was the class of goods you were wanting?"

"I wanted a set of imitation gems made to given shapes and dimensions to form a collection such as might be suitable for purposes of instruction in a technical school."

"Would the shapes and dimensions have to be exact?"

"Yes, quite exact. They are intended to be copies of existing specimens and the settings are already made."

Thorndyke's answer seemed to occasion some surprise, for the man to whom he made it reflected profoundly for a few moments and then looked round at a younger man who was sorting samples from the stock at a side-bench.

"Odd, isn't it, Fred?" said the former.

"What is odd?" inquired Thorndyke.

"Why, you see, sir, we had someone come in only a few days ago making the very same inquiry. You remember him, Fred?"

"Yes, I remember him, Mr Lambert. Crinkly-faced little blighter."

"That's the man," said Mr Lambert. "I rather wondered at the time what his game was. Seemed to know a lot about the trade, too; but you have to mind what you are about making strass facsimiles."

"Of course you have," Thorndyke agreed, "especially when you are dealing with these crinkly-faced people."

"Exactly," said Mr Lambert. "But, of course, sir, in your case we know where we are."

"It is very good of you to say so," rejoined Thorndyke. "But I gather that you are not often asked to make sets of facsimile imitations."

"No, not sets. Occasionally we get an order from a jeweller to duplicate the stones of a diamond necklace or tiara to be used while the original is in pawn, or for safety in a crowd. But not a collection such as you are speaking of. In fact, during all the thirty-five years that I have been in the business, I have only had one order of the kind. That was between four and five years ago. A gentleman named Scofield wanted a set to offer some local museum, and he wanted them to be copies of stones in various public collections. He got the shapes and dimensions from the catalogues – so I understood."

"Did you execute the order?"

"Yes; and quite a big order it was."

"I wonder," said Thorndyke, "whether he happened to have selected any of the stones that are on my list. Mine are mostly from the Hollis collection. But I suppose you don't keep records of the work you do?"

"I expect all the particulars are in the order book. We can soon see."

He went over to a shelf on which was ranged a row of books of all ages, and running his hand along, presently drew out a leather-backed volume which he laid on the counter and opened.

"Ah! Here we are," said he, after a brief search. "Mr Scofield. Perhaps you would like to glance over his list. You see there are quite a lot of them."

He pushed the book across to Thorndyke, who had already produced a note-book from his pocket, the entries in which he now proceeded to compare with those in Mr Scofield's list. Mr Lambert watched him with close interest as he placed his finger on one after another of the entries in the book, and presently remarked:

"You seem to be finding some duplicates of your own lot."

"It is most remarkable," said Thorndyke – "and yet perhaps it isn't – but his selection coincides with mine in over a dozen instances. May I tick them off with a pencil?"

"Do, by all means," said Lambert. "Then I can copy them out afterwards – that is, if you want me to get the duplicates cut."

"I do, certainly. I will mark off those that I want, and when you have cut those, I will give you a further list. And I may add that I should like you to use the best-quality strass that you can get. I want them to be as much like real stones as possible."

"I should do that in any case for good cut work," said Lambert; and he added: "I suppose there is no special hurry for these stones?"

"None at all," replied Thorndyke. "If you will send me a card to this address when they are ready, I will call for them. Or, perhaps, if I pay for them now you could send them to me."

The latter alternative was adopted, and while the prices were being reckoned up and the bill was being made out, Thorndyke occupied himself in making, in shorthand, a copy of the list in the order book. He had finished and put away his note-book by the time the account was ready; when, having laid a visiting-card on the counter, he paid his score and began to put on his gloves.

"By the way," said he, "your customer would not happen to be Mr Scofield of the Middle Temple, I suppose?"

"I really couldn't say, sir," replied Lambert. "He never gave any address. But I had an idea that he came up from the country. He used to give his orders and then he would call, at longish intervals, and take away as many of the stones as were ready. He was a middle-aged man, a bit on the shady side; tallish, clean-shaved, iron-grey hair, and not too much of it."

"Ah, then I don't think that would be the same Mr Scofield. It is not a very uncommon name. Good-afternoon."

With this Thorndyke took up his stick and, emerging from the shop, set a course southward for the Temple, walking quickly, as was his wont, with a long, swinging stride, and turning over in his mind the bearings of what he had just learned. In reality he had not learned much. Still, he had added one or two small items to his stock of facts, and in circumstantial evidence every added fact gives additional weight to all the others. He sorted out his new acquirements and considered each in turn.

In the first place, it was clear that Mr Scofield's collection was a facsimile of the missing part of Hollis'. The list in Lambert's book was identical with the one in his own pocket-book; which, in its turn, was a list of the forgeries. The discovery of the maker of the forgeries (a result of extensive preliminary scouting on the part of Polton) was of little importance at the moment, though it might be of great value in the future. For, since the forgeries existed, it was obvious that someone must have made them. Much more to the point was the identity of the person for whom they were made. Whoever "Mr Scofield" might have been, he certainly was not John Osmond. And this set Thorndyke once more puzzling over the really perplexing feature of this curious case. Why had Osmond absconded? That he had really done so, Thorndyke had no doubt, though he would have challenged the use of the word by anyone else. But why? There had been nothing to implicate him in any way. Beyond the hairs in the boxes – of which he could not have known and which were not at all conclusive – there was nothing to implicate him now but his own flight. All the other evidence seemed to point away from him. Yet he had absconded.

Thorndyke put to himself the various possibilities and argued them one at a time. There were three imaginable hypotheses. First, that Osmond had committed the robbery alone and unassisted; second, that he had been an accessory or worked with a confederate; third, that he had had no connection with the robbery at all.

The first hypothesis could be excluded at once, for Mr Scofield must have been, at least, an accessory; and Mr Scofield was not John Osmond. The second was much more plausible. It not only agreed with the known facts, but might even furnish some sort of explanation of the flight. Thus, supposing Osmond to have planned and executed the robbery with the aid of a confederate in the expectation that, even if discovered, it would never be traced to the office, might it not have been that, when, unexpectedly, it was so traced, Osmond had decided to take the onus on himself, and by absconding, divert suspicion from his accomplice? The thing was quite conceivable. It was entirely in agreement with Osmond's character as pictured by Mr Wampole; that of a rash, impulsive, rather unreasonable man. And if it were further assumed that there had been known to him some incriminating fact which he had expected to leak out, but which had not leaked out, then the whole set of facts, including the flight, would appear fairly consistent.

Nevertheless, consistent as the explanation might be, Thorndyke did not find it convincing. The aspect of Osmond's rooms, with their suggestion of hardy simplicity and a robust asceticism, still lingered in his memory. Nor had he forgotten the impressive face of the gentlewoman whose portrait he had looked on with such deep interest in those rooms. These were, perhaps, but mere impressions, of no evidential weight; but yet they refused to be lightly dismissed.

As to the third hypothesis, that Osmond had not been concerned in the robbery at all, it would have been quite acceptable but for the irreconcilable fact of the flight. That seemed, beyond any question, to connect him with the crime. Of course it was conceivable that he might have some other reason for his flight. But no such reason had been suggested; whereas the circumstances in which he had elected to disappear – at the exact moment when the crime had been traced to the office – made it idle to look for any other explanation. And so, once more, Thorndyke found himself involved in a tangle of contradictions from which he could see no means of escape.

The end of his train of thought coincided with his arrival at the entry to his chambers. Ascending the stairs, he became aware of a light above as from an open door; and a turn of the staircase showed him that door – his own – framing a small, restless figure.

"Why, Polton," he exclaimed, "you are early, aren't you? I didn't expect you for another hour or two."

"Yes, sir," replied Polton, "I got away early. But I've seen it, sir. And you were perfectly right – absolutely right. It is a sparrow-hawk, stuck in a little log of cherry wood. Exactly as you said."

"I didn't say a sparrowhawk," Thorndyke objected.

"You said, sir, that it was a stake or a bec iron or some kind of small anvil, and a sparrowhawk is a kind of small anvil."

"Very well, Polton," Thorndyke conceded. "But tell me how you managed it and why you are home so early."

"Well, sir, you see," Polton explained, fidgeting about the room as if he were afflicted with St Vitus' dance, "it came off much easier than I expected. I got to his house a good hour too soon. His housekeeper opened the door and wanted me to call again. But I said I had come down from London and would like to wait. And then I told her about the buttons and explained how valuable they were and asked her if she would like to see them; and she said she would. So she took me upstairs to his sitting-room and there I undid the parcel and showed her the buttons.

"Then I got talking to her about the rooms; remarked what a nice place Mr Wampole had got and how beautifully it was kept."

"Really, Polton!" Thorndyke chuckled, "I had no idea you were such a humbug."

"No more had I, sir," replied Polton, with a complacent crinkle. "But you see, it was a case of necessity; and besides, the room was wonderfully neat and tidy. Well, I got her talking about the house, and very proud she seemed to be of it. So I asked her all the questions I could think of: whether she had a good kitchen and whether there was pipe water or a pump in the scullery, and so on. And she got so interested and pleased with herself that presently she offered to let me see over the house if I liked, and of course, I said that there was nothing in the world that I should like better. So she took me down and showed me the kitchen and the scullery and her own little sitting-room and a couple of big cupboards for linen and stores, and it was all as neat and clean as a new pin. Then we went upstairs again, and as we passed a door on the landing she said, 'That's a little room that Mr Wampole does his tinkering in.'

" 'Ah!' says I, 'but I'll warrant that room isn't quite so neat and tidy. I do a bit of tinkering myself and I know what a workroom looks like.'

" 'Oh, it isn't so bad,' says she. 'Mr Wampole is a very orderly man. You shall see for yourself, if it isn't locked. He usually locks it when he has a job in hand.'

"Well, it wasn't locked; so she opened the door and in we went; and the very moment I put my head inside, I saw it – on the table that he used for a bench. It was set in a little upright log, such as you get from the trimmings of fruit trees. And, my word! it was fairly riddled – like a sponge – and where it stood on the bench there was a regular ring of powder round it.

" 'That's a rare old block that his anvil is set in,' says I, going across to look at it.

" 'Not so old as you'd think,' says she. 'He got it about five years ago, when we had the cherry tree lopped. You can see the tree in the garden from this window.'

"She went over to the window and I followed her; and as I passed the bench I picked up a pinch of the dust between my finger and thumb and put my hand in my pocket, where I had a pill-box that I had brought in case I should get a chance to collect a sample. As we were looking out of the window, I managed to work the lid off the pill-box and drop the pinch of dust in and slip the lid on again. Then I was happy; and as I had done all that I came to do, I thought I would rather like to clear off."

"Why?" asked Thorndyke.

"Well, sir," said Polton in a slightly apologetic tone, "the fact is that I wasn't very anxious to meet Mr Wampole. It wouldn't have been quite pleasant, under the circumstances, to present those buttons and have him thanking me and shaking my hand. I should have felt rather like Pontius Pilate."

"Why Pontius Pilate?" asked Thorndyke.

"Wasn't he the chap – or was it Judas Iscariot? At any rate, I had a sudden feeling that I didn't want to hand him those buttons. So I looked up my timetable and discovered that I couldn't wait to see him. 'But, however,' I said, 'it doesn't matter. I can leave the buttons with you to give him; and I will leave my card, too, so that he can send me a line if he wants to.' So with that I gave her the roll of buttons and nipped off to the station, just in time to catch the earlier train to town. I hope I didn't do wrong, sir."

"Not at all," replied Thorndyke, heartily. "I quite understand your feeling on the matter; in fact, I think I should have done the same. Shall we look at that pill-box? I didn't expect such good fortune as to get a specimen."

Polton produced the little box, and having opened it to make sure the contents were intact, handed it to Thorndyke, who forthwith made a preliminary inspection of the dust with the aid of his lens.

"Yes," he reported, "it is evidently the same dust as was in the other samples, so that aspect of the case is complete. I must compliment you, Polton, on the masterly way in which you carried out your really difficult and delicate mission. You have made a brilliant success of it. And you have been equally successful in another direction. I have just come from Lambert's, where I had a very instructive interview. You were perfectly correct. It was Lambert who cut those dummy stones."

"I felt sure it must be," said Polton, "when I had been round to those other lapidaries. He seems to be the only one who specializes in cutting strass gems. But did you find out who the customer was, sir?"

"I found out who he was not," replied Thorndyke, "and that was as far as it seemed wise to go. The rest of the inquiry – the actual identification – will be better carried out by the police. I think if we give Mr Lambert's address, with certain other particulars, to Mr Superintendent Miller, we can safely leave him to do what is necessary."

Chapter Eighteen

The End of the Clue

It was nearing the hour of six in the evening when five men made their appearance on the stretch of pavement on which Mr Woodstock's office door opened. They did not, however, arrive in a solid body, but in two groups – of two and three, respectively – which held no mutual communication, but kept within easy distance of one another. The larger group consisted of Dr Thorndyke, Mr Lambert, the lapidary, and a tall, powerful man of distinctly military appearance and bearing; the smaller group consisted of a uniformed inspector of the local police and Mr Lambert's assistant "Fred".

"I hope our friends are punctual in coming out," Thorndyke remarked as he stood with his two companions ostensibly inspecting the stock in a bookseller's window. "If we have to wait about long, we are likely to attract notice. Even a bookseller's window won't explain our presence indefinitely."

"No," the tall man agreed. "But there is a good deal of traffic in this street to cover us up and prevent us from being too conspicuous. All I hope is that he will take things quietly – that is, if he is the right man. You are sure you would know him again, Mr Lambert?"

"Perfectly sure, Superintendent," was the confident reply. "I remember him quite well. I have a good memory for faces, and so has my man, Fred. But I tell you frankly that neither of us relishes this job."

"I sympathize with you, Mr Lambert," said Thorndyke. "I don't relish it myself. We are both martyrs to duty. Ah! Here is somebody coming out. That is Mr Woodstock. I mustn't let him see me."

He turned to the shop-window, presenting his back to the street, and the solicitor walked quickly past without noticing him. A few moments later Mr Hepburn emerged and walked away in the opposite direction, furtively observed by Fred, who, with his companion, occupied a position on the farther side of the office door. He was followed after a short interval by two young men, apparently clerks, who walked away together up the street and were narrowly inspected by Fred as they passed. Close on their heels came an older man, who emerged with an air of business and, turning towards the three watchers, approached at a brisk walk.

"That the man, Mr Lambert?" the superintendent asked in a low, eager tone, as the newcomer drew near.

"No," was the reply. "Not a bit like him."

Two more men came out, at both of whom Mr Lambert shook his head. Then came a youth of about eighteen, and after his emergence an interval of several minutes, during which no one else appeared.

"That can't be the lot," said the superintendent, with a glance of anxious inquiry at Thorndyke.

"It isn't unless some of them are absent," the latter replied. "That would be rather a disaster."

"It would, indeed," the superintendent replied. "What do you say, Doctor, to going in – that is, if the door isn't locked?"

"Not yet, Miller," Thorndyke replied. "Of course we can't wait indefinitely, but, if possible – Ah! here is someone else."

As he spoke, an elderly man came out and stood for a few moments looking up and down the street. Then he turned and very deliberately locked the door behind him.

"That's the man!" Lambert exclaimed. "That is Mr Scofield."

"You are quite sure?" demanded Miller.

"Positive," was the reply. "I recognized him instantly"; and in confirmation, Fred was signalling with a succession of emphatic nods.

Superintendent Miller cast an interrogative glance at Thorndyke.

"Your man, too?" he asked.

"Yes," replied Thorndyke. "Mr Wampole."

The unconscious subject of these observations, having locked the door, slowly pocketed the key and began to walk at a leisurely pace and with a thoughtful air towards the three observers, closely followed by Fred and the inspector. Suddenly, he became aware of Thorndyke; and the beginnings of a smile of recognition had appeared on his face when he caught sight of Mr Lambert. Instantly, the smile froze; and as Superintendent Miller bore down on him with evident purpose, he halted irresolutely and cast a quick glance behind him. At the sight of Fred – whom he evidently recognized at once – and the inspector, his bewilderment changed to sheer panic, and he darted out into the road close behind a large covered van that was drawn up at the kerb.

"Look out!" roared Miller, as Wampole passed the rear of the van; but the only effect of the warning was to cause the fugitive to cast a terrified glance backward over his shoulder as he ran. And then, in an instant, came the catastrophe. An empty lorry was coming up the street at a brisk trot, but its approach had been hidden from Wampole by the van. As the unfortunate man ran out from behind the latter, still looking back, he charged straight in front of the horses. The driver uttered a yell of dismay and tugged at the reins; but the affair was over in a moment. The pole of the lorry struck Wampole at the side of the neck with the force of a battering-ram and flung him violently down on the road, where he lay motionless as the ponderous vehicle swerved past within an inch of his head.

A number of bystanders immediately gathered round, and the carman, having pulled up the lorry, climbed down from his high perch and came hurrying, white-faced and breathless, across the road. Through the gathering crowd the inspector made his way and piloted Thorndyke to the fatal spot.

"Looks a pretty bad case, sir," said he, casting a perturbed eye down at the motionless form, which lay where it had fallen. "Will you just have a glance at him?"

Thorndyke stooped over the prostrate figure and made a brief – a very brief – inspection. Then he stood up and announced curtly:

"He is dead. The blow dislocated his neck."

"Ha!" the inspector exclaimed. "I was afraid he was – though perhaps it is all for the best. At any rate, we've done with him now."

"I haven't," said Miller. "I've got a search-warrant; and I shall want his keys. We will come along with you to the mortuary. Can't very well get them here."

At this moment the carman presented himself, wiping his pale face with a large red handkerchief.

"Shockin' affair, this, Inspector," he said, huskily. "Poor old chap. I couldn't do no more than what I done. You could see that for yourself. He was down almost as soon as I see 'im."

"Yes," the inspector agreed, "he ran straight at the pole. It was no fault of yours. At least, that's my opinion," he added with official caution. "Just help me and the constable here to lift the body on to your lorry and then he will show you the way to the mortuary. You understand, Borman," he continued, addressing the constable. "You are to take the body to the mortuary, and wait there with the lorry until I come. I shall be there in a minute or two."

The constable saluted, and the inspector, having made a note of the carman's name and address, stood by while the ghastly passenger was lifted up on to the rough floor. Then, as the lorry moved off, he turned to Miller and remarked:

"Your friend Mr Lambert looks rather poorly, Superintendent. It has been a bit of a shock for him. Hadn't you better take him somewhere and give him a little pick-me-up? We shall want him and his assistant at the mortuary, you know, for a regular identification."

"Yes," agreed Miller, glancing sympathetically at the white-faced, shaking lapidary, "he does look pretty bad, poor old chap. Thinks it's all his doing, I expect. Well, you show us the way to a suitable place."

"The Blue Lion Hotel is just round the corner," said the inspector, "and it is on our way."

To the Blue Lion he accordingly led the way, while Thorndyke followed, assisting and trying to comfort the shaken and self-reproachful Lambert. From the hotel they proceeded to the mortuary, where Lambert having, almost with tears, identified the body of "Mr Scofield," and the dead man's keys having been handed to Superintendent Miller, the latter departed with Thorndyke, leaving the inspector to conduct the carman to the police-station.

"You seem to be pretty confident," said Miller as they set forth, guided by Polton's written directions, "that the stuff is still there."

"Not confident, Miller," was the reply, "but I think it is there. At any rate, it is worth while to make the search. There may be other things to see besides the stones."

"Ah!" Miller agreed doubtfully. "Well, I hope you are right."

They walked on for some five minutes when Thorndyke, having again referred to his notes, halted before a pleasant little house in a quiet street on the outskirts of the town, and entering the front garden, knocked at the door. It was opened by a motherly-looking, middle-aged woman to whom Miller briefly but courteously explained his business and exhibited his warrant.

"Good gracious!" she exclaimed. "What on earth makes you think the missing property is here?"

"I can't go into particulars," replied Miller. "Here is the search-warrant."

"Yes, I see. But couldn't you wait until Mr Wampole comes home? He is due now, and his tea is waiting for him in his sitting-room."

Miller cleared his throat. Then, hesitatingly and with manifest discomfort, he broke the dreadful news.

The poor woman was thunderstruck. For a few moments she seemed unable to grasp the significance of what Miller was telling her; then, when the horrid reality burst upon her, she turned away quickly, flinging out her hand towards the staircase, ran into her room, and shut the door.

The two investigators ascended the stairs in silence with an unconsciously stealthy tread. On the landing they paused, and as he softly opened the three doors and peered into the respective apartments, Miller remarked in an undertone: "Rather gruesome, Doctor, isn't it? I feel like a tomb-robber. Which one shall we go in first?"

This one on the left seems to be the workshop," replied Thorndyke. "Perhaps we had better take that first, though it isn't likely that the gems are in there."

They entered the workshop, and Thorndyke looked about it with keen interest. On a small table, fitted with a metal-worker's bench-vice, stood the "sparrowhawk," like a diminutive smith's anvil, in its worm-eaten block, surrounded by a ring of pinkish-yellow dust. A Windsor chair, polished by years of use, was evidently the one on which the workman had been accustomed to sit at his bench; and close inspection showed a powdering of the pink dust on the rails and other protected parts. On the right-hand side of the room was a small woodworker's bench, and on the wall above it a rack filled with chisels and other small tools. There was a tool cabinet ingeniously made from grocer's boxes, and a set of shelves on which the glue-pot and various jars and small appliances were stowed out of the way.

"Seems to have been a pretty handy man," remarked Miller, pulling out one of the drawers of the cabinet and disclosing a set of files.

"Yes," Thorndyke agreed; "he appears to have been quite a good workman. It is all very neat and orderly. This is rather interesting," he added, reaching down from the shelf a box containing two earthenware cells filled with a blue liquid, and a wide jar with similar contents.

"Electric battery, isn't it?" said Miller. "What is the point of interest about it?"

"It is a two-cell Daniell's battery," replied Thorndyke, "the form of battery most commonly used for making small electrotypes. And in evidence that it was used for that purpose, here is the jar filled with copper sulphate solution, forming the tank, with the copper electrode in position. Moreover, I see on the shelf what look like some gutta-percha moulds." He reached one down and examined it. "Yes," he continued, "this is a squeeze from a coin. Apparently he had been making electrotype copies of coins; probably some that had been lent to him."

"Well," said Miller, "what about it?"

"The point is that whoever stole those gems made an electrotype copy of Hollis' seal. We now have evidence that Wampole was able to make electrotypes and did actually make them."

"It would be more to the point if we could find the gems themselves," rejoined Miller.

"Yes, that is undoubtedly true," Thorndyke admitted; "and as we are not likely to find them in here, perhaps we had better examine the sitting-room. That is much the most probable place."

"I don't quite see why," said Miller. "But I expect you do," and with this he followed Thorndyke across the landing to the adjoining room.

"Good Lord!" he exclaimed, stopping to gaze at the neatly-arranged tea-service on the table, "just look at this! Uncanny isn't it? Teapot under the cosy – quite hot still. And what's under this cover? Crumpets, by gum! And him lying there in the mortuary! Fairly gives one the creeps. Don't you feel a bit like a ghoul, Doctor?"

"I might, perhaps," Thorndyke replied, dryly, "if there had been no such person as John Osmond."

"True," said Miller. "He did do the dirty on Osmond, and that's the fact – unless Osmond was in it, too. Looks rather as if he was; but you don't seem to think so."

"As a mere guess, I do not; but it is a puzzling case in some respects."

He stood for a while looking about the room, letting his eye travel slowly along the papered walls as if in search of a possible hiding-place. From the general survey he proceeded to the consideration of details, turning the door-key – which was on the inside and turned smoothly and silently – and examining and trying a solid-looking brass bolt.

"You notice, Miller," he said, "that he seems to have been in the habit of locking and bolting himself in; and that the bolt has been fixed on comparatively recently. That is somewhat significant."

"Yes; seems to suggest that the swag was hidden here at one time, if it isn't here now. I suppose we may as well look through these cabinets, just as a matter of form, for he won't have hidden the stuff in them."

He produced the dead man's bunch of keys, and having unlocked the hinged batten which secured the drawers of one, pulled out the top drawer.

"Coins," he announced; "silver coins. No! By jingo, they're copper, plated, and no backs to them. Just look at that!"

"Yes," said Thorndyke, taking the specimen from him, "a silver-faced copper electro, taken, no doubt, from a borrowed coin. Not a bad way of forming a collection. Probably, if he had been skilful enough to join the two faces and make a complete coin, it would have been the original owner who had the electrotype, and Wampole would have kept the genuine coin. While you are going through the cabinets, I think I will explore those two cupboards. They seem to me to have possibilities."

The cupboards in question filled the recesses on either side of the fireplace. Each cupboard was built in two stages – a lower about three feet in height, and an upper extending nearly to the ceiling. Thorndyke began with the right-hand one, throwing open both its pairs of folding doors, after unlocking them with the keys, handed to him by Miller. Then he cleared the shelves of their contents – principally stamp albums and back numbers of *The*

Connoisseur – until the cupboard was completely empty, when he proceeded to a systematic survey of the interior, rapping with his knuckles on every part of the back and sides and testing each shelf by a vigorous pull. Standing on a chair, he inspected the top and ascertained, by feeling it simultaneously from above and below, that it consisted of only a single board.

Having thoroughly explored the upper stage with no result, he next attacked the lower story, rapping at the back, sides, and floor and pulling at the solitary shelf, which was as immovable as the others. Then he tested the ceiling or top by feeling it with one hand while the other was placed on the floor of the upper story.

Meanwhile, Miller, who had been systematically examining the row of home-made cabinets, shut the last of the multitudinous drawers and stood up.

"Well," he announced, "I've been right through the lot, Doctor, and there's nothing in any of them – nothing, I mean, but trash. This last one is full of buttons – brass buttons, if you'll believe it. How are you getting on? Had any luck?"

"Nothing definite, so far," replied Thorndyke, who was, at the moment, taking a measurement of the height of the lower story with a tape-measure; "but there is something here that wants explaining. The internal height of the lower part of this cupboard is two feet ten inches; but the height from the floor of the lower part to the floor of the top part is three feet one inch. So there seems to be a space of three inches, less the thickness of two boards, between the ceiling of the lower part and the floor of the top part. That is not a normal state of affairs."

"No, by jingo!" exclaimed the superintendent. "Ordinarily, the floor of the top part would be the ceiling of the bottom part. Carpenters don't waste wood like that. Either the floor or the ceiling is false. Let us see if we can get a move on the floor. That is the most likely, as it would be the lid of the space between the two."

He passed his hands over the board, feeling for a yielding spot, and craned in, searching for some indication of a joint, as he made heavy pressure on the edges and corners. But the floor showed no sign whatever of a tendency to move. He was about to transfer his attention to the ceiling underneath when Thorndyke stopped him.

"Wait," said he. "Here is another abnormal feature. This moulding along the front of the door is fastened on with three screws. They have been painted over with the rest of the moulding, but you can make out the slots quite plainly."

"Well?" queried Miller.

"Carpenters don't fix mouldings on with screws. They use nails and punch them in with a 'nail-set' and stop the holes with putty. Moreover, if you look closely at these screw-heads, you can see that they have been turned at some time since this moulding was painted."

As the superintendent stooped to verify this observation, Thorndyke produced from his pocket a small leather pouch of portable tools from which he took a screwdriver and the universal handle. Having fitted them together, he inserted the screwdriver into the slot of the middle screw and gave a turn.

"Ah!" said he. "This screw has been greased. Do you see how easily it turns?"

He rotated the tool rapidly, and as the screw emerged he picked it out and exhibited it to Miller.

"Not a trace of rust, you see, although the paint is some years old."

He laid it down and turned to the left-hand screw, which he extracted with similar ease. As he drew it out of its hole, the moulding became visibly loose, though still supported by the mitre; but when the last screw was extracted, the length of moulding came away in his hand, showing the free front edge of the floor, or bottom-board. This Thorndyke grasped with both hands and gave a steady pull, when the board slid forward easily, revealing a cavity about two inches deep.

"My eye!" exclaimed Miller, as Thorndyke drew the board right out. "This puts the lid on it – or rather takes the lid off."

He stood for a moment gazing ecstatically into the cavity, and especially at a collection of small, flat boxes that were neatly packed into it; then he grabbed up one of the boxes, and sliding back the hooked catch, raised the lid.

The expression of half-amused astonishment with which he viewed the open box was not entirely unjustified. As the receptacle for a robber's hoard, it was, to say the least, unconventional. The interior of the box was divided by partitions into a number of little square cells; and in each cell, reposing in a nest of black or white velvet according to its colour, was an unmounted gem.

The superintendent drew a deep breath. "Well," he exclaimed, "this knocks anything I've ever come across. Looks as if he never meant to sell the stuff at all. Just meant to keep it to gloat over. Is this what you expected to find, Doctor? I believe it is, from what you said."

"Yes," Thorndyke replied. "This agrees exactly with my theory of the robbery. I never supposed that he had stolen the gems for the purpose of selling them."

"Didn't you?" said Miller. "Now, I wonder why."

"My dear Miller," Thorndyke answered, with a smile, "the answer is before you in those cabinets which you have just examined. The man was a human magpie. He had a passion for acquiring and accumulating. He was the born, inveterate collector. Now, your half-baked collector will sell his treasures at a sufficient profit; but the real, thoroughbred collector, when once he has got hold, will never let go."

"Well," said Miller, who had been meanwhile lifting out the boxes and verifying their contents with a supercilious glance into each, "what is one man's meat is another man's poison. I can't see myself hoarding up expensive trash like this when I could swap it for good money."

"Nor I," said Thorndyke. "We both lack the acquisitive instinct. By the way, Miller, I think you will agree with me that all the circumstances point to Wampole having done this single-handed?"

"Undoubtedly," was the reply. "This is a 'one-man show,' if ever there was one."

"And, consequently, that this 'find' puts Osmond definitely out of the picture?"

"Yes," Miller agreed; "I think there is no denying that."

"Then you will also agree that, although we might wish it otherwise, the whole of the circumstances connected with this robbery must be made public. That is necessary as a matter of common justice to the memory of Osmond. He was publicly accused and he must be publicly exonerated."

"You are quite right, Doctor," Miller admitted, regretfully; "though it seems a pity, as the poor devil is dead and we've got the swag back. But, as you say, justice is justice. The innocent man ought to be cleared."

He took out the last remaining box, and having opened it and looked in, handed it to Thorndyke and cast a final glance into the cavity.

"Hallo!" he exclaimed, reaching into the back of the space, "here's something wrapped in paper – a key, by Jove!"

"Ah," said Thorndyke, taking it from him and inspecting it curiously, "the key of the strong-room. I recognize it. Quite a well-made key, too. I think we ought to hand that to Woodstock at once; and perhaps it would be as well to hand him the gems, too, and get his receipt for them. We don't want property of this value – something like a hundred thousand pounds – on our hands any longer than we can help. What do you say?"

"I say let us get rid of them at once if we can. But we must seal the boxes before we hand them over. And we must seal up these rooms until the property has been checked by Hollis. Let us put the books back in the cupboard and then, perhaps, you might go and find Woodstock while I keep guard on the treasure-trove."

They fell to work repacking the cupboard with the albums and magazines which they had taken out; and had nearly finished when they became aware of voices below and then of hurried footsteps on the stairs. A few moments later the door was flung open and Mr Woodstock and Mr Hepburn strode into the room.

"May I ask," the former demanded, glaring at Miller, "who the deuce you are and what is the meaning of this indecent invasion? The housekeeper tells me that you profess to have come here to search for missing property. What property are you searching for and what is your authority?"

The superintendent quietly explained who he was and exhibited his warrant.

"Ha!" exclaimed Woodstock with a withering glance at Thorndyke. "And I suppose you are making this ridiculous search at the suggestion of this gentleman?"

"You are quite correct, sir," replied Miller. "The warrant was issued on information supplied by Dr Thorndyke."

"Ha!" was the contemptuous comment. "You obtained a warrant to search the private residence of a man of irreproachable character who has been in my employ for something like a score of years! Well, have you made your search? And if so, what have you found?"

"We have completed the search," replied Miller, "and we have found what we believe to be the whole of the stolen property, and this key – which I understand is the key of your strong-room."

As the superintendent made this statement, in studiously matter-of-fact tones, Mr Woodstock's jaw fell and his eyes opened until he appeared the very picture of astonishment. Nor was his colleague, Mr Hepburn, less amazed; and for a space of some seconds the two solicitors stood speechless, looking from one another to the wooden-faced but secretly amused detective officer. Then Woodstock recovered somewhat and began to show signs of incredulity. But there was the key and there were the boxes; and it needed only a glance at the contents of the latter to put the matter beyond all question. Even Woodstock could not reject the evidence of his eyesight.

"But," he said with a puzzled air and with new-born civility, "what I cannot understand is how you came to connect Wampole with the robbery. Where did you obtain the evidence of his guilt?"

"I obtained it," Thorndyke replied, "from the dust which I collected from your office floor."

Mr Woodstock frowned impatiently and shook his head. "I am afraid," he said, coldly, "you are speaking a language that I don't understand. But no doubt you are right to keep your own counsel. What do you propose to do with this property?"

"We had proposed to hand it to you to hold pending the formal identification of the gems by Mr Hollis."

"Very well," said Woodstock; "but I shall want you to seal the boxes before I put them in my strong-room. I can't accept any responsibility as to the nature of the contents."

"They shall be sealed with my seal and the superintendent's," Thorndyke replied, with a faint smile; "and we will hope that the seals will give more security than they did last time."

This understanding having been arrived at, the boxes were gathered up and distributed among the party for conveyance to the office; and after a short halt on the landing while Miller locked the doors and sealed the keyholes, they went down the stairs, at the foot of which the tearful housekeeper was waiting. To her Mr Woodstock gave a brief and somewhat obscure explanation of the proceedings and the sealed doors, and then the party set forth for the office, the two solicitors leading and conversing in low tones as they went.

Arrived at their destination, the formalities were soon disposed of. Each box was tied up with red tape, sealed on the knot and on the opening of the lid. Then, when they had all been conveyed into the strong-room and locked in, Mr Woodstock wrote out a receipt for "eight boxes, containing real or artificial precious stones, said to be the property of James Hollis, Esq., and sealed with the seals of Dr Thorndyke and Superintendent Miller of the CID," and handed it to the latter officer.

"Of course," he said, "I shall communicate with Mr Hollis at once and ask him to remove these things from my custody. Probably he will write to you concerning them; but, in any case, I shall wash my hands of them when I get his receipt – and I shall take very good care that nobody ever saddles me with portable property of this kind again."

"A very wise resolution," said Thorndyke. "Perhaps you might point out to Mr Hollis that the boxes ought to be opened in the presence of witnesses, one of whom, at least, should be an expert judge of precious stones. I shall write to him tonight, before I leave the town, to the same effect. We all want the restitution to be definitely proved and acknowledged."

"That is perfectly true," Woodstock admitted; "and perhaps I had better make it a condition on which I allow him to take possession of the boxes."

The business being now concluded, Thorndyke and the superintendent prepared to take their departure. As they were turning away, Mr Hepburn addressed Thorndyke for the first time.

"May I ask," he said, hesitatingly, and with an air of some embarrassment, "whether the – er – the dust from our office floor or – er – any other observations of yours which led you to this surprising discovery seemed to suggest the existence of any – er – associate or – er – confederate?"

"No," Thorndyke replied, decisively. "All the evidence goes to show, very conclusively, that Wampole carried out this robbery single-handed. Of that I, personally, have no doubt; and I think the superintendent agrees with me."

"Undoubtedly," Miller assented. "I, too, am perfectly convinced that our late lamented friend played a lone hand. You are thinking of John Osmond?"

"Yes," Hepburn admitted, with a frown of perplexity. "I am. I am wondering what on earth can have induced him to go off in that extraordinary manner and at that particular time."

"So am I," said Thorndyke.

"Well, I'm afraid we shall never learn now," said Woodstock.

"Apparently not," Thorndyke agreed; "and yet – who knows?"

Chapter Nineteen

Thorndyke Connects the Links

Early in the afternoon – at forty minutes past twelve to be exact – of a sunny day in late spring, a tall, hatchet-faced man, accompanied by a small, sprightly lady, strolled at a leisurely pace through Pump Court and presently emerged into the cloisters, where he and his companion halted and looked about them.

"What a lovely old place it is!" the latter exclaimed, letting her eyes travel appreciatively from the porch of the Temple Church to the façade of Lamb Buildings. "Wouldn't you like to live here, Jack?"

"I should," he replied. "It is delightful to look at whichever way you turn; and there is such a delicious atmosphere of peace and quiet."

She laughed merrily. "Peace and quiet!" she repeated. "Peace, perfect peace. That has always been the desire of your heart, hasn't it? Oh, you old humbug! Before you had been here a month you would be howling for the sea and someone to fight." Here her glance lighted on the little wig shop, tucked away in its shady corner, and she drew him eagerly towards it. "Let us have a look at these wigs," said she. "I love wigs. It is a pity they have gone out of fashion for general use. They were such a let-off for bald-headed men. Which one do you like best, Jack? I rather fancy that big one – full-bottomed, I think, is its proper description. It would suit you to a T. It looks a little vacant with no face inside it, but it would have a grand appearance with your old nose sticking out in front. You'd look like the Great Sphinx – before they knocked his nose off. Don't you think you'd look rather well in it?"

"I don't know that I am particularly keen on wigs," he replied.

"Unless they are on the green," she suggested with a roguish smile.

He smiled at her in return, with a surprising softening of the rather rugged face, and then glanced at his watch.

"We mustn't loiter here staring at these ridiculous wigs," said he; "or we shall be late. Come along, you little babbler."

"Aye, aye, sir," she responded; "come along, it is," and they resumed their leisurely progress eastward across the court.

"I wonder," he said reflectively, "what sort of fellow Thorndyke is. Moderately human, I hope, because I want him to understand what I feel about all that he has done for us."

"I shall want to kiss him," said she.

"You had better not," he said, threateningly. "Still, short of that, I shall look to you to let him know how grateful, beyond all words, we are to him."

"You can trust me, Jack, darling," she replied, "to make it as clear as I can. When I think of it, I feel like crying. We owe him everything. He is our fairy-godmother."

"I don't think, Betty, dear," said Osmond with a faint grin, "that I should put it to him in exactly those words."

"I wasn't going to, you old guffin!" she exclaimed, indignantly. "But that is what I feel. He is a magician. A touch of his magic wand changed us in a moment from a pair of miserable, hopeless wretches into the pet children of Fortune, rich in everything we desired, and with the whole world of happiness at our feet. Oh, the wonder of it! Just think, darling! While you, with that ridiculous bee in your silly old bonnet, were doing everything that you could to make yourself – and me – miserable for life, here was this dry old lawyer, whose very existence we were unaware of, quietly, methodically working away to dig us out of our own entanglements. We can never even thank him properly."

"No. That's a fact," Osmond agreed. "And, in spite of Penfield's explanations, I can't in the least understand how he did it."

"Mr Penfield admits that he has only a glimmering of an idea himself; but as he has promised to extract a full explanation today, we can afford to bottle up our curiosity a little longer. This seems to be the house; yes, here we are: '1st Pair, Dr John Thorndyke.' "

She tripped up the stairs, followed by Osmond, and on the landing was confronted by the open "oak" and a closed inner door, adorned by a small but brilliantly burnished brass knocker.

"What a dinkie little knocker!" she exclaimed; and forthwith executed upon it a most impressive flourish. Almost instantly the door was opened by a tall, dignified man who greeted the visitors with a smile of quiet geniality.

"I have no need to ask who you are," he said, as, having saluted the lady, he shook hands with Osmond. "Your resemblance to your mother is quite remarkable."

"Yes," replied Osmond, a little mystified, nevertheless. "I was always considered to be very like her. I should like to think that the likeness is not only a superficial one."

Here he became aware of Mr Penfield, who had risen from an armchair and was advancing, snuff-box in hand, to greet them.

"It is very delightful to meet you both in these chambers," said he, with an old-fashioned bow. "A most interesting and significant meeting. Your husband's name has often been spoken here, Mrs Osmond, in the days when he was, to us, a mere abstraction of mystery."

"I've no doubt it has," said Betty, regarding the old lawyer with a mischievous smile, "and I don't suppose it was spoken of in very complimentary terms. But we are both absolutely bursting with gratitude and we don't know how to put our feelings into words."

"There is no occasion for gratitude," said Thorndyke. "It has been a mutual exchange of benefits. Your husband has provided us with a problem of the most thrilling interest, which we have had the satisfaction of solving, with the added pleasure of being of some service to you. We are really your debtors."

"Very kind of you to put it in that way," said Osmond, with a faint grin. "I seem to have played a sort of Falstaffian part. My deficiency of wit has been the occasion of wit in others."

"Well, Mr Osmond," Thorndyke rejoined, with an appreciative side-glance at the smiling Betty, "you seem to have had wit enough to bring your affairs to a very happy conclusion. But let us draw up to the table. I understand there are to be mutual explanations presently, so we had better fortify ourselves with nourishment."

He pressed an electric bell, and, as his guests took their places at the table, the door opened silently and Polton entered with demure gravity to post himself behind Thorndyke's chair and generally to supervise the proceedings.

Conversation was at first somewhat spasmodic and covered a good deal of mutual and curious inspection. Betty was frankly interested in her surroundings, in the homely simplicity of this queer bachelor household, in which everything seemed to be done so quietly, so smoothly and so efficiently. But especially was she interested in her host. Of his great intellect and learning she had been readily enough convinced by Mr Penfield's enthusiastic accounts of him; but his personality, his distinguished appearance, and his genial, pleasant manners were quite beyond her expectations. It was a pleasure to her to look at him and to reflect that the affectionate gratitude that she must have felt for him, whatever he had been like, had at least been worthily bestowed.

"My husband and I were speaking as we came along," she said, "of the revolution in our prospects that you created, in an instant, as it seemed, in the twinkling of an eye. One moment our affairs were at a perfectly hopeless deadlock; the next, all our difficulties were smoothed out, the tangle was unravelled, and an assured and happy future lay before us. It looked like nothing short of magic; for, you see, John had done everything that he possibly could to convince all the world that he was guilty."

"Yes," said Thorndyke, "that is how it appeared; and that is one of the mysteries which has to be cleared up presently."

"It shall be," Osmond promised, "if utterly idiotic, wrong-headed conduct can be made intelligible to reasonable men. But still, I agree with my wife. There is something quite uncanny in the way in which you unravelled this extraordinary tangle. I am a lawyer myself – a pretty poor lawyer, I admit – and I have heard Mr Penfield's account of the investigation, but even that has not enlightened me."

"For a very good reason," said Mr Penfield. "I am not enlightened myself. I am, I believe, in possession of most of the material facts. But I have not the special knowledge that is necessary to interpret them. I am still unable to trace the connection between the evidence and the conclusion. Dr Thorndyke's methods are, to me, a source of endless wonder."

"And yet," said Thorndyke, "they are perfectly normal and simple. They differ from the methods of an orthodox lawyer merely in this: that whereas the issues that I have to try are usually legal issues, the means which I employ are those proper to scientific research."

"But surely," Betty interposed, "the purposes of legal and scientific research are essentially the same. Both aim at arriving at the truth."

"Certainly," he replied. "The purposes are identical. But the procedure is totally different. In legal practice the issues have to be decided by persons who have no first-hand knowledge of the facts – by the judge and jury. To them the facts are furnished by other persons – the witnesses – who have such first-hand knowledge and who are sworn to give it truly and completely. And on such sworn testimony the judges form their decision. The verdict has to be 'according to the evidence,' and its truth is necessarily subject to the truth of the testimony and the competence of the witnesses.

"But in scientific research there is no such division of function. The investigator is at once judge, jury, and witness. His knowledge is first-hand, and hence he knows the exact value of his evidence. He can hold a suspended judgement. He can form alternative opinions and act upon both alternatives. He can construct hypotheses and try them out. He is hampered by no rules but those of his own making. Above all, he is able to interrogate things as well as persons."

"Yes," agreed Mr Penfield, "that is what has impressed me. You are independent of witnesses. Instead of having to seek somebody who can give evidence in respect of certain facts, you obtain the facts yourself and become your own witness. No doubt this will become evident in your exposition of this case, to which I – and our friends too, I am sure – are looking forward with eager interest."

"You are paying me a great compliment," said Thorndyke; "and as I hear Polton approaching with the coffee, I need not keep you waiting any longer. By the way, how much may I assume that our friends know?"

"They know all that I know," replied Mr Penfield. "We have had a long talk and I have told them everything I have learned and that you have told me."

"Then I shall assume that they have all the main facts, and they must stop me if I assume too much." He paused while Polton poured out the coffee and partially disencumbered the table. Then as his familiar retired, he continued: "I think that the clearest and most interesting way for me to present the case will be by recounting the investigation as it actually occurred, giving the facts observed and the inferences from them in their actual order of occurrence."

"That will certainly be the easiest plan for us to follow," said Osmond, "if it will not be too wearisome for you."

"On the contrary," replied Thorndyke, "it will be quite interesting to me to reconstitute the case as a whole; and the best way will be to treat it in the successive stages into which the inquiry naturally fell. I will begin with the information which was given to me when the case was placed in my hands.

"A number of sealed boxes had been deposited by Mr Hollis in the custody of Mr Woodstock, who placed them in his strong-room. These boxes were stated by Hollis to contain a number of valuable gems, but the nature of the contents was actually known only to Hollis, who had packed the boxes himself. After an interval the boxes were returned to Hollis; and it was agreed by all the parties, including Hollis, that all the seals were then intact. Nevertheless, on opening the boxes, Hollis found that most of the gems had been abstracted and replaced by counterfeits. Thereupon he declared that a robbery had been committed while the boxes were reposing in the strong-room; and this view was, strange to say, accepted by Mr Woodstock.

"Now, it was perfectly obvious that these statements of alleged fact were mutually irreconcilable. They could not possibly be all true. The question was, Which of them was untrue? If the stones were in the boxes when they were handed to Woodstock and were not there when he returned them to Hollis, then the boxes must have been opened in the interval. But in that case the seals must have been broken. On the other hand, if the seals were really intact, the boxes could not have been opened while they were in Woodstock's custody. Woodstock's position – which was also that of Hollis – was a manifest absurdity. What they alleged to have happened was a physical impossibility.

"So far, however, the legal position was quite simple, if Woodstock had accepted it. The seals were admitted to be intact. Therefore no robbery could have occurred in Woodstock's office. But Woodstock accepted the impossible; and thereupon a certain Mr John Osmond proceeded very deliberately to tip the fat into the fire."

"Yes, didn't he?" agreed Betty with a delighted gurgle. "You were an old guffin, Jack! Still, it was all for the best, wasn't it?"

"It was, indeed," assented Osmond. "Best stroke of work I ever did. You see, I knew that there is a Providence that watches over fools. But we mustn't interrupt the exposition."

"Well," continued Thorndyke, "the disappearance of Mr Osmond settled the matter as far as Mr Woodstock was concerned. He swore an information forthwith, and must have grossly misled the police, for they immediately obtained a warrant, which they certainly would not have done if they had known the real facts. Then Woodstock, distrusting his own abilities – very justly, but too late – consulted Mr Penfield. But Mr Penfield took the perfectly sound legal view of the case. The seals were admittedly unbroken. Therefore the boxes had been returned intact and there had been no robbery in the office. But if there had been no robbery, the disappearance of Osmond had no bearing on the case. Of course, neither Woodstock nor Hollis would agree to this view, and Mr Penfield then recommended that the case should be put in my hands.

"Now it was obvious that the whole case turned on the seals. They had been accepted as intact – in spite of the absurdity – without any kind of inquiry or examination. But were they really intact? If they were, the case was against Hollis; and I could see that my friend Professor Eccles suspected him of having engineered a sham robbery to evade a bequest to the nation. But this seemed to me a wild and unfair suspicion, and for my own part I strongly suspected the seals. Accordingly, I examined a whole series of them, minutely and exhaustively, with the result that they proved to be impressions, not of the matrix in Mr Hollis' ring, but of an electrotype matrix made from a wax impression.

"This new fact brought the inquiry to the next stage. It proved that the boxes had been opened and that they had been opened in Woodstock's office. For when they came there they had been sealed with Hollis' seal, but when they left the office they were sealed with the forged seal. Things began to look rather black as regards Osmond; but, although I was retained ostensibly to work up a case against him, I kept an open mind and proceeded with the investigation as if he did not exist.

"The second stage, then, started with the establishment of these facts: a robbery had really occurred; it had occurred in Woodstock's office; and, since the boxes had been kept in the strong-room, it was from thence that they had been abstracted. The next question was, By whom had the robbery been committed? Now, since the property had been taken from the strong-room, and since the strong-room had not been broken into, it followed that the thief must have had, or obtained, access to it. Now, there were three persons who had easy access to it: Woodstock, who possessed the key, Hepburn and Osmond, both of whom occasionally had the key in their custody. There might be others, but if so, they were at present unknown to me. But of the three who were known, one, Osmond, had apparently absconded as soon as the robbery was discovered and connected with the office. Moreover, the commencement of the robberies apparently coincided in time with the date on which he joined the staff.

"Evidently, then, everything that was known pointed to Osmond as the delinquent. But there was no positive case against him, and I decided to proceed as if nothing at all were known and seek for fresh data. And my first proceeding was to make an exhaustive examination of the boxes, the wrapping-paper, and the inside packing. As to the paper, I may say that I developed up a large number of finger-prints – on the outside surface only – which I never examined, as the occasion did not arise. The investigation really concerned itself with the dust from the insides of the boxes and from the packing material. Of this I collected every particle that I could extract and put it aside in pill-boxes numbered in accordance with the boxes from which it was obtained. When I came to examine systematically the contents of the pill-boxes, I made two very curious discoveries.

"First, every pill-box – representing, you will remember, one of the gem-boxes – contained one or more hairs; usually one only and never more than three. They were all alike. Each was a hair from a moustache of a light-brown colour and cut quite short, and there could be no doubt that they were all from the same individual. Consequently they could not be chance hairs which had blown in accidentally. The gem-boxes had been packed at various times, and hence the uniformity of the hairs connected them definitely with the person who packed the boxes. In short, it seemed at first sight practically certain that they were the hairs of the actual robber; in which case we could say that the robber was a man with a short light-brown moustache.

"But when I came to reflect on the facts observed I was struck by their singularity. Moustache hairs are shed very freely, but they do not drop out at regular intervals. One, two, or more hairs in any one box would not have been surprising. A man who was in the habit of pulling or stroking his moustache might dislodge two or three at once. The surprising thing was the regularity with which these hairs occurred; one, and usually one only, in each box, and no complete box in which there was none. It was totally opposed to the laws of probability.

"The point was highly significant. Anyone can recognize a hair. Most men can recognize a moustache hair. A detective certainly could. If these boxes had been opened by the police, as Hollis had originally intended, these hairs would almost certainly have been seen and eagerly fastened on as giving what would amount to a description of the thief. They would have been put in evidence at the trial and would have been perfectly convincing to the jury.

"The more I reflected on the matter the more did I suspect those hairs. If one assumed that they had been planted deliberately, say by a clean-shaved or dark-haired criminal, their regular occurrence in every box would be quite understandable. It would be a necessary precaution against their being overlooked. Otherwise it was unaccountable. Still, the fact of their presence had to be noted and the individual from whom they came identified, if possible.

"The second discovery that I made was, perhaps, even more odd. In every one of the boxes I found particles of the fine dust which falls out of the holes in worm-eaten wood; sometimes only a few grains, sometimes quite a large number of grains, and in the aggregate a really considerable quantity."

"But how astonishing," exclaimed Betty, "that you should be able to tell at once that these tiny grains came from worm-eaten wood."

"I make it my business," he replied, "to be able to recognize the microscopical appearances of the different forms of dust. But your remark indicates a very significant point. I imagine that there will be very few persons in the world who could identify these particles in a collection of miscellaneous dust. And therein lay the value of this discovery; for if the significance of the hairs was open to doubt, that of the wood-dust certainly was not. There was no question of its having been purposely planted. It had certainly found its way into the boxes accidentally, and the person who had unconsciously introduced it was pretty certainly unaware of its presence. It was undoubtedly a genuine clue.

"The discovery of this characteristic dust raised several questions. In the first place, how came it into the boxes? Dust from worm-eaten furniture falls on the floor and remains there. It is too coarse and heavy to float in the air like the finer kinds of dust. In a room in which there is worm-eaten furniture, you will find the particles of dust all over the floor; but you will not find any on the tables or chair-rails or mantelpiece. But these boxes must have stood on a table or bench when they were being packed and when the dust got into them. Then the dust must have been on the table or bench. But how could it have got there? It was possible that the bench, itself, might have been worm-eaten. But that was not a probable explanation, for the dust tends to fall, not to rise. It would have fallen, for the most part, from the under-surface on to the floor. The most likely explanation emerged from a consideration of the next question; which was, how could one account for the large quantity that was found?

"The quantity was extraordinarily large. From the whole set of boxes we collected something approaching a quarter of a thimbleful; which seems an enormous amount if you consider that it must all have got into the boxes during the short time that they were open for packing. What could be the explanation?

"There were two factors which had to be considered: the nature of the wood and the nature of the object which had been fashioned from it; and both were important for purposes of identification. Let us consider the first factor – material. Now, these wood-boring insects do not bore through wood as the bookworm bores through paper, to get at something else. They actually feed upon the wood. Naturally, then they tend to select the kind of wood which contains the most nourishment and which, incidentally, is usually the softest. But of all woods those of the fruit trees are richest in gum and sap and are most subject to the attacks of the worm. Walnut, pear, apple, plum, and cherry all have this drawback, and of these cherry is so inevitably 'wormy' that it has usually been shunned by the cabinet-maker. Now, the quantity of the wood-dust pointed to some excessively worm-eaten object and suggested one of the fruit woods as the probable material, and the balance of probability was in favour of cherry; and this was supported by the pinkish colour of the dust. But, of course, this inference was purely hypothetical. It represented the general probabilities and nothing more.

"And now we come to the second factor. What was the nature of this wooden object? A piece of ordinary furniture we could dismiss for two reasons: first, the dust from such a piece will ordinarily fall upon the floor, from whence it could hardly have got into the boxes; and, second, no matter how badly wormed a piece of furniture may be, the quantity of dust which falls from it is relatively small and accumulates quite slowly, being practically confined to that which is pushed out of the holes by the movements of the insects within. This process would not account for the great quantity indicated by these samples of ours. My feeling was that this worm-eaten object was an appliance of some sort, subject to frequent and violent disturbance. Let us take an imaginary case as an illustration. Let us imagine a mallet with an excessively worm-eaten head. Whenever that mallet is used, the shock of the impact will send a shower of wood-dust flying out on the bench, where it will rapidly accumulate.

"But, of course, this object of ours could not be a mallet for the reason that mallets are always made of hard wood; and jewellers' mallets are usually made of box-wood, lignum vitae, or horn, none of which is subject to the 'worm'. Thinking over the various appliances used by jewellers – since it was with a jeweller we were dealing – I suddenly bethought me of one which seemed to fulfil the conditions exactly. Jewellers and goldsmiths, as you probably know, use a variety of miniature anvils, known as stakes, bec-irons, sparrowhawks, etc. Now, these little anvils are usually stuck in a block of wood, just as a smith's anvil is planted on a tree-stump. These blocks are not usually hard wood; indeed soft wood is preferable as it absorbs the shock better. A favourite plan is to get a little log of wood and set the spike of the stake or sparrowhawk in a hole bored in the end grain; and the most abundant source of these little logs – at least in the country – is the pile of trimmings from old fruit trees. Such a log would tend very soon to become worm-eaten; and if it did, every time it was used a ring of wood-dust would form around its base and would soon spread all over the bench, sticking to everything on it and straying on to the hands, arms, and clothing of the workman.

"This inference, you will observe, was, like the previous one, purely hypothetical. But it agreed perfectly with the observed facts and accounted for them in a reasonable way; and as I could think of no other that did, I adopted it with the necessary reservations. But, in fact, the correctness or incorrectness of this hypothesis was at present of no great importance. Apart from any question as to its exact origin, the wood-dust was an invaluable clue. We now knew that the unknown robber was a person whose clothing was more or less impregnated with wood-dust; that any places that he had frequented would yield traces of wood-dust from the floors, and that the place where the boxes had been packed abounded in wood-dust and contained a badly worm-eaten wooden object of some kind.

"The next proceeding was obvious. It was to find the places which had been frequented by that unknown person, to seek for the worm-eaten object, and, if possible, to identify the individual who appeared to be connected with it. The suspected places were two: Mr Hollis' house and Mr Woodstock's office. I did not, myself, suspect Hollis; but nevertheless I determined to examine his house as narrowly as the other. Accordingly I asked Mr Penfield to obtain facilities for me to visit both places to make inquiries on the spot; which he did.

"Perhaps, before I describe that voyage of exploration, it may be as well to pause and consider what knowledge I now possessed and what I was going to look for. There was the wood-dust, of course. That was the visible trail that I hoped to pick up. But there were other matters. I knew that there was a man, in some way connected with the robbery, who had a short, fair moustache. I had to find out who he was. Also if there was any source from which some other person might collect specimen hairs from that moustache – a hair-brush, for instance – and if such source existed, who had access to it.

"Then there was the personality of the thief. One knew a good deal about him by this time. He was an ingenious man; a fairly good workman, at any rate, with metal-worker's tools, but not a skilled jeweller. He must have been able to make a key from a wax squeeze – unless he were Woodstock himself, which he pretty certainly was not; for none of the others had sufficiently free access to the strong-room to do what had been done. Then he must have had at least a simple working knowledge of electric batteries, since we could be fairly certain that he made the electrotypes himself; he would never have run the risk of putting the forgery out to trade. He was clearly a secretive, self-contained man. The only fallacy that I had to guard against was the possibility of a confederate outside the office, who might have done the actual work; but this possibility seemed to be negatived by the whole character of the robbery and especially by one very odd feature in it, which was this: Professor Eccles had noticed with surprise that many of the stones which were taken were of quite trifling intrinsic value, so trifling that, if they had been sold, they would hardly have realized enough to pay the cost of replacing them with the specially-made counterfeits. Indeed, in one case, at least, the thief must have lost money on the transaction, for he had taken a fine moonstone and replaced it with an inferior one of the same dimensions. But the value of the original was only about ten shillings, and he must have spent more than that on the replacement. The professor was greatly puzzled by this, having assumed, of course, that the gems were stolen to sell. But to me, this rather anomalous feature of the robbery offered a very curious suggestion; which was that no sale of the booty had ever been contemplated. It looked like a collector's robbery; and if there had been a collector in any way connected with the parties, I should have given him my very close attention. But, so far as I knew, there was none. Nevertheless, this peculiarity of the robbery had to be borne in mind when I came to make my investigations on the spot.

"Let me now briefly describe those investigations. Their main object was to ascertain whether there were any traces of wood-dust in the premises of either Hollis or Woodstock, and the method was this: in each case, a rough ground-plan of the premises was made; then small areas of the floors were cleaned thoroughly with a specially constructed vacuum cleaner and the dust from each area put into an envelope marked with a number, which number was also marked in the plan on the spot from which the dust had been collected. The collection was carried out by my laboratory assistant, Mr Polton, whom you have seen, leaving me free to make inquiries and to inspect the premises. Of course, the samples of dust had to be brought home to be examined in the laboratory, so we were hampered by the circumstance that we did not know at the time whether any wood-dust had or had not been obtained. But this proved to be of no importance.

"We operated first at Mr Hollis' house, regardless of his scornful protests. Then we went on to Mr Woodstock's office; and there I had a rather remarkable experience. As I entered with Mr Woodstock, I saw an elderly man engaged in repairing an electric bell; and a glance at his hands and the way in which he manipulated his tools showed the unmistakable facility and handiness of the skilled workman. It was a little startling; for here were two of the characteristics of the unknown person I was endeavouring to identify. This man had evident skill in the use of metal-worker's tools and he clearly knew a good deal about electric batteries. And when I learned that this Mr Wampole was the office-keeper and that he evidently had a key of the premises, I was still further impressed. I began to revise my opinion as to there being no confederate; for the fact remained that Osmond had absconded and that his disappearance – until it was otherwise explained – undeniably connected him with the robbery. I began to think it possible that there had been a partnership and that he had been used as a cat's paw. Meanwhile, I had to find out as much as I could about him, and to this end I sat down by Wampole, as he worked at refitting the batteries, and questioned him on the subject of Osmond's appearance, habits, temperament, and circumstances. It is only fair to him to say that he scouted the idea of Osmond's having committed the robbery and gave excellent reasons for rejecting it. On the other hand, his description of Osmond made it clear that the hairs which I had found in the boxes were Osmond's hairs; and when I expressed a wish to inspect Osmond's desk, he took me to it readily enough, and as it was unlocked, he threw up the lid and showed me the interior. The most interesting thing in it, from my point of view, was a pair of hair-brushes; from which I was able to extract several moustache hairs which appeared – and subsequently turned out to be – identically similar to those found in the boxes.

"The examination of Osmond's desk suggested a similar examination of all the other desks in the office, finishing up with that belonging to Mr Wampole. And it was in examining that desk that I did really receive somewhat of a shock. For when we came to turn out its contents, I found that these included, in addition to a number of metal-worker's tools, a workman's linen apron and some battery terminals and insulated wire, a stamp-album, a tray of military buttons and badges and old civilian buttons, and another tray of old coins.

"The coincidence was too striking to be ignored. Here was a man who had free access to these premises night and day, and who corresponded in every particular with the unknown robber. We had already seen that he had the skill and special knowledge that were postulated; now this stamp-album, these buttons, badges and coins, wrote him down an inveterate collector. If I had looked on Mr Wampole with interest before, I now regarded him with very definite suspicion. Whatever significance the hairs had seemed to have was now entirely against him; for there were the brushes, easily available, and he knew it.

"I must confess that I was greatly puzzled. Every new fact that I observed seemed more and more to confuse the issues. With the exception of the hairs – which were, at least, doubtful evidence – I had found nothing whatever to incriminate Osmond; whereas Wampole presented a highly suspicious appearance. But Osmond had absconded; which seemed to put Wampole outside the inquiry, excepting as a confederate. And when I went with Wampole to Osmond's rooms, my inspection of them only left me more puzzled; for the personality that they reflected was the very opposite of that indicated by the nature and method of the robbery. Instead of the avarice and cunning that characterized the robber, the qualities suggested were those of a hardy, adventurous, open-air man, simple to austerity in his tastes and concerned with anything rather than wealth and worldly possessions. The very photographs on the mantelpiece proclaimed the incongruity, especially that of his mother, whom Wampole informed me he strongly resembled; which showed the face of a dignified, strong, resolute, courageous-looking lady, whose son I found it hard to picture, first as a thief, and then as a panicky fugitive. Yet the fact remained that Osmond had absconded.

"However, when we got home and proceeded to question the samples of dust in the laboratory, they gave an answer that was unmistakable. The results were roughly thus: the samples from Hollis' house contained no wood-dust; those from Osmond's rooms contained none; that from the inside of his desk contained none and that from his office floor barely a trace. Those from the floor of the clerks' office yielded a very small quantity, but that from the floor by Wampole's desk contained quite a large amount, while the dust extracted from the interior of his desk was full of the castings – derived, no doubt, to a large extent from the apron which he had kept in it. So the murder was out. The man who had packed those boxes was Mr Wampole, and the hairs which I found in them had come from Osmond's brushes.

"One thing only remained to be done; the final verification. The wood-dust had to be traced to its ultimate source in Wampole's lair. This invaluable service was carried out by my assistant, Polton, who, with extraordinary tact and skill, contrived to get a glimpse into the workshop during Wampole's absence; and when he peeped in, the first object that met his eye was a sparrowhawk, planted in a little log of cherry-wood that was absolutely riddled by the worm. That concluded the inquiry so far as I was concerned, though some further work had to be done to enable the police to act. But no doubt Mr Penfield has told you about the lapidary and the police raid which resulted in Wampole's death and the discovery of the gems in his possession."

"Yes," Osmond replied, "I think we have had full details of the final stages. Indeed, Mr Penfield had given us most of the facts that you have mentioned, but neither he nor we were able to connect them completely. It seemed to us as if you had made one or two very fortunate guesses; but now that I have heard your reasoned exposition I can see that there was no element of guessing at all."

"Exactly," agreed Mr Penfield; "every stage of the argument rests securely on the preceding stages. I am beginning to suspect that we lawyers habitually underestimate the man of science."

"Yes," said Osmond, "I am afraid that is so. It is pretty certain that no lawyer could have solved this mystery."

"I have to remind you," Thorndyke remarked, "that the man of science was not able to solve it. He was able only to solve a part of it. The thief was identified and the stolen property traced to its hiding-place. But one question remained and still remains unanswered. Why did John Osmond disappear?"

Osmond and Betty both smiled, and the latter asked:

"Did you never form any guess on the subject?"

"Oh yes," replied Thorndyke, "I made plenty of guesses. But that was mere speculation which led to nothing. It occurred to me, for instance, that he was perhaps drawing a red-herring across the trail – that he was shielding the real criminal. But I could find no support for the idea. I could see no reason why he should shield Wampole – unless he was a confederate, which I did not believe. If the criminal had been Hepburn, it would have been at least imaginable. But there was never the shadow of a suspicion in regard to Hepburn. No, I never had even a hypothesis; and I haven't now."

"I am not surprised," said Osmond, with a slightly sheepish grin. "It was beyond even your powers to conceive the possible actions of an impulsive fool who has mistaken the facts. However, as I have put you to the trouble of trying to account for my unaccountable conduct, it is only fair that I should make it clear, if I can; even though I know that when I have finished, your opinion of me will be like Bumble's opinion of the Law – that I am 'a ass and a idiot.' "

"I hardly think that very likely," said Thorndyke, turning a twinkling eye on Betty. "As I said just now, you seem to have brought a most unpromising affair to an extraordinarily satisfactory conclusion; which is not at all suggestive of 'a ass and a idiot.' "

"But," objected Osmond, "the satisfactory conclusion which you are putting to my credit is entirely your own work. I set up the obstacles; you knocked them down. However, we need not argue the point in advance. I will tell you the story and you shall judge for yourself."

CHAPTER TWENTY
Osmond's Motive

"In order to make my position clear," Osmond began, "it is necessary for me to say certain things to you, my best and kindest of friends, which I should not confide to any other human creature. I shall have to confess to thoughts and suspicions which were probably quite unjust and unreasonable and which are now uttered subject to the seal of the confession."

The two lawyers bowed gravely in acknowledgement, and Osmond continued: "I was introduced to Mr Woodstock, as you know, by my brother-in-law, Mr Hepburn; and I may say I accepted the post chiefly that I might be near my sister. She and I had always been very devoted to one another, and from the time when I left Oxford up to the date of her marriage we had lived under one roof; and that was how she came to make the acquaintance of Hepburn.

"I did not encourage the intimacy, but neither could I hinder it. She was of a responsible age and she knew her own mind. The end of it was that, after an engagement lasting a few months, they were married, and there was nothing more to be said. But I was rather troubled about it. I had known Hepburn nearly all my life. We had been at school together and the greater part of our time at Oxford, where we belonged to the same college, Merton. Through all those years we were on the footing of intimate friends – rather oddly, for we were very different in temperament and tastes, and, indeed, had very little in common – and we knew one another extremely well. I don't know what Hepburn thought of me, but I must confess that I never had much of an opinion of him. He was a clever man; rather too clever, to my taste. An excellent manager, very much on the spot, and in fact decidedly cunning; fearfully keen on the main chance, fond of money and ambitious to be rich, and none too scrupulous in his ideas. At school he was one of those boys who contrive to increase their pocket-money by all sorts of mysterious little deals, and the same tendency showed up at Oxford. I didn't like his ways at all. I always had the feeling that, if he should ever be tempted by an opportunity to make a haul by illegitimate means, he might be led by his acquisitiveness to do something shady.

"However, his morals were not in my custody and were none of my business until he began to visit us at my rooms, where I was living with my sister. Then I gave her a few words of warning; but they took no effect. He made himself acceptable to her, and, as I have said, they became engaged and eventually, when Hepburn took up his job with Woodstock, they married. For a year or two I saw little of them, as I was articled to a solicitor in London; but when I was fully qualified Hepburn, at my sister's suggestion, offered to speak to Woodstock on my behalf, and the result was that I entered the office, as you have heard.

"And now I come to the particular transaction. Woodstock's office was, as you know, conducted in a rather happy-go-lucky fashion, especially as regards the strong-room. The key hung on the wall practically all day. Usually, Woodstock took it away with him at night; but quite frequently, when Woodstock was away for a night, it would be left in Hepburn's charge. Occasionally it was left with me; and on one occasion, at least, Wampole had charge of it for a night. And each of us four, Woodstock, Hepburn, Wampole, and myself, had a key to the outer door and could enter the premises whenever we pleased. You will remember, too, that the house was empty, out of office hours. There was no caretaker.

"Now, one night when I had been out on the river and got home rather late, I found that I had run out of tobacco. The shops were all shut, but I remembered that there was a nearly full tin in my desk at the office, so I ran round there to fill my pouch. I am always rather quiet in my movements, and perhaps, as it was late, I may have moved, instinctively, more silently than usual. Moreover, I still wore my rubber-soled boating-shoes. Well, I let myself in with my key and entered the office, leaving the outer door ajar. As I came in through the clerk's office I could see through the open doorway that there was a light on in Woodstock's office and that the door to the strong-room was open. A good deal surprised at this, I stopped and listened. There were sounds of someone moving about in the strong-room, and I was on the point of going in to see who it was when Hepburn came out with one of Hollis' boxes in his hand. And at that moment the outer door blew-to with a bang.

"At the sound of the closing door Hepburn started and whisked round to re-enter the strong-room. Then he saw me standing in the dark office, and I shall never forget his look of terror. He turned as white as a ghost and nearly dropped the box. Of course I sang out to let him know who I was and apologized for giving him such a start, but it was a minute or two before he recovered himself, and when he did he was decidedly huffy with me for creeping in so silently. His explanation of the affair was quite simple. He had been up to London with Woodstock, who had stayed in town for the night and had sent him down with a consignment of valuable securities which the firm were taking charge of. Not liking to have them in his personal possession, he had come on to the office to deposit them in the strong-room; and then, while he was there, he had taken the opportunity of checking Hollis' boxes, which he informed me he was in the habit of doing periodically and usually after office hours.

"The explanation was, as I have said, quite simple; indeed, no explanation seemed to be called for. There was nothing in the least abnormal about the affair. When I had once more apologized for the fright that I had given him, I filled my pouch and we went away together, and I dismissed the matter from my mind.

"I don't suppose I should ever have given the incident another thought if nothing had occurred to remind me of it. The months went by and it seemed to have passed completely out of my memory. Then Hollis dropped his bomb-shell into the office. Someone among us, he declared, had secretly opened his boxes and stolen his gems; and until that somebody was identified, we were all more or less under suspicion.

"Of course, Hepburn scouted the idea of there having been any robbery at all, and so did Wampole. They both pointed to the unbroken seals and declared that the thing was a physical impossibility; and I should have been disposed to take the same view, in spite of the strong evidence of the missing emerald. But as soon as I heard the charge, that scene in the office came back to me in a flash; and now, somehow, it did not look by any means so natural and simple as it had at the time. I recalled Hepburn's terrified stare at me; his pale face and trembling hands. Of course, my sudden appearance must have been startling enough to upset anyone's nerves; but it now seemed to me that his fright had been out of all proportion to the cause.

"Then, when I came to think it over, the whole affair seemed very characteristic of Hepburn; of his greed for money, his slyness, his cunning, calculating ways. The property which had been stolen was of great value, and I did not doubt that Hepburn would have annexed it without a qualm if he could have done so with complete safety. But it had been done so skilfully that the risk had been almost entirely eliminated. It was a very clever robbery. But for the merest chance the things would have gone back to Hollis' cabinet unchallenged; and when they had been there a week or two the issues would have become hopelessly confused. It would have been impossible to say when or where the robbery had been committed. The whole affair had been most cunningly planned and neatly carried out. I felt that, if Hepburn had been the robber, that was just the way in which he would have done it.

"Moreover, the robbery – if there had really been one, as I had no doubt there had – seemed to lie between three, or at the most, four of us: those who had easy access to the strong-room. But of these Woodstock was out of the question, Wampole had practically no access to the strong-room and was an old and trusted servant of irreproachable character, and as I was out of it, there remained only Hepburn. Whichever way I thought of the affair, everything seemed to point to him, and whenever I thought of it the vision came back to me of that scared figure standing by the strong-room door with the box of gems in his hand.

"But I need not go into any further detail. The bald fact is that it appeared to me beyond a moment's doubt that Hepburn was the thief, and the only question was, what was to be done. The fat was in the fire. The police would be called in. The stolen property would be traced and the crime pretty certainly brought home to Hepburn. That was how I forecast the probable course of events.

"Now, if Hepburn had been a single man it would have been no affair of mine. But he was my sister's husband and the father of my two little nephews, who had been to me like my own children. If Hepburn had been convicted of this crime, my sister's life would have been absolutely wrecked. It would have broken her heart; and as for the two little boys, their future would have been utterly and irrevocably damned. I couldn't bear to think of it. But was there any way out? It seemed to me that there was. I was a bachelor with no home-ties but my sister and the kiddies. I had always had a desire to travel and see the world. Well, now was the time. If I cleared off to some out-of-the-way region, the dangerous inquiries at the office would stop at once and the whole hue-and-cry would be transferred to me. So I decided to go. And the place that I selected as my destination was Adaffia, where I knew that an old friend of Hepburn's had settled as a trader.

"But I thought I would take Hepburn into my confidence and give him a chance of doing the same by me, only I am afraid I rather muddled the business. The fact is that, when it came to the point, I was a little shy of telling him exactly what was in my mind.

It is a delicate business, telling a man that you have discovered him to be a thief. So I hummed and hawed and approached the subject gradually by remarking that it looked as if there would be wigs on the green presently. But that cat didn't jump. Hepburn declined to admit that any robbery had occurred in the office. However, I persisted that we should presently have the police buzzing about the office and that then the position would become mighty uncomfortable for some of us. Still, he professed to be – and, of course, was – quite unconcerned; but when I went on to suggest that if I took a little holiday the state of affairs at the office would be made more comfortable for everybody, he stared at me in astonishment, as well he might. Of course, I could think of nothing but what I had seen that night when I caught him coming out of the strong-room, and I took it for granted that he realized what was in my mind, so that his astonishment didn't surprise me.

" 'Wouldn't it look a bit queer if you went away just now?' he asked.

" 'That is just the point,' I replied. 'If I hop off, they will leave the office alone and there will be no more trouble.'

"He seemed a good deal puzzled, but he didn't raise any objections; and of course he did not make any confidences, which again did not very much surprise me. He was the very soul of caution and secretiveness.

" 'Where did you think of going for your holiday?' he asked.

"I told him that I thought of running over to Adaffia to call on Larkom, the trader there, and suggested that he should send Larkom a letter introducing me. He didn't much like writing that letter, and he liked it less when I mentioned that I proposed to travel under the name of Walker. However, Larkom was an old friend whom he knew that he could trust, so, in the end, he agreed to write the letter. And that settled the affair. In due course I went off in the comfortable belief that he understood the position exactly, leaving him considerably surprised but quite confident that he knew all about the robbery. It was a very pretty comedy of errors; but it would have become a tragedy but for your wonderful insight and for the strange chance that the results of your investigations should have found their way into the newspapers. That is to say, if it was a chance."

"It was not a chance," said Mr Penfield. "As a matter of fact, Dr Thorndyke wrote out the account himself and broadcast it to all the papers, including those of the United States."

"Why did you do that?" Betty inquired, with a glance of intense curiosity at Thorndyke.

"For two reasons," the latter replied: "one obvious, the other less so. In the first place, Osmond had been publicly accused, and as there had been no trial, there had been no public withdrawal of the accusation. But he was a man of honourable antecedents and irreproachable character. Common justice demanded that his innocence should be proclaimed at least as widely as had been the presumption of his guilt. Even if he were dead, it was necessary that his memory should be cleared of all reproach. But in the second place, it was not at all clear to me that he was dead."

"The deuce it wasn't!" exclaimed Osmond. "I thought I had settled that question beyond any possible doubt. But you were not satisfied?"

"No. The report which reached me was singularly unconvincing, and there were certain actual discrepancies. Take first the general appearance of the alleged occurrences; here is a man, a fugitive from justice, whose purpose is to disappear. He lands at Adaffia and in the course of a week or two is reported to have died. Now, West Africa is a very unhealthy place, but people don't usually drop down dead as soon as they arrive there. On the contrary. The mortality among newcomers is quite small. Death is most commonly due to the cumulative effects of repeated attacks of malaria and does not ordinarily occur during the first year of residence. Osmond's death under the circumstances alleged was not in agreement with ordinary probabilities.

"Then the fact of death was not certified or corroborated. The officer who had reported it had not seen the body; he had only seen the grave. But to a man of my profession, the uncorroborated grave of a man who is admittedly trying to escape from the police is an object of deep suspicion. The possibility of a sham burial was obvious. This man, on leaving his home, had made a bee-line for Adaffia, an insignificant village on the African coast the existence of which was unknown to the immense majority of persons, including myself. How came he to know of Adaffia? and why did he select it as a hiding place? The obvious answer suggested was that he had a friend there. But as there was only one white man in the place – who must have been that friend – a sham death and burial would have been perfectly easy and a most natural expedient.

"Then there was the discrepancy. Osmond was reported to have died of blackwater fever. Now, this was almost an impossibility. Blackwater fever is not a disease which attacks newcomers. It lies in wait for the broken-down coaster whose health has been sapped by long-standing chronic malaria. In the immense majority of cases it occurs during, or after, the third year of residence. I have found no record of a single case in which the patient was a newcomer to the coast. It was this discrepancy that immediately aroused my suspicion; and as soon as I came to consider the circumstances at large, the other improbabilities came into view. The conclusion that I arrived at was that there was a considerable probability that the trader, Larkom, had carried out a sham burial; or, if there had really been a case of blackwater fever at Adaffia, the victim was Larkom himself, and that a false name had been put on the grave; in which case the man whom the officer saw must have been Osmond. You will note the suspicious fact that the name on the grave was 'John Osmond' – not 'Walker.' That impressed me very strongly. It met the necessities of the fugitive so very perfectly."

Osmond chuckled softly. "It seems to me, Dr Thorndyke," said he, "that you and I represent the two opposite extremes. You take nothing for granted. You accept no statement at its face value. You weigh, measure, and verify every item of evidence presented to you. Whereas I – well, I wonder what you think of me. I shan't be hurt if you speak your mind bluntly."

"There is nothing in my mind," said Thorndyke, "by which you need be hurt. It would, of course, be insincere to pretend that you did not display very bad judgement in taking so momentous a course of action on a mere, unconfirmed suspicion. But perhaps there are qualities even more valuable than worldly wisdom, and certainly more endearing; such as chivalry, generosity, and self-forgetfulness. I can only say that what you have told us as to your motives has made my little service to you a great pleasure to me; it has turned a mere technical success into a source of abiding satisfaction – even though you did seek to defeat the ends of justice."

"It is nice of you to say that, Dr Thorndyke," Betty exclaimed with brimming eyes. "After all, it is better to be generous than discreet – at least, I think so; and I don't mind admitting that I am proud to be the wife of a man who could cheerfully give up everything for the good of his kinsfolk."

"I think," said Mr Penfield, tapping his snuff-box by way of emphasis, "you have very good reason to be proud of one another."

"Thank you, Mr Penfield," she replied, smilingly. "And that brings me to what really was the object of our visit today. Only, here I am in rather a difficulty. I am commissioned to give thanks for all that has been done for us, and I really don't know how to express one-half of what we feel."

"Is there any need?" said Thorndyke. "Mr Penfield and I already understand that you enormously overestimate your indebtedness to us. Isn't that enough?"

"Well, then," said Betty, "I will just say this. But for you, Jack and I could never have been married. It was really you who gave us to one another. We wish to say that we are extremely pleased with your gift and we are very much obliged."

R Austin Freeman

The D'Arblay Mystery

When a man is found floating beneath the skin of a green-skimmed pond one morning, Dr Thorndyke becomes embroiled in an astonishing case. This wickedly entertaining detective fiction reveals that the victim was murdered through a lethal injection and someone out there is trying a cover-up.

Dr Thorndyke Intervenes

What would you do if you opened a package to find a man's head? What would you do if the headless corpse had been swapped for a case of bullion? What would you do if you knew a brutal murderer was out there, somewhere, and waiting for you? Some people would run. Dr Thorndyke intervenes.

R Austin Freeman

Felo De Se

John Gillam was a gambler. John Gillam faced financial ruin and was the victim of a sinister blackmail attempt. John Gillam is now dead. In this exceptional mystery, Dr Thorndyke is brought in to untangle the secrecy surrounding the death of John Gillam, a man not known for insanity and thoughts of suicide.

Flighty Phyllis

Chronicling the adventures and misadventures of Phyllis Dudley, Richard Austin Freeman brings to life a charming character always getting into scrapes. From impersonating a man to discovering mysterious trap doors, *Flighty Phyllis* is an entertaining glimpse at the times and trials of a wayward woman.

R Austin Freeman

Helen Vardon's Confession

Through the open door of a library, Helen Vardon hears an argument that changes her life forever. Helen's father and a man called Otway argue over missing funds in a trust one night. Otway proposes a marriage between him and Helen in exchange for his co-operation and silence. What transpires is a captivating tale of blackmail, fraud and death. Dr Thorndyke is left to piece together the clues in this enticing mystery.

Mr Pottermack's Oversight

Mr Pottermack is a law-abiding, settled homebody who has nothing to hide until the appearance of the shadowy Lewison, a gambler and blackmailer with an incredible story. It appears that Pottermack is in fact a runaway prisoner, convicted of fraud, and Lewison is about to spill the beans unless he receives a large bribe in return for his silence. But Pottermack protests his innocence, and resolves to shut Lewison up once and for all. Will he do it? And if he does, will he get away with it?

OTHER TITLES BY R AUSTIN FREEMAN AVAILABLE DIRECT FROM HOUSE OF STRATUS

Quantity		£	$(US)	$(CAN)	€
☐	Mr Pottermack's Oversight	6.99	12.95	19.95	13.50
☐	The Mystery of 31 New Inn	6.99	12.95	19.95	13.50
☐	The Mystery of Angelina Frood	6.99	12.95	19.95	13.50
☐	The Penrose Mystery	6.99	12.95	19.95	13.50
☐	The Puzzle Lock	6.99	12.95	19.95	13.50
☐	The Red Thumb Mark	6.99	12.95	19.95	13.50
☐	The Shadow of the Wolf	6.99	12.95	19.95	13.50
☐	A Silent Witness	6.99	12.95	19.95	13.50
☐	The Singing Bone	6.99	12.95	19.95	13.50
☐	When Rogues Fall Out	6.99	12.95	19.95	13.50

ALL HOUSE OF STRATUS BOOKS ARE AVAILABLE FROM GOOD BOOKSHOPS OR DIRECT FROM THE PUBLISHER:

Order Line: UK: 0800 169 1780
USA: 1 800 509 9942
INTERNATIONAL: +44 (0) 20 7494 6400 (UK)
or +01 212 218 7649
(please quote author, title and credit card details.)

Send to:

House of Stratus Sales Department
24c Old Burlington Street
London
W1X 1RL
UK

House of Stratus Inc.
Suite 210
1270 Avenue of the Americas
New York • NY 10020
USA

PAYMENT

Please tick currency you wish to use:

☐ £ (Sterling) ☐ $ (US) ☐ $ (CAN) ☐ € (Euros)

Allow for shipping costs charged per order plus an amount per book as set out in the tables below:

CURRENCY/DESTINATION

	£(Sterling)	$(US)	$(CAN)	€(Euros)
Cost per order				
UK	1.50	2.25	3.50	2.50
Europe	3.00	4.50	6.75	5.00
North America	3.00	3.50	5.25	5.00
Rest of World	3.00	4.50	6.75	5.00
Additional cost per book				
UK	0.50	0.75	1.15	0.85
Europe	1.00	1.50	2.25	1.70
North America	1.00	1.00	1.50	1.70
Rest of World	1.50	2.25	3.50	3.00

PLEASE SEND CHEQUE OR INTERNATIONAL MONEY ORDER.
payable to: STRATUS HOLDINGS plc or HOUSE OF STRATUS INC. or card payment as indicated

STERLING EXAMPLE

Cost of book(s):........................ Example: 3 x books at £6.99 each: £20.97

Cost of order: .... Example: £1.50 (Delivery to UK address)

Additional cost per book:................ Example: 3 x £0.50: £1.50

Order total including shipping:........... Example: £23.97

VISA, MASTERCARD, SWITCH, AMEX:

☐☐☐☐☐☐☐☐☐☐☐☐☐☐☐☐☐☐☐☐

Issue number (Switch only):

☐☐☐

Start Date: ☐☐/☐☐

Expiry Date: ☐☐/☐☐

Signature: ______________________

NAME: ______________________

ADDRESS: ______________________

COUNTRY: ______________________

ZIP/POSTCODE: ______________________

Please allow 28 days for delivery. Despatch normally within 48 hours.

Prices subject to change without notice.
Please tick box if you do not wish to receive any additional information. ☐

House of Stratus publishes many other titles in this genre; please check our website (**www.houseofstratus.com**) for more details.